SNAKE

PROLOGUE

Chapter One

Paul Sanonia had been touched by a nightmare, an unbelievable disaster that had manifested in reality where it shouldn't belong. Tonight, he was dwelling on the nightmare in St. Mark's Cathedral—it didn't matter that it wasn't a Catholic cathedral, at this point a mosque would do—and no matter how many times he turned it over in his mind, he couldn't see what the reason was behind it all, why his life had to have been touched, and why his cousin's life had to have been touched more.

"Oh Jamie." Paul murmured, putting his head in his hands. "What did they do to you? Why did it have to be you?"

Paul tried telling himself that it was final: *Jamie's dead. Jamie's dead.* But no matter how many times he repeated it to himself, Paul couldn't get himself to believe it. Jamie had only been his cousin, but they'd been like brothers, inseparable, thick as thieves and thicker than blood. Even though Paul had joined the Camerlengo family as a soldier after high school and Jamie had gone onto college and then law school, they'd still remained close. In fact Paul had glowed with pride when Jamie had become one of Mr. Camerlengo's *consigliere* and had been one of the first to congratulate him.

But now Jamie was dead. No, he was murdered. Paul flashed back to the funeral three days ago: the crying, the quiet respect of the mourners, the eulogies and the memories, the cameras flashing outside the gates of the cemetery, the reporters leaning against the security cordon, shouting their incessant questions. *Mrs. Sanonia! Do you think your husband was assassinated for his mob connections? Give us a comment, anything!*

What did it matter, anyway? Paul could only imagine what the humiliation must've been like for his sister-in-law. It didn't matter that Jamie had been a *consigliere* in the Camerlengo family; it didn't matter that he'd been found in the Hudson; and it certainly didn't matter that readers and viewers and the whole damn world wanted a fucking piece of James Sanonia now that he was dead. None of that mattered at all, at least from Paul's perspective.

No, what mattered now was that someone had murdered Jamie; that Jamie's wife was now a widow and eight months pregnant, and now he was dead, and he died in a manner that the police moles said somewhat resembled certain Russian mob hits.

What did that even mean, anyway? "Somewhat" resembled certain Russian mob hits. That could mean any number of things. And what did that thing on Jamie's chest mean anyway? For police moles, they weren't very good at their jobs. Weren't moles supposed to be good at passing along information or something?

Paul felt a buzz in his pocket and looked down. Through the fabric in his pants Paul could see the light from his phone's screen shining through. Paul reached into his pocket, pulled out his phone, and dove into a little alcove where he could take the call in peace. Without checking the number he pressed the talk button and brought the phone to his ear.

"Hello?" said Paul. From the other end all Paul could hear was a deep breathing, making him raise his eyebrows in suspicion. "Who is this?" He checked the caller ID, and saw only UNKNOWN NUMBER.

Suddenly the person at the other end of the phone spoke. "Men in your line of business have no right to be in a church, Mr. Sanonia."

Paul jerked his head away from the phone, surprised. Glancing quickly around the church, he saw only three people, and none of them were on their phones. How did this person know where he was and how did he get his number? He looked back at the phone and spoke into the mouthpiece. "Who the fuck is this?"

The man on the other end laughed, a rich, hearty laugh that for some reason chilled Paul's skin. "When your cousin James Sanonia died, he was shot in the head execution-style." said the man, his voice deep and affected with a heavy Russian accent. "Then after his death, several bones were broken all over his body. He was then taken from wherever he was killed and thrown in the Hudson. Dockworkers saw his body floating and pulled him up out of the water. By the time they got him though, there was nothing to identify your cousin's murderer. Except for one interesting detail, that is."

Paul froze, his heart beating loudly in his chest. Who was this guy? How did he know all that? "And what was that detail?" he asked through gritted teeth.

The man spoke, and Paul froze. "You killed my cousin." he hissed angrily. "You killed Jamie."

"Horrible thing, wasn't it?" said the Russian man. "I couldn't get what I wanted out of your cousin. But I'm sure you'll be much more helpful."

Paul was only half-listening now, looking around the church, trying to find someone—anyone!—on a phone. One of the other worshippers, a teenage girl with a skirt too short for the cold February weather, walked out of the church while texting. Besides her, no one else seemed to have a phone.

"Where the fuck are you, you crazy shit?" Paul whispered into the phone. "Come on out and face me like a man!"

"But there is no fun in that." replied the Russian man. "Besides, you're so much more amusing to watch."

Paul stepped out of the alcove, looking around the church. "Watch?" he repeated.

"Oh, didn't I mention it?" asked the Russian man. "I'm right in the church with you."

Chapter Two

Cold sweat broke out on Paul's forehead. "What did you say?" he whispered into the phone.

"I said," the Russian man replied, enunciating each word, "I'm in the church with you. Are you having trouble understanding me with my accent?"

Paul gripped the phone tightly in his hand, his rage threatening to overtake him. "Then why can't I see you?"

"Oh, but you did." said the Russian man. "Didn't you just watch me leave? I was texting on my phone."

"What the hell are you talking about—?" Paul stopped and flashed back to a few seconds ago. The girl who'd just left had been texting on her cell phone, hadn't she? If she was the one who was on the phone with Paul now—

He stopped himself before he went any further. Did this guy really think that just because Paul was angry he'd believe this bullshit and go ballistic on some teenager? Well, he certainly had another think coming. "Very funny, wise-guy." Paul told the Russian man. "There's no way you could be that girl. If you were, how could you talk to me while texting?"

The Russian man laughed. "But you just answered your own question." replied the Russian man. "It's not too difficult to take a phone and program an app into it that allows you to turn your texts into a voice. Plenty of young men and women these days can make an app like that. And even if I couldn't, it wouldn't be too hard for me to use my feminine wiles to get such a program, would it?"

Paul was stunned. He hadn't thought of that at all. But he didn't have time to be stunned. The Russian man was speaking to him again, his words coming slowly enough one after the other that Paul could believe a teenager was texting to him. "Leave the church and go to the northwest corner of Second Avenue and Seventeenth Street. Don't take your car, there is probably a GPS device built into it. Take a taxicab instead. I am already halfway there. If you wish to know why I killed your cousin—if you wish to know why one of the other *consigliere* had a price put on your cousin's head—then you'll meet me."

There was a click and the line went dead. Paul looked at the phone in disbelief for a fraction of a second before storming out of the church and into the night. *I don't know what this bastard's game is*, thought Paul, *but if he really is that girl, and if she really did kill Jamie, I'm gonna ring her tiny little neck! And what did he mean, one of the other consigliere put a price on Jamie's head? Why? That freak better have some answers. Now where the fuck's a cab?!*

As he left the church a small yellow cab appeared at the corner. Paul ran out and hailed it as the light changed. The cab pulled alongside the gate to the church and Paul got into the backseat. "Perfect timing!" he said to the cabbie. "Take me to the corner of Second and Seventeenth, and if you get me there quickly I'll throw in a big tip."

Without a word the cabbie stepped on the accelerator and the cab zoomed into traffic, turning right at the corner. Paul sat back in his seat and looked at the cab's ceiling. Like his anger therapist had been trying to teach him, Paul took deep, calming breaths, trying to get himself back under control before he met the Russian man. Or teenage girl, he wasn't sure which yet. *I really got to get control of my anger.* he thought to himself, his rage dissipating. *That bastard or bitch made me get into a cab just because they said they murdered Jamie. Doesn't matter if it's a prank or not though. I'll still make them pay. And if he's out to get me, then I'll show him what happens when you mess with the Sanonias!* This thought put Paul into a good mood as the cab zoomed through another intersection.

Suddenly the cab pulled over to the curb and stopped. The front lights and the dashboard went dim, leaving Paul and the cabbie alone in the dark. Paul looked around, trying to see if something in the road had made them pull over. When he didn't see anything, he turned to the cabbie, his anger powerfully reignited.

"What's the big idea, you fuck?" shouted Paul. "I told you, I gotta be somewhere!"

The cabbie replied in a voice tinted with a Russian accent, "You are surprisingly gullible, Mr. Sanonia."

Paul felt the hairs on the back of his neck bristle. *What in the hell—?*

Suddenly the cabbie threw himself over into the back seat, his hands reaching for Paul's throat. Paul tried to back away, but the man's arms reached his neck and started squeezing his windpipe. Paul tugged at the man's hands, beat at his arms, but the man only squeezed harder.

Paul felt his lungs screaming, his heart beating faster as his brain cried out for oxygen. And the man in front of him, his face swathed in shadow, just quietly choked him, staring at Paul with two large, shiny blue eyes.

Finally Paul's hands grew weak and he collapsed against the back seat. The man let go of Paul's neck and Paul slipped into the dark.

Paul's eyes fluttered open, but for a second he thought that his eyes were still closed, it was so dark. When he realized his eyes were indeed open, Paul also realized that he was lying on his back and there was some sort of gag in his mouth too. Paul poked his tongue against the gag but he couldn't figure out what it was. All he could tell was that the gag was round, rubbery, and a bit smaller than a tennis ball. He tried to move his arms but they were bound behind him by what felt like handcuffs. Paul tested his legs and realized his ankles were bound too.

Lifting his head up as high as it would go, Paul tried to call out for help, but the gag in his mouth muffled his shouts. *What's going on?* thought Paul. *Who the hell did this to me?* Then he remembered the call he'd received in the church, the Russian man identifying himself as Jamie's murderer and as the teenage girl who'd been texting as she left, and the cab driver who'd choked him. Paul's eyes widened as he grasped what had happened: he'd been set up.

Suddenly there was the sound of footsteps from somewhere nearby. Paul looked around, trying to pinpoint the location of the feet in the darkness. The footsteps stopped, replaced by the clack of something metallic being set down somewhere. Then there was a clicking sound and a bright light burst into life, banishing the darkness.

Paul closed his eyes, the light burning beneath his eyelids. When he opened them, he saw the light was coming from an electric lantern set down by a stone support column. The light shone in all directions, illuminating what looked like a construction site, all concrete and wood frames and plastic sheets. Beyond the lantern's glare was utter darkness, giving no clue as to where Paul had been taken.

Paul looked around, trying to find the person who'd lit the lantern. As he did, he saw that someone had stripped him down to his boxers and laid him face-up on a black tarp. Paul felt fear clutch at his being as he realized what this meant for someone in his line of work and started screaming through the gag. "Ahm-ah-ee! Ai-ee-ah-ee! Awuh ih!" *Somebody! Anybody! Help me!*

"No one will come to your rescue, Mr. Sanonia." said a deep voice. From his right Paul saw a man walk into the lantern's light, taking slow, quiet steps as if he knew he had all the time in the world. As the man came closer Paul got a good look at him: the man must've been at least six feet tall, broad-shouldered and long-legged. Everything he was wearing—his boots, pants, leather jacket, gloves—were jet black, and on his face, the man wore a black leather mask that came down over his face like an executioner's hood, only tighter and more form-fitting. The only parts of his face that Paul could see were his eyes, small, brilliant blue orbs that shone with malice.

"It's just you and me, Mr. Sanonia." said the man. Paul shivered, feeling a chill not from the air crawl up his spine. The man's voice was the same voice that he'd heard over the phone, only in person it sounded much more sinister. "And you and I are going to have a little discussion. Well, it is more accurate to say we will have a little…interrogation. And how it goes is all dependent on you."

Paul struggled against his restraints, shouting through the gag in his mouth. "Ai ah oo oo-ih ih!" *Why are you doing this!*

"*Do stupayet t'ree ga stovit seriynyy ubiytsa.*" said the Russian man. When Paul just stared at the man, the man said, "It's Russian." The man walked closer to Paul and bent his knees till he was hovering a few inches above Paul's head. "It means, 'it takes three to become a serial killer'. Three murders, that is."

Paul's eyes grew wide, panic coursing through his system. "Ooh-uh!" he shouted. *Murders!*

"Yes, indeed." said the Russian man. "Murders. You see, I'm not working for your *consigliere*, or anyone from your family. I'm doing this for my own reasons. But do not worry, your death shall not be in vain. Far from it, actually. You will become a message to your boss. A message that, well…people are dying to spread." The Russian man turned Paul onto his stomach and placed a hand on Paul's right pinkie finger.

"Tell me, Mr. Sanonia." said the Russian man. "Are you familiar at all with the term *zamochit*?"

Paul stopped struggling as the word reverberated through his brain. *Zamochit*. He knew what that word meant: it was a Russian slang term meaning *to be quiet* or *to shut up*. However among Russian mafia families *zamochit* took on a much more sinister meaning as a punishment in which every bone in a person's body was broken one at a time, usually while the victim was alive. Jamie had had something similar done to him, but he'd been dead when it happened.

And that same killer was threatening to do the same thing to him. Only this time, Paul had a feeling he wasn't going to be dead during the torture. With renewed vigor, Paul started struggling again, the Russian man holding onto Paul's pinkie the whole time.

"I guess the medical examiner who took care of your cousin told you and your police informants of what I did to him." said the Russian man. "Good, I would hate to lie to you and tell you this will not hurt at all."

The Russian man twisted Paul's pinkie finger in its socket, turning it one-hundred and eighty degrees with a sickening crack. Paul screamed, his head shooting off the ground. "*Ras*." said the Russian man, taking ahold of Paul's ring finger. "*D'va*." Another twist, another sickening crack; Paul screamed louder, hoping to God somebody would hear him.

"Scream all you want, Mr. Sanonia." said the Russian man, moving onto Paul's middle finger. "This construction site is one of several around here, and all of them were abandoned due to the economy. Not to mention this is the seventh floor of a skyscraper. No one's going to hear you scream, let alone come to your rescue. *T'ree.*" The Russian man twisted Paul's finger, squeezing hard as he spun the finger around in its socket farther than he had the previous two before letting go. Paul screamed until his throat felt raw, the pain unbearable.

When he finally stopped screaming, Paul's head fell back down against the black tarp, whimpering. His fingers throbbed painfully, like a thousand needles on his nerves. He was sure he had peed himself, though between the pain and the exhaustion from screaming there was no way he could tell.

The Russian man was standing over him, watching him. "That was a warning, Mr. Sanonia." said the Russian man. "If you do not cooperate, I will break more bones. If you do cooperate though...we may be able to put this night behind us both." The Russian man bent down again and grabbed the gag in Paul's mouth. "Now I'm going to ask you a question and take this ball gag out of your mouth. When I do, I want you to answer truthfully. If you do not..."

The Russian man left the rest of his sentence hanging. Slowly he bent down to Paul's ear and whispered something in it.

When Paul heard the Russian man's question, the emotion he registered was surprise. What did this man have to do with *that*?

The Russian man removed the gag from Paul's mouth. Paul sucked in a deep breath of air, feeling like he'd never known how wonderful it was to breathe through his own mouth until now. "I…I don't know…anything…about that." he gasped.

Behind him the Russian man sighed. "I thought I was being clear. I guess not." The Russian man bent down to insert the gag back into his mouth; Paul protested loudly as the gag went in. "I guess I'll have to explain it a bit more."

The Russian man grabbed Paul's index finger and shoved it backward against the back of Paul's hand; Paul screamed, trying to shake off the Russian man. The Russian man then took Paul's thumb and crushed it in his fist. The Russian man went on, counting each finger as he crushed, twisted, or pulled it back. By the time he was done, Paul's fingers felt like a big, bloody mess, and they must've looked like it too.

The Russian man removed the gag again and asked the same question. Paul sobbed where he lay, snot dribbling down his nose. "I swear I don't know." Paul cried. "Please believe me. I really don't know."

"Then who would know?" asked the Russian man. "Or do we need a little more explanation? You have no idea how important this is to me! Your cousin died because he wouldn't tell me about her!"

"No please!" Paul screamed as the Russian man grabbed ahold of his forearm. "I nuh—I know someone who was involved in that. Yeah, he told me about it on the phone the other day."

"Who?!" the Russian man squeezed Paul's forearm, his fingers massaging the bones as if looking for a weak point. Terrified, Paul gave his friend's name, shame mingling with the pain and humiliation that was already within him.

The Russian man relaxed his grip on Paul's arm as he heard the name. "Very good." said the Russian man. "I have no more use for you."

Paul felt his spirits soar at the sound of that. The man wouldn't torture him anymore, he'd let him go and—

"Now, it is time for you to become a message." said the Russian man, picking up the ball gag that he'd left on the tarp and stretching the strap.

"Wait!" Paul cried. "Please, I—!" His screams were cut off as the gag was put back in his mouth.

"That ball gag is a very dependable product, Mr. Sanonia." said the Russian man as he took hold of Paul's forearm again. "But I'm not surprised/ The bondage shop I bought it from is one of the legitimate businesses your boss controls. And we all know a Camerlengo business always sells the finest quality products, correct?"

The Russian man broke Paul's forearm, and from there Paul lost track of time, caught in a whirlwind of screaming pain and breaking bones. When the Russian man stopped, both Paul's arms and legs, his spine, and a few toes were mangled and destroyed. Paul felt himself trying to slip into the darkness, into the yawning void that was surely waiting for him.

The Russian man turned Paul back onto his back and Paul looked up into the Russian man's masked face. "I do not care to lie if I can help it, Mr. Sanonia." said the Russian man, pulling out a handgun. "So I will tell you, it was very personal."

The Russian man pointed the gun at Paul's forehead and squeezed the trigger. "*Spokenye Nocha*, Paul Sanonia." said the Russian man.

The world fell away.

Chapter Four

"*Spokenye Nocha*, Paul Sanonia." said the man who called himself the Snake. *Good night, Mr. Sanonia.* The Snake's body tensed as his excitement built to a peak, rising with the pitch of the music playing in his head. He inhaled and pulled the trigger, letting the bullet in the chamber end Paul Sanonia's life.

The music playing in the Snake's head shut off as he put his gun back in his jacket. All throughout the torture, he'd listened to the piano, the violins, the steady percussion, a small symphony orchestra only he could hear. Now that the *zamochit* had finished, there was no need to listen to the music anymore. Even so, Snake hummed the tune under his breath as he pulled out his hunting knife. He wondered if Paul Sanonia would've known what tune the Snake was humming if he were still alive.

Probably not. After all, how many Italian mafia soldiers were fans of amateur slasher films, let alone knew the names of the movie scores made for them? Very few, if any.

But the Snake knew it. He knew the music and he loved it, just as he loved the films the music came from and just as he loved all slasher films, be they the famous American franchises like *Friday the 13th* and *Nightmare on Elm Street*, or the Canadian cult hits such as *My Bloody Valentine* or *Happy Birthday to Me*. They were great inspiration for Snake's own kills, along with a mass of other horror and thriller stories. Those stories were his Bible, his guide, as he went about doing what must be done.

The critics say that slasher films do not contribute anything, that all they do is mess up children's heads and make them into serial killers in turn. the Snake thought. *Maybe so, but for once, slasher films will be responsible for saving lives. With their power, I will protect what is most important to me.*

The Snake gripped the handle of the hunting knife and steadied it over Paul Sanonia's belly. Slowly he sliced in, the knife sinking in up till the hilt. Snake went about his work carefully, carving the letters into the skin so that they would be noticeable but neat. When he was done, he wiped the blade on the edge of the tarp and surveyed his work. On Paul Sanonia's belly, in large, jagged, bloody lines, were the letters S, N, A, K, and E.

The Snake felt a great satisfaction. Tonight had gone a lot better than it had a week ago with James Sanonia. No fear, no nervousness or squeamishness, and certainly no derisive laughter from his intended victim about how he was too weak to kill him.

The Snake stood up and picked up the edge of the tarp, the piano melody from another amateur horror movie now playing in his head as he worked. It was time to dispose of the body and then make sure it was found.

PART ONE
THE NEW YORK MAFIA KILLER

Chapter Five

Blake Harnist stepped off the elevator into the thick of the Organized Crime Control Bureau's Manhattan branch. Around the squad room, officers went over evidence files, detectives made phone calls and chased down leads, and one or two ADAs could be seen arguing with private lawyers over case aspects and plea deals. It was a constant stream of people coming and going, quiet voices mingled with loud telephones, and the smell of swill that looked like coffee.

Harnist walked through the maelstrom to his desk, taking off his heavy coat and slinging it over his shoulder. As he passed he was aware of the eyes on him as he walked. Harnist ignored them, heaving an inward sigh. *You'd think after three months they'd forget about it and have other things to stare at.* he thought, taking a seat at his desk.

Harnist had only made detective a month and a half ago, but the reason why he'd made detective had quickly become legend within the New York Police Department. Three months ago, Harnist, still a regular officer barely making enough to pay rent, had been heading back to the precinct from a lead that hadn't gone anywhere when he'd stopped at a gas station to fuel up. While at the pump, Harnist had seen someone he'd recognized as a leader in the Irish mob crossing the street in a rush. Harnist, curiosity and instinct aroused, had followed the man to the seventh floor of an apartment building. There, Harnist had seen the mob boss arguing with a man, their voices growing louder and angrier as the argument continued. Harnist had pulled out his smartphone and filmed the entire exchange using the phone's camera, right up until the moment when the boss had abruptly brought out a gun and shot the man he'd been arguing with.

Harnist, startled by the sudden change in events, was somehow able to put away his phone and pull out his Glock, yelling to the boss to drop his weapon and raise his hands above his head. The boss, without bodyguards and startled that he'd been caught in the act of committing a murder, had dropped the gun in surprise and had come quietly.

The man who'd been shot survived, and had agreed to testify against the boss, who was brought up on attempted murder charges. With Harnist's footage as evidence, the boss had accepted a plea deal, gave up a bunch of members of the Irish mob and was put away in a state prison rather than a federal one. Meanwhile, Harnist's arrest and video recording had fast-tracked him, so that within a few weeks he'd been promoted from regular police officer to Detective Grade-3. At just twenty-eight years old, it was quite the feat, and many recent academy graduates still came up to Harnist asking if he had any tips for them.

What I need are a few tips. thought Harnist, checking his email. *For instance, how do you get rid of unwanted admirers in the workplace? Or perhaps get me a girlfriend whose schedule syncs up with mine?*

Harnist felt a tap on his shoulder and saw his sergeant, James Pacine, standing behind him. "Captain wants to see you, Harnist." said Pacine.

"And good morning to you, Sarge." said Harnist. "I see those classes on small-talk are paying off."

Pacine grunted nonchalantly. All those who knew him agreed that Sergeant Pacine was a private guy and never said much more than what needed to be said. Fifteen years on the force, and not even his former partners could say they knew much about the man. The only thing everyone agreed on was that Pacine could take the constant ribbing about how quiet he was with grace and never make a fuss over it.

Harnist glanced over to Captain Patton's office, the blinds drawn down a signal that the captain was in a meeting and only those who were invited could enter, lest they risked getting their head bitten off. Harnist looked back at Pacine, who looked like he wanted to get back to whatever he'd been doing before he'd been sent to retrieve Harnist. "Any idea what he wants me for?"

Pacine shrugged. "Something to do with the case you're working?" he offered.

"I'm just tracking down the cousin of a gun smuggler." said Harnist. "How is that worthy of getting invited into one of the captain's meetings?"

Pacine gave another noncommittal shrug and gestured that Harnist should hurry up and meet with the captain. Harnist slid out of his seat, walked quickly over to the captain's office, knocked on the door and went in. Inside the office Captain Patton sat behind his desk, while two people Harnist didn't recognize, a serious-looking man in a black three-piece and a pretty brown-skinned woman wearing a grey-and-white pantsuit, sat in the seats facing the desk.

Captain Patton gestured for Harnist to come in, and then motioned to the two people sitting in the chairs. "Blake, these are Section Chief Alan Gramer and Special Agent Angela Murtz." he said. "They're with the FBI."

Harnist shook hands with Gramer and Murtz. "Does my current case have something to do with the FBI?" Harnist asked his captain.

Captain Patton shook his head and started stroking his beard, the sign that everyone in the OCCB recognized as the sign that something was troubling the captain. "No, you're off that case."

"Off the case?" Harnist repeated, surprised. "Why?"

"Are you familiar with the Sanonia murder?" asked Gramer, speaking for the first time since Harnist had joined the meeting.

"James Sanonia?" said Harnist. "Everybody in OCCB has. He was murdered a week ago. We've been having competitions about who can do the best Italian accent while saying, 'he gotta whacked'."

Patton, Gramer, and Murtz stared at Harnist, who blushed and said, "Sorry, we were all kind of upset that Sanonia was murdered before we could bring him to justice, and so some of us were trying to find ways of making it funny. Stupid way to let off steam. Sorry."

"Don't worry son, we sympathize." said Gramer. "We at the Bureau are pretty mad about it too, seeing as we were conducting an investigation trying to link Sanonia with the murder of a black market antiques salesman. Unfortunately, his murderer got him before we did."

"And his cousin too." said Patton.

Harnist stared at his captain. "His cousin?"

"This morning," said Murtz, handing Harnist a large manila file folder, "a phone call came into your dispatch about a body floating in the Central Park pond. Body was still fresh when CSU and uniforms arrived. There was a driver's license stuck between the victim's teeth. The photo on the license matches the face of the victim. It's definitely Paul Sanonia."

Harnist opened the file folder and scanned the contents. Among the items within was a coroner's report on James Sanonia (cause of death was a single gun-shot wound to the forehead), a CSU report on Sanonia's body (negative for prints, DNA, or fibers due to water contamination), and a photo of a mangled body, clipped to a close-up shot of the corpse's belly. Someone, presumably the murderer, had carved the word SNAKE into Sanonia's belly in big capital letters.

"I didn't know Sanonia's killer had carved 'snake' into his stomach." said Harnist, not looking up from the file.

"It was a detail we decided to keep hidden from most of the department." said Patton. "Since the Camerlengo family is supposed to have a mole or two in every section of OCCB, we wanted to keep things quiet." Patton scoffed and went on, "Doesn't mean they don't already know about it, though."

Harnist nodded in understanding. The Camerlengo Family was one of the most powerful families in New York. They dealt mainly in the sex trade, and most of their legitimate businesses involved things like fetish shops, dating services, and a few places where you could "look but not touch". They'd been around for only eighteen years, but the power they'd amassed in that time was enough that even some of the NYPD's top brass spoke carefully when discussing the Camerlengos.

It was also the family that James Sanonia had been a *consigliere* and public spokesman for.

Harnist looked up from the file and said, "So the latest victim is his cousin?"

Murtz nodded. "Paul Sanonia." she said, flipping through her own manila file folder. "He was a recruiter for one of the Camerlengos' escort services."

"Same company, different departments." said Harnist.

"Yes, but according to our sources, they were close." said Gramer. "They often ate together five nights out of the week, and drank at the same bar every night but Saturday."

"And we're sure it's the same person?" asked Harnist.

"All but certain, pending autopsy." said Murtz. "The coroner is holding the body for us down at the crime scene."

"Us?" said Harnist. "Does that mean everyone in the room or just a couple of us?"

"You and Agent Murtz." Gramer answered. "Murtz has degrees in psychology and criminology and has worked for the

Behavioral Analysis Unit for twelve years. She's here to help profile the perp."

"Criminal profiler, huh?" said Harnist. "Ever work a mafia-related case?"

"One time in Georgia." said Murtz, pulling back a strand of the luxurious black hair that fell onto her shoulders. "I helped to figure out that the wife and mistress of a mob boss in Atlanta were working together to scam every member of the family and a few politicians out of their savings."

"Hey, I know that case." said Harnist. "The Thomas/Lourdes Scammers. You were on that?" When Murtz nodded, Harnist nodded appreciatively. That case had made headlines last year, and plenty of law enforcement officials had let out wistful sighs when they heard the money trail had led to the arrest of several powerful criminals through a strange twist of luck. Pleased to be working with someone from that case, Harnist turned back to the file. "So what can you tell us about our killer?"

"From the file alone?" asked Murtz. "Not much. Just that he most likely has a grudge against the Camerlengos."

"The Camerlengos?" said Harnist. "Not just the Sanonias?"

"If it was just the Sanonias, James Sanonia's wife would've probably been killed, and probably before Paul Sanonia." Murtz replied.

"Not to mention that James Sanonia's parents live in the Bronx and haven't so much as received a death threat." Gramer added.

"Okay, so he's angry at the Camerlengos. But what does 'snake' mean?" asked Harnist. "Is he calling the Camerlengos snakes? Because considering the business they're in, I can see where he'd come up with that."

"Either that or he's leaving a signature." answered Murtz. "We'll know more when we get to Central Park."

"Keep us updated." said Patton.

"Will do sir." said Harnist, opening the door. "Your car or mine?"

"Yours." said Murtz. "Mine's still in the shop, and sometimes these mechanics make Godot look on time."

Chapter Six

"So how did you become a cop?" asked Murtz, as Harnist turned the car onto Fifth Avenue.

"You're not psychoanalyzing me, are you?" asked Harnist; he looked like he was making a joke, but the look in his eyes said he was somewhat serious.

"No I'm not." Murtz replied. She knew most law enforcement agents, like many people, were leery of psychologists because they were afraid of being labeled as "insane", so having to work with one might make Harnist nervous. She had seen it so many times she was used to it. "The only person I'm going to psychoanalyze is our perp once we catch him. No, I'm just curious about why you went into law enforcement. It's like asking about your major; you're always guaranteed an interesting conversation."

"If you put it that way, then I'll tell you." said Harnist. Although the young cop wasn't trying to show it, Murtz could tell he was relieved she wasn't profiling him. "There was this hold-up at a bank in my hometown when I was a kid. The robbers got their money, but when they tried to get away, the cops showed up about a couple minutes earlier than they suspected. So when they tried to take a hostage, this one police officer just rushed in, disarmed all three robbers, and did it all without firing a single shot."

"Let me guess: you were in that bank when it happened." said Murtz.

"It was like watching John McClane right before my very eyes." Harnist replied. "I heard the officer who saved us all caught hell for breaking protocol and endangering lives later, but from then on he was considered a hero in town. I've wanted to be a cop ever since." Harnist pulled over into a parking space on Sixty-Fifth Street. On either side of the street there were concrete walkways surrounded by grass and melting snow. "What about you? Why criminal profiling?"

"Well, my family didn't grow up with a lot of money, but we always had enough cash for a single Christmas present for everyone." said Murtz, unbuckling her seatbelt. "And I always asked for a puzzle. Didn't matter if it was a jigsaw puzzle, a word puzzle, or a math puzzle, I just loved the feeling of putting the pieces together, solving a riddle, seeing the order hidden in the chaos."

"And the human mind's the greatest puzzle of all, right?" said Harnist.

"And the mind of the criminal is like a puzzle with extras added in." Murtz replied with a nod. "What motivates a person, what makes them commit a crime, it's always been the most fascinating part of my work, and especially when I'm trying to gauge whether or not a person is fit to stand trial."

"Does the work always stay interesting for you?" asked Harnist.

"And sometimes scary." added Murtz. "You should hear about the rapist I handled in Hartford once. I still get the chills every time I think of it." As the crime scene started to come into view, Murtz said, "So why the walk? We could've parked closer."

"Something my training officer used to do." said Harnist, his voice taking on a wistful quality. "He used to always park a little farther away from the crime scene, have a moment to collect himself before facing a dead body. He called it 'the ready stroll'. I tried to park closer once when he was in the hospital after a surgery, and it was one of the worst experiences I ever had. So now I always do the ready stroll."

"Sounds like a Zen thing." Murtz observed.

"That's what my ex-girlfriend said." said Harnist. "She was a yoga nut."

Harnist and Murtz flashed their credentials to the uniforms surrounding the scene and stepped under the yellow tape. All around the pond, cops with large cameras were taking photos of the crime scene and everyone who'd come to ogle it, while CSU techs combed over the area looking for anything out of the ordinary. At the edge of the water, a lone figure with a clipboard stood next to a body bag on a gurney. It was still pretty early and except for the sound of busy law enforcement officials the air was still. Not even the news crews had shown up yet, giving the area a sort of peace rarely found at high-profile crime scenes like this one.

"Dr. Mohawk!" called Harnist called to the man wearing a medical examiner's uniform standing by the lakeside. "How's your morning been?"

"Cold." replied the medical examiner, gesturing with his clipboard to the body on the gurney. "I got woken up at five in the morning just for this sucker. I had to wait half an hour here while NYPD and the feds hammered out a jurisdiction agreement before I could start examining the body. Who's your friend?"

"Agent Murtz, this is Dr. Ross Hillbrook." said Harnist. "Dr. Mohawk, this is Special Agent Angela Murtz with the FBI."

"Why do they call you 'Dr. Mohawk'?" asked Murtz, shaking the medical examiner's hand.

"I guess it's because I'm a Mohawk Indian and proud of it." Dr. Mohawk replied. "Now, how about I give you guys a quick run-down of the body and then I can get out of here to do an autopsy?"

"Fire away." said Harnist.

"Good. Now, as far as I can tell, we're not dealing with a copycat." Dr. Mohawk began. "The bullet hole in the forehead is the same size as the one in James Sanonia, probably the same caliber bullet too. It also looks like the knife that carved these letters here was the same type of knife as last time." Dr. Mohawk indicated the large and jagged letters on Paul Sanonia's belly, an exact copy of the letters on his cousin James. "The victim also had his driver's license between his teeth, just like his cousin. Early guess at time of death is sometime last night between eleven and one."

"So it's the same guy?" asked Murtz.

"Well, a few things are bothering me." said Dr. Mohawk. "First is that the victim has some bruising over his neck. It indicates somebody tried to strangle him before he was killed. And then there are the broken bones."

"What about them?" said Harnist. "He looks pretty broken up if you ask me. Just like his cousin."

"No, it's not how broken up he is." Dr. Mohawk explained. "It's that the bones on James Sanonia were broken right after he was murdered. The bones on his cousin though…well, they were broken before he died, and it wasn't as quick and haphazard a job as on James Sanonia." Dr. Mohawk slipped his clipboard under his arm and motioned for two assistants to come over and help him. "I'll know more once I perform an autopsy. Don't expect much from me though. After all, this guy was floating long enough to erase physical evidence, just like his cousin."

Paul Sanonia's body was wheeled to a waiting van, where it was loaded into the back and taken away. As the coroner's van drove away, Harnist looked at Murtz and said, "Well, you're the expert. What kind of killer are we dealing with?"

"This type of case?" said Murtz, her brain kicking into overdrive, considering the possibilities and drawing on her many years of working with criminals and the insane. "Probably just one killer, not two using similar MO's. And most likely we've got a vigilante type, someone who feels he can do a better job than the police at getting rid of crime. To that end he's chosen the Camerlengos, easily one of the most powerful and dangerous families in the city, and he's making sure everybody knows that he's bringing his own brand of justice to them."

"A serial killer with a hero complex." said Harnist. "And to think I almost found myself admiring him for getting rid of filth."

"Oh, but it gets worse." Murtz replied. "He may seem like he's doing good, and he may be telling himself that he's doing good, but in the end he's just getting high off all the attention we're giving him. It's garden-variety psychopathy, really. These sort of killers do what they do because they like the feeling of people noticing them."

"So he's like that Broadway actress I dated, only deadlier." said Harnist. "Let's head back to the Bureau. I'll call a judge and get Paul Sanonia's phone records and financial statements, see if there's anything strange there—oh hell."

As Harnist was speaking, a crowd of people started running towards the pond, many toting notepads, microphones, and cameras of every imaginable design and use. Leading them was a tall, blonde-haired woman with bright red lipstick and a smile that seemed to gleam in the early morning air.

"The circus is here." said Murtz.

"And Candace Berman, reporter and police-basher extraordinaire, is in the lead." Harnist added. "She never misses a moment to make herself look good at our expense."

The uniforms moved to intercept the crowd as they got closer to the pond. However Berman and her cameraman managed to get under the yellow tape and rush to Harnist and Murtz.

"Detective Harnist!" she said cheerily, as if she and Harnist were old friends. "You remember me? I covered your big arrest three months ago. So, can you tell us who might be behind the death of James Sanonia's cousin?" Berman broke right into her questioning before Harnist could even speak.

"We're chasing down several leads, and when we know something, we'll give you guys a call." Harnist gave the standard reply for reporters who were asking too much too soon.

"But is it true there may be a serial killer targeting the Camerlengo family?" asked Berman, following Harnist and Murtz as they tried to leave.

"What put that idea in your head?" asked Harnist. He and Murtz increased their speed, hoping to leave Berman behind. "You should really leave before you contaminate evidence."

"But we got a call from someone claiming to be the killer." said Berman.

Harnist and Murtz stopped and turned around to face Berman, who nearly ran into the both of them as she stopped. "You got a call?" said Murtz.

"Yeah, on our tip line. Oh Joel, get a close-up." said Berman, gesturing to her cameraman. "Yes, we got a call saying that the cousin of James Sanonia was in Central Park pond, and that the person calling had killed both of the Sanonia cousins." Berman brought her microphone closer to Harnist and Murtz, looking like a cat playing with a juicy mouse that has nowhere to go. "So, is there a serial killer in New York hunting down mobsters?"

Chapter Seven

On the other side of Central Park, far from the earnest police and the intrusive paparazzi, the Snake ran on one of the park's jogging paths, just another person among several who managed to enjoy the park even on a cold February morning such as this. Unlike the others enjoying the park though, he was very different from the rest of them. He was a monster, a creature that wore human skin but on the inside was as dark and as dangerous as Legion. If anyone else knew what he was, what he'd done in order to become this monster, any love or compassion they might have for him would be lost in overwhelming fear and disgust.

Except perhaps for one person. One who could see his good side. It was that person who was motivating the Snake in his crusade, though they probably didn't know it yet. But they would, and by then all of the Camerlengos would feel his wrath.

The Snake stopped by a tree and took a long sip from his water bottle. Beside him a large dog with grey hair and a long tail was panting, looking pleased to be out and about getting exercise in a place full of so many different smells. Around them, people pointed and stared at the large dog, as if it were an alien rather than a canine.

You'd think none of these dura'ki *have ever seen an Irish wolfhound before.* the Snake thought, swallowing his water. "Linda." he said to the dog. "*Be'gi.*" *Let's go.*

With a yip Linda starting running, the Snake jogging beside her. He'd trained Linda from the time she was a small pup, taught her to obey his commands in Russian. The training had paid off well and the Snake was pleased. Although Linda was normally docile, at a single command or even a whiff of danger to her master she could become a dangerous attack dog and a vicious homage to her ancestors who had hunted and killed wolves in the Irish forests and fields of old.

Just as he turned a bend, Snake caught sight of someone whose face he recognized, someone whom he'd searched for and found on the internet last night. *Bozhe moy*, he thought. *What luck! How unexpected!*

The Snake slowed to a walk, Linda pulling up next to him to match his pace. Seeing a nearby tree, Snake sat down and pulled out a tennis ball from his sweatshirt. Linda saw the ball and immediately started wagging her tail in joy. The Snake teased her for a second, then raised his arm and threw the ball in a direction with few people in the way. Linda bounded after the ball, her long legs catching up to it in seconds.

The Snake played with Linda for a while, lobbing the ball away from him while she ran to fetch it and bring it back. And while they played, the Snake listened to the conversation of his next target, Thomas Luiso, as he conversed in Italian to the two friends he had met with, unaware that the man sitting by a tree and playing with his giant dog was fluent in Italian.

As he listened he stole a glance at Luiso, a large, beefy man with a military buzz cut, puckish lips, and a shark tattoo on his left hand. The Snake thought Luiso looked like a bald fish on land and wondered if he smelled fishy too. Not that he wanted to check, of course

As the Snake turned his head away he heard Luiso address a question to one of the two men with him. "So, is it true that James Sanonia's cousin was murdered?"

"It looks to be that way." said one of the men with Luiso. "And he was murdered by the same man too, it seems."

Luiso swore in Italian. "The man who might be a Russian." he said. "Mr. Camerlengo will not be happy when he hears this. If we don't find this bastard soon, the other bosses and their families will start to think they're better than us. Especially those fucking Russians! *Dio Maledetto!*"

The Snake had to stop himself from laughing. *You're worried about your reputation?* Snake thought. *Not what I would be worried about if I were you. But you'll learn. You'll all learn what happens when you take what's most precious to me!*

And the Snake would be careful when he taught them. He would not allow the police to find him, he would not leave any trace evidence pointing to him. He would not do anything more than alert the police to the bodies he'd leave behind, and he would not seek publicity. He knew from too many movies and books that the moment the villain tried to let people know he was the villain, that was the moment it was assured he would fail.

And the Snake would not fail. More importantly, he could not fail. There was too much at stake.

As the men continued speaking in Italian, Snake caught Luiso saying that he needed to get going. One of the men asked if they were still having dinner at Luiso's home that weekend. Luiso indicated yes and gave the address. Snake felt his spirits soar as he heard the address. Now he knew where his target lived! It was as if God Himself was helping him bring his target to a very painful end.

As the men parted ways and Luiso headed towards Fifth Street, the Snake followed behind with Linda, keeping a steady distance. On Fifth Street Luiso got into a cab, which drove down the street, turned left, and out of sight.

Snake watched calmly with Linda. For now, everything was going well. His first two victims had served their purpose, he hadn't been caught yet, and the Camerlengos were getting angry and nervous and were looking for him.

Of course, they'd never find him. After all, only the Snake knew the truth about himself. Most importantly, he knew the one thing that everyone assumed was true was false. He was no Russian adult in the mob like they probably guessed he was. He wasn't even an adult yet! He was an eighteen-year-old American teenager who hadn't even graduated high school yet!

Chapter Eight

Allison Langland struggled with the men carrying her, screaming through the sackcloth bag and struggling with the restraints around her wrists. One of the men carrying her commented, "She's a fighter, aint she?"

"She won't fight so much once she finds out what's in store for her." said another, eliciting laughs from the rest. Allison ignored the laughter. She'd been quiet and docile for too long while she'd been kept in that office, but now she planned on fighting back. Like these men had guessed, she was a fighter by nature and from the sound of things they weren't planning on killing her, so she might as well take advantage of that fact and give them some grief.

The men carried her along for a while longer, struggling to keep their grips as Allison tossed and shook, before she felt herself being let down and righted by her captors. As the restraints around her wrist were undone, Allison slipped her hands free and took a wild swing with her right arm, connecting with a stubble-covered cheek.

There was a loud cry as one of the men holding her let go. Shaking off the pain in her hand, Allison curled her fist again and took another swing. As her arm sailed through the air, she felt a hand grab her wrist and give it a hard twist.

Allison cried out through the sackcloth that was still over her head. One of the men said, "Hey don't hurt her too much. She's valuable merchandise."

A moment later the sackcloth was lifted off her head and Allison found herself in a small, window-less room, surrounded by four men in business attire who looked anything but cheerful. One of them was holding his cheek while glaring daggers at her.

"You sure are feisty." said one of the men, the one holding her wrist. "But that'll change soon enough, once you learn what's in store for you."

The man let go of her wrist, putting his hand into his pocket and bringing out a lighter and cigarette. Allison rubbed her wrist as the man lit up, taking in a deep breath and then releasing a puff of smoke in her face. Allison coughed as the putrid fumes filled her nose.

"Aww, does the wittle girl not like cigawette smoke?" asked one of the men in a mocking baby-talk voice. "Does she think she should be tweated bettuh than this?"

"Well, that's tough." said the man Allison had punched, lunging at her. Before she could react the man was holding her in an arm lock, her arm threatening to break under the pressure. The other men laughed while the one with the cigarette came forward and held the lit end right up to Allison's nose. Allison felt her heart begin to pound as she watched the cigarette sizzle and burn and felt the heat coming from the lit end.

"You're lucky the boss doesn't want us treating you too roughly." he said. "Otherwise, you'd be dead just like your dad."

Allison looked at the man, a wave of shock mixing with the fear inside her. "My dad's—?"

"Your daddy was too unreliable." said the man holding Allison. "He might've gone to the police. We had to have him…taken care of."

"And the boss might've had you taken care of too," said the man with the cigarette, "if he didn't think you could be useful to him. So he decided to let you off easy. But what did it get him? Nothing except you trying to rock the boat. So now you have to face the consequences of your actions."

"I was scared." said Allison, feeling her heart skip a beat every time the cigarette got a little closer or a little further to the left or right. "I thought the policeman could help me."

"You thought wrong." said one of the men. "And now you're going to suffer a fate worse than death."

The man with the cigarette dropped the still-smoking butt on the ground and put it out with his shoe. "And that's the only reason we don't stick that cig anywhere on your cute body." he said.

"Otherwise, we'd poke you with it all over and do worse things besides."

"Someone else will get that honor, though." said the man holding Allison, throwing her to the ground. As Allison got up the men were leaving the room, the man who had held the cigarette bringing up the rear. As he took the door handle he looked back at Allison and said, "See you again…when your turn comes up."

Before Allison could ask what he meant, he closed the door shut behind him, leaving Allison alone in the room. A second later the lock rattled and something slid into place. From the other side of the door came the sound of cruel laughter.

Allison ran at the door, tried turning the knob, and when that didn't work she began kicking the door and pulling at the frame. "Come back here!" she called. "You can't do this! Come back in here and talk to me!" Now that nobody was holding a cigarette up to her face, Allison felt her fire return, the same fire her boyfriend had always admired and said made her special, or if she was angry enough, downright dangerous.

The men on the other side seemed to realize this or perhaps they didn't hear her, because the lock didn't rattle and the door didn't open. It was at this point Allison realized something: her father was dead and she had no idea where she was.

She was alone.

Sliding down to the floor, Allison crossed her arms and huffed angrily. *When I get out of here, those men are going to get it!* she thought. In the meantime she could wait. She could take care of herself. In fact, Allison had been doing it for years, learning to cook for herself and keep the home tidy while her dad worked and her mom lay sick in the hospital and she was alone with a nanny more concerned with soap operas than with her charge. Allison had grown up quickly, especially after her mother had died, and that was why she could wait for these men to come back for her and do…whatever they thought she was going to let them do to her.

Even so, Allison felt a tear welling up in her eye, the first tear she'd shed since her mother had died when she was eight. Slowly the realization that her father was dead and that she'd never see him again came over her. Allison cried, feeling like a little girl again.

For a while she let herself mourn before sniffling and taking some deep breaths to get herself back under control. Summoning her strength, Allison began looking around methodically, looking for a tool, an advantage, anything to get herself out of this box. She'd get out of here, she'd be exactly unlike the twits in the movies her boyfriend liked, the scary ones where the girls couldn't do shit without screaming their heads off. He was always complaining about those girls, so she would do the exact opposite of what they would do. He'd be so impressed. She'd make him so impressed he'd forget to call her Al in his awe. But first, what in this room could she use—a bucket! Allison went to the bucket sitting on the corner of the room, picked it up to see what she could do with it, and—noticed a horrible smell coming from it.

Allison dropped the bucket as she gagged from the smell, feces and urine mixed together and grown old together. Why was such a bucket in here—? Allison felt a sense of horror overcome her. She hadn't been the first girl they'd thrown in a room, had she? And these girls…they'd kept them long enough that they'd put a bucket in the room for…that.

Allison shivered and put the bucket back in the corner. She'd avoid using the bucket, either for escape or for…that. Putting the bucket out of her mind, Allison turned around the empty room, looking for something to get out of here.

Chapter Nine

Harnist and Murtz stepped off the elevator and made a beeline for Captain Patton's office. It was nearly five in the afternoon, and they'd spent the whole day combing over financial and phone records for both James and Paul Sanonia, only stopping at three to go to city hall to get the autopsy report for Paul Sanonia. In addition, Murtz and Harnist had listened to the recordings made of the 911 calls that had alerted the police to where they could find the bodies, the calls that had been made to the media alerting them to the bodies and had interviewed the Sanonia's relatives, who obviously didn't seem to want to talk to the cops, cutting the meetings short before telling them anything helpful.

As they made their way to the office, Murtz held a notepad in her hands, her analysis of the suspect and his likely character traits written in a neat, curly script. Harnist glanced at the pad and said, "Are psych profiles as good as they're made out to be on TV?"

Murtz had shaken her head in response. "They're only approximations." she explained. "We take what little data we have and, based on previous cases, experience, and what we consider most likely, try to match it all together to create a working profile."

"So you're making guesses." said Harnist. "Good guesses, but guesses."

"It can seem that way." Murtz replied. "But they can be quite accurate. Remember the case in Georgia? The police caught those two women based entirely on a profile." Then Murtz said, "But as my teacher at the academy said, you don't really know everything about a suspect until you sit down and talk to them. Only then does the picture become really clear."

As she knocked on Patton's door and opened the door, Murtz hefted the notepad under her arm and sat down in one of the chairs in front of Patton's desk. Patton sat in his chair, while on a large electronic screen behind him Section Chief Alan Gramer looked at them through a video-conference camera.

"How's your day been?" asked Gramer. "Learn anything?"

"A bit." said Harnist, closing the door behind him. "Both our vics were spotted leaving public places at some point between ten and eleven the nights they died, and then show up dead after three in the morning, in water, with bones broken, bullets in their head, no clothes, and no evidence to help us track down our killer."

"The autopsies did turn up some interesting things, though." said Murtz.

"What sort of things?" asked Patton.

"Paul Sanonia's body." Murtz began. "Unlike his cousin, his bones were broken before he was murdered. Not only that, but whereas James Sanonia's broken bones span the length of his body,

53

Paul Sanonia's fractures are all below the shoulders. No damage at all to his neck or head."

"Plus Paul Sanonia was strangled at some point during all this." Harnist added.

"Does that mean we have a copycat after all?" asked Patton.

"No sir." said Harnist. "Dr. Mohawk says that the bullets from Paul Sanonia match James Sanonias. They were both murdered by the same forty-five millimeter Glock, so most likely they were murdered by the same person."

"When was the last time anyone saw these men alive?" asked Gramer.

"James Sanonia was clocked leaving a bar near his home the night he died a little after ten-thirty." Harnist answered. "The bartender remembers him not being that drunk as he left. Paul Sanonia was seen leaving the Episcopal Church of St. Mark last night and getting into a cab around that same time. But that's the interesting thing."

"What is?" asked Gramer.

"Right before Paul Sanonia left the church, he received a phone call on his cell." said Murtz. "The call was from a burner phone, so we can't trace it. However, right after he received that phone call, Paul Sanonia left the church and got into the cab."

"So Sanonia received a call, possibly from our killer, and was lured out to meet him in another location." said Patton. "Sounds like this guy doesn't like to be in the open and waits for his victims to be alone before doing anything."

"That would fit with my profile." said Murtz.

"Before we get to that though, you should know about the cab." said Harnist. "The medallion is registered to a man from Nicaragua who's been living in New York for three years. It took a lot of rusty Spanish, but I managed to figure out that his cab was stolen last night around nine, and he didn't report it because his cab company's getting audited and he was afraid a lost cab would cause problems."

"The cab was found this morning behind a dumpster two blocks from the church." said Murtz. "CSU's going over it now, but I'm willing to bet we won't find useful."

"He's probably using stolen cars to get around the city." said Harnist. "However unless we're able to find a car he used, there's no way to confirm that."

Patton sighed. "What kind of freak are we dealing with here? He knows just about every trick in the book."

"I think that might be because he's ex-military." said Murtz.

"Ex-military?" Gramer repeated.

Both Gramer and Patton fixed their attention on Murtz, who turned to the notepad resting on her lap. "Yes, but based on the phone calls he's not American military, but Russian." Murtz explained, glancing down at her notes every few seconds. "According to a professor from NYU, it's an authentic Russian voice on the other end of the call, so most likely he's a native Russian male, between the ages of thirty and forty-five, and has extensive experience with weapons, especially firearms. He's been in country at least ten years, might be a taxi driver himself if our hunch about the cars is right, and may or may not have ties to the Russian mob here."

"And he's killing because…?" asked Patton.

"He thinks he's better at delivering justice to criminals than the police." Murtz explained. "And he's doing it in such a way that both the police and the Camerlengos know about it. He craves attention, which is why he's contacting both police and the media. If we were to send him a message through TV news programs, he'd likely respond to it in the hopes we'd give him more press time."

"Let's hold off on sending this guy a love letter through the newspapers or television." Gramer instructed. "Candace Berman's already been on the news saying there might be a mafia-hunting serial killer on the loose in New York, only she said that in more idealistic terms."

"Sounds like something she'd do." said Harnist.

"See if anyone matches Murtz's profile here in New York." commanded Patton. "Contact INS and see if they have any Russian ex-military in their system. And Murtz?"

"Yes sir?"

"What's the likelihood this guy will kill again?" asked Patton.

Murtz looked Patton straight in the eye and said, "Likely. Extremely likely."

Chapter Ten

The Snake was in a good mood as he returned to his home with Linda. Despite the cold he had tailed Thomas Luiso most of the day, staying discreet and out of sight as the mobster had gone around Manhattan making sure that people were paying their loans on time. At some point Luiso had stopped for lunch with a pretty young woman in a nurse's uniform at a small café a few blocks from Bellevue Hospital Center. At the end of their meal, Luiso had kissed the nurse passionately on the lips before dropping her off at the hospital and leaving to collect more loans. At the end of the day Luiso had gone home and had hugged his wife hello. His wife, it turned out, was not the nurse from Bellevue.

In the morning the Snake would get up early and tail Luiso again. At some point the man would be alone and then the Snake would be able to take him. It was only a matter of time.

The apartment building where the Snake had been staying recently came into view. It wasn't the nicest building and the manager wouldn't have allowed Linda to live there without a healthy bribe of cash, but for now it suited the Snake's purpose and that was all that mattered to him.

The Snake entered the building and jogged up the stairs to the third floor, Linda padding merrily beside him. As he approached his apartment the Snake reached for his keys—and stopped. The door to his apartment was slightly ajar. Someone was in his apartment, and it looked like they were expecting him or they were very stupid if they were leaving the door open like this. Still, it was better to err on the side of caution.

Slowly the Snake replaced his keys in his pocket and pulled out his Glock and mask. Slipping on his mask and switching the gun's safety off, he looked down at Linda and whispered, "*Vnimaniye.*" *On guard.* At once Linda's sweet demeanor vanished as she began growling, eyeing the door as if an enemy were about to pop out of there at any given moment. Given the people the Snake had pissed off, he was counting on that.

The Snake backed against the wall and brought up his Glock to the level of his head, like he'd seen police do in the movies and on television. Slowly he inched his right foot in front of the door, his heart beating louder and louder with every passing second. The Snake paused, counted slowly to three, raised his foot, and swung it full force into the door, which opened with a loud creak, banging against the wall as it stopped.

Nothing happened. No gunshots, no footsteps. As far as the Snake knew, nobody was moving in the apartment. At least, there wasn't anyone moving in the apartment by the front door.

The Snake dared a peek past the door frame. Nobody by the coat rack or in the living room, which meant whoever was inside was either in the kitchen, the bathroom, or the bedroom. The Snake moved his head back from the door frame and issued another command to Linda, who gave a loud, commanding bark and disappeared into the apartment. There was a shout of surprise from the kitchen and Linda started barking loudly, every bark punctuated with a low-throated growl. The Snake pushed himself off the wall and walked into the apartment, gun pointed casually in front of him. He now knew he had nothing to fear. Whoever was here had not been expecting to be attacked, let alone expecting Linda to run in and corner them. That meant the intruder was probably unarmed, a deadly contrast to the Snake and Linda and if needed could be dispatched quickly.

The Snake closed the door behind him, hung up his coat and strode into the kitchen. In the corner by the stove, a tall man in an expensive-looking suit and jacket was grimacing at Linda, whose growling intensified every time the man in the corner moved.

The Snake recognized the man and immediately felt annoyed. *I almost would've preferred someone attacking me.* he thought to himself, pulling off his mask and switching his Glock back to safety. *This is the last person I want to see right now.*

The man in the corner noticed the Snake and yelled, "Get this mangy mongrel off of me!"

"Linda." said the Snake. "*Otpusti.*" At once Linda stopped growling and padded away from the man in the corner, who took a deep breath and glared menacingly at the Snake.

"Why the hell did that damned dog attack me?" he growled, a vein on the man's forehead popping out. "She should've known me!"

"Well, you're never at home, so she doesn't know you. Besides, you were intruding, and I wasn't sure whether or not the person in my apartment was hostile or stupid." the Snake replied simply, as if that response covered everything. The Snake sighed then, and said, in his regular American accent, "What are you doing here, Dad?"

Chapter Eleven

The Snake's father glared at his son, his face a portrait of fury. Then his face suddenly relaxed and a strange smile that looked out of place on the Snake's father appeared. The Snake knew what that look meant, that his father was extremely angry about something but trying to hide it and that was when he was his most unpredictable. Once upon a time that would have worried and even have scared the Snake.

Not anymore.

"What am I doing here? Well, let me think about it." said his father, walking around the kitchen counter toward his son. "I come home from a hard day's work, you know, because I don't want to be at that apartment that I bought for late nights at the office, and what do I find out from the housekeeper? That my son has run off with the dog and a suitcase, leaving his little sister in tears. And for what? An illusion."

The smile on his father's face disappeared and the frown returned, deeper and angrier-looking than before. "An illusion." he repeated. "A fucking illusion. And if that weren't enough, the little ingrate that I'd raised and fed and clothed and given the best education possible has stolen nearly twenty-five thousand dollars from a private safe in my office at home, and used it to rent a shitty apartment, bribe his landlord, and God only knows what else he's done with that money!

"So, I think I'm well within my rights as a parent to track down my son, using the serial numbers on the bills he stole and a connection at the FBI, and let him know how terribly disappointed I am in him before I drag him home."

The Snake sighed and said, "Is there a point to this little speech, besides how paranoid you have to be to write down all those serial numbers? Because I turned eighteen last month and I really don't have to listen to you anymore."

Snake's father swung his fist toward his son, but the Snake caught it easily in midair. Bringing the gun up to his father's chest, the Snake grinned malevolently at his father, who was looking down at the gun as if he were noticing it for the first time.

"Hitting a guy with a gun?" said the Snake. "For an investment broker you really aren't that smart. Lucky for you though, I took off my mask."

"What does that have to do with anything?" asked the Snake's father, his eyes never leaving the gun.

"Oh, it's everything." Snake explained. "It makes everything a movie, and I'm the most important actor. But most importantly, I can't cause you intense pain, let alone kill you, without it. That doesn't mean I can't cause you *any* pain though." As he spoke, the Snake squeezed and twisted his father's arm. The Snake's father groaned, collapsing onto his knees with a pained look. The Snake watched his father's expression for a moment before letting him go.

His father gasped, cradling his arm against his chest as if it threatened to fall off. "Let me rephrase what I said before." said the Snake. "I am no longer in your power. I don't have to listen to you anymore, and I certainly don't have to put up with any of your shit anymore."

"I'm your father!"

"What you are is a sociopath." said Snake. "The best thing you ever did for me was donate sperm for Ruby. The rest of the time, it's always been about you. Always you, never anyone else. Why do you think Mom left?"

"And what are you?" said the Snake's father. "If I'm a selfish sociopath, what does that make you?"

"Good question." said the Snake, sidestepping his father, going to the fridge, and grabbing a soda. "I'm mentally unbalanced, that's for sure. But it's not exactly a bad thing, being unbalanced. So far, it's served its purpose."

"What the hell are you talking about?"

"I killed two people, Dad." the Snake explained, pulling the tab on his soda. "One of them was an advisor for the Camerlengo family and the other was the advisor's cousin and a recruiter for an escort service connected to the Camerlengos." The Snake took a gulp of soda and turned to face his father, who had a shocked look of realization on his face. "I see you've heard of me. Oh, and nice approximation of looking horrified. You really are good at imitating people's expressions, you know."

"The New York Mafia Killer," whispered the Snake's father. "The New York Mafia Killer is my own son."

"Is that what they're calling me?" said the Snake. "I haven't been paying attention to the news. I've been too busy following my next victim. A serial killer's has to stay busy."

"This is because of those films, isn't it?" said the Snake's father. "Those disgusting films where teens are senselessly murdered? I knew I should never have let you watch those films—!"

"Oh for God's sake, stop your sanctimonious bitching." the Snake cut in. "I know you don't believe what you're saying right now, and that you had no hand in me watching those movies, and they aren't the reason why I've become a murderer. I was born unbalanced…and you didn't exactly help."

"And what exactly brought on this murderous rage?" asked the Snake's father. "What's so important that you felt you needed to abandon your sister, your school, your future, and murder the members of a powerful organized crime family?"

"Well, you brought that up earlier." the Snake answered. "My 'illusion', as you called it, is my motivation, and it's half the reason why I'm doing things the way I'm doing them. But the other half...if you knew the other half, you'd know just how disturbed I am. And you know what the best part is?" The Snake sidled up to his father, standing about an inch or two above his father's head. "You can't tell anyone. Otherwise your oh-so precious reputation goes in the tubes. And you won't allow that."

The Snake's father looked apoplectic. "I should never have come after you." he said after a pause. "You're disowned. Don't ever come back to my house again, and never go near your sister again."

"Don't think you'll be rid of me." said the Snake, his face inches away from his father's. "The serial killers never go away. Look at all the bad sequels out there. I'll find a way to get Ruby away from you once this business is over, one way or another. Now get out before I'm forced to do something I would be all too happy to do." As he spoke, the Snake's voice became deeper, a Russian accent creeping into the words.

The Snake's father brushed past his son, opened the door, and slammed the door behind him. The Snake was glad to see him go. He'd been an inch away from putting on his mask and getting custody of his sister through murder.

Chapter Twelve

The Snake went to the door and locked it. He did not want his father getting back in, though for what reason that sorry excuse for a human being would want to come back in, the Snake did not want to guess. All the Snake cared about was that his father could become unpredictable when angry, and that was something the Snake did not want to deal with right now. He'd had to deal with it all the time when he was younger, his father shouting and throwing things and insulting him and his mother and a couple of times even beating them. The beatings had stopped when the Snake had begun to fill out and become bigger than his father, but as he had just witnessed, his father was still capable of swinging his fists when angry.

As the Snake turned away from the door, he wondered how his father had gotten into his apartment in the first place. He'd probably convinced the manager to let him in, and probably used a huge donation of cash in the process. He'd have to speak to the manager about that. The Snake couldn't allow anyone to interfere with his mission, and his apartment was a safe house between victims. It was a place that shouldn't and couldn't be violated if he were to continue using it.

The Snake downed the rest of his soda, threw the can into a small blue recycling bin by the kitchen counter, and then went to the cabinet and got out a treat for Linda, who accepted it graciously with a big wet kiss. The Snake laughed, rubbing her on the head. "Don't worry girl." he said. "We'll finish what we set out to accomplish. And then we'll get Ruby away from the big, nasty man."

Linda did not respond, too intent on her dog biscuit to care very much. However the Snake was sure that she missed Ruby, the sweet little girl they'd left behind at the Snake's father's home. The Snake was pretty sure that his father wouldn't vent his rage on Ruby, and that she'd be taken care of by Georgia the housekeeper, but the Snake worried about her. His little sister seemed so bright and cheerful, but deep down he knew she hurt without a mother and only her uncaring father. With her brother and Linda, the people she loved the most, gone to fulfill a very important mission, she had no one to take care of her—

Don't go there. thought the Snake, shaking his head to rid himself of the thought. *You've got important work to do. You can't fail because of doubts or regrets. There's too much at stake.*

The Snake took off his shirt and got out the bench press and weights. He then went to the stereo he'd installed next to the small TV he'd bought the other day, and turned up the volume. At once heavy metal music came blaring out, filling the Snake's body from his ears to his very core as he listened. With a sigh of contentment, he blotted out his thoughts, went to the bench press, and started lifting. He'd been a health freak before, eating only vegetarian food and working out whenever possible, but since he'd resolved to get back what he'd lost and take down the Camerlengos, he'd been a fanatic to stay fit and strong, and his determination had shown not only in his physique, but in how brutally he tortured and killed his victims.

I won't stop. he thought, the Russian accent creeping into his thought patterns as it always did when he was focused on his mission. *That* chudovishche *who calls himself my father may see what I strive for as an illusion, but I know the truth. It's stronger than me, and I'll do anything to preserve it, even if I have to kill to do it.*

Chapter Thirteen

Night in the Bronx was never easy for Carla Scarusco. After the office closed and everybody went home, she was often plagued by insomnia and tonight was no exception. In fact, tonight was worse, because tonight Carla was burdened by more than just her own regrets and broken dreams. Tonight, Carla was wracked with guilt as she sat in her chair with her back to the dark office.

Well, "office" was a pretty loose term for what they did here. Some of the girls had their own names for this big room they all worked in: the "call-for-sex center"; the "talk-and-fuck shop"; and probably Carla's least favorite, the "best brothel on the phone lines". And someone had thought it clever to call Carla the Central Sexecutive Officer because she ran the whole thing.

What had happened to her? How'd she end up working in this dump, leaving her office every night at eleven to go next door to her suite, only to come back here when sleep eluded her? She'd had dreams once: dreams of bright lights and Broadway and men who would give her flowers just because she could deliver a line with just the right amount of zing.

But the roles didn't come and she'd had to go to her uncle Christopher Camerlengo for help, even though she wasn't an official member of the Camerlengo Family. She'd begged and groveled for him to help her get back on her feet. And what had he done? "Sure Carla, I'll help you. You just got to help me for a while." That's what he'd said to her. And that had been seven years ago. She was never leaving this dump. Once you were indebted to the Camerlengo family, you were indebted for life, and that was especially so if you were indebted to Christopher Camerlengo.

And now look what I've done. thought Carla, tears spilling into her hot cocoa. *I could've helped that poor girl, and I just stood by out of fear. I'm a horrible person.*

Carla flashed back to when two of her uncle's flunkies had appeared in the office a couple of weeks ago. Having anyone from the family visit her was a rare occasion, as they usually only showed up to let her know she was late with a payment or that the payment rates were being adjusted, so Carla was very surprised when two members of the family appeared, shoving a girl in front of them at gunpoint.

One of the flunkies, whose name Carla was sure was Veretti or something like that, had said that the girl would be working in the center from now on, and that she'd be living in the building too. Veretti had also mentioned that the girl was a "special case", so Carla had to take good care of her. Carla knew what the words "special case" meant: that whoever this girl was, she could be dangerous but would be allowed to live if she behaved.

"Surely you can handle that, can't you Carly?" the other flunky had asked, the one whose name Carla could never remember. They'd left laughing like it was one big joke, like leaving a girl who posed a threat to the family under close surveillance at a phone-sex service was just as funny as calling Carla "Narly Carly, who enjoys phone-sex as much as horses enjoy oats and barley". Pricks.

The girl they'd brought in had looked around fearfully, as if she was surrounded by lions in a Roman arena. Carla had merely sighed, learned that the girl's name was Allison, and then showed her what they did at the office.

Allison had got used to living with Carla in the building, and wasn't half-bad at operating the phones in the sound-proof booths they used. Some of the other girls had even started calling her "Little A", on account that the girl was so young and naïve when it came to sex and yet there she was working as a phone-sex operator. Even Carla had come to like the girl a bit, though she wouldn't say anything in case it somehow got back to the Camerlengos.

And then today, several of the Camerlengos had shown up unexpectedly and dragged Allison out of her booth in the middle of a call. They'd carried her out of the office, kicking and screaming, while all the other girls watched in dumb amazement. Then one of the men who'd come for Allison had pulled out a gun, held it out at arm's length, swept his gaze around the room, and said that if anyone said anything about this incident, "they could kiss their lives goodbye".

Then the men had left. No reason, no explanation, not even a hint of where they might be taking the poor girl. But Carla had a hunch, and she did not like it one bit. *Oh Little A.* she thought. *I'm so sorry. I hope to God you come out of this alright. Please forgive me.*

A siren cried in the gloom and Carla watched as an ambulance passed down below her window. She cried and more of her tears fell into her cocoa as she contemplated suicide for the thousandth time since she'd started working in this office, this time with more seriousness than she had ever contemplated suicide with before.

Chapter Fourteen

The Snake watched from his hiding place as Luiso stepped out the front door of his house, whistling merrily in a thick leather coat and a red ski cap. From inside the house the Snake could hear Luiso's wife yell, "Bowl a strike for me, sweetie."

"Will do!" Luiso called, closing and locking it behind him. Luiso walked to the corner and turned right, crossing the street and out of sight. The Snake counted to five and then, followed by Linda, went in the same direction as Luiso. Together, the Snake and Linda caught up with Luiso, keeping several yards behind him, avoiding the illumination of headlights and streetlamps as they weaved behind cars and bushes. It was a dark night, and dressed entirely in black, the Snake might have looked like a floating head bobbing alongside a lone miniature pony to any passerby that happened to be out.

Suddenly Luiso took a left turn, away from the nearest bowling alley. The Snake stopped and watched as Luiso crossed the street again, moving farther and farther away from the nearest bowling alley with each step. The Snake was perplexed, but he was also excited. If Luiso wasn't going bowling like he'd told his wife, then where was he going?

The Snake followed after Luiso, Linda padding quietly along behind him. Luiso walked down a few more blocks, still whistling merrily to himself. No other walkers passed Luiso or the

Snake as Luiso lead them farther away from his house and any bowling alley. Once a car drove by, but Snake and Linda were able to hide before the driver could see them. And as Luiso continued walking, the Snake felt curiosity biting at him. Where was he going? Who was he meeting? Would the Snake be able to take him tonight?

After a while, Luiso turned right and started up the steps to the front porch of a small blue house with potted flowers hanging from the windows. He cleared his throat and then knocked on the front door. A moment later the door swung open and the pretty nurse that the Snake had seen Luiso with two days ago threw her arms around him. The Snake watched as she led him into the house, closing the door with a tittering laugh.

The Snake waited for a minute, then he and Linda ran from their hiding place to behind the house. Under the window, he and Linda listened to their conversation, mixed with the clink of silverware and the uncorking of a bottle.

"...my wife won't let me leave, she's a major Catholic that way. But I'll find a way to leave and get the kids away from her, just you wait."

"Don't worry, Tom. I believe in you. Now how about some champagne and chicken alfredo?"

The Snake tuned out their conversation and motioned for Linda to follow him. Behind the house they found several large rose bushes and hid behind them. The Snake peered behind the gap between two of the bushes, watching them in the kitchen as they ate, drank, and flirted. Linda lay down on the ground and stretched out her enormous body. She knew they'd be waiting for a while by watching her master's body language, a sign of how well the Snake had trained her.

The Snake couldn't hear what Luiso and his mistress were saying, but the way they acted with each other—the kisses, the laughs, their body language—brought back memories for him. Slowly he felt himself drifting away from the present and into the past, to when he'd started down this dark path. The backyard faded and he was in a happier time.

PART TWO

HUNTING IN THE CONCRETE JUNGLE

Chapter Fifteen

Eleven days ago

Central Park was a thin blanket of white with spots of green poking out in different spots. Small flakes drifted down from the sky, landing on the ground and in hair and fur and onto the surfaces of lakes and ponds before being swallowed up by the murky liquid. The air was quiet and still and the cold bit at even the most heavily covered patrons of the park.

At the same pond where Paul Sanonia would be dumped in and then found a few weeks later, a pair of teenagers walked arm in arm, close to each other as if only by holding each other close they could escape the air's icy grip on them. Ahead of them, wearing a hat and a scarf, a large Irish wolfhound led the way, connected to the teens by a long leash that the boy held in front of him with one outstretched arm. There was nobody else around, and it was quiet, and it seemed perfect, just them and the dog walking through Central Park on a cold winter's day.

"So, did your dad find a date for tonight's...what'd you call it again?" asked the boy. He was average in looks, his air was that of someone who was unremarkable and liked it that way, and his name was so ordinary you were likely to forget it after you heard it. Until recently, he had hardly been known outside the film club at his prep school, and he hadn't even attracted the attention of bullies who preyed on unassuming kids like him, though they would get a nasty surprise if they ever tried to attack him.

"Societal gathering." said the girl, who was beautiful, with long red hair and a stunningly smooth face with skin that looked as white and as soft as cream. "That's what he calls it, anyway. If you ask me, it's just an excuse for him to get dressed up and talk to people who have more money than he does so he can get more money than he already has. And to answer your question, he did not get a date."

The boy looked at the girl, a small part of him still unable to believe their arms were linked like this. Her name was Allison Langland, and if her beauty didn't make you remember her name, her personality would: she was a confident girl, one who didn't back down from a challenge or from something that scared her, and who put flirts to shame with her comebacks to their come-ons. She was also a very fiery young woman, whose anger could scare her teachers into submission if they were unfortunate enough to be on the receiving end of her rage. Despite all this, many boys wanted Allison, which led to them being surprised and very upset when they found out she was dating a very unremarkable boy.

The boy groaned as he heard the news about her father. "You're his backup, aren't you?"

"I'm not happy about it either." said Allison. "All the boys our age who will be there will be looking at me like a piece of furniture for sale, the girls will be looking at the boys like they're succulent hors d'oeuvres, and anyways, I can't stand my dad's friends."

"Aren't they all mafia types from his military academy days?" said the boy.

"Yeah, and I don't like them one bit." said Allison. "But you know my dad, he can't go alone, and I made a promise."

"Ruby's going to be disappointed you can't come over tonight." said the boy. "She was looking forward to you watching *High School Musical* with us for the thousandth time."

Allison laughed. "I'd prefer to hang with you and your sister than with the mafia." said Allison. "Though I got to admit, the mafia doesn't normally ask to hear how you and I met like it's the greatest story ever."

"You mean it's not?" asked the boy with a laugh, remembering to the day he'd met Allison. It had been a simple study hall last spring, no different than any other. The boy had been hunched over his laptop, doing research for a documentary the film club would be entering into a contest for high school film societies. Their documentary would be covering the history of organized crime in New York City, and the boy would be directing, something he'd done before and something that most members of the film club agreed was a talent of his, among others.

The boy scrolled over a recent article a professor at Hudson University had sent him, one that dealt with the links between organized crime and prostitution over the past fifteen years. *...during this period, the number of arrests for prostitution, promoting prostitution, soliciting prostitution, and similar crimes fell with each month, with only 62 arrests for the specified crimes in May 1996, compared to 204 arrests for those same crimes a year ago!*

"Uwaah!" The boy was startled as someone slammed their books down a few chairs to the left of him and looked to see a girl with red hair and a pretty face seething with rage as her hands clenched her books. "That bastard is so unfair!"

For a moment the boy considered not getting involved, but then he noticed the girl's beautiful body underneath her school uniform and asked, "Everything alright?"

The girl looked at him as if she'd forgotten there were other people in the library with her. "Oh, I'm sorry." she said, looking slightly embarrassed. "I'm just a little frustrated. I've got a history test tomorrow, and my teacher just sprung on us that the test will be entirely essays."

"You've got Henderson, don't you?" said the boy, feeling a sense of déjà vu as he remembered being upset the year before just like this girl was now. The girl looked surprised again, but nodded her head anyway. The boy smiled and said, "I had him last year for history. If you want, I can help you. I know how to pass his essay exams."

"I know how to write an essay." said the girl, looking a little insulted.

"Do you know how to write an essay for Henderson?" asked the boy. "Because he likes only a certain type of essay, and I happen to know what it is. And it's not the kind they teach us to write for the SATs."

The girl's eyes narrowed and she pursed her lips, which the boy knew meant that the girl was trying to decide if she should allow the boy to help her. The boy had always been good at reading people's body language, a talent born from watching his dad to see if he was in a hitting mood when he was younger, and he could tell everything that was going through this girl's mind just from looking at her.

The boy noticed a sudden release of tension in the girl's shoulders, and knew before she had opened her mouth that she'd decided to let him help her. The boy moved down closer to the girl and gave her his name and his hand to shake. The girl took it and said, "Pleasure to meet you. I'm Allison Langland."

The boy knew of course who this girl was. Allison Langland, unlike himself, was a very remarkable person, beautiful and studious, and part of a group of girls who were also very beautiful and studious. He'd also heard that many a hunky jock or self-styled ladies' man had asked her out, only to be rejected and walk away looking like a beaten dog.

But now that the boy was shaking her hand and they had been formally introduced, he couldn't help but notice that her smile was full of confidence and pride, and the way her forehead had knitted when she'd been considering his offer for help had been very cute, but a cute that was different than the cute his dog or the cute his sister had. It brought strange feelings to the boy's chest, feelings that weren't like the curious lust he'd felt a few moments ago and that he wasn't very well-acquainted with but decided he liked these new feelings all the same.

Over the next thirty minutes, he showed her how to write an essay that Allison's picky history teacher would enjoy. To the boy's surprise, they were getting along very well, laughing at Mr. Henderson's funny mustache and complaining about his teaching methods. Then Allison asked what he was doing on his computer, which led to a discussion about the film club and their documentary project, which led to the boy inviting Allison to a meeting of the film club. The bell rang, but before Allison left she said she'd consider going to the meeting, which only made the feelings in the boy's chest intensify.

He was so happy when she showed up later that day at the club's meeting, the only person in the room not surprised to see the famous Allison Langland at a film club meeting. Allison stayed through the meeting, showed up at the next one, and even ended up helping to finish the documentary. As he'd spent more time with her, the boy and Allison became friendlier with each other, and eventually, based on her body language, he'd guessed that she had feelings for him, which made him happy and made the boy realize he'd had feelings for her. This had led to the boy gathering up the courage to ask Allison out on a date. The rest, as he told Ruby every time he recounted the tale to her, was history.

"You know why I decided to go to the film club, even though I'd never consider it my thing?" said Allison suddenly, taking the boy out of his memory of their first meeting and all that had happened afterward.

"You know, I never asked about that." said the boy. "I was just happy you decided to come to that meeting."

"It was because you didn't flirt or just assume I'd go out with you." said Allison. "I hadn't seen that in a guy since elementary school. I was hoping that if I got to know you a little better, you'd stay that way."

"You went to the film club just so you could see if we could be friends?" asked the boy.

"Well, at first." Allison replied. "But as time went on...let's just say that when I auditioned for the summer movie, I was really happy when you asked me out afterwards. What about you? Did you just want to be friends when we first met? Or were you hoping we'd start going out?"

The boy remembered how he'd been slyly checking out Allison's body the first time he'd met her and wondered if the blood was rushing to his cold cheeks. "Going out, I guess?" said the boy. "I don't know."

"You don't know?"

The boy stopped walking, shut out his thoughts about Allison's body when he'd first met her, and turned so that he was hugging Allison to him. "I don't know, and I don't really care." said the boy. "All I know is I'm happy when I'm around you, my sister adores you, you never get weirded out or anything when I get excited by slasher films or horror novels. You're amazing, and I thank God I got such an awesome girlfriend every day."

"Ah, that's sweet." said Allison, kissing the boy on the lips. "I'm pretty sure you took that line from a lot of movies and songs, but it's still very sweet. And for the record, I think the reason I started to fall for you is that you're different from other boys I've dated, which I like. And when I say different, I don't mean your little eccentricities."

"Is it the dog and the cute little sister?" asked the boy with a wry smile. "Or the fact that I can talk about your good qualities in seven different languages and two dialects?"

Allison laughed. "Come on, Linda looks like she wants to smell that bush." They walked a little farther on before reaching the edge of the park. In one of the parking spaces they could see Allison's father in his black Jetta, waving to her from the driver's seat.

"Looks like I have to go." said Allison, turning to the boy. "I'll call you tonight when I get tired of the conversation and I want to talk to someone's who's more than a pretty face."

"Am I even that?" asked the boy.

"Okay, that's a little too self-deprecating." said Allison. "You'll be available later tonight right, 'kay?" Even though she phrased it as a question, the boy could tell that she was demanding it, for the sake of her sanity as well as for the sake of their relationship.

The boy smiled. *She's not afraid to say what she wants from somebody.* he thought. *I adore her for that.* "Okay, Al. Whatever you say."

"I wish you'd stop calling me that, you know." groaned Allison. "It's annoying."

86

"But your nose scrunches up in the cutest way when you're annoyed." said the boy.

"No it does not." said Allison. She must have noticed something on the boy's face, because then she said, "What's up? You look like you want to say something."

The boy looked Allison in the eye and said, "I love you."

Allison smiled when she heard that and said, "I love you too." She kissed him again, held for a second, and then let go, leaving a pleasant warm tingling on the boy's lips. "Call you later."

Allison hugged him, patted Linda on the head, and ran to her father's car. She climbed into the passenger seat and waved to the boy as the car drove away from the park. The boy waved back, touching his hand to his lips, the feel of her kiss still there.

Chapter Sixteen

The Snake broke out of his reverie as he noticed Luiso and the nurse moving out of the kitchen and out of sight. The Snake watched as the nurse turned off the kitchen lights before leading Luiso somewhere in the house. A moment later the lights came on in an upstairs room, and the Snake could see silhouettes coming together and then falling out of sight.

"Linda." said the Snake, his voice deepened and accented. Next to him the dog woke up and looked at her master with a grunt. "Get ready to go, Linda." With a yawn Linda stood up and stretched her large body before joining the Snake at the bush. The Snake put on his mask and watched as the silhouettes appeared briefly before the lights in the upstairs room went out.

The Snake guessed that Luiso and his nurse were probably in the middle of a good fuck and decided that the situation was perfect. Luiso would be unguarded while in the throes of passion, he would not expect someone to attack him. He would be an easy target.

The Snake stepped out of the bushes and crept to the back door, listening for sounds of others. Linda followed, sniffing the air as she went. Walking on tiptoe, the Snake strode up the steps to the door, tested it, and found it locked. No matter; he had planned for this.

The Snake reached into his pocket and pulled out a small key. To anyone who didn't know better, the key might've belonged to a house, a car, or a box lock. In actuality, the key in the Snake's hand was a bump key, a key specially made to force open many different locks. It could be used over and over, and if one knew what they were doing they could break open a lock quickly and quietly.

The Snake inserted the bump key into the lock, the lock tumblers stopping the key after the first tooth. The Snake took a deep breath, counted to three, and then pushed the key in, rotating the lock to the right as he did so. There was a click, the key went in, and the door opened. The Snake grinned and stepped inside the house, giving Linda the command to stay outside and keep guard.

As the Snake stepped into the dark and empty kitchen, music started playing in his head. He recognized the music: it was the theme at the beginning of the Jack the Ripper film he had made the semester before he'd met Allison. The Snake had composed the music with a friend who studied musical composition, and it had been one of the highlights of the film, according to the critics. This particular section of the musical score was from the scene when Jack is about to sneak up on Mary Jane Kelly and have his identity revealed. While the Snake wasn't planning on revealing his identity or stopping his murderous rampage with Luiso, he could see how the music fit the situation.

You will suffer. the Snake thought as he found the stairs. *I will put you through pain as I get what I want from you, and then you will change from a mere thug into a wonderful message for your master, Christopher Camerlengo.*

The Snake crept up the stairs, touching each stair with the tip of his shoe to see if it creaked before actually getting on the step. In a few minutes he was on the second floor, right outside the room where he'd seen the silhouettes minutes before. The Snake stood outside the door, taking deep breaths to calm himself. He listened, waiting for the lovemaking to reach its peak. As the moans grew louder in their intensity, the Snake readied himself to spring.

There was a final yell and then Luiso's voice saying, "Oh, that was great."

The Snake entered the room with his gun pointed at Luiso, still hovering over his mistress nurse in her bed. "*Dobrei vecher*, Mr. Luiso." he said. *Good evening, Mr. Luiso.*

Luiso turned around in shock while the mistress nurse screamed. The Snake fired off a shot, and the bullet zipped through the silencer and into the wall above the head of the nurse. Luiso's mistress saw the bullet hole two inches above her head and fell over in a dead faint. Meanwhile, Luiso looked from his unconscious mistress to the Snake, back to his mistress, and then finally back to the Snake, who said, "Hope I'm not interrupting anything."

Chapter Seventeen

Luiso stared at the Snake as if he didn't know who or what he was looking at. Then he started shaking in anger and said, "Who the fuck do you think you are?"

"That is irrelevant." the Snake replied. "Now, you can give up easily and we can do this cleaner than I usually do, or we can—"

Luiso jumped out of the bed and threw a punch at the Snake. The Snake caught the punch with his left hand, brought his knee up into Luiso's flabby stomach, and pushed him away with his boot. Luiso flopped onto the bed, holding his gut and groaning.

The Snake laid his gun on a vanity table beside the door and shook his head as music began to fill his head, a dark, visceral music that called to mind a bloody attack by a terrifying killer. *Looks like I'll have to do this the hard way*, thought the Snake.

The Snake strode over to Luiso, who was just getting off the bed. Luiso looked at him and cursed in Italian. "You son of a bitch." he growled. The Snake ignored him, reaching for Luiso's neck.

Just then Luiso spun, kicking the Snake in the knee. The Snake stumbled backward, hitting his head against the wall. Luiso ran at him, swinging his fist. The Snake dodged, moving his head to the right to avoid Luiso's fist, which went into the wall with a sickening crunch. Luiso pulled on his hand, but it looked stuck.

The Snake smiled from beneath his mask and grabbed Luiso's meaty left nipple, giving it a hard twist. Luiso screamed in pain, grabbing the Snake's arm weakly with the hand not stuck in the wall.

Letting go of the nipple, the Snake pulled back his fists and punched Luiso in the gut and face. Luiso groaned with each impact, looking more and more on the verge of fainting every time the Snake hit him. The Snake kept up the barrage, his excitement building. *How much longer can you go?* he thought. *How much more can you struggle before I beat you into submission?*

As the Snake was considering letting up a little on Luiso, Luiso swung a fist at the side of the Snake's head, hitting him right in the ear. The Snake fell over, holding his ear as if it were about to fall off. With a loud crunch, Luiso freed his other hand from the wall and turned to the Snake. "You are so *morto*, freak." said Luiso. "Teach you to mess with me!"

The Snake saw Luiso take a step towards him and threw himself at Luiso's large belly, sending the man backwards and over. Luiso fell onto the ground with a loud thump, shaking the room as he hit the carpet. The Snake crawled onto Luiso's chest, straightened himself up, and began punching Luiso's face. Blood flew as the Snake broke Luiso's nose and knocked out a few teeth.

It was a while before the Snake realized that Luiso was knocked out. Standing up off the man's expansive belly, the Snake looked at Luiso and wondered if he should steal a car and take him somewhere where they wouldn't be disturbed or—

Then the Snake noticed there was a bathroom attached to the bedroom, one with a large bathtub and several fluffy white towels. An idea came to the Snake's head, something he'd always wanted to try, and here was the perfect opportunity for it.

The Snake grabbed his gun from the vanity table and, hooking his arms underneath Luiso's armpits, dragged Luiso into the bathroom.

Chapter Eighteen

The Snake lifted Luiso's body into the bathtub, his head lolling right underneath the faucet. The Snake felt the excitement building up in him, transforming from the thrill of the hunt to the thrill of the kill. This was a unique opportunity to try something new, and the Snake was not about to let it go to waste.

The Snake went into the linen closet in the bathroom and grabbed a pillowcase and sheets. Heading back into the bedroom, the Snake stuffed the pillowcase into Luiso's girlfriend's mouth and tore up the sheets intro strips to tie her up. Couldn't have her waking up and screaming with all the noise he and Luiso were going to be making in the bathroom.

The Snake headed back into the bathroom, grabbing a fluffy white hand-towel and stuffing it into Luiso's mouth. Then the Snake felt along Luiso's right arm until he found the bones he'd been looking for. Counting to three in Russian, the Snake squeezed Luiso's arm and twisted, breaking the bones.

With a scream Luiso woke up, sitting upright in the tub with a wild-eyed stare. The Snake swung a leg over the rim of the tub and drove it into Luiso's chest, forcing him back down. Bending over the Snake grabbed Luiso's left arm and snapped the bones in it. Luiso screamed again, writhing violently underneath the Snake's foot.

"Oh, stop squirming." said the Snake, reaching for Luiso's leg. "It's only about to get worse. If you expend any more energy, you'll fall unconscious again." The Snake took Luiso's calf in his hands and twisted it hard to the left, breaking both the tibia and the femur in one simple move. Luiso screamed again, his cries muffled by the towel in his mouth. As if there wasn't a man underneath him screaming and struggling in pain, the Snake broke the other leg with the same move and stepped out of the tub.

"You think this is painful?" asked the Snake. "*Nyet*, it's only going to get much worse. By the time I've finished with you, you're going to wish I would kill you. And then, in my mercy, I will."

The Snake bent down and took the towel out of Luiso's mouth. Luiso gasped and looked at the Snake, his eyes full of rage and hate. "Who are you?" he shouted, his voice raspy. "What the fuck do you want with me?"

"I am the Snake." said the Snake. "I am the one who killed Paul and James Sanonia. And I am the one who will kill you."

Luiso stared at the Snake, his expression disbelief. "You?" he said. "You killed the Sanonias?"

The Snake nodded. "Before he died, Paul Sanonia mentioned your name." said the Snake. "He said you might be able to help me find what I'm looking for."

"He said what?" said Luiso.

"There will be time for that later." said the Snake, replacing the towel in Luiso's mouth. Luiso fought to keep the towel out, but the Snake eventually forced it in. "First, there's something we need to establish: you either cooperate, or this will happen." The Snake placed his hand under Luiso's head and lifted it to the faucet. A look of realization dawned on Luiso's face and he started shaking his head vigorously, screaming out muffled *no*'s from the gag. Ignoring him, the Snake reached for the cold water tap, and turned it on.

At once water flowed out of the faucet, soaking the towel and seeping rapidly into Luiso's mouth. The Snake took his free hand off the tap and pinched Luiso's nostrils closed, cutting off his oxygen supply. The Snake grinned from beneath his mask, watching Luiso writhe as he struggled for air. Eventually, his lungs would fill with water and he would drown unless the Snake intervened. Which the Snake would, if Luiso cooperated.

The Snake sensed Luiso was near the breaking point and moved his head from out under the faucet and over the edge of the tub. Releasing Luiso's nostrils, the Snake took the towel out of Luiso's mouth and hit his back with the palm of his hand. Luiso vomited, a small puddle of water and bile pooling on the floor.

"Now you will answer my questions." said the Snake. "Unless of course, you *like* being waterboarded."

Luiso spat out some more water and then said, breathing hard between words, "What do you want to know?"

The Snake leaned in close to Luiso's ear and whispered, "Where is Allison Langland?"

Luiso looked at Snake, his eyebrow raised. "What did you say?"

"Where is Allison Langland?" The Snake raised his voice, enunciating each word.

"I heard what you said." said Luiso. "But I don't know anything about that. You're wasting your time with me."

"*Liar!*" the Snake roared. The Snake squeezed Luiso's nose shut, stuffed the towel back in Luiso's mouth, and thrust Luiso's head under the water. Luiso squirmed, trying with his broken arms to reach the Snake's hands and pull him off. The Snake held on, ignoring Luiso's feeble attempts. Finally the Snake decided that Luiso had had enough punishment and released him from the faucet. Once the towel was off Luiso heaved, releasing a fresh stream of vomit on the ground.

"Paul Sanonia said your name." said the Snake when Luiso had finished vomiting. "He said your name after being thoroughly tortured. Why would he say your name if you weren't involved?"

"Look, I know a lot of people." gasped Luiso, spitting out some vomit. "I'm friends and acquaintances with a ton of family members. One of them might've even been involved with the Langland girl. Why do you even care, anyway? She's probably dead by now. Hey, what are you doing? Hey!"

The Snake grabbed Luiso by the neck and thrust him against the opposite end of the tub. "How dare you!" growled the Snake, pulling out his hunting knife from his jacket. Luiso saw the light reflected off the knife and his eyeballs widened until they looked like they were going to pop out of his skull.

The Snake raised the knife high above his head and brought it down between Luiso's legs, sinking into the tender, fleshy meat above Luiso's penis. Luiso screamed as blood spurted out of the wound, spraying the Snake and the side of the tub. Heedless, the Snake raised the knife again, bringing it down deeper into Luiso's groin. Luiso screamed in pain as the Snake brought down his knife over and over again.

"She is not dead!" the Snake raged, slicing through the meat with angry vigor. "I know she's not! I can still…feel…her…kiss!" With a final thrust Luiso's penis and scrotum were detached from his body, falling into the tub with a sickening, bloody *plop!* Luiso screamed, tears rolling down his face as he tried with his broken arm to reach for his lost member.

The Snake went to the linen closet again and grabbed another towel. Bending over the edge of the tub, the Snake stuffed the towel into the hole that had once been Luiso's genitalia, eliciting a groan from Luiso, who looked on the verge of passing out. Then the Snake took Luiso's head, stuffed the towel that had been in his mouth back in, and said, "You brought that upon yourself. Now tell me, if you don't know anything about it, then who does!"

The Snake put Luiso's mouth under the faucet, jolting Luiso awake again. When the Snake thought Luiso had had enough, he released him from the water and took out the towel. Luiso heaved, coughed up blood, cried, looked at the Snake desperately. "Please!" he whispered. "Just kill me!"

"Then answer my question." said the Snake.

"Alright." sobbed Luiso. "I have this friend named Roman Veretti. He's new to the family. He mostly does pimp duty, you know, making sure the prostitutes give us our cut, but he also does odd errands for the top brass every now and then. He said he had something to do with the Langland girl."

"What was that 'something'?" asked the Snake.

"I don't know!" cried Luiso. "That's all I know! Please, just kill me! You've already taken away my manhood! what more can you do to me?"

"Good question." said the Snake. "How about we find out together?" The Snake stuffed the towel back in Luiso's mouth and ducked him under the faucet. As Luiso squirmed, the Snake took his fingers off Luiso's nose, reached for his gun, and placed the end of the silencer on Luiso's forehead.

"*Spokoynoy nochi*, Thomas Luiso." said Snake, pulling the trigger and sending Luiso to the afterlife full of terror.

Chapter Nineteen

The Snake let go of Luiso's head as if he was letting go of a basketball. The head fell into the drain, blood slowly seeping out of the bullet wound. The Snake examined his glove and sleeve, noticing the bloodstains. He'd have to get rid of anything that had blood on it, put it in cold water so that the DNA could be destroyed and erased.

Good thing that I bought extras of everything in case this happened before I started hunting James Sanonia. thought the Snake, holding up the bloody knife again. *Hell, I even have another knife in case I have to get rid of this one.* The Snake bent over into the tub and carved the letters into Luiso's stomach.

S. N. A. K. E.

With a few quick strokes, the Snake had turned Luiso into a message.

And now I'm a full-fledged serial killer. thought the Snake, grabbing cleaning fluids from underneath the bathroom sink. *I've joined the ranks of Fish and Gein and Dahmer and Bundy. And I will bring fear into the hearts of the Camerlengos when I come calling.*

The Snake went about cleaning the bedroom and bathroom, ignoring the staring eyes of Luiso's mistress. He poured cleaning solution and bleaches on the floor, filled the tub with cold water and mixed in more bleach for good measure. In nearly half an hour he'd cleared the scene of anything that might lead back to him, including the blood on his knife.

There was a groan from the bedroom and the Snake peeked out and saw Luiso's mistress—make that former mistress—staring at him with murderous rage as she tried in vain to break her bonds. T=Ignoring her, the Snake checked over his work to see if he'd missed anything, was satisfied, and left the house.

Once outside Linda greeted him with a happy bark. "Did you miss me? Were you cold?" asked the Snake, taking off his bloody glove to rub her head. "I'm sorry girl. Come on, let's go."

The Snake walked a few blocks away from the nurse's home before selecting a car. He got out another bump key, one designed for cars, got into the driver's seat, and hot-wired the engine. The Snake drove for an hour, getting out twice to steal a new car, getting out several more times to notify news outlets of Luiso's death, and at one point stopping on a bridge so he could dump his bloody clothes.

When they finally dumped the last vehicle in a place that was far enough away from the Snake's apartment building that nobody, especially the cops, would come around asking about it, the Snake felt so exhausted he wanted to just jump into bed as soon as he got to the apartment.

Instead the Snake went into the bedroom and stared out the window, where the sky was just beginning to lighten. The Snake thought back on the three men he'd killed. First he'd killed James Sanonia before he could get any information out of him. Then he'd killed Paul Sanonia when Paul had given up someone who might have information on Allison. And then Thomas Luiso had pointed him in the direction of someone who'd actually been part of what had happened to Allison. He hoped Roman Veretti might be able to tell him where Allison actually was.

The Snake brought his fingers to his lips and felt their soft, tender flesh. Just as he'd told Luiso, the sensation of Allison's kiss was still there, warm and sweet. *I'm getting closer, Al.* thought the Snake. *Just hold on until I get there. I'll save you, and I'll kill anyone who gets in my way.*

Chapter Twenty

Eleven days ago

"Ruby, what do you see in this?" the boy asked. They were halfway through *High School Musical* and once again, the basketball and scholastic teams were working *together* to keep two of their members *apart*, which the boy thought was stupid and a little ironic. "What is it that makes you want to watch these musicals over and over? I just don't get it."

"I don't know." said Ruby, a small girl with green eyes and brown hair that she was growing out to look like Allison's hair. "Why do you watch horror movies so much and always take notes afterwards about what worked and what didn't?"

"Because I want to be a totally awesome horror movie director when I grow up." the boy answered. "Do you want to direct high school musicals someday?"

"No!" replied Ruby. "I want to be a princess."

"With Zac Efron as your Prince Charming?"

"Yes please!" said Ruby, earning her an appreciative laugh from her older brother.

"Well, I'll see what I can do to make you a princess." said the boy, hugging his sister. "But if I can't get Zac Efron to be your prince, who do you want instead?"

"I don't know." said Ruby. "Maybe you?"

"I'm your brother." the boy replied. "And I thought you wanted me to marry Allison."

"Yeah, I know." said Ruby. "But you're really nice and you always take care of me, even if you always watch scary movies whenever you have the chance."

"Oh thanks, Ruby." said the boy. "That means so much to me."

"Hey, can I ask you something?" said Ruby suddenly. "Why do you like scary movies so much? I get nightmares from *The Nightmare Before Christmas*, but you watch the really scary ones like teachers grade papers."

'Where did you come up with that phrase?" said the boy. "You know, I've thought about it for a while, I've tried to figure out why I like scary movies, and I think it might have something to do with our dad."

"You mean how he's never around and he's not very nice when he is?" said Ruby, her lower lip trembling. Whenever their mom and dad were brought up, Ruby always looked like she wanted to cry, which her brother couldn't blame her for, considering their family situation.

105

"Yeah." said the boy. "I think it might be because I always thought that he was a kind of monster. And I…well, I guess I discovered the movie monsters and—I don't know, I guess I would rather feel a connection to these vampires and serial killers and demonic spirits than I would to our dad. Even if they were chasing after me, I'd rather have them, I guess."

"I don't get it." said Ruby, furrowing her brow.

"I don't think I really get it either." said the boy. "But hey, don't worry about it. Whatever the reason is, it doesn't change that I love you and I always will, right?"

"Right!" said Ruby. "Hey, your phone's buzzing."

The boy looked at the coffee table and saw that his phone was vibrating. On the screen, a picture of Allison dressed as a cowboy from their school's Halloween party four months ago shined up at him. The boy smiled, remembering their date today, the kiss at the end of it, and how the warm sensation of the kiss was still present on his lips.

"It's Allison." said the boy, grabbing the phone and heading to the hall. "She must've gotten tired of the party."

"Tell her I said hi." said Ruby, returning to her movie.

"Will do." the boy replied. The boy unlocked his phone, punched in his password, and pressed the talk button. "Hey Al. How's the shrimp and cocktails?"

"Now's not the time for small talk!" said Allison. She was breathing hard, making her voice come through the phone rough and crackly. "I just ran three blocks in a long dress and high heels. I'm hiding behind a department store right now!"

The boy stared at the phone in his hand in disbelief. Was Allison playing some sort of joke on him? "Allison, what's going on over there?" asked the boy. "Is some mob boss's son being too aggressive or something?"

"Oh, I wish that was the problem." said Allison. There was a pause and an inhalation before Allison continued. "I got tired of these three debutantes talking about a vacation to Italy, so I went to the restroom to get away from them. The party's in this fancy hotel, so on the way back I passed by this conference room. As I was passing by, I thought I heard someone say the N-word."

"Someone said the N-word?" asked the boy. "In the conference room?"

"Yeah, and I stopped to listen. The door was thin, so I could hear everything going on inside. Turns out my dad's old army buddy, Christopher Camerlengo, was talking with some...business partners, I think—anyway, they were talking about killing this black cop who was getting too close to something of his, I think it might have been something to do with smuggling."

"Smuggling what?" asked the boy, totally drawn into Allison's story. By now he was sure this wasn't a joke, Allison's sense of humor did not involve telling people she overheard something she shouldn't have and then coming up with some lame punch line. The boy wondered what was at the end of this story before asking, "Did they say what they were smuggling?"

"I don't know!" Allison replied. "But I thought I should record it on my phone, you know, to turn it over to the police? I mean they were talking about killing someone! And I managed to record enough of their conversation that I thought it might get them convicted, but as I was leaving, so were they! They asked me if I'd heard anything and I said no, but they were acting suspicious, like they didn't believe me. So I got out of the building and ran!"

"Did you get leave out the front or the back?" asked the boy, feeling apprehensive, as if some sort of ghost of ill omen was hanging over this conversation.

"Um...the front?" Allison answered.

The boy groaned. "They probably had that entrance videotaped. A side door or the back exit would've worked better."

"I'll keep that in mind the next time I feel like my life's in danger!" said Allison, sounding annoyed.

"I'm not accusing or blaming you. I'm just saying." said the boy, trying to quickly to repair the situation before it became an unnecessary fight. "Listen, send the recording to my phone. That way there won't be only one copy."

"Okay." said Allison. "I'm sending it to your phone. Hang on a sec, alright?"

"Alright." the boy replied. "Also, I think you should get farther away from that hotel."

"How far away?" asked Allison.

"A dozen blocks would probably work."

"A dozen blocks!" Allison repeated.

"Al, they're going to be looking for you!" said the boy. "Right now you're too close to that hotel, and around the hotel is where they're expecting you to be. Just stick to the shadows, don't cross the street unless there's a crowd of people to cross with you, and don't stop till you need a cab to go back the way you came in a timely manner!"

"How do you know all this?" asked Allison. "From those movies of yours?"

"And books." the boy answered. "You'd be surprised what sort of great tips and ideas you can get from movies and books, especially when you mix in a little common sense."

"Alright, I'm about to send you the audio. Tell me when you got it—*ayiee*!" There was a scream on the other end of the line. The boy listened, terror-struck, as he heard men shouting—"It's going into the drain! Grab that phone!"—Allison crying for help, and then a clatter and a splash. The boy brought the phone away from his ear and looked at the screen: CALL LOST.

The boy stared at the screen, unable to believe what he'd just heard. Allison had been...Allison was—

The boy felt weak suddenly and he fell to his knees. Behind him he could hear Ruby and Linda coming towards him, Linda whining as she nudged him, Ruby asking what was wrong. He didn't pay any attention to them, though. All he could think about was that Allison had called him, she had screamed, and then he'd lost the call and lost her.

Chapter Twenty-One

Murtz jumped out of her car before she had even turned off the engine. Slamming the car door shut, she flashed her FBI badge at the uniform guarding the perimeter of the crime scene and trooped up the front steps of the walkway. Harnist was waiting for her at the front door, looking sleepy but determined.

"How'd you get here so fast?" asked Murtz, huffing as she joined Harnist inside the house.

"I took a shortcut *and* turned my siren on." Harnist answered, handing Murtz a pair of latex gloves. "Anyway, call came in about fifteen minutes ago, from the owner of the house. Said that she had woken up and had found her boyfriend in the bathtub. He was dead, and had our boy's signature word on his chest."

"And our victim is…?" said Murtz.

"Thomas Luiso." Harnist replied, pausing to watch Sergeant Pacine walking down the stairs, a hand over his mouth, his face a greenish hue. "One of the Camerlengo's loan sharks, a mafia socialite, and a womanizer to put Tiger Woods to shame, if the rumors about him are true."

"Sergeant Pacine, are you okay?" asked Murtz. "You look ill."

"And you just said something funny." added Harnist. "Let me guess, you saw the body?"

"It's not pretty." said Pacine. For a moment he looked like he was about to heave, but thankfully he managed to suppress it and rushed out the door with a well-mannered "Excuse me."

"What's wrong with the body?" asked Murtz.

"Nothing." said Harnist. "Except that it shows how cruel our boy is. You wanna come up and see it with me?"

"Lead the way." said Murtz. "What's a mafia socialite?"

"It's someone who knows everybody or almost everybody in the family." Harnist explained, grabbing the banister and setting off up the stairs. "Most do it for the connections. Luiso was one of those types. He was either a friend or an acquaintance of many of the Camerlengo Family's members. It's possible he even knew one or both of the Sanonias."

"Which may be a lead on our killer." said Murtz, following behind Harnist. "What do we know about what happened?"

"Besides the socialite connection, nothing helpful." said Harnist. "The house belongs to Milly Close, a nurse at Bellevue and Luiso's latest mistress, though from the way she told it Luiso was just a poor man who'd been pressured into marrying a horrible bitch and was trying to leave the marriage for true love.

"Anyway, Luiso came over for dinner this evening, they'd wined and dined and went upstairs to have some fun. Meanwhile, the killer breaks in through the back door and sneaks upstairs where Luiso and Close are doing the nasty. Apparently he walked in after they were done, fired off a round, Luiso and the guy get into a fight, and then the killer drags Luiso into the bathroom and does a number on him."

"Ms. Close told us all that?" asked Murtz,. "I'm surprised he let her live!"

"It wasn't Close who told us all that." Harnist explained. "The crime scene and the body did. Apparently after the round was fired and embedded itself in the wall above her head, Ms. Close fainted and woke up tied up. Didn't see a thing, though she heard a lot of crying and screaming. Guy probably used a silencer, seeing as none of the neighbors called to report a gunshot."

"What happened after he 'did a number' on Mr. Luiso?" said Murtz.

"Cleaned up and left." Harnist answered simply. "Guy's really nitpicky about cleaning up the evidence. Apparently he cleaned up the whole bedroom and bathroom while there was a corpse in the tub and a living woman in the bed. Left before Luiso's girlfriend could untie herself."

"Let me guess: when she did wake up she went to the bathroom, saw the body, screamed and then called for help." said Murtz.

"Hey, you really are a mind reader, aren't you?" said Harnist. "Anyway, we sent her off in an ambulance to be checked over, but we don't think he really did anything to her."

"Thank God for small favors." said Murtz, processing the information. She wondered what it meant that the killer would attack Luiso but not the mistress. Did he think it was unnecessary to hurt her? Could he not hurt women at all? Or was she a better form of identification than a driver's license?

Murtz and Harnist walked into the bedroom, where a team of CSI techs were combing over every carpet fiber and every tile of marble for clues. In one area of the wall Murtz noticed a fist-sized hole that a techie was examining with a penlight.

"Who made that?" asked Murtz, pointing to the hole. The tech looked up and said, "According to the coroner, most likely our vic. There's some blood and bruises on his knuckles, and if he hadn't taken a bath, I'd say we'd have some drywall dust on his hand too."

"Actually he did make that hole!" called a voice from the bathroom. Dr. Mohawk appeared in the doorway, wearing a coat and latex gloves. "And did I mention I hate the smell of bleach this early in the morning?"

"Dr. Mohawk." said Murtz. "I hear the body is much worse off than the other two victims."

Dr. Mohawk scoffed and said, "That's an understatement. This guy didn't just bruise or break some bones. No, he brought to life every man's worst nightmare." Dr. Mohawk motioned for Murtz to come forward and said, "Take a look, if you dare."

Murtz stepped into the bathroom and looked into the tub. Draped over the side of the tub, the head lolling on a shoulder as if he had fallen asleep while taking a bath, was a large, pale man wearing the sheen of the recently-bathed, a bullet hole in his head. The man's body was bloody and bruised and had the familiar SNAKE carved into his chest. And between his legs, Murtz noticed that—

"The killer castrated him." said Murtz.

"Yep, he cut off his wiener." said Dr. Mohawk. "And quite brutally too, I might add. The guy literally hacked through the skin and muscle like he was using a machete to cut through jungle brush—Harnist, calm down, I know it's tough to stomach this, but I'm going to be with this guy in the morgue all morning and I'm going to thinking about lost manhoods when I go home to my wife and kids. If anyone should be looking like you do right now, it's me."

Murtz ignored Dr. Mohawk's complaining and bent down to get a closer look at the body. Just as Dr. Mohawk had said, the wound was bloody and mangled. Murtz could almost understand Dr. Mohawk's and Harnist's disgust and fear at the sight, and she definitely felt sorry for the victim. But more importantly, she felt a sense of realization, an insight into the killer.

"Our boy has a rage." she said, standing back up and turning back to look at Harnist and Mohawk. "He's upset with the Camerlengos, and something about our vic here really set him off, which is why he castrated him. He's not just killing out of a sense of justice, he's doing it for revenge."

"So this guy's a psychopathic Batman." said Harnist, taking a second look at the body before looking away again. "But what set him off?"

"I think you should be more concerned about who this killer is." said Dr. Mohawk, as a gurney for the body was carried into the bathroom. "There must be at least a hundred thousand people in the five boroughs alones with a grudge against the Camerlengos. Finding which one is capable of murder is going to be difficult for you guys. Excuse me."

As Dr. Mohawk went to help his assistants lift the body onto the gurney, Harnist's and Murtz's cell phones rang at the exact same moment. Murtz picked up her phone and left the room to take the call. "Murtz." she said, pressing the talk button.

"Angela, it's me." said the familiar voice of Alan Gramer. "This just got bigger."

Murtz sensed concern and unease in Gramer's voice, something she was not accustomed to hearing from him. "Alan—I mean Chief, what's wrong? What's gotten bigger?"

"This case." Gramer explained. "We weren't just investigating Sanonia, we were investigating Luiso too. We think he might've been running a heroin business on the side, quite possibly working with some Mexican cartels. We'd been trying to trace his ring with Customs and the DEA for almost eight months, and now we'll never know the details of the ring."

"So what does that mean for this case?" asked Murtz.

"You know how the higher-ups are appraised of the big cases we investigate whenever something big comes up in the case?" Gramer replied. "They got wind of this and now they're pissed. They called the commissioner at his house and decided they can't let this guy go on killing."

"Alan, what are you saying?" asked Murtz. "What are the higher-ups planning?"

"They're setting up a joint task force between NYPD and us." Gramer answered. "Just to catch this guy before he gets in the way of any other investigations. And guess what? You're on it as the chief forensic psychologist."

For a moment Murtz didn't know what to say, surprised that things had developed so quickly. Finally she opened her mouth and said, "I see."

"You'll get all the details when the sun comes up." said Gramer. "Looks like you're going to have your hands full with this, Angela. I'll call you later."

"Talk to you later, Chief." said Murtz, hanging up. When Murtz turned around she saw Harnist with a strange look on his face. "You heard?" she asked.

Harnist nodded. "Looks like things are going to get crazy from here on out." he said. "If they aren't already, that is."

Chapter Twenty-Two

Roman Veretti was whistling as he turned off the main road and onto the scenic route to Connecticut. The sun was shining, the view was beautiful, the minivan was warm and toasty, the XM radio was playing some of Roman's favorite jazz and big band songs, "A Gal in Kalamazoo" and "What a Wonderful World", among others, and there were no other cars on this secret route Roman loved so much.

Best of all, taking the scenic route meant another hour until Roman got to Connecticut, a place Roman wouldn't have even considered visiting if his wife hadn't insisted they go and visit her parents that weekend. It wasn't as if they were bad people—Roman thought that Lizzy's father was a hilarious storyteller and philosopher—but the house smelled heavily of cleaning products, and Lizzy's mother always found some way or another to suggest that Roman was a poor choice of husband for her daughter and that Lizzy could do better without actually coming out and saying it. In truth, Roman preferred making sure the prostitutes under his watch made their quota each day rather than spending an entire weekend smelling dish soap and hearing criticisms about his paycheck.

Just wait till I get off pimp duty and get into a real position in the family. Roman thought, drumming his fingers along the steering wheel as he listened to the music. *Mr. Camerlengo's getting to be real fond of me, and I'm sure that once this whole serial killer thing blows over, I'll be able to get a job with money enough to shut up that old bat.*

Up ahead on the road Roman noticed a car pulled over, its hood up and the lights blinking. The driver was waving his arms in the air, trying to signal Roman as he approached. For a moment Roman considered driving on, but the possibility of a few more minutes away from Lizzy's mother excited him enough that he flipped on his turn signal and pulled over to the side of the road next to the car. The driver of the car ran up to the driver's side door as Roman turned off the engine and stepped out of the minivan.

"You saved me!" said the driver, a young man who looked unremarkable save for a pair of brilliant blue eyes. "I can't tell what's up with my car and the battery on my phone is dead. Do you think you can help me?"

"Let me see the car." said Roman. "My dad was a mechanic, so I used to help him out all the time."

"Well, isn't that a stroke of luck!" said the driver. "Perhaps you can tell me how much this is going to cost me in repairs. I figured that son of a bitch was conning me when he sold me this piece of crap."

"We'll see about that." said Roman, sidling on over to the open hood. Peeking in, he examined the engine. To Roman's confusion, the engine looked brand-new, and nothing he could see indicated any maintenance issues or repair needs.

"I don't see any problems with the engine." said Roman, ducking his head out from under the hood. "What'd you say was wrong with it—?"

WHAM!

There was a bright flash of light and Roman felt a sharp pain in the side of his head. He pressed his hand to his temple before he staggered and fell over, darkness clouding over his vision. The last thing he saw was the driver of the stalled car putting on a strange-looking mask before Roman closed his eyes and the world fell away.

Chapter Twenty-Three

The Snake threw down the lug wrench he'd used on Veretti and stared at his prey with dark satisfaction. *Durak*, the Snake thought. *You never considered you'd be the next target, did you? Not once did you notice the man who snuck into your car while you went to harass one of your prostitutes and looked at your GPS to see where you were going after you were done. Nor did you notice there was a guy outside your house listening to everything you said to your wife that same morning, telling her you'd take the scenic route you both so loved and enjoy it for the both of you. All those mistakes allowed you to get caught in my trap, and in the end it'll prove fatal for you.*

The Snake grabbed Veretti under the shoulders and pulled him along, throwing him in the backseat of Veretti's minivan. Digging into the unconscious man's pockets, the Snake found Veretti's car keys and slipped into the front seat. Turning on the ignition, the Snake switched the XM radio to a hard rock and heavy metal station. Driving back onto the road, the Snake took off his mask and put on a wig and heavy sunglasses he'd stowed away in his coat with his gun and hunting knife.

"Enjoy the music, *moi dorogoy droog*." said the Snake to the unconscious Veretti. "I guarantee it'll be the last music you'll ever hear."

Chapter Twenty Four

Harnist sat down next to Murtz as the newly-formed task force filed into the large conference room that had been designated as the headquarters for the joint NYPD-FBI search for the New York Mafia Killer. From a window Harnist could make out the Hudson, where only a little a week and a half ago James Sanonia had been found floating in the river naked with a bullet in his head.

"So, ready to work together for the common good?" Murtz asked with a sly wink. Harnist chuckled in understanding: cooperation between different law enforcement organizations was always difficult to come by, as both parties wanted to be responsible for solving the crime and putting away the bad guys. Anytime two groups such as the police and the federal investigators, worked together on an investigation there was always a pull-and-tug as each group tried to have their say in the running of the investigation.

In this case though, both parties had much to lose if their target continued unstopped, and even more to lose if they bickered over the details for the sake of credit. This time, they'd have to put their differences aside if they wanted to catch the Snake killer, protect their investigations, and save face with the public.

There was a shift in mood and all eyes turned to the back of the room, where Captain Patton and Chief Gramer were walking in, each holding a large file in one hand and a cup of coffeehouse coffee in the other. The two men strode to the front of the room and assessed the thirty-five members of the task force before them.

"Alright, stop looking like we're about to give an Oscar-winning speech." said Patton. "We've come here for a purpose, and we're going to make sure it gets done without any-interagency bickering, so sit down." There was a collective chair-scraping and the task force sat, leaving Patton and Gramer the only ones standing.

"Now, here's why we've been assembled." said Gramer, holding up a small black remote. He pressed a button on it and the projector attached to the ceiling lit up, shining right into Gramer's and Patton's eyes. Both men stepped out of the way of the light as Gramer again pressed a button on the remote. The projector made a loud *click!* and a picture appeared on the wall, a close-up of the chest of one of the victims—Harnist thought it might be James Sanonia—and the eerie carving that had been placed there: SNAKE.

"The Snake Killer." said Patton. "Known to the media as the New York Mafia Killer, no thanks to Ms. Berman's tireless reporting. What he does is target members of the Camerlengo family—we're still not sure if there's a pattern to his kills, or how he finds them, but he does—and he waits for them to be alone or in an isolated, vulnerable position before he strikes."

"Once he does have them alone," said Gramer, picking up the thread, "he breaks their bones as a means of torture, and after he tortures them he shoots them point-blank in the head. Then he carves the word 'snake' into their chests. He'll then strip his victims naked and dump them into a body of cold water in order to erase evidence. He also leaves some form of identification for the victim behind when he kills them, usually a driver's license, or in the case of Thomas Luiso, his girlfriend."

"What about the waterboarding last night?" asked an officer, raising his hand. "Or the...um, the castration?" There was a collective shudder from the men around the room as the officer spoke, and even Patton and Gramer looked a little unnerved.

"For that, we'll turn to our forensic psychologist." said Patton. "Agent Murtz, would you kindly come up here and give us your profile? You too, Detective Harnist."

Harnist and Murtz looked at each other, then stood up and strode to the front of the room while Gramer and Patton moved off to the side. Harnist cleared his throat and said, "Hi, I'm Detective Blake Harnist, this is Special Agent Angela Murtz. We were assigned to the Snake case before this task force was convened."

"We didn't detect a pattern for the killer until the second murder." said Murtz, opening her file. "Now judging by the broken bones, our perp is employing *zamochit*, a form of torture employed by Russian crime families. He's also very good about cleaning up after himself and employs a couple of methods in order to make DNA matching or fingerprinting impossible.

"This leads me to believe he may be an ex-military from Russia, and may or may not have ties to Russian crime families here in the US or in Russia. He's most likely between the ages of thirty and forty-five, has been in the country for at least five or ten years, is of average intelligence, and judging by how well he gets around town he may be a cab driver."

"Now, we checked with INS for people who match that profile." said Harnist. "According to their records, there are twenty-eight people residing in the tri-state area that match some, if not most, of these criteria. However half of them are suffering from war wounds, three have medical conditions that would make this sort of task impossible, six have gained too much weight or has lost the physicality necessary for this sort of work, another four have alibied out for all of the murders, and one of them died last year in a bar fight, so if our perp matches Agent Murtz's description, then he's probably here illegally."

"Our subject is also most likely a sociopath." said Murtz, continuing her profile. "He feels little or no emotion and probably derives pleasure from hurting others. He's probably acting in a vigilante manner, trying to say that he can clean up the streets better than the police, and he's letting the police *and* the mafia know it by going after one of the most powerful families in New York. He may also be thinking that he's acting in a heroic and virtuous manner. To put it another way, he sees himself as a Batman or Spider-Man of sorts, fighting crime for the good of the public, which is why he calls media outlets to let them know about the murders. Last night's murder of Thomas Luiso also indicated that our perp likely has a vendetta against the Camerlengos, and was acting out his revenge on Mr. Luiso. This would also explain why he's writing 'snake' on the chests of his victims, maybe calling them snakes or comparing them to snakes.

"Other features that may help us identify our perp is that he probably lives alone or he has a passive partner, a wife or female relative who doesn't care where her husband or male roommate is at all hours of the night; he may excuse himself by saying he's working a third-shift job in order to avoid attention; he may or may not have had trouble with the law in the past, depending on whether or not he feels that what he's doing is in the name of justice and therefore doesn't want to cross paths with the law; and he is most likely going to get bolder and bolder the longer we let him go on."

"Any questions?" asked Harnist. Nobody raised their hands or spoke up, allowing Harnist and Murtz to resume their seats while Patton and Gramer strode back up to the front of the room.

"Thank you, Detective Harnist and Agent Murtz." said Gramer. "Now, I want you all to keep that profile in mind while we work this case. Profiling is not always right one-hundred percent of the time, but it's employed for a reason. So when you talk to your informants to see if anyone is taking credit for these murders among the Russian families, keep the profile in mind."

"There are some other things we need to cover before we finish this meeting." said Patton. "One is that forensics came back on the broken lock that was used to enter the residence of Milly Close last night. Looks like our boy used a bump key to get into the house. We traced it back to a locksmith who makes bump keys on the side. However, he sells plenty of bump keys in a month and he happens to suffer from prosopagnosia."

"God bless you." said one of the FBI agents in the room.

"It's a neurological disorder." Gramer continued, ignoring the comment. "People who suffer from it are unable to recognize individual faces, which makes our locksmith unable to recognize whom he sells his products too."

"I didn't know about the prosopagnosia." said Murtz.

"Forensics called just as we were getting on the elevator." Patton explained. "Sorry we didn't have time to inform you about it, Agent Murtz. Why? Does it change your profile at all?"

"No, but it does reinforce my earlier assertion," Murtz replied, "that he's been in this country long enough to know how to get around and maybe make some connections. I'll add it to the profile anyway."

"Thank you, Agent Murtz." said Patton. "Now, there's one last thing we need to cover." Patton pressed the button on his little remote control again and the projection changed from a photo of

James Sanonia's chest to a video of Candace Berman, holding a microphone and smiling her most winning smile. Underneath her the caption read MAFIA HUNTING SERIAL KILLER IN NEW YORK: DANGEROUS VILLAIN OR BAD BOY HERO?

"A serial killer nicknamed the New York Mafia Killer has struck again, this time killing a man in his girlfriend's home." said Berman, using her most dramatic reporting voice. Midway through her first sentence the screen switched from Berman to the outside of Milly Close's home, showing yellow tape around the property and police going about their work. "The victim, a man believed to have connections to organized crime, was reported in need of medical attention by his girlfriend early this morning. By the time emergency medical personnel arrived, the victim had succumbed to his injuries. The victim's name is being withheld by authorities pending notification of kin and the ongoing investigation."

The front of the house was replaced by pictures of James Sanonia at a press conference and a close-up of Paul Sanonia that might've come from Facebook or his driver's license. Berman's voice continued in the same dramatic voice she'd been using since she started.

"This is the third murder in as little as two weeks. The first murder was of James Sanonia, a public spokesman for the Camerlengo Corporation, which is believed to have connections to organized crime. The second victim was Paul Sanonia, James

Sanonia's cousin, who was murdered nearly a week after his cousin. Both victims were killed with a single gunshot, and were then dumped in bodies of water. Police and media were alerted to the scenes by phone calls from eyewitnesses."

The shot returned to Berman, who was still smiling brightly at the camera as if everything were alright. "Now police and the FBI are investigating these murders, but at this time have not made any statements or released any news on the investigation. Some New Yorkers however, do *not* want law enforcement investigating or trying to capture the New York Mafia Killer." Berman placed extra emphasis on the word "not", as if she wanted to have the word appear on camera and underline it but couldn't.

The shot changed, showing a man in a heavy winter jacket and a bike helmet talking into a microphone while standing next to his bicycle. "Look, these mobsters are running around like mad in the city." said the biker. "Do I want them in my city? No! I'm glad someone's getting rid of them."

The shot changed again, this time to a woman in a sanitation worker's uniform standing over a sewer grate. "I don't believe in murder or the death penalty." said the woman as she fed an instrument into the grate. "But the police aren't allowed to touch these mobsters without getting in trouble themselves. Maybe this guy's reacting to all that."

Next there was a woman in a business suit carrying a briefcase; then a dad pushing a baby cart and holding a little boy in his arms; and finally a street musician playing the violin while collecting coins in a hat. Each said basically the same thing: even if they did or did not support the actions of the New York Mafia Killer, they did not like the mafia getting away with crimes in their city, and the police weren't doing enough to stop the mafia.

Finally the shot changed back to Berman, who wrapped up her report with a promise that they would release more news as the story developed. As the video ended, Patton pressed the button on the remote again and the projector turned off.

"This is what we're dealing with here." said Gramer. "The media is making this guy out to be some sort of vigilante hero, and some of the people you've sworn to protect are behind this guy. Be aware that you may encounter some supporters of him while investigating, but unless they assault you, be courteous and do your best to ignore them."

"That's all right now, and you have your assignments." said Patton, with an air of closing. "Hop to it and get to work."

Immediately the task force came to life, agents and officers leaving the room while others sat in their seats and went over their files or made calls on their cell phones. Harnist and Murtz were looking over their files together when Harnist felt his pocket buzz.

Unlocking his smartphone, Harnist put his ear to the receiver and said, "Detective Harnist speaking."

"Detective Harnist, this is Captain Trisha Davies with the State Police." said the person on the other end. "I think we might have something here that relates to that serial killer case you are working on in the Big Apple."

Harnist raised an eyebrow in surprise. What could the State Police have that related to the Snake killer? Nevertheless he said, "Go ahead, Captain. What do you have?"

"One of my patrol units was going down one of the lesser-used country roads when he saw a minivan pulled over by the side of the road. The car belongs to a Roman Veretti. In the back of the van there was a teenager who said he pulled over to help the driver of the van and got hit in the head before having his car taken. When he came around he said his assailant had a mask on. About ten minutes ago we got word that another car had been hijacked and the owner whacked on the head and left in the back of the hijacker's car, which apparently belonged to the teenager.

"Now, normally I wouldn't be calling, but when one of my officers did a background search on the name 'Roman Veretti', it came back with him being a new member of the Camerlengo mafia family. Does any of this mean anything to you?"

Harnist felt his breath catch in his throat. Could it be—?

Harnist bolted out of his chair and ran up to Captain Patton, telling Captain Davies on the other end of the line to hang on.

Chapter Twenty Five

Ten days ago

The boy ran up the stairs two at a time and found himself at the Langland apartment. Without stopping for a breath the boy pounded on the door. "Dr. Langland! Dr. Langland!" he shouted. The boy called out his name to the doctor and asked to be let in.

There was a sound of footsteps and then the door swung open with a soft creak. "The door wasn't locked, you know." said Dr. Langland. He was a slim and lanky man, a few inches taller than the boy, with a mustache and receding hair the same shade of flaming red as Allison's. To the boy he looked tired and grief-stricken, more than usual anyway.

"Please let me in." said the boy. "I need to talk to you."

Dr. Langland moved aside without a word and let the boy in. The boy dumped his coat on the living room sofa and began speaking. "I'm sorry that I didn't let you know that I was coming, but I've been freaking out since last night, so I came here to talk to you, and I was coming here from the back of the building and the maintenance door was wide open. I just walked in and started running up the stairs. But that's not important. It's about Allison, I think she's been kidnapped!"

"By the Camerlengos." said Dr. Langland. "Last night at the party, she heard something she shouldn't and was abducted to protect the secret. I know."

The boy stared at the man, disbelieving. "You know?" said the boy. "You know? Then why haven't you—?"

"Done anything?" said Dr. Langland. "Because I simply can't *do* anything. Allison overheard something she shouldn't and on top of that she tried to get it to the police. She's lucky she's not dead now."

"Allison's alive?" said the boy. Ever since Allison's phone had been broken, the boy had felt a great despair welling up in him. And underneath that despair, growing like a terrible cancer, was a hot, red thing, a swirling nexus of scarlet rage and destruction that the boy sensed as surely as he sensed his own existence and had to keep in check lest it break free and make him do something unthinkable

Now however, for the first time since last night, the boy felt a ray of hope break through the cloud of despair and pause the growth of the red thing.

"Yes, she's alive." said Dr. Langland. "But at a price: she's being held hostage, and I think we can thank my old friend Christopher for that. He said he can't let Allison go until he's sure she won't tell the police about what she overheard, so until then she's being kept under supervision and being made to 'be useful' to the family. And until she's released, I cannot see her or have any contact with her. What's more, I'm not allowed to go to the police or contact law enforcement in any way. If Allison disobeys her captors or if I contact the police in any way, they'll kill her and kill me too."

"They're holding her hostage until she learns to behave?" said the boy in disbelief.

"Yes they are." said Dr. Langland. "It's Christopher's strange concept of mercy. He'll have someone watched and made useful instead of killed, if he can. That's how he works."

"So you're just going to sit there and let them do whatever they want with Allison?" asked the boy, astonished. "You can't trust them! They're mobsters!"

"Don't you think I know that?" said Dr. Langland. "I know I can't trust them. They're probably going to kill her, if they haven't already. There's nothing left for me to do except join my Allison and her mother now."

"What?" said the boy, stunned. "Do you hear yourself? Join Allison and her mother? You're talking like she's dead. You're going to just…kill yourself? Just like that?!"

"It's not like that, I'm just being realistic about the situation—"

"Oh, to hell with realistic!" the boy shouted, his anger swelling. Realizing how loud his voice was, the boy took a deep breath and said in an even tone, "I love Allison. I *love* her. God, it nearly drives me crazy how much I adore her. From the first words we said to each other, I wanted to hold her and never let her go. I can be myself around her, I don't have to be the horror freak or the good older brother or the film club director with the vision. I'm just me with her, and that makes me so happy, and I'm even happier when she's happy. And..." the boy took another deep breath and continued. "And I can still feel her lips on mine. It's almost like we're bonded, and I know from that kiss she gave me she's still alive.

"So I can't let go and give up. I just can't give in to despair. I've got to keep believing that she's alive somewhere, okay and healthy. So please Dr. Langland, don't give up hope. There's still a chance to help her."

Dr. Langland was staring at the boy as if he couldn't believe that there was another person in the room with him. For a moment the boy thought he hadn't gotten through to the doctor, but then Dr. Langland sighed loudly and said, "You're more of a man than I am. God, I nearly gave up on Allison, the most important thing in the world to me. If my wife could see me now...how did you become so sensible?"

The boy shrugged his shoulders. "Maybe I've seen too many people in movies make stupid mistakes when the smart moves were right in front of them."

The doctor laughed. "You've got a tongue to you." said the doctor. "Alright, so how do we help Allison? They said I shouldn't contact the police or they'll kill her."

"Yeah, but they never said anything about me, did they?" asked the boy. "Do they even know I exist?"

Dr. Langland's face lit up and he said, "All those years training at medical school, and I'm finding myself confounded by a teenager! Hold on, I'll go get the phone and call the police this very instant."

"No, it's okay sir, let me just get my phone out—"

BAM!

As the doctor moved past a window to grab the phone from its cradle, there was a loud noise and the doctor stopped in his tracks. Flashes of scarlet spurted from the sides of his head as Dr. Langland turned around to look at the boy. The boy watched in horror as the doctor mouthed senselessly at him and then fell over in a heap.

Chapter Twenty-Six

The boy stared at Dr. Langland's body on the floor, blood pooling around the doctor's head. Stepping back, the boy fell against the door and slid down to the ground, hugging his knees as his breath came in short little bursts. "Dr. Langland." he whispered. "Oh my God, Dr. Langland."

"Sniper bullet, right? They probably didn't trust him to keep quiet." said a voice.

The boy looked around, startled. "Who-Who's there?" said the boy, his hand over his heart.

"Come here." said the voice, a strangely familiar voice that the boy thought he knew from somewhere but couldn't quite place. "Follow the sound of our voice."

The boy stood up, looking around. As far as he could tell the apartment was empty, and yet the boy had the unsettling feeling that he wasn't alone anymore, that someone or some*thing* was in the apartment with him. "Where are you?" said the boy, moving into the kitchen.

"Most likely the sniper used a silencer." said the voice, growing a little louder. "The noise we heard was the sound of the bullet passing through the glass. It's the middle of the day, and it's a weekday too, so nobody would notice the sound of a bullet killing Dr. Langland. Nobody except us, that is."

"Who are you?" said the boy, moving out of the kitchen and into the hallway. "How long have you been here?"

"We've been here this whole time." said the voice. "We saw Dr. Langland go from despair to hope, and from hope to death. And a quick death too, we might add. Right through the side of the head and into the brain. Apparently the only way to kill hope is to kill hope's vessels, isn't it?"

"You seem to be pretty casual about all this, considering we both just witnessed someone die." said the boy, walking past the bathroom.

"Of course I am." the voice responded, coming from right behind the boy. "For me, death is nothing more than the end of a character in a story."

The boy froze, chills running up his spine. The voice called the boy's name and told him to turn around. Slowly the boy turned, and beheld only himself, reflected back to him in the mirror attached to the bathroom door.

The boy stared at his reflection, stunned and confused. The boy's reflection stared back, a horrible sneer on its face.

"W-What is this?" said the boy.

"It's you." said the boy's reflection, using the boy's voice. "Or at least, a part of you. I'm every horror story, every scary movie and every campfire ghost story you know. I am the Hooked Man and the Slender Man, I am Bloody Mary in the mirror. I am the Red Dragon and the Cenobites promising you power. I am Freddy Kreuger and Jason Voorhees, Dahmer and Bundy and Gein. I am the red thing that has been growing in your gut since you got that call from Allison. I am you, and I am a nightmares nurtured through stories and fears."

The boy put a hand over his stomach; with every word his reflection spoke, the red thing that had been growing in his stomach pulsed, sending waves of anger and destructive urges throughout his system.

"You," said the boy, "you're madness. I've gone crazy, haven't I? Why else would I be talking to my fucking reflection only to have it talk back?"

"Well, you did just witness the murder of Dr. Langland." said the mirror-self. "Not to mention Allison's abduction has put you under a lot of stress. And then there's all that stuff that's been brewing underneath the surface in your subconscious."

The boy stared at his mirror-self. "What do you mean?"

"I mean all that rage you've repressed." said the mirror-self. "Why do you think you love horror movies so much? Why do slashers appeal to you when they gross out and upset others? It's not because you wanted to hang out with those monsters; it's because you wanted to *be* those monsters. You wanted to embody them, to become Jason and Michael Myers and Freddy. You wanted to have the cojones to kill like Robert Hansen and like Son of Sam. You wanted to be them, and there's no denying that."

"Why would I want to be a monster?" asked the boy.

"Because you were already facing a monster." said the mirror-self. "Your father, the psychopath who neglected and abused you, and hurt your mother so bad that after Ruby was born she left and you never saw her again. You were alone, and you took care of Ruby because nobody else would. Oh, you were a good big brother, a better parent than your parents ever were, but you hated your father, you hated him for scaring your mother away, and you resented your mother for abandoning you and your sister.

"And then you discovered the monsters of movies. So strong, so powerful, and only virtuous people, people who did not exist in the real world, could kill them. That is, these nonexistent people could kill the monster if they were lucky. And you wished to be a monster, because although you knew the heroes of movies didn't exist in the real world, in the real world monsters did exist, and in order to defeat a monster, you had to be some sort of monster yourself. You loved them…because you wanted to embody their power."

The boy stared at the mirror-self. Could it be true? Was the reason he loved monsters and scary movies so much was because he had had some Freudian urge to kill his father? Did he like Jason so much because Jason could not be killed, not even by another monster? Did he enjoy horror so much because he wanted to commit those horrors in real life? Was that all because of the boy's father?

"Why are you telling me all this?" asked the boy.

"Because you are placing your hope in the wrong people." answered the mirror-self. "You wanted Dr. Langland to go to the police. That would be the last place you want to go. The police have been trying to bring down the Camerlengos for years, but the Camerlengos have power, money, and connections. The police are unable to touch them, and as long as the police are bound by their codes and morals, the Camerlengos will live in their little Garden of Eden, free to roam around and hurt others like the monsters they are.

"But what destroys monsters?" asked the mirror-self.

"Other monsters." the boy replied immediately.

"Good." said the mirror-self. "Very good. Now let me ask you this: what if there was another monster? One that nobody had ever encountered before? And if that monster were to go searching for Allison, and then destroy any monsters that came after her, what would that monster be?"

"I-I don't know." the boy responded.

"Of course you do!" said the mirror-self. "It would be an avenging demon, a monster that took revenge and dispensed justice at the same time. Unbound by moral codes and ethics, the monster would be able to accomplish what others could not: the rescue of Allison and the destruction of the Camerlengos!

"And you could be that monster." said the mirror-self. "You could be that avenging demon."

"M-Me?" said the boy. "Why me?"

"Who else?" asked the mirror-self. "You know everything there is to know about monsters. You are young and strong, and you even know how to break bones, you researched that in case you ever wanted to use it for a movie. Anything you don't know, you can find out through steady research. Why should you leave it up to the imperfect justice system, when someone from outside the system, someone who truly cares for Allison, someone uninhibited by restrictive regulations and morals, can do the job so much better?

"You can be that person, my friend." said the mirror-self. "You can be the avenging demon."

"How?" asked the boy.

"By accepting me." said the mirror-self. "By accepting your darker nature and letting it grow and become a full part of you, you can become the ultimate monster, a creature that is every monster combined. With me, you can enter the Garden of Eden that the Camerlengos inhabit, and burn it to the ground. Most importantly, you can save Allison, save her before the Camerlengos kill her…or do worse things to her."

The boy could not believe what he was hearing, what he was seeing, what he was witnessing with this senses. And yet it was happening, his reflection in the mirror was offering him a deal that was most definitely a deal with the devil. Every sense of propriety that had been hammered into the boy over the years was telling him to run and not listen to this devil. But even so, the temptation to listen to his reflection and take the deal was great.

"How do you know we won't get caught?" asked the boy, trying to find a flaw in the deal, perhaps make it easier to get out of it. "By police or Camerlengos? How do you know we won't get cocky?"

"Because I am a part of you." the mirror-self answered. "And like you, I love Allison, more than words can describe. Most monsters only kill and hurt for their own selfish wants and needs, and that leads to them getting caught. But a monster that fights for someone else's safety and well-being will work their hardest to make sure they don't get caught. They'll cover their tracks and erase all fingerprints and DNA after they finish murdering someone in a dark, secluded place. They'll go to great lengths so that nothing can be traced back to them. They'll stay hidden, even while striking fear into the hearts of their victims."

"And we would be that monster?" said the boy.

"Correct."

"But how will they know that they are being hunted by a single person?" asked the boy. "Every mobster with a gun or knife has their own way of killing someone. How do you know we just won't blend into the scene?"

"Well, how about this? We're going up against the most powerful mafia family in the Big Apple, so let's give them a killer with enough of an individual killing style that they'll know they're not dealing with some average freak." suggested the mirror-self. "We've always admired the Russian mafia for its brutality. How about we take some of that brutality for ourselves, huh?" As the mirror-self talked, its voice deepened and a Russian accent crept in.

"What are you saying, we use *zamochit*?" asked the boy.

"Yes, but in order to separate us from other killers who employ that style, we'll only break their bones to the point where they are near death." explained the mirror-self, still speaking with a Russian accent. "Then when they do not expect it, we'll kill them with something other than broken bones. A gun, perhaps?"

"Where'd we get a gun—you know what, don't answer that, there are plenty of ways to get a gun illegally." The boy was finding it harder and harder to deny that the mirror-self's argument made sense, and it was getting more and more difficult to poke holes in the argument. If he didn't find a hole soon that couldn't be plugged up, he wouldn't be able to resist his reflection's offer. "Okay, we could go after Allison. But if we go to the police, they could..."

The boy stopped as a dark thought occurred to him.

The mirror-self nodded, as if he'd anticipated the boy's thought process. "The Camerlengo family may have spies within the ranks of the police." said the mirror-self. "As soon as they know the police are looking for Allison, they will assume the worst and make it so that we never find Allison. She'll be lost to us, and if they don't kill her, they'll find ways to make money off of her. You know what business they are in."

The boy did know what sort of business the Camerlengos were in. And the thought of them doing that to Allison...selling her...shipping her overseas...forcing her to be some man's sex slave...

The boy looked at his mirror-self. "Let's do it." he said, knowing he had no other choice. "Let's become the avenging demon."

The mirror-self smiled. "Wonderful." The image in the mirror began to dissolve as the red thing in the boy's stomach—the madness of monsters—exploded and spread through his system. As the red thing explode the dissolved image in the mirror flew out of the glass in a blinding swirl of light, entering the boy's nostrils and mouth.

The boy felt hot and cold, like he was experiencing summer and winter battling within himself. His limbs shook, his vision slid in and out of focus. He was having trouble breathing, as if something was squeezing his lungs from the inside, and yet it was ecstasy, as if the boy knew no pain or terror or anger, only pure pleasure. He could feel strength that had been held in check for fear of hurting others being released in a flood, coursing through his system in an angry torrent. And underneath all the ecstasy, the strength, was the desire and the urge to kill all that stood in his way.

Finally the boy collapsed, the powerful sensations dissipating. As he lay on the floor, breathing hard, he felt light, as if a great weight that he'd never noticed before had been lifted from him. Readjusting himself into a sitting position, the boy stared at himself in the mirror. His reflection stared back, wearing a crazed smile.

His smile. The boy's smile.

The boy stood up, giggling. As he went to get his coat from the living room, the giggles became full-throated chortles. The boy closed the door to the apartment behind him, laughing madly.

I have evolved. the boy thought to himself as entered the stairwell. Two flights down he passed some men in suits who were carrying bags with them. As the men walked by them, the boy smelled cleaning solutions coming from the bags and thought they might have been sent to dispose of Dr. Langland's body. He considered going to kill them, but decided to let them be for now. He'd kill them as surely as he would kill anyone else in his way later.

I am more now. the boy thought, walking down the stairs two at a time. *I am the Snake in the Garden of Eden.*

As the boy exited through the maintenance door, he looked around at all the skyscrapers and cars of New York City, all pieces of the Garden of Eden that the Camerlengos inhabited. He could not wait to burn it to the ground.

Chapter Twenty-Seven

Roman Veretti awoke with a scream. Throwing his head back, he howled as waves of pain shot up his arm. Before he could catch his breath, there was another blast of pain from the other arm and Veretti screamed again, his eyes watering, his head swimming in a sea of agony.

"*Dobroye utro*, Roman Veretti." said a voice, and a figure appeared in front of Veretti, a man wearing black leather and a mask that showed only two brilliant blue eyes.

Gasping through the pain, Veretti looked up at the figure and said, "What'd you say?"

"I said 'rise and shine' in Russian." said the figure, speaking with a deep, Russian accent. "Do you know who I am? I am the Snake."

Veretti's eyes widened in horror and shock. Was this the serial killer who'd killed three members of the family? Was Veretti the next victim now?

"Judging by your reaction, I see you've heard of me." said the man who'd called himself the Snake. "Then you must know what I'm going to do to you."

Veretti hesitated to speak for a moment, then said, "You're going to kill me."

"Precisely." said the Snake. "But you have options: if you tell me what I want to know, you will die quickly, and you'll only be discovered in the state you are in presently."

"The state I'm in presently?" Veretti repeated. It was only then that Veretti noticed he was tied with strips of tightly-knotted fabric in the fetal position, and that he wasn't wearing any clothes.

"If you think you can endure mind-numbing torture, then I will kill you slowly, and when I do kill you…" The Snake took a pause, and then said, "Well, you and your family members will have to look forward to a closed-casket funeral."

Veretti stared defiantly up at the Snake, who was looking down at him like Veretti was just a bug to him, a puny insect. "Go fuck yourself." said Veretti. "Mr. Camerlengo's been nothing but good to me. I'll honor him to the grave!"

"Suit yourself." said the Snake, as if he'd been expecting that answer. "But I'm afraid you're out of luck. You see, if you'd taken a look at your surroundings, you'd realize you're in the worst place ever to go against a sadistic serial killer."

It was only then that Veretti looked around him and saw that he and the Snake were in an old barn, the ceiling rotting in places, the remains of stables lying on the ground, and on the wall—

"Ah shit." said Veretti. On nearly every bit of wall space, there were farm tools and mechanic tools and other pieces that could be used for torture in the right hands, rusted with age but still deadly looking.

"You can say that again." said the Snake, striding over to the wall on Veretti's left and touching a large ax. Letting his hand pass over the blade of the ax like he was stroking it, the Snake continued speaking, "I saw this old barn and its farmhouse from the road while I was searching for a place to…take care of you. I thought I was lucky, since it was abandoned. But when I got us over here and opened her up, I was ecstatic!" The Snake laughed, grabbed the ax, and swung it down in front of Veretti's face. The blade of the ax sunk into the ground, nearly an inch from Veretti's nose.

"I mean, it's like a dream come true!" said the Snake, as if he hadn't just missed decapitating Veretti by about ten inches. "I've always loved American slasher films, and this is a treasure trove of weapons, just lying abandoned in a single barnhouse! I'm still wondering if I'll find a chainsaw around here somewhere!

"But of course you know what this means, don't you Mr. Veretti?" said the Snake. "There are a thousand ways I can torture you, and I can pick any single one I want."

Veretti followed the Snake with his eyes as the masked man walked around Veretti and grabbed a long length of climbing rope that had been lying on the ground next to Veretti.

"Now this rope was from the last car I stole while carrying you around." said the Snake as he looped the climbing rope around Veretti's chest several times and tied it into a knot. "As was the motor oil I found in the truck. Now, I can guess some of the things the owner of the car used those for: he obviously took care to always have some spare oil for his car and he liked to go climbing or rappelling when he got the chance. But for my purposes, they will be used in a much different manner."

The Snake threw the rope over a ceiling beam and pulled, forcing Veretti's body off the ground. Slowly Veretti was lifted into the air, looking down now from just below the ceiling beam to where the Snake was tying the rope to a hook on the wall.

"Instead of all these fun little toys, I'd like to use a classic method of torture on you, Mr. Veretti." said the Snake, grabbing a long, metal pole that looked to be at least eight feet long and whose purpose Veretti could not fathom, either for the farmer that had owned this barn or the man who held the pole now. "And it's also a method I might not have the opportunity to use for a very long while, so I might as well use it now."

The Snake circled below Veretti, looking up at him as he spoke. "In the seventeenth century, Vlad the Impaler, ruler of Wallachia and the inspiration for Dracula, took several thousand of his enemies and impaled them on wooden stakes. However, he didn't just impale them: no, he impaled them in the cruelest manner possible." The Snake grabbed a bottle of motor oil hidden behind a shovel, and opened the lid, pouring the amber contents on one end of the pole. "No, he impaled them *vertically!*"

Veretti's eyes widened as he realized what the Snake meant to do to them. "No, you can't do this!" said Veretti. "You crazy bastard, you're insane!"

"Tell me something I don't know." said the Snake. Standing directly underneath Veretti, the Snake lifted up the pole so that the oiled end was facing upwards, and plunged it into the ground. Veretti watched with horror as the Snake pushed the pole deeper into the ground, and then grabbed several implements off the wall to support it.

"Do you know why I left your legs unbound, Mr. Veretti?" asked the Snake. "Because it's not going to be easy getting you on the pole like this. And with only one person, it'll be even more difficult to force it in you while you're in the fetal position."

"Please." said Veretti. "Stop. Don't do this to me. I've got a wife, for chrissakes!"

"She's a widow now." said the Snake. Veretti watched as the Snake went over to the hook he'd tied the rope too, and undid the knot. Slowly the rope started to unfurl from the hook, and Veretti began to swing downward, closer to the pole. The Snake caught his legs, and despite Veretti's screams and struggles, directed him over the pole.

As another coil of the rope loosed itself from the hook, Veretti jerked and fell a few inches down, where the Snake grabbed his thighs and forced him down on the pole. Veretti screamed as he felt the tip of the pole touch his anus, and then screamed louder as the Snake went behind him and forced the pole into him.

Chapter Twenty-Eight

The Snake watched calmly as Veretti slowly slid down the pole, Veretti screaming in agony. "We can end this, you know." said the Snake. "Just tell me what I want to know."

Veretti only cried out in response. The Snake shrugged. "Suit yourself," he said, going over to the wall on his right to examine some of the implements there. There was another axe, a rake, a pitchfork, a small sickle, and...

The Snake's eyes widened as he saw what was hidden behind the pitchfork. Slowly he moved the pitchfork aside and felt the handle with his palm, beautiful wood painted black with hardly any wear or scratches. The Snake slowly, gingerly pulled it out, latched his fingers around the handle and held the machete in the air, looking at it in awe, triumph, and excitement.

While Veretti screamed in the background, the Snake took the machete over to the rotted and broken horse stables. The machete felt good in his grip, the blade only barely rusted. The theme music from *Friday the 13th* was playing in his head, screeching strings and deep-throated horns, and the breathing of a prowling, patient killer.

I've always wanted the weapon of Jason Voorhees, the Snake thought to himself. *Jason was always my favorite. Nothing could kill him, not even Freddy! He lived, even when he was dead, and even if only in the memories of the people he couldn't kill. He was pure malignant power. Plus, he didn't have a father ruining his life.*

The Snake looked at the broken stables and in his imagination they morphed into a bunch of thugs, big and ugly and stupid. Behind them, Allison cowered, one slightly-bigger thug holding a gun to her forehead. The Snake slashed through the thugs, not making a single sound as he slew them. One by one the thugs fell in bloody streams, until just the one holding Allison hostage was left. The slightly-bigger thug was shaking in his fancy shoes, while the gun was shaking twice as much. Allison just stared at him silently, begging him to save her with her eyes.

The Snake swung his machete, and cut the slightly-bigger thug's arm off in one fluid strike. The gun slipped out of the man's hand as the limb flopped uselessly to the ground while the thug himself held his stump as blood fountained out of his shoulder. The Snake grinned underneath his mask, and cut off the man's head. The head rolled away into a corner, the body fell sideways onto the ground, and Allison stepped over it as she ran into his arms—

"You son of a bitch!" shouted Veretti. "What family are you working for? What information could I possibly have that your bosses would want! Tell me!" Veretti screamed again, his screams echoing in the large barn.

The Snake turned away from the rotting stables with their new damage, and rested the blunt side of the blade on his shoulder. "I hope you interrupting my fantasy is a sign that you're ready to talk?" asked the Snake. "Otherwise, I'll just ignore you."

"Any fantasy you have must be sick as hell." called Veretti. Looking at him from behind, Veretti's body already looked distorted and bruised as the pole moved backwards through his digestive system. "Ah God—what could I possibly tell you that you'd want to know?"

"Well, that's an easy question, *droog*." said the Snake, walking around to Veretti's front, which looked even worse off than the back. "You can tell me about Allison Langland."

Veretti stared at Snake, surprise on his face. "The Langland girl?" said Veretti. "Why the hell would your bosses want to know about that? She's not important or anything, and the proof she had against us is in the drain." Then a look of realization crossed Veretti's face, and he said, "Unless...unless you're..."

"For a goon on one of the lower rungs of the family, you catch on quick." the Snake noted. "Yes, this is my own personal vendetta, my own mission to recover what I've lost. The deaths along the way are a form of karma, delivered by me acting in a role for my own personal movie."

"And everyone who was murdered..." said Veretti, stopping only to scream in agony.

"I asked them the same question." said the Snake. "But thanks to my nervousness, I killed James Sanonia before I could get anything from him. So I went after his cousin, who alerted me to Thomas Luiso, a friend of everyone in the family, and Lusio alerted me to you, one of the people who actually kidnapped Allison.

"Now, you can tell me where Allison is and die quickly," said the Snake, pointing the tip of the machete at Veretii's breastbone, "or you can keep quiet and die a slow and painful death. Either way, you're death is inevitable."

The Snake hefted the machete back onto his shoulder and turned away from Veretti. From behind the Snake, he heard Veretti stop screaming for a second and say, his breathing heavy, "Alright, I'll tell you what you want to know."

The Snake turned around to face Veretti, who looked down at the Snake from atop the pole. "The Langland girl," said Veretti, "is dead. We raped her tight little body, then slit her throat like the pig she was and threw her in the river."

Veretti laughed loudly even as he slid a little on the pole. But the Snake wasn't laughing; he'd seen Veretti's eyebrows twitching, noticed how much his eyes blinked as he spoke. The

Snake raised his machete and said, *"Ty uveren?" Is that how you want to play it?*

Before Veretti could realize the huge mistake he'd made, the Snake swung the machete, slicing into Veretti's thigh muscle and breaking the bone. Veretti screamed as the Snake pulled the machete out of the meaty muscle, sending a spray of blood into the air that narrowly missed the Snake.

"What do you expect to happen when you anger a serial killer with a lie?" asked the Snake. "Flowers? Now you've just increased your chances of dying a slow and painful death, possibly by gangrene or blood loss now."

"Do what you want to me." spat Veretti, gasping in agony between each word. "You'll never break me."

"Maybe not." said the Snake, realizing that what Veretti said was true. He decided he would have to try a different tactic and said, "But I doubt your wife will have your willpower."

Veretti's grin disappeared as he heard what the Snake said. "My wife?" he said. "You wouldn't!"

"Oh yes I would." said the Snake, pleased Veretti had bought his bluff. "I'm a serial killer with an obsession for slasher films. The killers in those films *always* kill several women and girls before the end of the movie. If they can, why can't I? Oh, and I'll make her death more painful than yours, you can be assured of that.

I'll make her torture worse just to punish you for not telling me what I wanted to know. Would you like to hear my various ideas on how I will go about doing this—?"

"Stop!" said Veretti. "Don't touch my wife! She's not involved in the family."

"But maybe you told her things after making love." said the Snake. "All sorts of things can pass between a couple during pillow talk, and unlike you, your wife won't lie to save your boss's skin. But if you talk to me, I'll leave her be. It's all up to you, Roman Veretti."

Veretti looked like he was torn between loyalty to his wife and loyalty to his boss, when he let out an ear-piercing wail, a fresh bruise forming on his torso. "Alright!" said Veretti, beginning to sob. "You win. I'll tell you about the Langland girl."

"I'm glad you saw sense, Mr. Veretti." said the Snake. "Now start talking."

Veretti gave another loud sob, as if the fact that he was betraying his boss to save his wife hurt more than the torture he was going through, and began to speak. "I-I was on the team that took the Langland girl away from the party." he said, giving a little moan near the end as he slid another inch down the pole. "We found her a few blocks away from where the boss's party was happening. Anyway, we take her and she drops her cell phone into the sewer.

My buddy and I went to a warehouse and hid the girl there in a freezer for a couple of hours while we waited for instructions on what to do with her. Then we got the call and we were told she was going to be kept under watch. Look, I was only there to make a few extra bucks. It's not as if I had a thing against the girl or anything."

"What does 'under watch' mean?" asked the Snake, ignoring Veretti's excuses.

"It meant we were going to keep her with someone outside the family, but someone who could be trusted and wouldn't let her get away or whatever." Veretti explained. "In this case we let her stay with Carla Scarusco, she's like the boss's cousin's kid or something. She runs this phone-sex service, out in the Bronx."

"Where is it?" asked the Snake. Veretti gave him the address, giving a yelp of pain as he slid further down the pole again. Underneath his mask the Snake smiled triumphantly. Finally, he had a real, tangible lead, an actual location, for where Allison might be. "Good. Now, is there anything else you want to tell me, before I consider swearing that I won't touch your wife?"

Veretti nodded. "One more thing." he said. "The other day I heard there was some sort of problem involving the Langland girl and a police officer. He was a guy on our payroll, some cop named Jay Kasmet."

The Snake raised his eyebrows, surprised. What role did a crooked cop play in all this? "You said his name was Jay Kasmet?" said the Snake. "What role does this Jay Kasmet play in it?"

"I don't know." Veretti whined, tears spilling down his cheek. "I'm only going on hearsay. All I know is the results were pretty bad. Will you leave my wife alone now?"

The Snake considered what he'd heard and said, "Yes, I will leave your wife alone." Veretti smiled, looking relieved.

"However," said the Snake, "you still need to go through some more pain before I kill you." The Snake grabbed Veretti's hips and pulled him down the pole. Veretti screamed loudly, raising his head in a horrible howl. The Snake raised the machete again and swung it into Veretti's other leg, sending another fountain of blood arcing into the air, followed by a series of punches to Veretti's tense abdomen, where the pole was moving ever so slowly through his digestive system. Veretti screamed and cried, and the Snake didn't let up, throwing the machete this time into Veretti's arms, feeling his rage course through his body as he vented it out on Veretti's helpless body.

Finally, when Veretti looked fit to pass out, the Snake reached into his coat and pulled out his gun. Breathing hard, the Snake lifted the gun up so that the tip of the silencer was against Veretti's forehead. Veretti barely registered it, only moaning quietly in pain.

"Thank you, Mr. Veretti." said the Snake, cocking the hammer. "You've given me my first real lead to go on. If anyone asks, I'll tell them you were a joy to talk to." The Snake squeezed the trigger, and Roman Veretti ceased to exist.

Chapter Twenty-Nine

The Snake looked at Veretti's lifeless body, everything above the stomach slumped forward while everything below was kept upright by the pole within Veretti's system. The effect made Veretti look like some grotesque puppet, abandoned by its puppeteer and placed in some strange storage room.

The Snake sighed. "Your wife will never know how much help you were to me this evening, Mr. Veretti." said the Snake, patting the corpse on the cheek. "Then again, she must've been a total fool, if she didn't realize what a degenerate bastard you were, keeping company with prostitutes and crooks. But that's beside the point." The Snake hooked the machete's strap around his shoulder and replaced his gun in his coat, switching it out for his knife. "Let's get you ready. I think there's a nice little lake a few miles up the road. Perfect place for you, Mr. Veretti."

As the Snake brought his knife up to Veretti's chest, there was the sound of choppers in the air and a bright light shining through the holes in the ceiling. The Snake jumped out of the light, startled. What was going on here—?

Suddenly a bullhorn sounded from outside the barn. "This is the New York Police Department and the Federal Bureau of Investigation." said whoever was holding the bullhorn. "Let any hostages you have go free, and then come out with your hands in the air. Otherwise, we will be forced to come in for you."

The Snake turned to the doors, the direction from which the bullhorn was coming, and swore in Russian. This was going to get difficult.

Chapter Thirty

Harnist and Murtz stood waist-deep in wild grass several yards from the barn the New York Mafia Killer had holed up in. Both were wearing full Kevlar outfits and were hiding behind large, heavy police shields with bullet-proof windows. Up until a few seconds ago, screams had been coming from the barn, but now everything was silent. The entire task force had been set to go in while the screams were going on, but as soon as they had died out the command had been given to hold back. Now they were just standing there, waiting for something—*anything*—to happen.

"An abandoned barn in the middle of nowhere." said Harnist. "Reminds me of some stupid horror film I saw back in high school."

"It's isolated, and he's unlikely to be interrupted." said Murtz. "If he really does have Roman Veretti, then it'd be the perfect place for him to do whatever he's doing in there."

"But I thought serial killers usually have a comfort zone." said Harnist. "You know, they have a certain area they like to kill in, and they don't like to leave it. That's what I heard, anyway."

"Some do." Murtz answered. "But not all serial killers are restricted to a single area. Ted Bundy is a pretty good example. Besides, I bet the fact that his target was alone was too good to pass up and the killer attacked him. He probably drove around a lot looking for the perfect place to be alone with his victim afterwards."

"Yeah, you couldn't hear the screams unless you got off the road and walked into this field." said Harnist, looking around the field, which until last year had belonged to a farmer when the property had gone into foreclosure. "Too bad the bastard didn't know this field's a popular spot for local delinquents to get high and hook up."

"Thank God for small favors." Murtz replied with a sarcastic roll of her eyes.

There was a squawk on Harnist's shoulder, and Patton's voice crackled through the radio. "Choppers will be here in less than thirty seconds." said Patton. "As soon as they arrive, get ready to move in."

"Roger." said Harnist into the radio. Turning back to Murtz, Harnist said, "So, what's your prediction on this guy, Doc? You think he'll go quietly?"

"I can't really say." Murtz replied. "If he does go quietly, it'll probably be because he wants to be recognized as the killer. If not…well, let's be glad we have ambulances on standby."

There was a loud swishing noise and two choppers appeared in the sky, searchlights trained on the barn. From another area of the field, Patton's voice could be heard clearly as he shouted instructions to whoever was in the barn through the bullhorn. Quietly, members of HRT and the police tiptoed through the grass, closer and closer to the barn.

Patton shouted again for the New York Mafia Killer to come out of the barn, but there was no response from within. A tense two minutes passed. Harnist was feeling antsy, and from the looks he was getting, some of the others in the field were getting antsy too. Looking behind him to the road, Harnist could see the huge mobile command center where the people in charge of the operation were watching safely. Next to the van was a canine unit vehicle, along with several police, SWAT, and HRT cars.

What're you waiting for? thought Harnist. *It's obvious he's not coming out. We have to go in there!*

"Looks like he doesn't want to come out." said Murtz. "Get ready, he's probably up to something."

There was another wait. Finally the radios on everyone's shoulders buzzed. "First wave, you are go. Repeat, you are go!"

At once, members of the HRT and police gathered together in front of the barn, one of them lifting up a small battering ram and smashing it into the barn doors. The doors crashed open, swinging on their hinges as the man holding the battering ram moved away from the doors. The rest of the HRT team went into the barn, holding up their submachine rifles, searching for targets.

From inside the barn there came a hissing noise and a thick white smoke filled the doorway, obscuring everything inside. A moment later, there were several small popping noises, followed by several loud screams.

Chapter Thirty-One

The Snake was cornered. Even if he couldn't see the people outside the barn, he knew they were there, probably holding up metal shields and submachine guns, if his research of SWAT and HRT weaponry was still up to date. The Snake's breathing was coming slowly, as if he was trying to sniff out how many enemies he was facing through the mask. But of course he couldn't smell how many enemies he had through the mask. He wasn't a werewolf, was he? And he certainly wasn't Linda!

He wondered when they would come in, if they would use a battering ram when they did, if they would come in firing, or wait till they had sight of a target. Did they use laser sight, or was it all done manually—

The Snake shook his head, trying to focus his thoughts. *Now is not the time to be analyzing the FBI's attack strategies!* thought the Snake, snapping back to attention. *Allison's waiting for you. Don't get caught now!*

The Snake turned, walked past Veretti's corpse and climbed up a ladder into the loft of the barn, where he'd hidden a duffel bag he'd bought just for today. Unzipping the bag, he found his extra revolver, a pair of semiautomatics, a flare gun, several cartridges, a new disposable lighter, and several cans of whipped cream and Mountain Dew.

At least, the cans used to contain whipped cream and Mountain Dew. And neither the whipped cream cans nor the Mountain Dew cans had had corks in their mouths when he'd first bought them.

The Snake hid his revolver under the cuff of his pants, tucked the flare gun against his waist, loaded the cartridges into the semiautomatics, strapped the guns against his chest, and arranged the whipped cream and Mountain Dew cans by the edge of the loft. Lying down on his stomach, the Snake waited, watching the door. Outside the only sound were the sounds of the choppers hovering over the barn.

Ya- Zmeya, zmeya iz rayskogo sada. Davaj lovi menya, esli mozhesh, the Snake thought. *I am the Snake in the Garden of Eden. Come and get me, if you dare.*

The Snake saw shadows shifting beyond the door and reached for the lighter and a whipped cream can. Pulling out the cork, the Snake inserted the barrel of the lighter into the bottle and squeezed the trigger. The liquid concoction inside the can reacted to the flame and turned into a thick white smoke. The Snake threw the can into the air, the smoke leaking out and spreading throughout the barn.

The Snake grabbed another whipped cream bottle and pulled out the cork. *Sometimes chemistry really is like cooking.* he thought as he lit the solution in the can and threw it down below.

Just need to know what you want to make and what you need to make it with.

He threw the last of the whipped cream cans into the barn below as the federal agents and police stormed in, obscured by the smoke that had filled the barn. The Snake smiled underneath his mask as he noticed he could only make out their silhouettes, which meant that the feds and the police couldn't see him either, and that meant he could use the Mountain Dew cans without having to worry about being spotted and stopped.

Reaching for a can, the Snake pulled out the cork, quickly inserted the lighter, squeezed the trigger, and threw the can below. Before it hit the ground, the can exploded, the contents flying in all directions. Several screams went up as the volatile liquid hit some in the face, while others screamed as the liquid set the hay on the ground on fire.

Nothing personal. thought the Snake, lighting another can and throwing it down below before it could explode in his hands. *I just can't afford to get caught while I'm looking for Allison. I'm sure you'd do the same for the love of your life.*

The Snake lit one more can and put it inside the now-empty duffel bag. Putting the lighter down the Snake grabbed the machete off his back, stood up, and jumped before the can could explode. Landing on his feet, the Snake ran at the entrance, knowing that there were agents waiting for him out there but not caring. As he slashed through two of the FBI agents in his way, the Snake stepped outside and prepared for what was waiting for him.

Chapter Thirty-Two

"Somebody respond!" Patton's voice squawked over the radio as several more screams were heard coming from radios and from the barn. Harnist tried to see inside, but the white smoke was clouding everything. Occasionally Harnist thought he saw flickers of orange, but he couldn't be certain what they were or if he was actually seeing something in the smoke at all.

Suddenly there was another hiss of static on the radio and Harnist heard someone say, "He's lit the barn on fire! He's got a machete!" There was another loud hiss and then nothing.

"Oh damn." said Murtz. Both Harnist and Murtz stared at the barn as black smoke began to pour out of the front of the barn and two holes in the roof. The flickers of orange that Harnist had been seeing earlier were now more apparent, and they were definitely not the imagination. Something was burning in there.

As they watched, three men stumbled out of the barn, two holding their hands over their faces and screaming loudly, while the third flailed around wildly as flames ate at his pants and back. As four men stepped forward to help the three who had come out, two more emerged from the barn, which was now emitting a bright, eerie scarlet light. One was a member of HRT, holding his stomach as he staggered out of the barn, coughing up blood. The HRT member fell into the grass in front of him, while the second figure just stood there, as motionless as a statue.

It was then that Harnist noticed that the person standing in the entrance to the barn wasn't wearing anything that resembled an NYPD or HRT combat suit, and that the person was also holding two submachine guns pointed out in front of him.

Harnist grabbed the radio on his shoulder and shouted into it, "Suspect's in the doorway! He's heavily armed. I repeat, suspect's in the doorway and he's heavily armed!"

"Take him down!" came the reply from Patton. No sooner had the command come that the person in the door sprinted forward, firing off shots in all directions. Murtz hid behind her shield while Harnist ducked down to his knees, the whizzing sound of a bullet passing by where his head had been less than a moment ago.

As Harnist straightened, he searched the field for the figure he'd seen, and spotted him heading towards the woods beyond the abandoned field. He raised his gun, took aim, and fired off a round. The bullet flew out the barrel, and a moment later the figure running towards the woods staggered. Harnist thought for sure he'd fall over, but then the figure straightened, threw down the semiautomatics, and continued running, pulling something off his back.

Harnist, along with several others, fired off as many shots as they could, trying to hit the person running into the woods again. None met their mark. A moment later the figure disappeared, blending effortlessly into the woods.

Harnist grabbed the radio again and called the mobile command center. "Suspect has fled into the woods." he said. "I think I hit him. Repeat, suspect has been hit and has fled into the woods."

"After him!" came the command. "We're sending canine units in too. Take him, but try to take him alive!"

"Dr. Murtz!" said Harnist, turning to her. "You coming too?" Murtz was still hiding behind her shield, but quickly straightened and looked Harnist in the eye.

"I can't. You go after him." she said. "BAU profilers don't normally go to take-downs. I'm overstepping my bounds just by staying in this field a minute longer. Go catch that guy, and make sure I get a chance to sit down and pick his brains!"

Harnist nodded and turned to the woods, running in with several other agents and at least four large, fierce-looking dogs.

Chapter Thirty-Three

The Snake swore under his breath in Russian. His shoulder was killing him, and he could just imagine a thousand different infections trying to get into him now through that bullet wound. Oh, if he could only get his hands on the cop that had shot him—

That would have to wait. They were coming after him, and if they caught him, he'd be put into a hospital or, if he was treated on-site, in a jail cell under maximum security in the hopes that after he recovered he would tell the police and the FBI why he had killed so many different members of the Camerlengos. Of course, that was if the Camerlengos didn't get to him first in the hospital or through a jailhouse connection.

Oh, this is worse than the FBI sting in Jason Goes to Hell! *At least Jason had a magic heart that time.* thought the Snake. *What I wouldn't do for some magic right about now!*

The Snake ran, inhaling sharply with each stab of pain from his shoulder. The dead leaves under his feet crackled loudly, kicking up little clouds of leaf-bits as he went and alerting probably the whole fucking forest to his location. In the distance he could hear the police dogs they'd loosed getting closer, their barks and howls filling an otherwise-silent forest.

The Snake spied a log in his path and jumped over it. As his feet rose over the log, a branch sticking out of the fallen tree snagged his pants cuff and sent the Snake falling to the ground. The Snake cried out, his hands stinging as he put them out in front of him. He pulled his leg free, but his revolver fell out, landing with a soft thud on the earth.

The Snake reached to grab it, but then he heard the barking of the dogs, and it sounded much closer than from before he'd fallen. Standing up, he left the revolver where it was and started running again, praying that if there was a god of any sort still looking out for him, they'd put a river or a stream in front of him so that he could cross it and the dogs would lose his scent.

He could hear the dogs getting closer, the sounds of their barks and their paws in the leaves getting louder and heavier. The Snake's wounded shoulder was taking away all his energy, the bullet wound sending wracking pain throughout his body. As the Snake looked behind him, he counted four large, nasty-looking dogs behind him. The Snake turned his head forward again, looking for anything to save him—

—and instead fell over a cliff, rolling head over body in a wild somersault before he landed painfully on his back. The Snake raised himself with an effort off the ground, looking around, trying to find his machete…which was behind a large, brown-coated boxer, which was growling at the Snake even as it was lifting itself off the ground.

The Snake stared at the boxer, and the boxer stared back. The moment seemed to freeze in time, just the two of them glaring at each other menacingly. Then the dog bounded forward, barking loudly. The Snake grabbed it by the neck, trying to hold it away from his face even as the dog scratched him and leaned forward to bite him.

The Snake growled and channeled his strength into his arms. Slowly he began to push the dog back, despite the protest coming from his shoulder. As the boxer got further away from his face, the Snake squeezed the dog's throat with his fingers, pressing his thumbs into its windpipe. The dog's growls became muted whimpers as its air supply was cut off. The Snake squeezed harder, and the boxer's eyes began to roll. Finally it stopped moving and its eyes shut. The Snake released the dog's neck and stood up off the ground. He looked at the dog lying on the ground, panting weakly as it tried to regain its breath. The Snake shook his head, feeling pity for the poor creature. He hated hurting animals, and he'd had to nearly kill this one so he could live and continue to search for Allison. At least he'd let the dog live so it would live to chase down criminals another day.

The Snake turned away from the dog and looked for the machete. As he picked it up, he heard growling behind him and turned around. The three other dogs had appeared, and they were just as big and as angry-looking as the boxer had been.

Chort vozmi, thought the Snake. *The boxer must've gone over the cliff with me while these mutts took their time getting down here.* The Snake lifted up the machete, his shoulder screaming at him even as waved the machete in front of him. The dogs tensed their back legs, ready to jump forward.

Suddenly the dogs scattered and ran off, whimpering as if they were in pain. The Snake stood there for a second, stunned, before looking around himself for something to make the dogs run off like that. As he looked behind him, he saw a state trooper standing a few yards off, holding a round, yellow whistle up to his lips.

The Snake stared as the trooper, who tipped his hat, took the yellow whistle out of his mouth and said, "Special dog whistle meant to keep wolves and foxes away from farms. I bought one off a farmer who has a security system 'round his property that uses these every time wild animals get to close." The trooper smiled and then added, "Anyway, I thought you could use a hand."

Chapter Thirty-Four

The Snake turned to face the state trooper, a tall man around the same height as him, with a round face and short hair. *What is this man trying to do?* the Snake wondered. *Why would a state trooper help a wanted criminal? It doesn't make any sense.*

The trooper took a step towards the Snake, causing the Snake to raise his machete with both hands and pointed the tip at the trooper. "Don't come any closer!" the Snake commanded.

The trooper stepped back and raised his hands in the air. "Okay, okay." he said. "Just take it easy. I'm here to help you."

"Help me?" said the Snake. "Give me one good reason why I should let you help me. You're a police officer. What I do usually angers police officers."

"What you do is causing a much-needed wave in the criminal underworld." the state trooper replied. "For once, the bosses of the families are shivering in their expensive shoes, and it's all because of you." The trooper stared hard at the Snake, and continued, "And if you think I'm going to help give the families some peace of mind by aiding your capture, then you've got another think coming."

The Snake stared back at the state trooper, suspicious. "What do you stand to gain from helping me?" asked the Snake.

"Nothing." said the trooper. "I might even lose my job. But I've already lost the most important things in my life, so what else can be taken from me?"

The Snake was taken aback by what the state trooper had said. *I've already lost the most important things in my life...* that sounded so much like the Snake himself it was uncanny. And the trooper had said that the Snake was causing a wave in the criminal underworld. Did this trooper really admire the Snake?

Slowly, the Snake lowered the machete, not taking his eyes off of the trooper. "The moment I think you're about to betray me," said the Snake, "you can say *do svidanya* to that pretty little head of yours."

"Fair enough." said the trooper. "Come on, before the police and the FBI catch up to their pooches."

The Snake ran up to the trooper, who turned and motioned for the Snake to follow. "So what are you?" asked the Snake, gripping the machete tightly. "An admirer? Do you pin my stories in the newspapers up on your bedroom wall?"

"If anyone should be asking questions, it should be me." said the trooper between breaths The trooper was leading the Snake uphill, and the Snake was holding his shoulder as he trailed a little behind the trooper. "A mask-wearing serial killer with a Russian accent. There was nothing in the papers about that."

"There's plenty that's not in the American newspapers." said the Snake. "Where are you taking me?"

"To the highway." answered the trooper. "My motorcycle's parked there. We can escape with that. Come on, it's just a little way away—Jesus!"

There was a loud bang and a bullet passed between the trooper and the Snake, boring a deep hole in the leaves as it struck the ground. The Snake ducked behind a large oak while the trooper hid behind a thick pine a few yards away. Looking at each other, they slowly peeked out from behind their trees in the direction the bullet had come from.

A crowd of police and federal agents were running in their direction, rifles held high and pointed forward. One of them, perhaps the cop that shot the Snake, held up his hand and the pursuing crowd pulled to a stop.

"This is Detective Harnist of the NYPD." shouted the cop. "Come out with your hands up and we swear, you won't be hurt."

"Ah shit." said the trooper, softly enough that the Snake almost couldn't catch it. The Snake and the trooper had pulled their heads back behind their trees, the trooper taking off his hat to wipe his forehead. "They got us surrounded."

"Not for long." said the Snake, reaching for the flare gun which was somehow still tucked into his pants against his hip despite all that had happened. The Snake had envisioned using the flare gun as an actual weapon, perhaps trick an enemy into thinking it was a real gun. But it could work very well for this situation.

The Snake stepped out from under the protective canopy of the oak and pointed the flare gun skywards. "Close your eyes." he said to the trooper, closing his own eyes as he spoke. The Snake squeezed the flare gun's trigger and a bright light shot out of the barrel, lighting up the night sky as it burst through the treetops and into the open air.

There were several screams and the Snake opened his eyes, looking in the direction of the cops. All had their eyes covered with their hands, moaning loudly as the glow of the flare cast a color-muting glow on them.

"Let's go!" shouted the Snake to the trooper. They started running, the trooper leading the way as the Snake followed behind, holding his real gun in one hand and his machete in the other. Behind them the sounds of their pursuers were once again becoming louder, but much more slowly than when before the flare gun.

Finally they broke through the trees and onto a lonely stretch of highway. There, standing on the side of the road like a lonely statue, was a white motorcycle with STATE TROOPER in yellow letters across the side.

The trooper, panting loudly, looked at the Snake and said, "Let's get going."

"You sure about this?" asked the Snake. "I could make it look like I forced you and then knock you out. No one would have to know about your involvement with me."

"And miss the chance to help you?" said the trooper. "Plus, I was in the hospital just last week for a spill down the stairs with a suspect. I don't need to go there again."

"I think what you both need right now is a good lawyer." said a voice. The trooper and the Snake turned and saw two police officers, both outfitted in Kevlar vests and helmets and pointing guns at the Snake and at the trooper.

"This ends now." said one of the cops, a middle-aged man with a mustache. "We're placing you both under arrest."

Chapter Thirty-Five

The two police officers stepped towards the Snake and the trooper, one of the officers sending a message through his radio that they had two suspects along the highway. The other officer, the one with the mustache, was pointing his gun at the Snake's machete. "Drop your sword." he said. "Put it slowly on the ground."

The Snake sighed and said, "It's a machete. Learn the difference, *ti durak*." Even as he was speaking, the Snake was lowering the machete onto the ground, wearily watching the police officers as the mustached one watched the Snake and the other officer was putting handcuffs on the trooper.

I can't get arrested. thought the Snake, panic threatening to take his mind. *I just found out where Allison might be!* Suppressing the urge to just pick up the machete again and slash through the police officers, the Snake took a deep breath and forced himself to calm down. He'd made it out of the barn by staying calm. He'd find a way out of this situation by being calm too.

"Hey Pacine, can you believe this?" said one of the officers, whose voice the Snake recognized as belonging to the officer that had called out to him in the woods. Harnist was his name, if the Snake remembered correctly, and he had just cuffed the trooper and forced the trooper to his knees. "A dirty cop helping a serial killer. What is this world coming to?"

"Oh, I'm the bad guy?" said the trooper. "Do you know how much the Camerlengos make in prostitution in a year? Enough to buy off the NYPD and give perks to the politicians who work for them. It's a scandal! I was only trying to work for the people instead of my own bank account, for chrissakes!"

"Yeah, and you did it illegally. Look where it got you." said the mustached officer, the one Harnist had called Pacine, who was examining the Snake's machete where it lay on the ground. "You're going down for aiding and abetting a wanted criminal. And if you helped this guy kill anyone, your good fortune will get even better."

"Wow Pacine, you're really chatty this evening." said Harnist. "What's got you talking so much?"

The Snake wasn't listening to the conversation anymore. He'd just had an idea, and he was determined to make it work.

"Alright." said Pacine to the Snake, bringing out a pair of handcuffs. "Turn around nice and slowly—hey, what the—?"

The Snake raised his right arm into air, shaking his arm like it was experiencing its own miniature earthquake. "Oh shih!" said the Snake, purposely slurring his words. "Mwuh bwub pweshuh!" The Snake leaned over and fell to the ground, not moving a muscle. Pacine swore and Harnist said into his shoulder radio, "We need a bus here! Got a stroke!"

As Pacine leaned down to help the Snake, the Snake sprang up again, looping his arm around Pacine's neck in a nasty chokehold. The Snake kicked Pacine's legs and Pacine fell against the Snake, the officer's legs splayed out in front of him. "Do not move!" shouted the Snake as Harnist reached for his gun again. Reaching down, the Snake grabbed Pacine's gun from the ground and pointed it at Harnist, even as he gave Pacine's neck another tough squeeze. "I could easily kill him. To me you're all just in my way."

"You'd kill a cop?" said Harnist.

"He said he'd kill me if he thought I'd betray him." said the trooper.

"Shut up!" said Harnist to the trooper.

"*Tiha*." said the Snake to the trooper.

"Don't do what he says, Harnist!" said Pacine, which only earned him another squeeze from the Snake.

"Let Sergeant Pacine go." said Harnist. "We don't have to do this."

"You're right." said the Snake. "We don't have to do this. So let me go in peace and free Mr. State Trooper over there."

"Can't do that." said Harnist.

"Then he'll die." said the Snake, tightening his hold on Pacine's neck.

"You're not a cop killer." said Harnist, the gun in his hand starting to wobble a little. "I know you're not a cop killer. You're not the type."

"You're right, I'm not." said the Snake. "Do you really want to make me the type to kill a cop though?"

There was a long pause, during which Harnist and the Snake faced each other with stares and will. Finally it seemed like Harnist was about to break, his lips opening and closing like a fish in water. Before Harnist could speak though, there was a loud scream and the trooper barreled into Harnist's side with his head in a nasty tackle. Harnist was knocked off his feet, the trooper sending him smack into a tree. There was a nasty cracking sound and Harnist fell face-forward, a line of red falling down his forehead.

For a moment, the Snake and Pacine didn't know how to respond. Then the Snake regained his composure and dislocated Pacine's shoulder, at the same time releasing Pacine from the chokehold. Pacine fell over, holding one shoulder as he let out a loud moan. The Snake stood up off ground, dusting himself off as he did, and strode over to the trooper.

"Did you kill the man?" asked the Snake, taking hold of the trooper's wrists. "Hold still." The Snake brought up his foot and then brought it down again on the chain holding the handcuffs together, severing it in two. As the Snake released his hands the trooper rubbed his wrists and shook his head.

"No, I didn't kill him." he said. "Might've, if I'd put a little more force into it. Speaking of force, you're pretty strong yourself. Former body builder?"

The Snake ignored the question and said, "Why'd you do it? You didn't know you would knock him out."

To the Snake's surprise, the trooper just smiled. "Couldn't let you become a cop killer." he said. "I told you, you're scaring the criminal underworld silly by killing the Camerlengos and getting away with it. If you started scaring the police too...I really don't want to think about what would happen if that occurred."

The Snake was silent for a moment. Then he said to the trooper, "What is your name?"

The trooper looked surprised for a second. Then he smiled and said, "Armentrout. Will Armentrout."

The Snake nodded. "Will Armentrout." he said. Then the Snake began, "My name is—"

"Don't tell me." said the trooper Armentrout. "If we get caught, it'll be trouble."

The Snake nodded, surprised he hadn't remembered that fact. It was amazing what a little camaraderie could do for you in situations like this. "I'm beginning to like you, Mr. Armentrout. Come on, let's get going. We have a lot to discuss. And call me Snake, if you're going to call me anything."

Armentrout smiled at the Snake. Pulling out his keys from his pockets, he said, "Happy to make your acquaintance, Snake. Let's get going—"

BANG!

Armentrout fell over, clutching his back with a pained look. The Snake looked down at the state trooper, before looking up and seeing police and FBI agents coming through the woods. "Oh, *chort vozmi.*" said the Snake.

The Snake felt something being put in his hands and looked down to see Armentrout placing the motorcycle keys in his hand. "Go!" said Armentrout. "Get out of here!"

The Snake didn't hesitate, but instead grabbed the keys from Armentrout, ran to the motorcycle, and drove out into the other side of the woods as the agents and police tried to shoot him in the back again.

PART THREE
SEARCH & RESCUE

Chapter Thirty-Six

Chort vozmi! thought the Snake, twisting the throttle a little harder. The bike sped up and the woods blurred around the Snake, creating more distance between him and the police. *I finally found someone I thought I could trust, someone who's willing to give me a lift out of here and aid me in my fight against the Camerlengos, and he gets captured! It's a good thing I already know how to ride these ebati motorcycles, or I'd be ebat!*

The Snake slowed down long enough to fish his phone out of his jacket and check his location. As the screen lit up in the dark, the Snake checked for bars, saw one small bar, and pulled up the GPS. Seeing a rest stop and motel a few miles to the northeast, the Snake put away his phone and changed direction.

As the woods cleared, the Snake began to make out several cars and trucks, a twenty-four hour diner with a few patrons inside, and a motel that looked like it had seen better days. The Snake hid the motorbike inside some bushes and headed into the parking lot, completely sealed by the night and the massive vehicles surrounding him. As he walked he held his shoulder, which was still throbbing like crazy.

I'll have to get to a hospital soon. thought the Snake, looking beyond the front of an orange semi before running across to the next row. *Or find some other way to fix myself up. If I don't, I could get lead poisoning or—hello, what's this?*

The Snake looked over into a black minivan with Florida license plates he'd been walking past. Nestled between two car seats was a large blue box with a red and white cross painted on it.

The Snake considered the alternatives and then broke in. It was a start.

As soon as the Snake had applied alcohol and had wrapped up the wound, he closed the first aid kit and car door and climbed over into the driver's seat. Breaking open the cover over the steering wheel, the Snake found the right wires and brought their ends together. The car sputtered and then roared into life, the lights in front shining onto the Jeep across from it.

Smiling, the Snake sat in the driver's seat, shifted gears, and reversed out of the parking spot. Driving away from the parking lot, the Snake turned the radio to a news station, where a live update of what happened at the barn was being broadcast.

"...although police are not speaking right now to journalists, there is evidence to support that the operation being held tonight was to capture the New York Mafia Killer, the same man who has killed three men associated with the Camerlengo Family in New York. It is unknown who the current victim is or if they are also associated with the organized crime family, but if it is the New York Mafia Killer, we can be sure that whoever it was, they most likely did not survive the encounter. It is also unknown whether or not the New York Mafia Killer was apprehended, but judging by the dejected look on the faces on some members of the team tasked with the capture, the killer has not been caught yet. We will have more updates as time passes on. I'm Candace Berman, reporting live from the old Adams farm here in Suffolk County."

The Snake smiled underneath his mask. *When this is all over, I'll have to send Candace Berman a bottle of vodka or something.* he thought, turning off the highway into a suburban neighborhood. *She's doing more to spread my fear than anyone else in the entire media.*

The Snake drove into a street lined with shops and restaurants, most of which were dark and closed at this time of night. The Snake looked for anything that might help him, a clinic or a medical supply store—*tam!* There!

The Snake saw a veterinarian's office up ahead and pulled into the back parking lot where the minivan couldn't be seen. Uncoupling the wires, the Snake slipped out of the front seat, disabled a security camera, and slipped into the building through the back door with the help of his bump key.

Chapter Thirty-Seven

The Snake walked past a staff lounge, a storage closet, and into a large room covered in grey tile with a big, metal table in the center of the room. Several cabinets and desks lined the wall, each with a lock in them. A veterinarian's operating room.

Turning on the lights, the Snake took off his coat, shirt, and mask, setting them in a neat little pile on top of one of the taller cabinets. Slipping the bump key out of his pocket again, the Snake started opening cabinets, looking for supplies. *Scalpel...sutures...disinfectant...face-mask and hairnet...*

The Snake set all the supplies onto the table and, unwinding the bandages around his shoulder, began scrubbing the wound with antiseptic. Grabbing a scalpel, the Snake cut into the bullet wound, widening it up and letting the blood flow again. The Snake cried out as he put the scalpel back onto the table, breathing hard.

Fighting a wave of nausea, the Snake took some clamps and did what he hoped was a half-decent job at closing the blood vessels around his wound. Then, taking a pair of forceps, he reached into the wound in his shoulder and dug for the bullet.

As the forceps went in, the Snake groaned aloud. Bog. he thought. *Shit. I'm going to need a lot of painkillers when I'm done.* The Snake dug in deeper, reaching deeper and deeper for the bullet. The blood began to flow faster, dripping down his pants and onto the floor. There was a heady sensation and the Snake wondered if he was going to faint.

Finally, the forceps grabbed onto the bullet and the Snake began to pull the forceps out. With a loud squelching sound the forceps came out in a spray of blood, the bullet clamped right between their teeth. The Snake stared at the bullet for a second, finding it hard to believe that something so small could cause him so much pain and trouble.

Placing the forceps and the bullet back onto the table, the Snake took the clamps out of his shoulder, and grabbed the sutures and needle and began to sew up the wound. Working with a mirror, the Snake watched as the bloody wound became a thin slit on his back, the needle disappearing into and then out of his skin, causing a blast of pain every time it went in and out.

Finally, the Snake cut and tied the string, cleaned the area around the wound, and wrapped it up in fresh bandages, hoping against hope he'd done a half-decent job at doing surgery on himself. If not, he'd be in trouble later.

The Snake took a few light painkillers, pocketing the bottle they'd come in. Then, putting on his clothes and mask again, the Snake began cleaning up the operating room, removing his blood and DNA from any surface it might've landed on. When he was done, he put the tools and soiled cotton and bandages he'd used during the surgery in a bag and walked out of the operating room, only going back to the minivan in the parking lot in order to make sure he hadn't left any evidence in there that could lead back to him.

A few blocks north of the commercial district, the Snake found a residential area with cars out on driveways, the car's owners sleeping inside their homes unconcernedly. Breaking into one of the cars, the Snake hotwired the engine and began the long drive back to Manhattan.

Chapter Thirty-Eight

"Hey!" shouted Allison. "Hey somebody! Open up and let me out now! I need to use the bathroom!" Allison pounded her fists on the door, but no one came. She wasn't surprised though: in the three days since they'd left her in this room, Allison hadn't been visited by anyone, the viewing slot had remained closed, and only the small panel at the base for sliding food in had seen any use the past three days.

And the whole time Allison had been stuck in this room, she hadn't figured out a way out. There were no windows and no furniture. The door wasn't crooked or had a gap that could be exploited to open the door or rusty hinges or anything. The only thing in the room was the poop bucket, and Allison had refused to touch that at all.

But now Allison had a bigger problem. She'd used the bathroom before she'd been abducted from Carla Scarusco's office, so she hadn't had to go the first day in the room. The second day she'd been able to hold it somehow, thank goodness the men had been feeding her only dry crackers and water so the need to go hadn't really increased, and her pride helped keep her need to go at the back of her mind.

But now the need to go was overwhelming. It filled her thoughts, kept her awake when she wanted to sleep, and was now threatening to cause her bladder and her butt to explode if she didn't go soon. But the thought of using the bucket...Allison could not allow herself to do that. There was no way in hell that she would use the bucket. It was gross, it was unsanitary, and it was just plain disgusting! No way.

But if she didn't hurry and sit down on a toilet soon, she'd have a problem. Allison took a deep breath, aware that every movement brought a painful tremor from her bladder and her butt. With another swing of her fists, Allison hit the door again. "Open up!" she shouted. "I needed to use the bathroom!"

There was a grating sound and to Allison's surprise a pair of big, piggish eyes stared out at her from the viewing slot. "Cut it out, red." said the man, looking Allison up and down as he looked at her. "That's what the bucket's for, don't you know? Use that."

"I am NOT using a bucket." said Allison. "Now take me to a real bathroom."

"Sure, sure." said the man. "Whatever you say, Your Highness. But only if you do me a favor in return."

Allison raised an eyebrow, suspicious. "What sort of favor?" she asked.

"Well, I'm a lonely kind of guy." said the man. "We wouldn't have to go all the way, but if you'll just give me a little head—"

"Go give *yourself* some head, you creep!" said Allison, stepping away from the door and crossing her arms as if to keep this disgusting man's aura away.

The man only shrugged. "Suit yourself, red." he said. "Hope you like shitting your pants." The man laughed cruelly as he slid the viewing panel closed. Allison stared at where the man's eyes had been for a full minute, directing all her anger and revulsion at him before she realized that she still needed to use the bathroom.

And now there really was no way of getting out of that room unless she—

Allison shook her head and looked at the bucket, considering it as a serious option for the first time in three days. It was either using the bucket or giving into that man. Another twinge from her bladder had Allison decided. With a groan she ran to the bucket, turned it over onto its end, and slid her pants and underwear off. Lowering her butt over the bucket, Allison felt herself crying as she let herself go in the bucket.

Pain, release, and humiliation coursed through her system as Allison emptied her bladder and her anus. How had it come to this? Why was this happening to her? When it was over Allison pulled her underwear and pants up and ran into the corner farthest away from the bucket and the smell, now worse than when she'd first been thrown in the room.

This isn't happening. Allison thought, huddling into a ball on the cold floor and rocking back and forth. *This isn't happening. This isn't happening!* Desperately, Allison tried to find a way out of her situation. Eventually she found herself in her memories, reliving her first date with her boyfriend. Instead of in the cell, she was in a coffee shop in the Village; instead of a sweater, jean pants and a pair of sneakers, she was wearing a bright green blouse, a white skirt, and white flats; and instead of fear and humiliation, Allison felt nervous and excited as she spotted the guy who would be her boyfriend.

"Did I keep you waiting long?" he said. "Because if I did, I'd like to blame my cab driver getting lost on the way here."

"No, you're fine." Allison replied, happy to be here than in the cell. "I just got here. Hey, what's with that look?"

Her boyfriend was looking at her with a funny look on his face. Finally he said, "You look very nice."

Allison beamed when he said that. "Thanks." she said. "I really appreciate that." As they ordered drinks, Allison hoped that she could stay in her memories for as long as possible before she had to return to reality. Because when she did, she felt—no, she *knew*—that she'd never be able to return to this place and time again.

Chapter Thirty-Nine

Murtz, Patton, and Gramer surveyed what was left of the crime scene, feeling terribly dispirited. Not only had the Snake killer gotten away from a whole task force of NYPD officers and FBI agents, he'd left a trail of blood and destruction in his wake. So far, eight officers were reported as injured, an attack dog had nearly been strangled to death, and the barn where the Snake's latest victim, probably Roman Veretti, had been gutted by flames and then soaked with water by responding fire crews. The chances of getting anything useful from this crime scene were close to zero.

"How could he do this?" asked Patton.

"Which part?" asked Gramer, his voice a disheartened mutter.

"All of this!" Patton replied, his voice rising in anger. "How could one man turn the police and the FBI into a bunch of fools? This isn't supposed to happen, especially when the guy's completely surrounded! This is something out of a really bad movie or something."

"I wish I had an answer for you, Captain." said Murtz, watching as techs tried to pull anything salvageable from the wreckage of the barn. "But I don't. All I can say is we're not dealing with your average killer, but one with either a very fine intuition or a lot of luck or both and we're going to have to plan more carefully next time."

Gramer let out a deep sigh, to which Murtz replied with a consoling pat on the back. What most people didn't realize was that Gramer and Murtz had come up in the Academy at Quantico together and were old friends. Even as he had moved up and she had settled into the BAU, they'd stayed friendly, and even called each other by their first names on occasion. On this occasion though, a pat on the arm seemed to do better than the use of first names, as Gramer seemed to brighten a little and nod appreciatively at Murtz.

"You're right, Murtz." said Gramer. "We will plan more carefully for next time. And we'll also have to get a better handle on this guy. Like you said, he's not the average killer."

"You're also going to have to notify Mrs. Veretti of her husband's passing before you start planning for intuition or luck." said a familiar voice. Murtz turned to see Dr. Mohawk coming towards her, Patton, and Gramer, a tired look on his face. "That's definitely Roman Veretti on that stake. His face matches the photo of him released to the news when he went missing earlier today. Of course, the photo given to the news teams doesn't have as much pain on it. Or a bullet hole in the forehead."

"How did that guy get Veretti onto a stake like that anyway?" asked Patton, eyeing the body on the stake with distaste. "He'd need an accomplice to help him."

"I'm not so sure." said Dr. Mohawk, looking back at the body. "You see, Veretti's arms and legs were broken pre-mortem, just like Thomas Luiso. Not only that, but Veretti's arms were tied behind his back, further limiting his ability to struggle. And you see that rope tied around his chest? That's the same type of rope my wife and I used when we went mountain-climbing on our second honeymoon.

"Now this is not my department," said Dr. Mohawk, turning back to Gramer, Patton, and Murtz, "but I'm going to guess that the Snake killer lifted Veretti up with that rope, and then impaled him from underneath, somehow getting Veretti onto the stake while controlling the rope. How he did it, probably some use of physics that I haven't figured out yet, but he obviously was able to plan it so he could get Veretti onto the pole without any help. It's the only possible explanation."

"And it would certainly work with my profile." said Murtz. "A loner who really likes to cause pain."

"Makes you wonder why he didn't kill the officers or the dog." said Patton, stroking his chin thoughtfully. "You'd think he'd get off on killing them."

"If it had just been the officers, I'd say it went against his moral code. Remember, if he's the type who sees himself as a sort of hero, he wouldn't want to be the bad guy by killing a good guy. But," said Murtz musingly, turning it over in her head, "the fact that he only injured the dog does put this in a different light. After all, these sort of killers start out hurting animals and then graduate to humans. Killing an attack dog should've been easy for him once he'd started choking it."

"Maybe he didn't have time to kill it." suggested Dr. Mohawk.

"Or maybe I'm looking at him all wrong." Murtz shook her head, as if by that alone, she could clear the fog in her head and solve this mystery. "I'm going to have to get back to you on this when I've had at least six hours sleep and some coffee to perk me up."

"Good luck getting either of those at this rate." said Gramer. "Agent Fallmouth, what news do you bring?"

One of the agents from the task force was running over to them, talking on his phone as he ran. When he arrived, he cut the call and said, "Just got word from the hospital. The agents that just got cut by our perp are going to be fine, though those cuts that machete made on them are going to put them out of commission for a while. And the ones who got acid on their faces…it's not pretty. The son of a bitch blinded them. They're whole lives have been upended because of him! Not to mention their careers are in the toilets!"

"While very unfortunate, that's not our major concern at the moment." Patton commented. "What else?"

"Well, we've confirmed that the state trooper is a Will Armentrout, and that he was definitely in league with our perp, sir." said the agent. "Don't know what the relationship is though, because he's currently knocked out and on his way to the emergency room to get a bullet out of his back."

"Bastard will probably lawyer up once he's out of the OR." said Gramer. "Keep security on the guy anyway. He's a valuable asset now, and we don't want him getting away."

"Or getting killed by a friend of Veretti." Patton added.

"It's already been ordered, sir." said Fallmouth. "Oh, and there's one more thing."

"And that is?" asked Gramer.

Fallmouth took a deep breath before responding, "Detective Harnist and Sergeant Pacine were injured. They were the officers who'd caught the killer and Armentrout before the killer got away."

"Harnist and Pacine?" repeated Murtz. "Are they alright?"

"Detective Harnist will be fine, ma'am." said Fallmouth. "He'll need a few stitches though, and I don't think he'll be doing any heavy-duty work anytime soon. Sergeant Pacine...well, that's another story. The perp dislocated his shoulder and then knocked him out. He's going to be off-duty for a little while."

Patton groaned, covering his eyes with his hands. "Pacine's one of the best on my staff." said Patton. "How the hell am I going to get anything done without him?"

"I think we've got bigger things to worry about now, if you don't mind me saying, sir." said Dr. Mohawk, walking past Agent Fallmouth and out of the barn. A second later he reappeared and said, "Like the circus out on the highway."

"Circus?" repeated Murtz. Patton, Gramer, Murtz, and Fallmouth joined Dr. Mohawk outside the barn, and saw what he meant: a whole mob of media types were stationed on the highway, being kept back only by barriers and crowd control units. Murtz could see cameras flashing, people talking, shouting, and asking questions, while from above helicopters flew over and surveyed the scenes below them.

"Oh great." said Patton. "This'll be a PR nightmare. That political suck-up of a commissioner will be all over my ass in the morning asking why we looked so bad in front of the cameras."

"So will my AD." said Gramer. "He's a climber, and this won't look good for his FBI Director dreams."

"I'm more worried about the criminal underworld's reaction at this point, truth be told." commented Dr. Mohawk. "Imagine what'll happen when they see this cluster-fuck on the eleven-o'clock news."

As soon as he'd said it, Murtz, Patton, and Gramer all looked at each other, a horrifying idea passing between them. They'd let the New York Mafia Killer get away with murder again, even after sending in SWAT, HRT, and everything else they could've mustered. And now the news teams were reporting it live to everyone in New York, and quite possibly in the nation. What would happen once the crime families realized that the Camerlengos' biggest threat in years was going around killing left and right, and nobody could stop him? What would the people of New York think of the authorities? When Murtz thought of the various possibilities, all she could fear was a dark dread.

Chapter Forty

The Snake trudged up the stairs to his apartment, his whole body aching from the exhaustion that had finally caught up with him. Even worse, his shoulder was still throbbing horribly, as if to remind the Snake that he was only mortal and that his luck wouldn't always last.

But it was worth it. thought the Snake, pulling his keys out of his pocket and turning them in the lock. *I finally have a bead on where Allison might be.*

As the door swung open, there was a bark and Linda bounded over to the Snake, skidding on the linoleum as she pulled up in front of the Snake.

"Nice braking." said the Snake, bending down to rub Linda's head. Linda whined happily and licked his face, eliciting laughs from the Snake. "Did you stay up for me, girl? That's very kind of you. Guess what? I've got a good lead this time! Tomorrow we'll be heading out. We might just find out where Allison is!"

Closing the door to the apartment, the Snake stripped and went to the bathroom, where he gave himself the best wash he could without letting the water seep into the bandages. As he took a sponge from a cabinet, poured soap and water on it, and started scrubbing, the Snake went over the events of the night to see if there was anything he could've done better.

In actuality, there was plenty he could've done better than what he did, including not getting shot, or taking less time to interrogate and murder Roman Veretti. But at least he'd covered his tracks: the barn would probably not contain any DNA or anything that could be tied back to him, thanks to the fire. If they'd called for fire crews, which they probably did, then the water would've also erased any evidence the police could've gathered to use against him.

Not only that, but he'd made sure the minivan and the car he'd stolen and dumped afterwards hadn't had any of his DNA on him, and anything he'd touched or used that could be used against him on had either been dumped, taken, or scrubbed clean. And the instruments and waste he'd taken with him from the veterinarian's office were probably now floating down a sewer line to either the ocean or a treatment facility, where any usefulness they might've had would be destroyed.

So far, he was still in the clear. For now, anyway. He'd have to be much more careful next time and think more in-depth about his escape routes. He'd also have to find out how the police and the FBI had been alerted to where he was. Perhaps with that information, he could avoid having the police summoned to him again.

Finishing his sponge bath, the Snake put on some pajamas and climbed into bed. Linda climbed on top of the covers as he settled in, stretching her limbs so that she was lying across half the bed. For once, the Snake decided to let her sleep in the bed with him, too tired to say otherwise.

Setting his alarm for seven-thirty, the Snake settled back into the sheets and laid his head against the pillow. As Linda began to snore, the Snake closed his eyes and dreamed of Allison's face. *Don't worry, Al.* he thought, reaching out in his dream to stroke the cheek of that lovely face. *I'm coming for you. I'll get you out soon.*

The dream-face smiled back at him, filling the Snake with happiness.

Chapter Forty-One

"Alright." said Dibacca, looking out the window as he talked on his phone. "Uh-huh. We get it, sir. You be careful as well. See you at the meeting on Wednesday. Bye." Dibacca shut his phone and sighed. "Goddammit."

"What happened?" asked Cabrera as he sat behind the wheel, signaling that he wanted to make a lane change. "Is it...you know?"

Dibacca groaned from the passenger seat, rubbing his hand up and down his face. "Yep, it is." he growled. "The New York Mafia Killer. The bosses just got word that Roman Veretti was the latest victim. The crazy bastard really did a number on him, too."

"Jesus Christ." said Cabrera, moving into the right lane. "I knew Veretti. We played poker together on Thursday nights. Cleaned me out more than once, too."

"I bet he did."

"What sort of number did he do on him?"

"I didn't ask, you dummy." Dibacca replied. "Could you turn on the radio or something? I don't want to think about the New York Mafia Killer or the Veretti kid right now."

"Yeah, sure thing." Cabrera leaned over in his seat and punched the audio dial. As the display screen lit up, a woman's voice came over the speakers. "...sources say that the New York Mafia Killer evaded an entire force made up of police and FBI agents, injuring at least ten members of the task force and one attack dog. It is unknown how the suspect managed to evade the entire force, or how seriously injured the officers are. Law enforcement officials are at this time not commenting on what has transpired here this evening. From Suffolk County, I'm Candace Berman, reporting to you at the scene of the crime."

Dibacca and Cabrera stared at each other. Finally, Dibacca broke the silence and said, "Turn it off."

"Huh—w-what?"

"I said turn it off!" Dibacca shouted. Cabrera sputtered to life and pressed the audio dial, his left hand turning the steering wheel sharply to the right. The car drifted to the right and almost off the road.

"Get off the curb, you idiot!" shouted Dibacca. Cabrera took back control of the wheel and righted the course of the car, smoothly exiting off the highway and pulling off to the side of the road.

Dibacca and Cabrera sighed in unison as Cabrera put the car into park. "Oh my God." said Cabrera. "That was crazy."

"What were you doing?!" shouted Dibacca, slapping Cabrera in the head. "Trying to get us both killed?"

"Jeez, I'm sorry!" said Cabrera, rubbing the spot where Dibacca had slapped him. "No need to go ballistic."

"Can we just hurry up and get this over with?" asked Dibacca, a vein pulsing in his forehead. "I wanna get home. 'Sides, the higher-ups want everyone on pimp duty home early."

"Early?" Cabrera repeated. "Why do they want us to be home early?"

Dibacca gave a loud cry of frustration before turning to his partner and shouting, "Because of the killer, you moron! Think about it, he's killed four of our guys, and he evaded an entire team of feds and cops! Of course they want us home early! What, did you think they wanted us to study for a quiz on The Colbert Report?"

"Why would they do a quiz on The Colbert Report?" asked Cabrera. "Jon Stewart's a thousand times funnier."

"Just drive, you numbskull!" shouted Dibacca.

When they finally reached the pick-up location, the sky was beginning to brighten a little, becoming a soft purple. Dibacca and Cabrera got out of the car and looked around for the girls under their watch. Not a soul was around.

"Where the hell are they?" growled Dibacca.

"I don't know." said Cabrera. A second later, Cabrera had lifted his hands to his face and was shouting, "Chontelle! Cassidy! Euphie!"

"What the hell are you doing?" snarled Dibacca.

"I'm just calling for the girls." said Cabrera.

"No you're not!" said Dibacca, stomping over to Cabrera. "You're alerting the serial killer and all his fans to where we are just so you can see that thing you've been seeing on the side!"

"Huh? Wait, I don't know what you're talking about—!"

"I know you're seeing that slut Euphie on the side!" Dibacca cut in. "And she may be some sweet Kansas girl, but she's nothing but bad news! Getting involved with any whore is bad news. Especially when you happen to have no brains in that thick head of yours!"

"What'd you just say about Euphie—?"

"Sheesh, what's with all the noise?" said a voice. Dibacca and Cabrera turned to see three men in expensive suits. One of them, a dark-skinned man wearing a gold ring and a goatee, strode towards Dibacca and Cabrera, grinning from ear to ear.

"This neighborhood must really be going to the dogs," said the man, his voice matching the one that had spoken earlier, "if two grown men can stand around arguing at the top of their lungs about the quality of golden-hearted whores. Euphie…was she by any chance the one with the cheap rose earrings? Cute girl. Last one to leave after we chased those girls off. Kept saying she wanted to see her Eddie. That you, hotshot?"

"Who the hell are you?" asked Dibacca, the vein in his forehead pulsing again. "In case you haven't noticed, I'm not really in the mood to entertain, so why don't you just tell us where we can find our whores and we can be on our merry way."

The man with the goatee clicked his tongue and said, "Oh, where are my manners? I'm Danny Baldwin, these two are Gomez and Gold, and we're the new owners of this spot."

"What the hell is he talking about, D?" asked Cabrera. "This is Camerlengo land. Everybody knows that."

"First off, I told you to lay off with that stupid nickname. Save it for the fantasy basketball league, you moron." said Dibacca. "Second, I've heard of you, Baldwin. You work for the Cromlin group. And none of Cromlin's men would ever pick a fight with us."

"That's how it used to be." said Baldwin, flashing another grin. "But things have changed. After all, the New York Mafia Killer is going strong, and he's killed four of your men. Most don't even get past planning to kill one. So, if he can get away with four…"

Baldwin snapped his fingers and his partners pulled out handguns from within their suit jackets, pointing the guns at Dibacca and Cabrera.

"…why can't we?" Baldwin finished.

Cabrera and Dibacca glanced at each other, and a silent message passed between them. Striding forward to Baldwin, trying to give off his most powerful alpha-male air, Dibacca smoothed his hair back and said, "Look pal, I know the serial killer's got everybody on edge. But don't take that as some stupid excuse to go and pick a fight with us. After all, the Camerlengos are still top dog, last I checked. So why don't you and your pals do the smart thing and scoot out of here? We're both busy men who've got to collect from our whores, and we don't want to waste any more time on you."

To Dibacca's surprise, Baldwin just laughed. "Oh, I'd do just that…except my boss wants me to 'knock out your support beams'." Baldwin replied, making quotation marks in the air.

"Cromlin said that?" said Dibacca, disbelieving.

"Yeah." Baldwin answered. "And in any way we can."

Dibacca felt something poke him in the belly. A second later there was a loud bang and Dibacca felt something hot and painful pierce through his stomach. Looking down, he saw a small river of blood forming just beneath his suit jacket. Feeling dizzy, Dibacca fell over, holding a hand to his stomach.

"Dibacca!" Cabrera shouted, reaching into his jacket. Without a second's hesitation, Baldwin's companions cocked back the hammers on their guns and started shooting. Cabrera flailed around like a clown on a ball before falling over, his face and body riddled with holes.

Dibacca turned over and stared at Cabrera, his face stuck in a horrible expression of surprise, as if he hadn't seen his own death coming. *Ah shit.* thought Dibacca. *Even that numbskull didn't deserve this.* From behind him, Baldwin was talking as if he were discussing travel plans with a coworker.

"Once we take over this area of town, your regular customers will start paying us." he said, walking around Dibacca. "And if the other gangs and families are thinking like we are—strike now while the iron's hot—the Camerlengos will lose at least a third of their territory and your foreign contacts. That's millions in profits down the tubes if you can't sell girls overseas."

"You bastard." Dibacca growled, spitting on Baldwin's shoes.

Baldwin shrugged nonchalantly. "I've been called worse." he said, pointing his gun at Dibacca's head and squeezing the trigger.

The world ceased to be.

Chapter Forty-Two

BE-BE-BEEP! BE-BE-BEEP! BE-BE-BEEP!

The Snake opened his eyes and groaned as he realized Linda's front paw was lying right on his mouth. Sitting up and rubbing his eyes, the Snake looked at the clock. The LED numbers on the screen read 7:31 in the morning. *Big day today.* thought the Snake, swinging his legs over the edge of the mattress. As the Snake's shoulder gave a painful throb, he groaned and thought, *Better get something for this shoulder first.*

Turning off the alarm and trudging off to the kitchen, the Snake took a couple of mild painkillers and ate some cereal and hot chocolate. As Linda woke up and padded into the room, the Snake gave her some dog food and fresh water to keep her off the kitchen table. As the large dog chewed noisily, the Snake took a sip of his hot chocolate and said, "We're going on a trip today, girl. Going to go to the Bronx. Meet a woman named Carla Scarusco. She runs a phone-sex agency. Can't believe they hid Allison there, right? I certainly can't believe they hid her there…or that Al liked living in that sort of place."

Linda didn't reply, or even lift her head. The Snake rolled his eyes. *I can't wait to get Allison back.* he thought, taking another sip of hot chocolate. *The only person I have to talk too is my dog, and she's only concerned with her food. Not the best source of conversation in the world.* Deciding that he should do something productive with his time, the Snake went back into the bedroom to grab his smartphone. Walking back into the kitchen, the Snake turned on the search engine and put in the name "Carla Scarusco".

As the search results came up, the Snake raised a surprised eyebrow: there were no hits for Carla Scarusco, at least none that resided in New York and worked in the Bronx. The Snake browsed through Facebook, Twitter, LinkedIn, but there was nothing there. He wondered if that had something to do with the business she ran, or if it had to do with her connection with the Camerlengos. Perhaps it was a little bit of both.

Opening up the search-space again, the Snake input the name of the dirty cop Roman Veretti had given him, Jay Kasmet. Up came a Facebook page, which the Snake clicked on. A photo came up of a man with hair thinning around the front and a dark brown mustache. The status read "Tough work in the NYPD. Barely slept. Got bad guys to catch though so people can sleep at night. What you going to do?" The Snake squeezed the phone as he read the lie in the status and wondered how many of Kasmet's Facebook friends knew that Kasmet was one of the bad guys he was supposed to be chasing.

As the Snake finished up his breakfast, he went into the bedroom, got dressed, and hid his mask, gun, knife, a lighter, and some whipped cream cans in a messenger bag. Putting Linda on a leash, the Snake grabbed his keys, locked the door behind him, and started down the stairs.

The Snake and Linda walked around for a little while until they were a good distance away from the apartment building. When he felt they couldn't be traced back to the Snake's apartment, the Snake lifted his arm and called a cab, a minivan painted yellow and black, which pulled over to the curb right in front of the Snake. Rolling the front window down, the driver poked his head out and said, "That dog of yours trained?"

"Yeah, she can play Chopin on my dad's piano without rehearsing." the Snake replied, eliciting a wheezing laugh from the cab driver. "Can you take me out to the Bronx?"

"Sure, if you have the money to pay me." replied the driver. "Where do you both want to go?"

"Wakefield." the Snake answered, opening the car door. Linda bounded in with a bark, settling in between the two middle seats. "I've got a lady to meet and I'm going to meet her at her office."

"Hey, good luck to you." said the cab driver. "You known her long?"

"No." said the Snake. "Not very long at all. But I think we'll get along great."

Chapter Forty-Three

Jay Kasmet opened an email, called the city morgue, took down some notes, hung up the phone, received a fax, gave it to Sergeant Pacine's replacement, and told another officer to find his partner and go inform another family that their loved one had died of senseless violence, all between sips of coffee. Taking a large gulp of the bitter stuff, Kasmet sat down in his chair and heaved a big sigh.

At this rate, I'll be working all day and tonight! With a groan, Kasmet opened another email, rolling his eyes at the message. His future father-in-law had some questions and wanted to meet up. Kasmet clicked delete before reading down to the polite goodbye. The old fart could wait, both the police and the Camerlengos were depending on him to find out information on the serial killer, and the paychecks both parties were giving him came before any question from a man who'd already concluded that his daughter could do better than a cop, which was some pride considering the old fart was a mailman.

Rubbing his eyes, Kasmet looked around the spacious new room the task force had been assigned as of seven-thirty this morning, when the reports came flooding in of mass Camerlengo fatalities. As soon as the FBI and NYPD had seen the reports, the higher-ups stopped berating Patton and Gramer for fucking up an entire operation that had been placed under their command and instead moved the entire investigation to a large room in the FBI's enormous building at Federal Plaza and gave the task force fifty more cops and agents to help out.

So far, most of the new recruits were dealing with the new fatalities that the task force had learned about, deaths of Camerlengo members who had been killed on their own territory, and by members of rival gangs to boot. The message in these deaths was clear: *if the New York Mafia Killer could get away with these murders, why can't we?* So far, twelve men had been killed between the hours of two and ten this morning, while twenty-five had been reported in varying states of injury.

"The underworld is in chaos." said Kasmet aloud, opening the latest email from a source that worked in the bank where the Camerlengo Family stored most of their on-shore cash. The bank account for the Camerlengos had been hacked, and thousands of dollars had been siphoned off. Not a lot for the most illustrious organized crime syndicate in New York, but still large enough to show that they weren't as untouchable as before, which would make the Camerlengos even angrier than before and their enemies even bolder.

"You can say that again, Officer Kasmet." said a voice. Kasmet looked up from his seat and saw Agent Angela Murtz, the chief profiler on the task force. Richard Alvarado, Kasmet's connection to the Camerlengos, had been pestering him to get close to her for some insights into the New York Mafia Killer, but until now Kasmet hadn't spoken two words to her, which was either because this job made it difficult to have any sort of conversation that wasn't work-related, or because she was an attractive woman with legs that went all the way down from here to Mexico.

Trying not to look at Murtz's rack, Kasmet cleared his throat and said, "Did you need something, Agent Murtz?"

"No, I was just passing by and I heard what you said." said Agent Murtz, taking a sip of her own coffee. "Twelve deaths at the last count and more sure to come, plus some cyber-warfare and money maneuvers mixed in for fun. I could never have predicted this sort of reaction."

"Funny, I thought all you shrinks were full of fun facts and could decipher anything about freaks and psychopaths." Kasmet replied. "That's how it goes on TV."

"Don't believe most of the stuff on TV." said Agent Murtz. "That's just show writers trying to make police psychologists full of glamour and mystery. Though I do have a lot of fun facts on musical instruments from working in my uncle's pawn shop during the summer growing up. I've seen some pretty interesting guitars go through that shop."

"I'll bet." said Kasmet. "Hey, can I ask you something off-topic? About the Snake killer, I mean."

Agent Murtz seemed a little surprised but said "Sure" anyway.

"I'm still not sure why the Snake killer didn't kill those HRT guys, or kill that attack dog, either." said Kasmet, trying to sound as casual about it as he could. "I heard your explanation earlier, but could you explain it again for me?"

"Oh, no problem." said Agent Murtz, leaning against Kasmet's desk (*hoh boy, that's some ass*, thought Kasmet). "Well, I can't say for certain since I haven't had the chance to actually speak to the killer and make a definitive examination of his mental state, but I'd say that it's part of his code. In a way, he only kills those who have it coming to them, like the Camerlengo family. The police, while a nuisance to him, are only doing their job, and he doesn't hate them for that, so he only does what he needs to in order to get away. The dog, I'm assuming is because dogs and other animals are innocent, so they don't deserve to die."

"Interesting." said Kasmet. "And the rogue cop? Armentrout? Was he really trying to partner up with the guy?"

"Yeah, that's something that's been bothering me too." said Agent Murtz. "The Snake killer is obviously a psychopathic individual, but yet he's willing to team up with a complete and total stranger. Either he's really desperate, or…"

"Or what?" asked Kasmet.

"I'm not sure." said Agent Murtz. "I'm starting to feel like I'm missing something with my previous profile. I had him pegged at average intelligence, but the fact that he was able to create such complex chemical weapons in whipped cream and soda cans using household ingredients proves that he's smarter than I gave him credit. I also kind of expected him to not be so kind to police. I don't know, maybe I'm just looking at this the wrong way."

"Hey, don't be so hard on yourself." said Kasmet. "Maybe some source of inspiration will come along, and you'll come up with something that'll put the TV shrinks to shame."

Agent Murtz laughed. "I should hope. Oh, your phone's vibrating."

Kasmet looked down and saw that his phone was buzzing on the counter, the blue screen reading RICHARD A. Kasmet's eyes widened as he recognized the name and picked up the phone. "I've got to go take this." said Kasmet to Agent Murtz. "Excuse me, and thanks for talking to me."

"No problem." Agent Murtz replied. "I've got to talk to Gramer anyway."

Kasmet headed into the bathroom, and after making sure that nobody else was around, pressed talk. "It's me." he whispered, locking himself in one of the stalls. "What's up?"

"Any news?" asked Richard Alvarado in his gruff voice. Jay Kasmet had met Alvarado about a month and a half ago, when Alvarado had recruited him to be a watchdog in the Organized Crime Control Bureau for the Camerlengos. It hadn't been too hard to convince Kasmet to turn traitor: Kasmet was overworked, way underpaid, and until Alvarado had given him fifteen-hundred dollars and an off-shore bank account in the Caribbean to deposit the bribe in, he hadn't had the money to buy his fiancée a wedding ring. And since he'd turned in the Langland girl and had gotten into the New York Mafia Killer task force, the money in that account had only increased. With these benefits, Kasmet was surprised that more cops weren't on the Camerlengos' payroll.

"Only that twelve of your employees are dead, several more injured, someone's trying to make off with your money, and all of it was done by rival families." answered Kasmet. "But you probably already knew that, right?"

"It's being taken care of." growled Alvarado, his voice suggesting to Kasmet that he better change the topic. "Do you have anything useful?"

"Oh yeah." said Kasmet. "I mean, it's not exactly a revelation, but who knows? It might be prove itself useful later—"

"Are you going to tell me what it is, or are you going to beat around the bush?"

"Sorry, I talked to the profiler Murtz. She says that the reason why this guy doesn't kill police officers or dogs is because he thinks your employer and his company, quote-on-quote, 'have it coming to them'."

"Oh, do we?" said Alvarado. "And you cops don't have something you should be killed over?"

"Hang on, don't get angry. It's her words, not mine. She also says that she might be entirely off the mark about who the hell this guy is."

"You mean she could be pulling stuff out of her ass?"

"It's a possibility."

There was silence on the other end. Finally Kasmet cleared his throat and asked if there was anything else he could do.

"Yeah, can you make it down to Scarusco's office?" asked Alvarado. "In the next hour or so? We're making sure our little conglomerate doesn't break into pieces because of the New York Mafia Killer. And after the little fiasco with the Langland girl, a little police intimidation would work very well on Narly Carly."

"I'm sure I could sneak out for a little while." Kasmet replied. "What's the address?"

Kasmet input the address on his phone and hung up. Exiting the stall, Kasmet washed his hands in case he might've gotten something on them, and headed down to the parking lot to get his car.

Chapter Forty-Four

The cab pulled over to the side of the road at the intersection that the Snake had indicated. As the Snake handed the driver several twenties, the driver said, "Have fun, kid. Hey, you bring that dog everywhere with you?"

"You bet." said the Snake. "She's my good-luck charm."

"Oh, like a wing-dog?" asked the driver.

The Snake burst out laughing, holding his stomach with one hand. "That's good. That's really good. I've never heard that one before." he said. "Yeah, she's my wing-dog. You'd never guess how many girls ask for my number 'cause of Linda here."

"Well, good luck with this gal." said the driver.

"Thanks." said the Snake. "Hey, keep the change."

"Thanks." said the driver, looking at the bills as if he couldn't believe how generous his fare had been. The cab pulled away, getting into the turning lane and making a left. The Snake watched until the cab was out of sight, and then he and Linda started walking down the street, hidden among the crowd of people walking in the midday commute.

Well, not that hidden; few people could ignore a dog that was three feet at the shoulder.

After intentionally taking a wrong turn and wandering around for about a half-hour and making himself seen on a traffic camera walking away from Carla Scarusco, the Snake finally found the building where the phone-sex service Allison was supposed to be being kept was located. The building was a fifteen-floor skyscraper that, beyond a couple of stone lions out on the front porch, was as unremarkable as the next building. Perfect place to hide a phone-sex service and a kidnapped girl, in the Snake's opinion.

The Snake was about to head to see if the front door was monitored or had a security guard when a police car pulled up in front of the street. Out of the driver's seat came a uniformed police officer with thinning hair in front and a brown mustache.

Jay Kasmet.

The Snake gripped Linda's leash harder, feeling his anger rise. Linda looked up at him, giving a concerned whine.

Kasmet went to meet a man at the front entrance, a bald man with a tan suit and a briefcase in one hand. Kasmet shook the man's hand and they went into the building together, talking like a couple of old friends meeting at a church function.

The Snake's eyes narrowed. Who was that man? Was he a member of the Camerlengos? The Snake wondered if he would find out, and felt it was probable. After all, what were the chances that the same day the Snake came to find Carla Scarusco, the director of the Camerlengo-owned phone-sex service that Allison was being kept in, and Jay Kasmet, who had been involved in some sort of incident with Allison, would be visiting the same building, and that they'd come for different reasons?

Not very high.

The Snake decided to try for the back of the building, and led Linda on a circular route that avoided security and traffic cameras, eventually ending up at the back of the building. There were no cameras, and the back door was open as a large, tired-looking woman put trash bags into a dumpster. Indicating to Linda with a Russian phrase to be quiet, the Snake and Linda ran through the back door and into a service hallway while the maintenance woman's back was turned.

The Snake walked down the hallway, found a door that led to the stairwell, and began climbing the stairs. Linda bounded forward, her tail wagging happily at the cardio workout she was getting. The Snake matched her pace, counting floors as they reached each flight. Two...three...four...five...six...

The Snake rounded around the corner and stopped. Linda pulled up beside him, panting happily.

The seventh floor was where Roman Veretti had said the sex service was located.

Feeling a rush of excitement, the Snake reached into his bag and pulled out his mask.

Chapter Forty-Five

There were two loud knocks on the front door, startling Carla Scarusco and making her spill coffee all over the kitchen counter. Scowling at the mess she knew she'd have to clean up later, Carla power-walked over to the front door, trying to put on her most-winning smile and think up a biting zinger to let the visitor know he was disturbing her morning.

Pulling open the door, Carla flashed a smile and said, "Good morning and welcome to Naughty Princess Industries. We'll give you your fantasy, but only for three-ninety-five a minute—oh!"

"Hello Carla." said Richard Alvarado, flashing a smile. Next to him was a man in a police uniform who was looking Carla over with lecherous eyes. Without waiting to be invited the two men pushed their way in past Carla and started walking towards her office in the back.

As Carla watched the two men walking through the office, past soundproof booths where several women and a couple of men pleased callers with their voices, only one thought went through her head: *this cannot be good*. Richard Alvarado was one of Christopher Camerlengo's lieutenants, an extremely important man in the Family hierarchy. A word from him was an order, and it could only be countermanded by Camerlengo himself or one of the *consigliere* who advised the Family. The fact that he'd brought a cop with him only deepened the sense of gravity that Carla felt about this visit. It could only be bad news.

Closing the door, Carla ran after the two men as fast as her skirt would let her run, and joined them in the office, where Alvarado and the police officer were already getting comfy in the two chairs that sat in front of Carla's desk. Sitting down in her own chair, Carla looked at the two men and said, "What can I help you gentlemen with?"

"Oh, that's right." said Alvarado. "I forgot to introduce you to my associate. This is Jay Kasmet, a police officer whom I've…become friendly with over the past couple of weeks."

Carla's eyes widened as she heard the name. *Jay Kasmet*…the man that had gotten Little A taken out of here. The same man who had been transferred to Little A, mentioned he was a cop and then betrayed Little A when she'd asked for help. Carla could not believe that same man sat now before her.

Alvarado smirked. "I see the look on your face." he said. "You know my friend here." Alvarado's face turned serious, and he added, "Then you know what sort of problems he could cause for you."

Carla looked at both men, confused. "P-Problems?" she stammered.

"Well, you know how it is." said Kasmet, crossing his legs. "You hear about the New York Mafia Killer, and the chaos he's causing in the underworld, and you start to think funny things, like maybe showing your employers that they're not as strong as they think, or you try to jump ship and join a new team, or you try to bend the rules so that they work for you. I'm on the task force trying to catch the killer, so I kind of know what's been going on lately here in New York."

"And we know how much of a shock the Langland girl must've been." Alvarado picked up the thread, leaning forward in his seat towards Carla. "We can understand how that might make you question your loyalties."

"Loyalties?" Carla repeated. "I've been so busy running this place, I've had no time to think about loyalties!"

"That's good." said Alvarado. "Because if you did, we could make it so that you've been using your business to launder money, and make sure that the information comes in the form of a handy tip to Officer Kasmet."

Carla stared at Alvarado and Kasmet, shocked. "You'd frame me?!" she said, her voice rising an octave. "You can't do that!"

"Oh, but we can." Alvarado replied, pushing himself out of his seat. "And we can make it so the backlash falls only on you and not on the Camerlengo Family." Alvarado walked around Carla's desk so that he stood next to her, towering over her like some angry giant. "You see, serial killer or no serial killer, the arm of the Camerlengos stretches far. And you don't want to be on the receiving end of whatever that arm dishes out, do you?"

Carla stared up at Alvarado, unable to answer. She was about to ask him to back up a little bit and let her breathe when there was a hissing sound from the front of the office. Looking behind Kasmet, Carla saw what she thought were two whipped-cream cans spewing a white gas throughout the office, obscuring everything.

As both Alvarado and Kasmet noticed the gas, they all heard the sound of a large dog barking.

Chapter Forty-Six

The Snake walked through the thick fog, Linda rushing ahead of him with a loud bark. As the smoke cleared in front of him, the Snake spotted three people: one was the man in the tan suit, another was a woman with blonde hair that the Snake guessed was Carla Scarusco, and the third was Jay Kasmet.

Tsel Vid'na. thought the Snake. Target sighted.

The Snake gave a command in Russian and Linda attacked the man in the tan suit, standing up on her hind legs and ramming her front paws into tan suit's shoulders. Tan Suit fell over onto the desk, struggling under Linda as she tried to tear off his face with her teeth. Carla Scarusco screamed, huddling up against the windows with her hands over her eyes and neck.

"Son of a—!" shouted Kasmet, pulling out his gun. The Snake ran at him and tackled him to the floor, bringing up the knife above Kasmet's throat. "Jay Kasmet." said the Snake with his Russian accent. "Believe me when I say, the pleasure's all mine."

Kasmet's eyes went wide as he heard the Snake's Russian accent. "You!"

Underneath his mask, the Snake smiled. "Me." The Snake brought down the knife, intentionally missing Kasmet's neck by an inch. "And I have some questions to ask you, Officer Kasmet. I'm hoping you can answer them for me."

"You freak!" Kasmet replied. "I won't answer any questions for a sadist like you!"

"Ooh, it hurts me when you say that—oh!" Suddenly Kasmet threw himself forward and head-butted the Snake. The Snake, dazed by the blow, let go of Kasmet and fell backwards onto Linda. Dog and owner fell onto the floor, untangling themselves from each other and standing up to face Kasmet and the man in the tan suit, both of whom had drawn their weapons.

"I heard that Russian accent." said the man in the tan suit. The Snake was saddened to note that despite Linda's best efforts, Tan Suit had survived her unmolested. "You're the New York Mafia Killer, aren't you?" From where she was standing, Carla Scarusco gasped, staring at the Snake as if he were going to turn on her and try to kill her next.

"Correct." said the Snake. "And you are?"

"Richard Alvarado." said the man. "I work directly for Mr. Camerlengo."

"Ah yes, I've heard of you." the Snake lied. He hadn't actually heard of Alvarado, let alone most of the Camerlengo family, but if the man in the tan suit was someone important in the Camerlengos' organization, maybe he had valuable information to glean. In any case, he'd see what he could get out of Tan Suit, even if it was only a boost to his reputation. "Funny that we should run into each other this morning, don't you think?"

"Oh yeah, very funny." said Alvarado. "What the fuck are you doing here? You didn't recognize me, so I'm betting you weren't here to kill me. Were you after Kasmet?"

"Actually, I was here for Ms. Scarusco over there." said the Snake truthfully. Behind her desk, Carla Scarusco's face blanched and she stammered out, "M-M-Me?"

"You wanted to kill Carla?" asked Alvarado.

"The New York Mafia Killer doesn't kill women." said Kasmet. "I bet he's here for another reason, if he's really here for her. Right?"

"Correct." The whole time Kasmet was talking and he was replying, the Snake was weighing options, reading body language, trying to find a way to take this situation and turn it to his advantage. Maybe if he kept them talking, something would present itself. To his surprise and delight an opportunity did present itself, as Alvarado and Kasmet turned their bodies ever so slightly in the direction of Carla Scarusco.

"Correct? Correct?!" Alvarado repeated, glancing behind him at Carla, who wilted under Alvarado's glare. "Are you helping this bastard? Are you helping this sick fuck find his victims?! 'Because that's the only reason why I can think he'd come here."

"No!" cried Carla, tears forming in her eyes. "I have no idea why he's here! Please believe me!"

"Are you screwing him?" shouted Alvarado, ignoring Carla. "Is this your boyfriend? Your sick, serial killing boyfriend? Is this your gratitude for all we've done for you, Carla?"

"What you've done for me?" said Carla, glaring at Alvarado as if she couldn't believe what he'd said to her before turning her attention back to the Snake. "You haven't done shit for me! You just stuck me in here and left me here to rot!" Carla's face was livid for a moment, but as it dawned on her what she had just said, her face fell and she put a hand to her mouth with a soft "oh".

Alvarado turned his body and pointed his gun at Carla's chest, pulling the hammer back. "You ungrateful bitch." snarled Alvarado. "This job was too good for you."

"At least we now know how the Snake is getting his victims." said Kasmet, glancing quickly at Alvarado and Carla.

As he saw the attention in the room turn from the Snake to Carla, the Snake smiled and made a hand signal to Linda. At once Linda's lips pulled back in a snarl and she bounded forward, opening her mouth to bite Kasmet's hand.

Kasmet shouted and dropped his gun, trying to beat Linda off with his free hand. Linda only held on harder, growling loudly with every jerk of Kasmet's arm. Next to him, Alvarado dropped his shooter's stance and turned to see Kasmet struggling with the large dog. "What the fu—?"

The Snake pulled out his gun, and in one deft motion, unlocked the safety, pulled back the hammer, and fired at Alvarado's hand. With a muffled bang the bullet flew out the barrel of the silencer and into Alvarado's hand. Alvarado screamed as he dropped his gun, holding up his hand to his face, staring in horror at the small black hole in his hand.

The Snake ran forward and grabbed Alvarado's throat, squeezing the man's windpipe with his thumbs. Alvarado stared at the Snake as if he didn't know what was happening to him, but then he reached with his good hand and tried to pry the Snake's hands away from the Snake. To the Snake's surprise Alvarado managed to pry off one finger and was working on the next. The Snake squeezed Alvarado's windpipe harder, the pressure hurting his own thumbs.

Come on. thought the Snake, as Alvarado peeled off the second finger. Despite the fact that the man was struggling for oxygen, Alvarado was grinning from ear to ear. *Lose consciousness. Lose consciousness!*

Something hit and broke against the side of Alvarado's head with a loud crash. Alvarado stopped moving, blinked a few times, and then he became limp, his eyes closing shut. The Snake held the man up by the throat for a second before letting Alvarado fall to the floor, a dark, shiny spot growing on his temple. All around Alvarado on the ground, the Snake saw pieces of what looked like marble shards, each piece surrounded by little piles of white dust.

The Snake looked at Carla Scarusco, who was breathing hard and holding a look of triumph on her face. "What did you throw at him?" asked the Snake.

"A statue of Muhammad Ali that was here when I got here." Carla answered proudly. "And I've wanted to do that for years."

"Well done." said the Snake after a pause. Looking for Linda, the Snake turned and saw her on her hind legs, wrestling with Jay Kasmet, his forehead shiny with sweat and a bleeding cut on his lip. Despite himself, the Snake felt himself admiring Kasmet for lasting this long with Linda.

Still, this had to end. The Snake turned to Carla and said, "Got any more statures that you don't mind throwing?"

"Um...I've got a bust of Roger Moore." said Carla.

"May I use that?" asked the Snake. Carla nodded and handed the bust to the Snake, who bounced it up and down in his hand, getting a feel for its weight. Finally he looked back to Linda and Kasmet and yelled, "Linda! *Otpusti!*"

Linda heard the command and jumped off of Kasmet, running back to her master. Kasmet stared at the dog in wonder before looking at the Snake, who lobbed the small bust at Kasmet. The bust sailed through the air and bounced off of Kasmet's head with a loud smack, landing on the ground and shattering into several pieces. Kasmet wavered on his feet for a second before falling over, a black, shiny pool of blood forming on his forehead.

Satisfied, the Snake turned back to Carla and said, smiling under his mask, "I've been wanting to do that since breakfast." Carla looked at the Snake with a dumbfounded expression before bursting out laughing, holding her stomach as tears rolled down her cheeks. The Snake allowed her to laugh as he patted Linda and praised her for her hard work.

He couldn't be sure, but he felt that he had won Carla over to his side.

Chapter Forty-Seven

The Snake looked around the office and realized they were alone. Besides him, Carla Scarusco, Linda, and the two unconscious men on the floor, there was nobody else around. *The operators must've bolted when the smoke bombs went off.* he thought, his body tensing. *Which means it'll only be a matter of time before the cops arrive.* The Snake looked at the two men on the floor, wondering how the hell he was going to get them out of the building so he could interrogate both of them for any information they might have.

From behind him the Snake heard the clatter of blinds and turned to see Carla looking out the window. "We have to get out of here." she said, letting go of the blinds. "Someone on my staff will probably already have called the police. Who knows when they'll show up."

This woman's already in sync with me. thought the Snake. Looking back at Alvarado and Kasmet, the Snake thought, *I just need to find a way to get these two out of here without getting caught by the police—that's it!*

An idea forming in his head, the Snake grabbed Alvarado's limp body and dragged him to where Kasmet lay. Reaching down, the Snake withdrew Kasmet's handcuffs from his belt and cuffed Kasmet's right hand to Alvarado's left. Making sure the cuffs were tight around the men's wrists, the Snake grasped both men's pinkies and said, "*Vremya prosypat'sya.*" *Time to wake up.*

The Snake twisted the men's fingers with two sickening cracks and the two men awoke with agonized cries. The Snake stood up and pulled out his gun, cocking back the hammer at the two men. "Stand up." he commanded.

The two men looked back and saw the Snake holding his gun, and then they saw they were handcuffed together. When the Snake didn't put his gun away or point it somewhere else, the two men struggled to stand up, looking like a pair of awkward clowns in a tan suit and a police uniform as they did. Finally both men were on their feet, Kasmet facing the Snake while Alvarado faced the front of the office.

"Alright." said the Snake. "Move."

Before the men could ask where they were supposed to move, the Snake started striding forward, his gun held out in front of him. The men started walking away from the Snake, heading towards the door.

"Good. Just keep going like that." said the Snake. "Linda, we're leaving."

"Um…excuse me?" As Linda came toward the Snake, Carla walked around her desk and, looking like she was trying to keep her body from shaking, said, "M-May I come with you? If I'm here when the police arrive, Mr. Camerlengo is going to think I went with the police willingly, and I really, *really* don't want to be in this shithole a second longer—"

"I was going to have you come with me anyway." said the Snake, taking his eyes off of Alvarado and Kasmet. "I wish to speak with you about something very important to me."

Carla looked surprised and terrified, like she couldn't believe she could speak about anything that might be important to a serial killer and she was wondering what would happen to her during their conversation. "W-What do you want to t-talk about?"

The Snake paused, wondering if he should answer. Then he decided to hell with it, she might not want to go with him if she thought he was going to kill her, and said, "I have questions for you about Allison Langland."

Carla gasped. "Allison?" she said. "Little A?"

"The Langland bitch?" said Alvarado, his tone incredulous.

"That's what this is all about?" asked Kasmet. "Some kid who was giving the family trouble?"

The Snake returned his attention to the two men he'd handcuffed, his eyes narrowed menacingly at them. Both men shut up under the Snake's glare and watched the gun the Snake was holding, as if the Snake was going to point it at either one of them and shoot just for speaking.

"Both of you, be quiet." said the Snake. "We'll have plenty of time to discuss this later." Turning back to Carla, the Snake said, "Where is she?"

Carla's mouth opened and closed like a fish before she finally said, "I don't know. She was just taken the other day and...I haven't heard anything since."

"Then we'll have to ask these two gentlemen for their assistance in figuring out what happened to her." said the Snake. "But we'll need to go somewhere else. Are you still coming with me? I can protect you, for a short time anyway. And we may be able to help each other."

Carla only hesitated for a second before going and grabbing a coat off a rack on the wall of her office. Then, reaching into her purse, she pulled out a ring of jingling keys and said, "We can take my van, it's in the parking lot behind the building."

"Carla, you're really going to get it once the boss finds out what you've done." said Alvarado, even as the Snake prodded him forward with his gun and a growling Linda. "This bastard's gonna get it and then you're going to get it worse!"

"Keep talking," said the Snake as they left the office and headed to the service elevator. "It doesn't change the fact that you both are going to die after I torture you." Neither man deigned to reply.

As the elevator let them off on the ground floor, Carla took the lead, saying, "My van's just this way." Alvarado, Kasmet, Linda, and the Snake followed behind, Alvarado and Kasmet looking for someone to come to their rescue as they awkwardly made their way to the back exit while the Snake looked and listened for police or anyone who might get in his way.

As Carla opened the exit door, the Snake was hit by a blast of cold air and harsh, bright light. Shielding his eyes with his free hand, the Snake looked around and saw that there were no police vans around. Quickly they crossed the alleyway behind the building and into the parking lot, headed to a large, white van with rust stains on the sides. Unlocking the back, Carla moved out of the way as the Snake ordered Alvarado and Kasmet into the back. Once they were in, the Snake said something in Russian to Linda, who jumped into the back and circled around Alvarado and Kasmet, her lips drawn back in a vicious growl.

"What did you say to her?" asked Carla as the Snake closed the back of the van.

"I told her to guard them." said the Snake. "Trust me, she's not going to let them pull anything on us."

"You're not going to sit back there with them?" asked Carla, sounding as if she had rather hoped he would.

"I'll have plenty of time to ask them questions later." he said. "You as well. Now get in front and start driving. The police will show up soon."

Carla walked around the Snake and to the front seat, while the Snake got into the passenger seat. Adjusting the mirror and buckling herself in, Carla turned the keys in the ignition and the van roared into life, masking the sound of Linda's growling. As the van pulled out of its parking spot and started moving towards the exit, the Snake kept an eye out for police uniforms and flashing sirens.

As Carla drove around the side of the building and onto the street that faced the front of her office building, the Snake saw flashing reds and blues coming up the street and swore under his breath. "Do me a favor," said the Snake, keeping his gun in his lap. "Drive, and drive as fast as you can."

"No problem." Carla replied, her voice strong and without any quaver. The Snake glanced at her and saw Carla looking nervous and excited, like a runner before a race. He wondered if that was because she was sitting next to a supposedly-vicious killer who had been nothing but civil with her so far or if she was excited at the idea of possibly outrunning the cops. The Snake thought it might be both.

As the street cleared, Carla turned the wheel sharply to the right and sped out onto the road, moving faster than the light traffic around them. The Snake looked out the side-view mirror, watching as the police cars, growing tinier and tinier with every second, pulled up to the side of the building, with several cops going into the building while a few stopped to talk to a small group of people without coats standing outside the front entrance. The Snake guessed that most of those people, if not all of them, were Carla's employees.

"Where do you want to go?" asked Carla, making a hard left as the light began to change.

"Somewhere I can speak to our two friends in the back without being interrupted." the Snake answered, looking into the back. Despite the shaking of the van, both Alvarado and Kasmet were on their feet, watching warily as Linda paced in front of them, a furry grey beast with deadly teeth. The Snake wondered if his two prisoners would believe just how gentle the dog was when playing with his sister Ruby.

"Well, they're no friends of mine," Carla replied, "but I do know a place that won't have anyone around."

"Will we be heard from the outside?" asked the Snake.

"I don't think so." said Carla. "Not if we go to the second floor."

"Take us there."

At the next intersection, Carla made a right, pulled into an alleyway, backed out of the alleyway, and started driving back to the intersection. Turning left onto the road they had just been on, Carla drove them around for several minutes, away from the office building where she worked and closer to the Bronx River. Finally, Carla turned right past an empty strip mall with a second floor above the deserted shops and into the lot behind the strip mall, where she turned off the engine and got out.

"I had a friend whose family used to have a shop in this mall up until a few years ago." Carla was saying as the Snake slipped out of the passenger seat and went to meet her near the front. "Had the loveliest bakery this side of the Bronx. Then the economy went south and she had to move to Ithaca with her parents. It was such a shame."

I'm feeling tears, thought the Snake sarcastically, as he surveyed the area. It looked like a commercial district, but it seemed that years of economic strife had led to urban decay. Now only broken bottles, a few pigeons, and graffiti paintings showed any signs that humans had been here recently. The Snake approved.

"This shop has a second floor?" he asked.

Carla gave a little "mm-hmm" as she nodded, and said, "The upstairs kitchen was where my friend did her best work. I swear, some of her work could've gotten her a show on TLC or something. But they already have a baking show, so I guess not."

Carla opened up the back of the van, where Linda was still guarding the two handcuffed men plastered against the van's side.

"Linda!" called the Snake. "*Otpusti!*" At the sound of the command, Linda stopped growling and jumped out the back of the car, rubbing her head against the Snake's side. Pointing his gun at Alvarado and Kasmet, the Snake said, "Get out." The two men looked at each other and climbed out the back of the van, flinching as Linda barked angrily at them for getting too close to her master.

Carla closed the back doors and locked up the van, while the Snake went to the back door of one of the shops. Taking out his bump key, the Snake opened the door and gestured for Alvarado and Kasmet to go in and up the stairs. Linda followed up after them, her every stride putting three steps behind her. The Snake and Carla went up after Linda, the Snake closing the door behind them.

As they came out onto the second floor, the Snake took a look around. There were windows on the other side of the room, letting in warm, early-afternoon sunlight that highlighted the reddish-brown tiles covering the floor. The Snake spotted black squares indicating where the legs of appliances and tables had been nailed to the ground here and there, reminders that this had once been a working business.

But now this room would serve a whole other purpose.

The Snake put his gun back into his jacket and rolled his neck around, working out the kinks. As he finished, he looked at Carla and then at Alvarado and Kasmet; the Snake felt his excitement building within him. "Let's get to work." he said, hearing horror movie music playing in his head.

Chapter Forty-Eight

The Snake cracked his knuckles and stretched his arms out, hearing and feeling the creak of his bones as he stretched them. Straightening out his back, the Snake saw Alvarado, Kasmet, and Carla wince with every popping noise that came from his spine, as if the sounds coming from the Snake's body were oracles of what was to come.

Finished stretching, the Snake said, "Before we start, I'd like to establish something." Looking at Linda, the Snake said, "*Atu!*" Linda bounded forward, barking and snarling at Alvarado and Kasmet, who ran awkwardly to the corner of the room, crying out every time Linda barked and tried to bite their legs.

"You two are weak, pathetic men." said the Snake, talking over Linda's barking and the two men's shouts. "In a gun fight with cronies, or even in a fist fight, you usually have the advantage. But unfortunately for the both of you, I'm a serial killer with a dangerous guard dog along with a gun and knife." The Snake strode casually to Linda's side, watching Alvarado and Kasmet as they watched him. "Even worse, I've taken you to an isolated location, you're both handcuffed to each other, and you each have head wounds, have been bitten by my dog, and you both have broken fingers.

"So let me tell you how this is going to work," the Snake continued. "Ms. Scarusco shall leave the room if she so desires.

Then I will kill you, and you will suffer. How long till your deaths, and how much you'll suffer before you both die, is dependent on whether you want to tell me what I want to know.

"So Mr. Kasmet," said the Snake, striding forward and grabbing Kasmet's cheeks between his fingers and thumb. "How about you start?"

"W-What do you want to know?" asked Kasmet, his whole body trembling.

"Don't you dare say anything, Kasmet!" shouted Alvarado, even as Linda snapped at his belt buckle.

"Oh, I didn't mean first to talk." said the Snake. "I meant to scream." As a look of horrified realization crossed Kasmet's face, the Snake reached down with his free hand and twisted Kasmet's wrist. The bone broke with an angry snap, bending the hand at an awkward angle. Kasmet cried out, his face a portrait of anguish.

Smirking underneath his mask, the Snake took Kasmet's index finger and twisted, causing another round of screaming. His excitement growing, the Snake released Kasmet's cheeks from between his fingers and, with both hands, broke his shoulder. This time, all Kasmet could manage was a pitiful moan, his face drained of blood.

"I give all my victims pain." said the Snake. "But since you're a rotten, dirty cop, I'll give you more pain than usual."

Kasmet whimpered, tears flowing down his cheeks. "P-Please." Kasmet whined, looking beseechingly at the Snake. "Please don't do this to me. I've got a fiancée. I'm getting married!"

"She'll find someone better," said the Snake, breaking another finger and eliciting another scream from Kasmet. "Perhaps she'll marry a cop who is upright and virtuous and never takes bribes from organized crime. Someone a lot better than you.

"Now tell me," said the Snake, his mouth only a few inches from Kasmet's ear, "what did you do to Allison Langland?"

"Please." Kasmet whined. "I don't understand what you mean."

"Oh? Well let me remind you." said the Snake, punching Kasmet in the gut. "Allison Langland was being kept at Carla Scarusco's phone-sex service. I believe your master, Christopher Camerlengo, was trying to teach her that they could do anything to her and that silence and being in the family's good graces was in her best interest, especially since she was the child of a friend. But then something happened, and it involved you. What exactly happened?"

When Kasmet didn't answer, the Snake wrapped his fingers around the policeman's forearm. As he was about to twist, Kasmet said, "I just wanted a boost. You know, a pick-me-up. It was a tough morning, I thought I'd have a little fun while I could, and

Alvarado told me that if I said I was a friend of his, I could get some phone action free of charge."

"Kasmet, don't say anything." hissed Alvarado, his eyes flicking frantically between Kasmet and Linda.

Ignoring Alvarado, the Snake said to Kasmet, "So you called the service. What happened then?"

"Well, I got their switchboard, and they asked for my credit card number. I told them I was a friend of Alvarado's, they got the message, and I got redirected. The phone rang for a few seconds, and then I got this girl on the other end with a real sexy voice. She said her name was Allison, and she asked me what sort of fantasy I wanted."

"And what did you say?"

"Kasmet, you're getting into dangerous waters here!"

"Any more dangerous than defying a killer with obvious mental issues?" said the Snake to Alvarado. "Now shut up or I'll break one of your ribs." To Kasmet, the Snake repeated his question. "What did you say to Allison?"

"I-I said I was a cop." Kasmet answered. "I said I was a cop and I'd always had this fantasy about catching a burglar in the act and s-s-screwing his intended victim after she tried to show me her gratitude."

"What happened next?"

"Sh-She asked me if I was really a cop." said Kasmet. "I said yes, and asked if she wanted me to read my badge number. I was just showing off, I didn't think she'd actually tell me she was being held against her will! For the love of God, you gotta believe me!"

"Just tell me what happened!" said the Snake, grabbing an unbroken finger. "Before I have to give you some persuasion to tell me!"

"She-She started telling me that she'd been kidnapped!" Kasmet cried, his eyes wide with fear. "She told me everything that had happened to her. And...I just didn't know what to say! But then I realized that this was something Alvarado and his boss might want to hear, so I pretended to take down her information, and assured her I'd come with help."

"You lied to her!" said the Snake, squeezing Kasmet's finger.

"I'm sorry!" cried Kasmet. "But I needed the money, and I had a feeling I'd get paid a lot of money for reporting this. So as soon as I was off the phone, I called Alvarado, and he said he'd take care of it. That was all, I swear! I wasn't involved any farther than that! Alvarado took over after that!"

"You traitor!" shouted Alvarado.

"Thanks for volunteering that information, Mr. Kasmet." said the Snake, breaking the remaining fingers on Kasmet's hand. "I guess I need to ask you next, Mr. Alvarado, what happened." The Snake switched from Kasmet's to Alvarado's side, grabbing the mobster's free hand. In one quick motion, the Snake broke two fingers, squeezing the broken digits until they shattered for good measure.

Alvarado cried out and said, "I'm not going to talk to you, you freak."

"That's your choice," the Snake replied. "But just know, the more you don't talk, the angrier I become. And the angrier I become, the more likely it will be that what happened to Thomas Luiso and Roman Veretti will happen to you."

Alvarado stared defiantly at the Snake. "Do your worst." he spat.

The Snake was surprised that someone could be so defiant in the face of so much pain, but shrugged and said, "If that is what you wish, I shall oblige you." Pulling out his knife, the Snake aimed the blade in front of Alvarado's crotch. Alvarado and Kasmet, watched as the knife hovered in front of Alvarado's groin, Alvarado trying to put as much distance between his pants and the knife. Finally the Snake gripped the handle tighter, drew back a little bit, and—

"Wait!" said Alvarado. The Snake looked up from the knife and saw Alvarado looking down with wide eyes at the knife, his forehead sweating profusely. "I-I'll tell you what you want to know. J-Just don't—don't do that to me!"

The Snake did not take away the knife, but he did say, "What did you do with Allison Langland?"

"A-As soon as I got the call from Kasmet, I told the boss, and he told me that the Langland girl would...would have to be taken care of." Alvarado began, his eyes never leaving the knife hovering below his belt.

"What did your boss mean by 'taken care of'?" the Snake asked.

"N-Not what you think it means." Alvarado replied.

"How do you know what I think it means?"

"He—Mr. Camerlengo didn't want her killed." Alvarado explained. There was a pause, and then Alvarado continued, "He-He said she was going to be sold at an auction. That way she could still be useful to the family."

"An auction?" repeated the Snake, anxiety squeezing his chest. If Allison was sold somewhere, would he ever be able to find her again? "Where?"

"H-Here in New York." said Alvarado. "We'd do it overseas, b-but the police are watching the docks and our foreign contacts, so for now we have to hold them here exclusively."

"That's good news for you, believe it or not." said the Snake. "If it was being held overseas, I might just stab you out of anger. Where is this auction being held?"

"It's held in two parts." Alvarado explained. "The first part is where you bid, and the second part is where you pick up the girls. I don't know about the pick-up location, but I do know where the auctions are held."

"Why don't you know the pick-up location?" asked the Snake.

"It's not my department!" Alvarado answered. "Please, you have to believe me. I never asked about where the girls were dropped off. It never mattered to me."

"I guess it wouldn't," said the Snake. "Not unless someone important to you was being auctioned off. Where is the bidding done?"

"A-At this sports bar in Manhattan." said Alvarado. "The Racehorse, in Midtown. It's owned by one of our shell companies. All you have to do is go to the back door and give them a password. If you give them the password, they'll let you in, no questions asked."

"What password?" asked the Snake.

"It's...It's an Italian phrase." said Alvarado. "It's *bella costa tosto è rapita*."

"'A pretty thing is quickly taken'." the Snake translated. "How fitting. When is the auction where Allison will be sold?"

"The n-next auction is scheduled in two days." said Alvarado. "The Langland girl will probably be sold last, 'cause she's a virgin. They usually fetch a high price."

For a moment, the Snake didn't say anything, processing the information, what he'd need to get into the auction, what he would have to do in order that the police or the Camerlengos didn't find him afterwards.

"W-Well?" said Alvarado, his eyes going from the knife to the Snake and back again every few seconds. "Are you satisfied? You got what you wanted?"

"Yes I did." said the Snake, lowering the knife away from Alvarado's penis. "I got exactly what I wanted. I'll leave your cock intact."

Alvarado let out a sigh of relief as the knife dropped from view.

"Now you get to die." The Snake dropped the knife on the ground and with two hands broke Alvarado's shoulder, getting a loud scream from the lieutenant. Throwing the man to the ground, the Snake proceeded to break his arms and legs, dislocate his spine, and crush fingers in his fist. When Alvarado's screaming had reached its peak, the Snake pulled out his gun and shot Alvarado in the head.

As soon as he was sure that Alvarado was dead, the Snake turned to Kasmet, who was facing him in an awkward bow, his cuffed hand reached forward to Alvarado. Seeing the Snake looking at him, Kasmet screamed as the Snake lunged at Kasmet and threw him to the ground as well. The Snake strangled Kasmet, broke ribs, punched and kicked him in the stomach and groin. Then, as Kasmet's screams began to peter out, the Snake pulled his gun out again and killed Kasmet.

Replacing his gun in his jacket, the Snake surveyed his latest kills, blood dribbling out of the holes in Kasmet's and Alvarado's foreheads. Then, pulling out his hunting knife, the Snake tore open the shirts of the men and started to carve his mark in their chests. The wounds didn't bleed.

As he stood up and cracked his spine again, the Snake realized there was a sobbing noise coming from the other end of the room. There in the corner, Carla Scarusco was crying, her arm covering her eyes as she cried.

For a moment, the Snake didn't know how to respond. Then he said, "I'm sorry. I forgot you were here. I should've asked if you wanted to leave."

Carla looked up and said, "That's not why I'm crying. I should be, but I'm having trouble feeling any sadness for them. No, I'm crying for a different reason."

Underneath his mask, the Snake raised his eyebrows in surprise. "Are you crying because you fear me?"

Carla shook her head. "No, that's not why." she said. "It's just...I just realized who you are underneath that mask."

The Snake stared at Carla as she nodded her head and said, "It was when you first mentioned Little A. That was what we called Allison, we called her Little A. She was like the younger sister to the whole office. And one night, she told me about...about her boyfriend. About how he was really into scary stuff like horror movies and serial killers but was really cool and nice. And she mentioned he had a big dog. She said you could ride that dog like a small pony. And there you are, you're killing scary men but you didn't kill me or try to hurt me for failing to protect her, and your large dog is right by your side. You...You're looking for her, aren't you? That's why you're doing this, isn't it? I'm sorry, I just find it very romantic, don't you? It's very sick, but it's romantic too, like some strange horror-romance novel."

For a moment, the Snake didn't know how to answer. Then he said, "Come on, we have to move these bodies. I can't get rid of any DNA in this setting, so I'm going to have to get creative on how to get rid of the evidence."

Carla didn't move, but instead just watched as the Snake took hold of both bodies and started dragging them towards the stairs, Linda pulling on Alvarado's sleeve as if to help her master with the heavy load.

Chapter Forty-Nine

The Snake turned on the engine and shifted the gear into drive. The van rolled forward ever so slightly. Then the Snake dragged Alvarado's head across the floor at the front of the van, holding the mobster's head over the accelerator. Looking past the open door, the Snake made sure there was nobody in the way of the car or to witness him running away, and then dropped Alvarado's head on the accelerator.

The Snake jumped away as the van sped up tremendously, zooming toward the waterfront faster and faster. The Snake stayed long enough to make sure that it would go into the water before running away, heading to the place he and Carla had decided to meet. There, hidden in shadow, the Snake waited for Carla and Linda to arrive.

Time ticked away till it was almost dark, and finally a dark-haired woman wearing a brand-new coat and sunglasses appeared, Linda walking right beside her. The woman took off her shades and smiled at him. Although the Snake knew she couldn't see under his mask, he smiled back.

"So what are you going to do now?" the Snake asked Carla as Linda ran to him, barking happily.

"I think I'll head to California." said Carla, fingering her new dark locks. "Get as far away from New York as possible.

Maybe see if I can still get a career in showbiz, even if it's some self-important agent's secretary. Are you going to continue searching for Allison?"

"I have to." said the Snake. "I don't feel complete without her. Why?"

"Oh..well it's hard to put into words," said Carla. "It's just...normally I wouldn't approve of anyone doing what you do, but...you're different."

"Because I'm a love-struck fool with violent tendencies?"

"Something like that." said Carla. "Plus you saved me from that pig sty and didn't kill me. I really have to thank you for that. You cannot understand how depressed that place made me." There was a pause, and then Carla said, "When you find Little A—and I believe you will, if anyone can find her, it's you—will you tell her I'm sorry? For everything?"

The Snake nodded. "I'll tell her."

Carla nodded, whispered "Goodbye", turned around and left, as if that were the end of it. The Snake and Linda watched her go, and when she was finally swallowed by the shadows, they turned and went the other way.

Chapter Fifty

There was a stirring, a moan, and then Will Armentrout woke up, a pained expression on his face. Happy to see the former state cop awake, Detective Blake Harnist said, "Welcome back to the land of the living, Sleeping Beauty."

Armentrout started, then focused on Harnist standing in the doorway. Recognizing him, Armentrout said, "Well, fancy meeting you here."

"Not that hard to imagine." said Harnist, tracing the line of stitches on his forehead. "I asked to be treated in the same hospital as you."

Armentrout raised his eyebrows. "Oh?" His voice registered surprise, but no nervousness. He didn't think Harnist would hurt him, which was the truth. Pity though; it'd be easier to get information from him if he thought Harnist would hurt him.

"Yes, I did." said Harnist, taking a seat next to Armentrout. "And guess what? I've been cleared for active duty. And guess what else? My first job back on the force is to ask you some questions."

"Well, if it's about what happened by the highway, I've got nothing to say." said Armentrout, crossing his arms.

"So you admit you were there of your own free will?" said Harnist.

"Oh, don't play those games with me." Armentrout replied. "I'm a cop too, I know all the tricks."

"Really?"

"Yes, really." said Armentrout. "And let me tell you something, the New York Mafia Killer isn't just some madman, okay? He's doing some good in this city. He's doing what the police can't do!"

"You really seem to believe in him." said Harnist.

"Damn straight." said Armentrout. "My sister was a victim of the Camerlengos. She moved to New York to become a Broadway actress. Instead of going on stage though, the Camerlengos tricked her and sold her into slavery. Last we heard, she was last seen in Spain and then Interpol lost track of her. Nobody's found her, and nobody knows if she's dead or alive. My parents gave up on her and gave up on justice, but I haven't! I became a cop just for the express purpose of revenge, but because of my alimony, I can't pay rent in New York City, let alone fight organized crime in it! No, I'm stuck doing traffic work on state highways! So you know what? Good for the Snake! He's getting something done in this godforsaken city!"

"He called himself the Snake?" said Harnist.

Armentrout's face morphed into an expression of shock as he realized what he'd done. Leaning forward, Harnist looked straight into Armentrout's eyes and said, "Look, I know you support this guy, but you're in big trouble. We've got you helping this guy and assaulting officers of the law. Those are some serious charges. If you turn over whatever information you have, the US Attorney's office might be willing to cut you a deal. How about it?"

Armentrout was quiet for a minute, and Harnist thought he might seriously be thinking the offer over. Then he looked at Harnist defiantly and said, "I'm not saying another word until my lawyer gets here. Now get out!"

Harnist sighed and left the room, meeting with Patton and Murtz down the hall. Murtz handed him a cup of coffee and asked, "How'd it go?"

"As well as could be expected." Harnist answered, gratefully accepting the coffee. "He's supporting the New York Mafia Killer, and—oh, get this! When he was talking, he called our perp 'the Snake'. He said, 'good for the Snake'."

"Good for the Snake?" Patton repeated.

"Well, that's interesting." said Murtz thoughtfully. "I thought the word 'Snake' on the victims' chests was our killer's way of calling the Camerlengos dirty names. But maybe it's his name or what he calls himself, and he's leaving his signature on his work. I'm going to have to add this to the profile. Did he say anything else?"

"Yeah, he said 'Get me my lawyer'." said Harnist. "I don't think he's going to take any deal. Armentrout's really fanatical about this guy—what are they saying on that television?"

Murtz and Patton looked in the direction of the television Harnist had indicated, a small flat screen nestled in the corner of a waiting room. There on the screen, in big black words, read the byline NEW YORK MAFIA KILLER STRIKES AGAIN, DUMPS VAN IN RIVER. On the screen, a crane was shown pulling a white van out of a river, water gushing out from the doors and windows.

Without a word Murtz, Harnist, and Patton rushed to the television, where the voice of Candace Berman greeted them. "...officials have no word yet as to the connection between the van dumped in the Bronx River and an earlier incident today in which a gunman stormed the office of Naughty Princess Industries, a phone-sex service located in the Bronx and reportedly stole a van belonging to the manager of the service. Officials also have no word on the whereabouts of Carla Scarusco, the manager of Naughty Princess Industries or even if she is a suspect, hostage, or victim of the New York Mafia Killer. We will have more on this as the story unfolds."

There was a ringing noise and Patton pulled out his cell phone. "It's Gramer," he said, flipping it open. "Alan, what the heck's going on? Why wasn't I notified of this? Yes, I'm watching the news. Is this really our boy? Okay. Alright then. Sorry I yelled.

Wait, are you serious? Oh hell. Thanks for the warning. We'll be there soon. No, he did not talk. Talk to the AUSA, it's out of our jurisdiction. Okay. See you in few."

Patton ended the call and said, "The FBI will handle Armentrout from now on." said Patton. "As for our news clip, it's definitely his work. Candace Berman got a personal call from the killer broadcasting the location of the van. He also told her that the van belongs to a woman named Carla Scarusco, who hasn't been seen since a gunman stormed her office. Not only that, but her van was dumped in the river with two bodies in it."

"Two?" repeated Murtz.

"Yes, two." said Patton. "One of them was Richard Alvarado."

Harnist inhaled and muttered a curse under his breath. Richard Alvarado was one of the top lieutenants in the Camerlengos, and one of the most difficult people to prosecute in the Family. Both the OCCB and the FBI had been trying for years to tie him to several dozen cases, all with no luck.

"Who was the other?" he asked.

Patton paused before saying, "Officer Jay Kasmet. And get this: Internal Affairs had received a warning about Kasmet early last week. Something about him possibly being on the take."

Murtz and Harnist looked at each other, and a wordless message passed between them. Somehow, they knew things were only going to get worse after this bit of news.

Chapter Fifty-One

It was early morning in the Upper East Side, but no one in Christopher Camerlengo's personal study felt sleepy. Instead, the usual proud and haughty faces were full of terror, and the source of their terror was the aura of murderous rage that was coming from their boss, Christopher Camerlengo, who was sitting behind his desk in a large, padded leather chair.

An overpowering six-feet-eleven, Christopher Camerlengo had a hawk-shaped nose and skin that still had the deep tan of his Sicilian ancestors. His eyes were a sharp grey color, his mouth was long and thin, and his hands were big and meaty with manicured nails. Dressed in an impeccable white suit and navy shirt, he might've been mistaken for a well-dressed, dark-skinned ogre.

In all his years leading this organization, Camerlengo had met with all his subordinates and his *consigliere* only one other time, and that was after he had taken control of a small escort operation from a lawyer who used the organization to pay for bills and a drug habit. Taking the lawyer out had been easy, but expanding her operation had been difficult. Eventually Camerlengo had had to bring in family members, then friends, and as the operation expanded into a real organization, complete strangers from the Sicilian community.

It had been difficult keeping control for eighteen years and grow this organization into the giant it was today. He'd had to endure police investigations and intimidations, coups and power struggles, and constant danger and death threats and assassination attempts. And yet he had stayed calm, he'd endured, he'd made a name for himself and he'd given his wife and children everything they'd ever wanted. His wife now ran her own real estate business, made possible by Camerlengo's own generous donations to his wife's start-up capital. His son had graduated top of his class from Catholic school and NYU, and was at Ohio State training to become a cardiac surgeon.

But the past two and a half weeks had shaken up his entire organization, and he had had to endure attacks on all sides by police investigators, rival gangs, and possibly even conspirators within his own organization. It was enough that Camerlengo was having trouble controlling his anger. And if his anger did manage to get out of control, he might revert to the hotheaded youth who had terrorized his hometown of Vittoria in Italy.

No, he would not let that happen. He'd learned to control his anger when he'd emigrated at fourteen and had made himself a powerful man by keeping himself calm. He'd stay calm now and would make this threat to his organization go away. As soon as he did, things would go back to normal. The universe would right itself. Only if he stayed calm though.

Camerlengo eyed his lieutenants and his *consigliere*, and was pleased to see that each of them showed fear as they registered that he was looking at them. Fear in his subordinates was a good thing: as much as the police were hated and feared, all those in Camerlengo's inner circle were well aware of what their boss was like when his anger was roused, of the men who'd been maimed and crippled by his anger in Sicily, and that was enough of a deterrent to keep most of them from thinking of mutiny or jumping ship.

Clearing his throat, Christopher Camerlengo said, "Find a new mole for the task force. We need to know any information that they can give us. The sooner we find the New York Mafia Killer, the sooner we can avenge Alvarado and our brothers."

"I'll get right on it," said Alex Rocca, the new lieutenant who was replacing Alvarado. Camerlengo fixed him with a hard stare, which elicited a nervous gulp from Rocca. Satisfied, Camerlengo moved onto the next subject.

"I also want the reward for the killer's head doubled." said Camerlengo. "It doesn't matter if he's dead or alive. The man has killed five of our men. They deserve revenge. And have those warnings to the other bosses been sent out?"

"Yes." said James Maffuci, one of the other lieutenants. "A hand from a member of each of the families. They should be arriving this morning."

"Excellent." said Camerlengo, rubbing his hands together with a sick, joyful anticipation. "This will remind them that we allow those third-class cunts to exist in the first place. They shouldn't forget that. Now, is there anything else we should be worried about?"

"The auction tomorrow night, sir." said John Battua, one of the *consigliere*. "Based on all that's been going on, we should probably cancel it."

"Cancel it?!" repeated Camerlengo with a growl, rising from his seat. At once the whole room stepped away from Battua, as if he'd just revealed he carried a deadly plague. "And show the world that we're actually afraid of this man? No! It will go on as usual, and we shall rake in a profit, as usual. If there are any problems, we shall have them taken care of. Is that clear, John?"

"Clear." said Battua, his voice cracking. "Crystal clear."

For a moment Camerlengo just stood behind his desk, his knuckles resting on the wood. Then he let out a quiet "Good," and sat back down, his chair creaking audibly as he sat. "Oh, and Joseph?"

"Yes sir?" said Joseph Rabuano, whose men were to be running the auction tomorrow night.

"You know that some of our...merchandise is very special." said Camerlengo, his fingers tip-to-tip in a steeple formation. "So with that in mind...well, you get the idea what will happen if anything should go wrong, correct?"

Rabuano gulped and said, his voice cracking, "Y-Yes sir."

"Good." said Camerlengo, his smile sending shivers down the spines of his men. At the same time Camerlengo took a deep breath, letting the oxygen relax his system and drive away the anger. "Very good."

He would weather this. It was only a matter of patience.

Chapter Fifty-Two

The Snake pulled out his cell phone and dialed a number. The phone rang twice before someone picked up. "Honey, do you know how much trouble you're in?" said Alberta, her voice coming through in a whisper.

"Oh, you have no idea." said the Snake. "Why are you whispering?"

"Well, it's your father. He's—hold on." There was a clatter and the Snake heard someone on the other end shouting at someone else.

"I don't want to hear his name in the house ever again! You hear me? Don't mention him again!" The Snake winced as a door slammed on the other end, followed by an uncomfortable silence. Finally Alberta came back on, her voice full of relief.

"My Lord, your father is a menace!" said Alberta. "He's scared Ruby to tears! God bless the child for not peeing herself."

"Has he hit her?" asked the Snake, his grip tightening on the phone.

"Honey—"

"Did he hurt her?" the Snake demanded, struggling to keep himself from shouting.

There was a pause, and then Alberta said, "No, thank God. But sometimes I worry he might. He's a monster, your father."

"That's a total understatement." said the Snake. "What did Ruby do that pissed off my dad?"

"She asked about you."

"Oh Ruby." said the Snake, feeling pity for the poor girl. "Put her on the phone, okay Alberta?"

"Why can't you just come home and apologize to your father?" asked Alberta, sounding more like she was giving an order than a request. "He might just return to his normal level of evil if you do."

"Even if my pride and conscience allowed me to do that, I doubt he'd allow me to come home." said the Snake. "I don't think he'd feel safe around me, to tell you the truth."

"What do you mean by that?" asked Alberta.

"Look Alberta," said the Snake, rubbing his temples as he felt his annoyance starting to rise, "could you just put Ruby on the phone? I'd really like to talk to her."

Alberta groaned, but a moment later the Snake heard her feet going up two flights of stairs and knocking on the door. "Ruby, sweetheart? Your brother's on the phone."

The phone passed hands and the Snake heard Ruby say, "Is that you?"

"No, it's Sherlock Holmes." said the Snake. "How you doing, Ruby?"

"When are you and Linda coming home?" asked Ruby, her voice pleading.

"Soon, hopefully." said the Snake. His heart broke that he couldn't come home to her, but if he gave up now, how could he face her? "I'm really close. I should be able to find Allison tomorrow night."

"Really?" Ruby's voice perked right up at the mention of Allison's name. "And then you can come home?"

"Hopefully." said the Snake. "I'll have to beat up all the bad guys first."

"Are you going to beat them up like that one guy in the TV show?"

"What TV show was that?" The Snake listened for the better part of three minutes as Ruby told him in detail how the superhero in her favorite cartoon had outwitted his nemesis by dropping a washbasin on his head. When she was done, the Snake just said, "I think I'll use martial arts instead. That doesn't rely on me learning how to stretch my legs so they can fit around a doorway."

"Can't you climb up like a ninja onto the ceiling and then drop the washbasin?"

"Who do you think I am? Batman?" said the Snake, laughing.

"No, you're Sherlock Holmes." said Ruby. "And you've got Linda with you, and you'll find Allison tomorrow."

"And first opportunity we get, we'll do whatever you want." said the Snake.

"I want to go to Coney Island!" said Ruby immediately, surprising the Snake. "And then I want to watch a movie with you and Allison!"

"Um…sure thing, kid." said Snake, immediately regretting making that promise to her. "Whatever you want. Count on it, okay?"

"Okay." Ruby replied. "I love you!"

"Love you too. Could you put Alberta back on the phone?"

"Okay." said Ruby. "Hey, can I tell you something?"

"Sure. What's up?"

"You're more like a father to me than Daddy is." said Ruby.

For a moment, the Snake didn't know how to reply. But then he smiled and, forcing back some tears, "Thanks, Ruby. That really makes me happy. Put Alberta on the phone now, okay?"

"Okay. Talk to you later. Bye!" Ruby took the phone back to Alberta, who came on and said, "Well, aren't you the lucky young man. Apparently you're a better parent than your own father."

"Don't rub it in, Alberta." said the Snake. "I had no idea I meant so much to her."

"I don't know why you're so surprised." Alberta replied. "When you're not here and I'm here with her, all she can talk about is you, Allison, and Linda. All three of you are her real family, not that monster who comes home once a week and is always in a bad mood when he does. So you get home as soon as you can and give that girl a hug so that all the hurt goes away. You hear me?"

"I hear you Alberta." said the Snake. "I'll be home as soon as I can. You still praying for me?"

"Every darn day, just like I promised you when you said you were going to look for Allison and I said I'd look after Ruby." Alberta answered. "As surely as I never answer the phone with a 'hello', I'm still praying for you."

"Yeah, I've been meaning to ask why you do that." said the Snake. "Why do you never say 'hello' to me when I call?"

Instead of an answer, there was a click and a dial tone. The Snake looked at the screen before hanging up himself, giving a nonchalant shrug and stroking Linda's head. "We'll be going home with Allison soon, Linda." said the Snake. "Just have to wait till tomorrow night."

The Snake looked out the window next to his bed, and watched the skyline. He could almost sense it in his gut. Allison would be back with him soon.

Chapter Fifty-Three

"Come on! Show us a fucking smile." said the photographer, running his fingers through his oily hair. "God, do we have to threaten you with a gun? You're the big prize tonight, so act like it, fuck-slut!"

Allison winced with every shout, but forced her face to smile. The photographer smiled and took a photo. The lights flashed and spots appeared in Allison's eyes. The photographer examined the photo in his camera's screen before looking up and saying, "Good. Now we're getting somewhere. Now put your hands on your top, like you're about to pull it off and show us your tits."

Allison's smile faltered. "W-What?"

"Put your hands on your top," repeated the photographer, enunciating each word carefully, "like you're about to pull it off and show us your tits."

"B-But I—"

"PUT YOUR HANDS ON YOUR TOP, YOU SOW!"

Allison shuddered, and put her hands on her breasts, her fingers curling around the strings of the golden bikini they'd forced her to wear for the photo shoot. Forcing her face to work itself into a smile again, there was another flash and the photographer checked the camera again. The photographer's mouth twitched upwards and

Allison thought she was done. But then the photographer looked at her, a dark glint in his eye. "Put a hand in your crotch." he said.

Allison's eyes widened. The photographer's brow furrowed as he sensed her hesitation, and Allison felt a pang of fear. Reaching down, tears welled in her eye as her hand went down below the straps of her bikini and into her pubic hair. The photographer's mouth twitched upwards again. "Lean forward." he said. "Let's get a good shot of those breasts."

Forcing herself not to cry, Allison leaned forward, her butt touching the pink tapestry behind her. The photographer's mouth twitched once more. "Tip your head up a little." Allison tipped her head up. "Good. Now smile and hold still." There was a flash, and the photographer gave a satisfied smirk before waving her off. Exiting the stage, Allison let her tears flow, her knees folding as she hugged her breasts.

"Yeah, cry now." said a voice to her right. Allison looked up and saw one of the women who'd been applying make-up to her and the other girls before the photo shoot. "Because trust me honey, you're not gonna have time to cry later."

"W-What do you know?" said Allison, her voice cracking as she tried to act as tough as she should be. Oh, why couldn't she stay in the past and in her fantasies? She'd prefer that to having to talk to this woman with the coiffed hair and lollipop between her lips.

"Ooh, there's that defiance I heard so much about." said the make-up woman. "Trust me, that attitude ain't gonna last much longer. You think being kept in a cell for a week, missing a meal when you're a bad girl, and shitting in a bucket is the worst? Puh-leaze! The men who buy girls in these auctions are the worst type of man out there. They see women as toys and possessions, and will do all sorts of shit to you when they play with you. You'll be lucky if you're bought by a lesbian. They're rough on the girls they buy, but they're a little less rough than the men, and actually pretend to care about their slaves. 'Least, that's what I heard."

Before Allison could reply, one of the men came and told the make-up woman to scram. The make-up woman gave the man some lip before stalking off in her clicking high-heels. Allison watched her go before she was herded back to the rest of the girls, where they had their hands cuffed behind their backs and told to walk to "the drop-off point". As Allison was led forward at gunpoint by one of the men, one with a gold earring and a distinctive birthmark above his eyebrow, she felt a hand on her butt and a voice in her ear.

"I wish I could buy you." said the man wistfully. Allison felt a chill run up her spine as she recognized the man's voice as the man who had promised her a real bathroom for sexual favors. What was he doing here? "Really wish it. You see, I've been watching you all week, red. I saw you when you took that first dump in that bucket we put in your cell, though you thought you were alone.

Your face as you pulled off your pants. And then those pubes. And just seeing those tears…man, you have no idea how hard I whacked off to that."

The man pinched Allison's butt cheek, giving a deep, disturbing laugh. Allison was too shocked and horrified to react. He'd been watching her? For how long? How did she not notice him?! Allison felt like she was going to throw up, but nothing came up. Was this what pure revulsion felt like?

As Allison was told to sit on a bench and be quiet, she began to cry again as she relived the memory of when she had had to use the bucket as a toilet and thought about how the man with the earring had been watching her as she'd done that. She wanted to wish that the agony and torment would end, but somehow Allison felt that would be nothing more than wishful thinking. It was just like the make-up lady had said: the worst was yet to come.

Chapter Fifty-Four

The Snake ambled over to the Racehorse, whistling as he walked. There were several people going in and coming out of the Racehorse, and most of the people going in seemed to be upper-class, judging by the quality of the clothes and the watches they wore. The Snake wondered how many of them were here for the auction, and which ones he might have to kill later.

As the front entrance came into view, the Snake paused to check his appearance one last time in the window reflection. He was wearing his usual gear, but he'd applied copious amounts of movie-grade makeup to his face and hands, effectively aging himself twenty years and giving himself a ruddy complexion. Add in the curly wig on his head and the false nose molded on with putty and painted the same color of his skin, and he looked like an entirely different person.

Taking a deep breath, the Snake went past the front entrance, into a side alley, and knocked on a door from which the sounds and smells of cooking were coming from. A moment later the door opened and a young man a few years older than the Snake with an apron on poked his head out. "Can I help you, sir?"

"*Bella costa tosto è rapita.*" said the Snake, putting his thumbs casually in his pants pockets.

The man with the apron said, "Hold on," and ducked back into the building. A minute later another man came out, this one wearing a blue dress shirt and a black tie. The man opened the door and gestured for the Snake to come in.

As the door closed behind the Snake, the man in the blue dress shirt pointed at a set of stairs behind a large oven and said, "Up the stairs, first door on your left. There's someone already up there."

The Snake was surprised but didn't let it show, instead just nodding and heading up the stairs. *Someone's already up there?* thought the Snake. *I thought this was an auction. Why's there only one person? Shouldn't there be a whole bunch of people?*

The Snake opened the door on the left and walked in. Inside, illuminated by a single light bulb on the ceiling, was a man in a T-shirt and cargo pants, sitting in front of a table with two computer monitors and several flashing electronic devices. The man sitting in front of the monitors looked at the Snake and smiled. "Hey, how you doing? I'm Fred." said the man, extending his hand. The Snake stared at him, a short twenty-something with thick-framed glasses and long hair that went down to his shoulders. Who was he and what was he doing here?

"Jay. I don't shake." said the Snake, looking around the room. It was a small room, with no windows and, except for the table with the computers and monitors, no furniture besides a chair by the table and another in the corner. There was no way an auction went on in this room. Had the man who'd sent him up gotten confused?

"Okay, that's fine." said Fred, turning back to his computer. "You're a germaphobe, that's cool. I was just trying to be friendly, is all. My uncle told me I wouldn't be needing security, but if you're here, things must be dire."

"Security?" repeated the Snake.

"Well yeah." said Fred, his fingers moving rapidly over the keyboard. "The New York Mafia Killer's killed like, four or five people in the past week. My Uncle Joseph is in charge of these auctions, and he said I probably wouldn't need security 'cause no one knows how these auctions are run or where they're even held. I guess my mom beat him into submission though, if you're here."

"Yeah." said the Snake, sitting in the chair in the corner and deciding it was better to play along for now and perhaps solve the mystery of the auction. "So what're you doing on the computer?"

"Setting up the auction." Fred answered, moving the mouse with one hand while typing out something on the keyboard with the other. "You know it's all electronic, right?"

Electronic? thought the Snake. *No I did not. Thanks for telling me.* The Snake cleared his throat, and said, "I heard it was electronic, but I don't know how it works."

Fred laughed, his eyes focused on the screens in front of him. "Well, let me tell you Jay, it's awesome," he said, pushing his glasses up his nose. "I run it all with these computers. The bidders come in downstairs, they give the bartender a password, and he gives them a web address, a username, and a password. They use their laptops, their mobile device, their tablet, whatever, to bid on items."

"It's done over the Internet?" said the Snake.

"Correct." Fred answered. "I've set it up so that not even the feds can get wind of it. They'd have to go through twenty different obstacles to get through, which leave the bidders safe from getting caught."

"Clever." said the Snake. "Do you just click on a button and raise your bid when you see something you like?"

"Something like that." said Fred. "I use an algorithm that ups the bid by a certain amount depending on quality of product, how many people are bidding, and a few other factors. I'm actually running a few studies on this. Nothing I can publish, obviously, but it's still pretty cool. Maybe my uncle can use it to find more products that people will buy."

"And what happens when you buy a product?"

"Well, if nobody bids within ten seconds of the last bid, then the last bidder is automatically the winner." said Fred. "If they win, they transfer money into an off-shore account. Once they do that, they receive a special passcode and the pick-up location. The guys at the pick-up location get the passcodes as soon as the girls are bought, so they know who bought what, and there's no confusion."

"And you do all this from here?" said the Snake. "Wow, that's a lot of skill."

"Thanks."

"And a lot of trust." said the Snake. "What do they do to keep you from using this to your own advantage?"

Fred turned around to face the Snake, pushing his glasses up his nose again. "I'm insulted by your insinuation." said Fred. "But if you must know, I get twenty-thousand every auction. That's enough to pay for all my expenses, and the stuff left over, I invest in popular Internet companies. I make do, thank you very much."

"Sorry!" said the Snake, holding up his hands defensively. "It's just that I find it hard to trust one person with such a big operation."

"Well, besides the pay, I get a few perks at Christmas and on my birthday." Fred replied, turning back to his computer. "It's enough that I don't feel like doing something stupid."

"I'll bet." said the Snake. *You computer-fucking, immoral ublyudok.* he thought, looking at the man he'd just called a bastard with distaste. Killing him wouldn't just be a treat, it'd be a mercy to the entire world.

"Alright, the auction is going to start." said Fred, rubbing his hands excitedly. "You wanna come up here and watch, Jay? The guy who does the photos of the products is a genius. Sometimes I save the photos they use and take them home with me, though don't tell anyone I said that."

"Sure, I'd love to watch." said the Snake, pulling his chair up next to Fred, who pressed a few more keys and then pressed ENTER. A program appeared on the left monitor, with a chat box near the bottom of the screen. At the top of the screen, a status bar said, 27 USERS LOGGED IN.

"Only twenty-seven? Usually there are more about now." Fred remarked, stroking his chin.

"Maybe they'll come later," the Snake suggested.

Fred shook his head. "It's set up so that once the auction starts, you can't log in late or back out early." said Fred. "It's designed that way to keep random people from miraculously hacking in or to keep people from getting cold feet. If either happens, I'll know about it, and I'll notify a security team I have on standby."

"How do you notify the security team?" asked the Snake. "That done on the computer too?"

Fred shook his head again. "I call them on my cell phone. If it's anyone within New York, it gets taken care of by morning. If it's outside the state, then it goes to an independent contractor. It's all quiet, and nobody's the wiser. Trust me, secrecy's important in these matters."

"I'll bet." said the Snake. "Maybe the New York Mafia Killer scared them off, though. I mean, if they know who's running this auction, maybe they're afraid it'll bite them in the ass if they do the auction."

"It's a possibility," said Fred, pushing up his glasses for the third time. "It's a stupid reason, but it's one I can imagine someone using as their excuse. Alright, let's start."

Fred began typing in the chat box, while looking through a list of JPEGs in a file on the right monitor at the same time. GOOD EVENING AND WELCOME. Fred typed. OUR FIRST PRODUCT IS AFRICAN-AMERICAN, 24. BREASTS ARE RATHER SMALL, BUT HER SKIN IS FLAWLESS. Fred dragged a JPEG to a box in the program on the left monitor, and a picture appeared of a dark-skinned girl against a bright pink background wearing a revealing striped bikini, her legs bent and her arms above her head for maximum exposure of her breasts and thighs.

LET'S START THE BIDDING AT $5,000. Fred typed. Almost immediately after the starting price appeared, a bidder's username appeared at the top of a column on the right side of the program. It was followed soon after by another bidder, and then another. After six bids the bidding stopped at thirty thousand dollars, and an orange bar with white letters saying ITEM SOLD appeared in the bidding column.

"One down, nineteen more to go," said Fred, bringing up the next girl for sale, a young girl from India who couldn't be older than fourteen.

The bidding went on and on, with the starting prices starting higher and higher, the bids going farther and farther up. As a dark-haired girl with large eyes and pouting lips sticking her ass out at the camera was sold for four-and-a-half million, Fred looked at the Snake and said, "Final item. They always save the best for last."

"Wonderful." said the Snake. "I can't wait." The Snake held back that he couldn't wait for it to be over. He'd seen nineteen women and girls sold off in the past hour or so as slaves and sex toys to anonymous buyers. The Snake was disgusted and wished he could do something for these girls as well, but he knew that he had to focus on saving Allison. Still, he hoped he'd get a chance later to pay back all the monsters who were causing these girls pain after he saved Al. In fact, watching Fred type in the information on the last girl, he'd consider it an honor to kill these bastards for them.

OUR LAST ITEM TONIGHT IS CAUCASIAN-AMERICAN, 17. SHE HAS BEEN DESCRIBED AS "DEFIANT", SO SHE IS YOURS TO BREAK. IN EXCELLENT HEALTH AND CERTIFIED PURE. BIDDING STARTS AT $2 MILLION.

Fred dragged the last JPEG over and put it up on the screen. The Snake's eyes widened. It was Allison.

Chapter Fifty-Five

The Snake stared incredulously at the picture of Allison. They'd dressed her in a revealing gold bikini, her hand on the strap of her top and her hand down beneath the fabric towards her pussy, leaning forward so that her breasts were heaving out of the top. All this was going on in the photo, but most disturbing of all was Allison's smile, and how forced it was, like her face would crack from trying to hold up that smile. Even if nobody else saw how hard she was struggling, the Snake saw it.

Allison, what have they done to you? he wondered, putting his hands under the table so that Fred wouldn't see how hard they were shaking. *When I get you back, I'll do whatever you want so you can forget this. Just tell me, I'll make it all better for you. Just wait a little longer, Al. I'll get you soon.*

"Hot damn." said Fred, licking his lips excitedly. "She's a real looker. I'm definitely taking a few copies of her home." The Snake was only just able to resist the urge to strangle Fred with his bare hands.

A username appeared in the bidding column: PL523 $2,000,000. A second later another name and number appeared: GIANT72 $2,500,000. A third person, RED1951, put down three million for Allison, only to be outdone by GIANT72, who was topped by LIZZIE78, then CLG3, and then GIANT72 again.

The Snake watched as the price on Allison kept going up, his eyes widening with each bid. Seven million…eight million…nine million…ten million…eleven-point-five million…thirteen million!

"Do people usually bid this much at the end?" asked the Snake as the bid went to eighteen million.

"You'd be surprised." Fred answered. As GIANT72 put down twenty million on Allison, there was a pause where no one else put down a bid. "Some people really go for virgins. They love planting the flag on a girl. There's something special about the first time, you know. Oh, looks like we have a winner."

Sure enough, nobody else put down a bid on Allison after GIANT72. The timer ran out, and the orange bar appeared, ending the bidding. Fred began typing as soon as the bar appeared, even as he was sending the picture of Allison to his email account. THAT ENDS TONIGHT'S BIDDING. CONGRATULATIONS TO ALL THE WINNERS AND THANK YOU FOR YOUR BUSINESS. YOU MAY PICK UP YOUR PURCHASES AT THE ADDRESS PROVIDED. PLEASE REMEMBER TO KEEP YOUR USERNAME AND PASSCODE IN ORDER TO CLAIM YOUR PURCHASE. THANK YOU AND HAVE A NICE EVENING.

Fred closed the bidding program and leaned back in his chair. "Well, that's that."

The Snake pulled out his gun and pressed it against Fred's forehead. "Indeed," said the Snake with his Russian accent. "That's that."

Chapter Fifty-Six

Fred froze as the barrel of the silencer touched his temple. "J-Jay?" he said, his whole body trembling. "This isn't funny, okay? I don't like these sorts of pranks."

"Nobody's laughing, Fred." said the Snake, pulling out his mask and slipping it on. "Especially not my previous victims."

"Previous victims?" repeated Fred. "What are you talking about—?"

"I've killed four or five people this past week! We were just discussing me!" the Snake growled. "God, for a computer genius you're not that smart, are you?"

A look of realization dawned on Fred's face and he said, "You're the—you're him?"

"Oh *now* you get it!" said the Snake, his eyes rolling. "And if you don't want to be tortured before you die, I suggest you tell me what I want to know."

"S-S-Sure." Fred stammered, sweat breaking out on his forehead. "W-What do you want to know?"

"Where's the pick-up location for the auction?" asked the Snake. "Where do I go if I want to retrieve one of the girls from the auction?"

"Why do you want to—wait, don't pull that trigger!" Fred said quickly as the Snake's eyes narrowed. "I-I don't know it off the top of my head, but I have it on the computer."

"Are you lying to me?" asked the Snake. "You could have an alarm on your computer. You could be trying to pull a fast one on me."

"No, I swear!" Fred cried, his whole body shaking. "It's in my records. I always get notified when they pick a new location for the pick-up! That way I know where to send the winners of the auction!"

The Snake scanned Fred's face and couldn't find a single indication that he was lying. "Bring it up." said the Snake.

Fred leaned forward and brought up a file from his hard drive. He clicked on it, and up popped a saved email with an address in it. The Snake read the address aloud and committed it to his memory. Turning to Fred, he said, "Thank you, Fred. Now I won't have to torture you and risk being discovered by anyone downstairs."

Fred looked at the Snake with a look full of relief and hope.

"However, you'll still die." said the Snake. "You don't deserve to live."

Fred's face changed from hope to despair and he said, "Please don't kill me. It's only a job. A single job in a large business."

"It's a bad job in a disgusting business," replied the Snake. "And it has its consequences." The Snake squeezed the trigger, and Fred fell out of the chair and onto the ground, his face frozen in an expression of terror. Standing up out of his chair, the Snake lifted Fred's shirt up and carved his name into Fred's chest.

Satisfied with his work on Fred, the Snake turned to the computer on the table and fired a round into it. The monitors flashed and went dead, followed by the rest of the system. Putting his gun and knife back in his jacket, the Snake took off his mask and left the room, skipping steps as he walked down the stairs and out the door.

He knew where Allison was now.

Chapter Fifty-Seven

The man with the earring approached Allison and said, "Lucky girl, you got bought for twenty million. Someone with money to spare really wanted you. Probably not as much as I wanted you, though."

"Stop messing with her, Joe." called one of the other men, one whom Allison thought might be in charge of this whole operation. "If the higher-ups got wind you were messing with other people's property, you'd find yourself in the Hudson by morning."

"Hey, I gotta have some fun in life." said Joe, fingering his earring.

"Then get it with your own paycheck," replied Joe's boss. "Now hurry up and get her ready; her new owner's going to be here soon."

"Alright, alright. Whatever you say." Joe stopped fingering his earring and grabbed Allison by the shoulder. "Come on, red." he said to her. "Let's get going. You're new master is on his way. Or maybe on her way. You see more women in these auctions nowadays. I wonder how freaky their tastes are."

I don't belong to anyone! That's what Allison wanted to say, but she was afraid to do so. Who knew what would happen if she reacted to the same guy who had gotten off watching her poop in a bucket?

As he pulled her along, Joe was running his fingers along her arm and back, his breathing becoming faster as he touched her. She had a feeling that if she tried to fight back against him or his friends and employers, her rebellion would only turn him on and then he would touch her more, and in other places, places she didn't want to be touched in.

The air got colder a second before Allison saw a docking bay for trucks, the corrugated steel door open without a truck in the doorway. Allison guessed she was in some sort of warehouse or factory, the first clue as to where she was being kept. Several other girls were already there, each being watched by a man who held tightly onto their arms.

Craning her neck to see beyond the docking bay door, Allison saw several expensive cars lining up outside in front of the door, with several men going to cars and speaking to the drivers before heading back to speak to the man supervising the whole operation.

A minute later one of the cars, a sparkling blue Lamborghini, was directed to the docking bay door, and the supervisor pointed to one of the girls, who was taken to the Lamborghini and pushed into the passenger seat. As soon as the girl was inside and the passenger door was closed, the Lamborghini sped off and out of sight. Allison felt her heartbeat speed up as she realized that soon, someone would be speeding off with her.

As the line of cars shrunk and the number of girls dwindled, Joe leaned down and whispered in Allison's ear, "Looks like it's almost time to say goodbye. How about leaving me a kiss before you go, huh?"

Before she could react, Joe had grabbed Allison's cheeks between his fingers and had pressed his lips to hers. Allison stared at him in horror as he held her for a moment and then broke away, licking his lips with a lecherous expression on his face. "Damn, you taste good! I'm really jealous of your new master now."

Allison turned her head to the side and spat, trying to get rid of the taste of those disgusting lips. Joe only laughed and said, "Oh come on, I'm not bad a kisser, am I?"

"Joe! I told you to cut it out!" shouted the supervisor. "If I catch you doing that one more time, I'll report it to Rabuano, and then your goose will really be cooked!"

"Sorry Jack," said Joe, holding up the hand that wasn't holding Allison's arm defensively.

"Anyway, her owner's here," said the supervisor, gesturing with a pen to the docking bay door. "In the red Mercedes. You better hope he didn't see you do that."

Allison felt her heart beating against her rib cage, her breathing coming in quick little inhalations. *He's here*, she thought. *I'm about to be taken away.*

As Allison was led to the Mercedes, she found herself hoping that, against all probability, her boyfriend was the person behind the wheel in the red Mercedes. Her boyfriend had a license, and could probably get his hands on a Mercedes and the money to pay twenty million for her, if his claims about having access to his father's accounts or his wealthy clients' accounts were true. Or maybe he would come swinging in like Indiana Jones with a whip or something, beat up all the bad guys, and let everybody go. He'd even have the perfect joke to tell when he did it. She knew it was an impossible fantasy, something that could never happen, something that could've only occurred in the fantasies she'd had when she tried to escape reality in the cell, but the thought of it filled her with hope and kept her heart from breaking out of her chest.

Maybe he's really here. she thought, as she stepped down out of the docking bay with the man with the earring and was led to the Mercedes. *Maybe he's come to save me, and then we'll ride away where no one will find me. Oh please let him be driving the red Mercedes. Please let him be driving the red Mercedes.*

The man with the earring opened the passenger door of the Mercedes and pushed Allison's head in. As Allison sat down, she looked at the driver, expecting to see her boyfriend smiling and saying, *Hey Al. Nice swimsuit*, or something stupid like that.

As she recognized the driver though, Allison felt icy cold fear grip her heart again. Although she knew who the driver was, as improbable as that was, it was not someone who could help her. In fact, Allison knew that her situation had gotten a lot worse.

The driver leaned over, fastened Allison in with the seatbelt, and stroked her cheek. "Hi there." he said, flashing her a maniacal grin.

Chapter Fifty-Eight

The Snake watched from a minivan he'd stolen after the auction as cars lined up in front of the pick-up location, a warehouse with a chain-link fence guarding the perimeter. The one gate in the fence had been rolled back, and several expensive cars were still rolling into line. As they rolled in, the Snake took some moist towelettes and worked on removing the make-up on his face, checking the rearview mirror after every wipe had been used.

The ups and downs of being in a wealthy private school's film club. the Snake thought, looking again in the mirror. *You learn where to get movie-grade make-up, you learn how to put it on by yourself, and you learn how hard it is to get off.* Satisfied with his face, the Snake stepped out of the car and threw the used towelettes in the dumpster where he'd already thrown the wig and fake nose. Then he took out a bottle filled with bleach and poured it over the wig and towelettes and fake nose. The Snake would've preferred to burn the evidence, but the smoke might've attracted unnecessary attention, so bleach would have to do . Returning to the car, the Snake watched as the pickup began.

First, a blue Lamborghini drove up to an open docking bay, where a young woman in a silver bikini was walked out and shoved into the passenger seat of the Lamborghini. As soon as the girl was in, the Lamborghini sped off, turning left at the chain-link fence towards the entrance and out again, driving away from the warehouse at speeds well above the speed limit.

The Snake watched the Lamborghini drive away and felt sorry for the girl who'd been picked up, even though he was only there for one girl in particular. He knew it was no consolation to the girl in the Lamborghini, but if the Snake was successful, no other girl would be sold by the Camerlengos ever again.

Another girl was picked up, and then another. Each time a car pulled up to the docking bay door, the Snake leaned forward, expecting to see Allison, but each time a different girl was picked up. The Snake was starting to get impatient when a red Mercedes pulled up. As the girl came forward, being led by a man with an earring, the Snake inhaled. He recognized that red hair and that gold bikini, even at this distance.

Allison! he thought.

The Mercedes rolled slowly to the gate, only speeding up as it passed beyond the chain-link fence and onto the street. Hotwiring the minivan, the Snake drove after it, going down an alleyway so that he could follow without being caught by any security. Pulling out onto a main road, the Snake came up a few cars behind the Mercedes, changing lanes so that he was just slightly behind and next to it.

As he drove, the Snake gripped the steering wheel hard. He was coming for Allison, and he would not stop until he had her again.

Chapter Fifty-Nine

On a rooftop, Fyedka Nabatov watched the pick-up of girls at the Camerlengos' warehouse. He'd been watching the pickup after every auction, once a month, for the past four months. The plan was to gather enough information on the Camerlengos' auctions that Fyedka's employers could pass on the info to the police or the FBI. Then, when the Camerlengos power had been sufficiently weakened, Fyedka's employers would move in and take some of that power for themselves.

Of course, they were still a long way from doing that. They still didn't know where they auctions were held or how they were conducted or who took part in them. Until they had that information, Fyedka and several others would have to continue these late night surveillance sessions.

But tonight, something was different. Shortly before the pick-up had started, a grey minivan had pulled up a short distance away from the warehouse, and a man had gotten out and thrown something away in a nearby dumpster. A few minutes later, the same man got out and threw something else into the dumpster.

Fyedka had been curious, but his priorities were to watch the auction, so he'd been watching and taking long-distance photos of the pick-up location, while peeking over the rooftop every few minutes to check on the minivan.

As the driver of a red Mercedes picked up his purchase and drove away from the warehouse, Fyedka heard an engine turn on and looked over to see the minivan rolling away and following after the Mercedes, going down another street but obviously trying to stay with the Mercedes.

Fyedka watched the minivan go and dialed his boss, who picked up the phone after the second ring. "What is it, Fyedka?" said Yulian Olovin, his voice nasally from a head cold.

"There's something weird going on here at the pick-up." Fyedka answered, looking away from the warehouse and pacing around the roof. "As I was watching the warehouse, there was a minivan in the street below me. As one of the cars was driving away, the minivan followed it, but in a way so that the driver of the car wouldn't see it."

"Do you think it was a private detective?" asked Dimitri. "Someone looking for their daughter or sister?"

"I'm not sure, but it could be." Fyedka replied. "What should I do?"

"Did you get the license plate number?" asked Dimitri.

"No, but I remember there was a 59 at the end, and that it was following a red Mercedes." said Fyedka.

"I'll send one of our men after it." Dimitri assured Fyedka. "If this is someone who's endangering our operation, we'll have to know. You stay where you are, Fyedka, and continue watching the auction. Keep up the good work."

"Yes sir." said Fyedka, hanging up. Returning to his view of the warehouse, Fyedka picked up his camera and started taking photos as the last couple cars received their purchases.

Chapter Sixty

The Snake followed the red Mercedes on the highway, careful not to be more than two or three cars behind but never less than one. His breathing was slow and steady, and with every breath he took, he repeated the same word in his head: *Allison...Allison...Allison.* It was almost like a mantra to him.

The Mercedes turned onto an exit, and the Snake followed, cutting off a black smart car that honked at the Snake. At the end of the exit, the Mercedes turned left into an area with many large, luxurious apartment buildings. The Snake followed at a distance, waiting an extra second at stop signs so as not to seem like he was following the Mercedes.

Finally the Mercedes stopped at a tall skyscraper, turning into an underground garage and out of sight. The Snake stopped and parked next to an Apple store, even though the sign next to the curb said NO PARKING. Resigning himself to the fact that the minivan might be towed and he might have to find a second car to hijack, the Snake put his mask back on and walked to the building that the Mercedes had gone into.

The Snake guessed that the building had twenty or twenty-five floors, with the upper floors reserved for the richest of the tenants. A sign out front read BARLOW HEIGHTS: A LOVELY PLACE TO LIVE. ASK ABOUT TOURS AND RATES. The Snake saw on a lower part of the sign that the building would be available to move into in mid-March. So what was the owner of the Mercedes doing here—?

The Snake realized who the owner of the Mercedes might be and immediately ran to the entrance of the garage. *Allison was bought by the owner of this building.* he thought as he saw a grated steel gate blocking the way into the underground garage. *And he probably lives here too if he's going to bring a sex slave he just bought here. Which means he's probably going to be found in the penthouse of this place. And that's where I'll find Allison.*

Looking for a different way into the building, the Snake walked around the perimeter, looking for an open door, a broken window. When he came across a back door, he saw it was electronically sealed, and didn't use a standard key, so he couldn't use the bump key. The Snake went around a second time, looking for something he could use to get in but finding nothing. He went around a third time, his frustration mounting. Still nothing.

The Snake was about to go around a fourth time when he saw it: an air vent, set into the dirt of a growing garden ringing the perimeter of the building. He'd missed it the first time because he'd been looking for a door, so obviously he wouldn't have been looking for anything in the ground. The shrubs growing in the ground must have obscured the vent the second and third time around.

Glad I found it this time, the Snake thought, going to the vent and testing the grate over it. To his delight, the grate lifted easily in his fingers, giving him enough room to slip in and jump into the vent. Landing on his feet, the Snake bent down and started crawling, feeling like a spy in an action movie.

As he crawled through, the Snake spotted a large grate in the vent to his right and turned toward it, his belly and legs sliding along the steel belly of the vent. As he got closer to the grate the vent around him opened up, becoming less tight and claustrophobic. Finally he reached the grate, beyond which he could see the garage. Repositioning himself in the vent so that he was in a sitting position, the Snake drew back his legs and kicked the grate. With a loud clatter the grate fell out of its frame, making an even louder clatter as one side hit the ground, then the opposite side, and finally all sides in one final *clang!* that, if this building were already lived in and staffed, might have roused security guards to his location.

As the Snake stepped out and stretched his legs, he was relieved to see nobody else around. Not even any cars, which made the Snake guess the Mercedes was somewhere else in the underground parking garage. Looking around, the Snake saw an elevator and ran towards it, pressing the button to go up when he got there.

The elevator hummed into life, a small display above the doors showing the car coming down from the top floor. At least the Snake had been right about what floor Allison was on.

Finally the doors opened and the Snake stepped inside, pressing for the top floor. As the doors closed, the Snake looked for a security camera. When he found one, he was relieved to see that its light was off. Nobody was watching. Good.

The doors opened again and the Snake stepped out into a brightly-lit hallway with two other doors, one a stairwell, the other the entrance to the penthouse. Going to the penthouse door, the Snake tested the knob and found it unlocked. Excellent. Turning the knob, the Snake let the door swing open and stepped in.

Chapter Sixty-One

The Snake stepped into a room with cream-colored carpet and yellow walls, fancy furniture and lights that were meant to look like floating white orbs. It was a different sort of upper-class living than what the Snake had grown up in, but it was still upper-class living, and the man who lived in it had about as much conscious as the Snake's father, making him wonder whether there was some sort of correlation between fancy living and being a total psychopath. Seeing a poker in the granite fireplace, the Snake grabbed it, letting his rage flow into his grip and into the handle.

The Snake moved through the penthouse, searching for its occupant. He had a feeling that whoever had bought Allison would probably keep her near them, too afraid to let Allison out of his or her sight. There was no one in the living room or the ornate, marble kitchen. Moving into the hallway, the Snake looked into a large playroom and entertainment center with a home theater, and then into a small bedroom that was probably a spare. Still nothing.

Moving up the stairs, the Snake found himself in a dark hallway, with a single lit room at the end, the door left slightly open. The Snake crept along the hallway, listening for any signs of life. As he got closer to the door, the Snake heard soft opera music, the patter of water from a shower head...and crying. The Snake stopped in his tracks and listened hard. Someone was sobbing and it sounded like a feminine voice.

Allison!

The Snake resumed creeping along the hallway, raising the poker up above his head. Looking in through the crack in the door, the Snake saw Allison on a bed, her limbs tied to the posts with leather bonds. She was still wearing the golden bikini, but somebody had put a dog collar around her neck, with a chain that had been slung over the headboard. Her face was tearstained, and the look of sadness and fear on her face was enough to break hearts. The Snake wanted to walk in and save her, but then the sound of the shower stopped and the Snake paused, waiting to see what would happen.

A minute passed without anything happening. The Snake was about to walk in and get Allison when a large, barrel-chested man appeared, fully naked and with a hard-on. The Snake looked at his face and saw he was wearing a mask, the transparent kind that somehow managed to obscure features through its thickness and curves. The man hummed along with the opera as he walked towards the bed, making little motions with his fingers like a conductor.

The Snake watched as Allison started struggling with her bonds, trying to scoot as far away from the man in the mask as possible. The man only watched and laughed. "Go ahead and struggle." he said, his voice reminding the Snake of a shark, dark and gravelly with a predatory edge to it. "It excites me. And soon, you won't have the energy to struggle. You'll be too busy pleasing me."

"I—I'll scream." said Allison as the man leaned over her.

"Go ahead, I like screamers," the man replied, putting a hand on Allison's shoulder, trailing a finger downward towards her breasts. "Nobody else is in the building anyway, so we won't be interrupted. And guess what else? I do all my important work from this apartment, so I'll be home with you most of tomorrow, and the next day, and the day after, and the day after that. That's plenty of time to train you to my liking."

The man bent down over Allison, lifted the mask off his face, and licked her belly, moaning with pleasure as his tongue slid from one side to the other. Allison gave a terrified scream.

The Snake felt his blood rise and he knew he couldn't wait any longer. He had to act.

Chapter Sixty-Two

The Snake kicked the door and ran in, the poker held high above his head. The man with the mask looked up and had enough time to say, "What the—?" before the Snake hit him with the poker, knocking the mask off his face and into a lamp next to the bed. Before the man could react, the Snake hit him again, this time in the temple. The man fell over, his body shaking the room as it hit the ground and causing the stereo system to skip. Standing over the man, the Snake hit him again and again in the head and back, not stopping until his arms began to tire.

Dropping the poker to his side, the Snake kicked the man lightly in the head. The man's head lolled to the side, but he showed no other reaction. Satisfied, the Snake threw the poker into a corner and turned around to face the bed.

At first, the Snake was so glad to see Allison he couldn't think of anything else. But then he saw she was crying again and trying to scoot away from him and he realized she was afraid of him. "P-Please." she said, looking at him with wide eyes. "D-Don't h-h-hurt m-me."

For a moment, the Snake had no idea how to soothe her, to let her know it was alright. Then, because he couldn't think of anything else, he took off his mask and said, "Al."

Allison stopped struggling and stared at him like she was staring at a ghost. Then her expression changed to disbelief. "No way." she whispered.

"Way." He said, smiling at her. Tears, flowing from her eyes, Allison said his name, his real name, and whispered, "You came. You actually came."

The Snake went to Allison and undid the collar around her neck. Throwing the collar and chain away from the bed, the Snake went to work on Allison's arms, undoing the knots around her bonds in seconds. Once Allison's wrists were free, he moved down to her feet, moving as fast as he could without becoming sloppy.

As Allison slipped her feet free of the leather restraints that had held her, the Snake extended his hand and pulled her off the bed. "We should move," said the Snake, speaking with his regular voice instead of his Russian accent. "Look, you grab a coat or something while I take care of this guy—whoa!"

Before the Snake could finish, Allison threw herself into his arms and started sobbing, wrapping her arms around his middle and crying against his chest. The Snake knew that they had to get out of the penthouse and quickly, but feeling the depth of Allison's fear and relief, he had to pause and return the embrace. "It's okay." he whispered, planting a kiss on top of her head. "I'm here. Everything's going to be alright."

"They told me my dad had died." said Allison, her voice quiet and racked with sobs. "They told me they killed him. I was so scared. I wanted you to come save me. When I was sold to him, I hoped you'd come and save me. And here you are."

Under other circumstances, the Snake might've been happy that Allison had been thinking about him, but at the moment all he could do was worry about her and comfort her. Tipping her chin up to look at him, the Snake kissed her lips and said, "Don't worry, I'm going to get you out of here. You'll be safe from now on. I'll protect you. Now go get a coat or something so we can leave—oof!"

Something grabbed the Snake from behind and threw him against the wall, ripping Allison from his arms as he was thrown. Turning around and drawing his gun out, the Snake saw the man with the mask holding Allison in his arms as if he meant to crush her. Allison was looking at him beseechingly, her eyes tearing up with fear again. "So you're her boyfriend, huh?" said the man raspily. "Come to play Prince Charming? Not in my penthouse."

The Snake recognized the man and stared. Finding his voice, the Snake coughed and said, "Yeah, I'm her boyfriend. And you're a sicker man than me."

The Snake couldn't believe who was in front of him, but there he was, holding Allison like he meant to kill her. It was Owen Barlow, a former pro football player that most of New York had loved. But a few weeks ago, Barlow's wife had left him and taken their two daughters with him. Not too long after that, the news came out that he had abused his wife with his fists and his words, and had abused his daughters sexually. According to the police they had a lot of evidence to convict Barlow, though the latter claimed he was innocent and that his wife was "crazy" and "after his money and a name for herself."

The Snake had remembered reading about the story and feeling sorry for the daughters while wishing his mother could've been like Mrs. Barlow. He hadn't realized that Barlow himself was out on bail, or that he had the freedom to go out and take part in an auction of human beings without being noticed by the cops or the press. How had this happened?

Barlow's lips pulled back in a snarl as he noticed the Snake watching him. "Do you know who I am?" he shouted. "My slut of a wife may have humiliated me in front of the nation, but that doesn't mean I can't cream a guy! No one can beat me, because I beat everybody!" The man arms tightened around Allison, who gasped in pain, looking at the Snake with pleading eyes. "Do you know what happens to people who get on the wrong side of me?"

"Of course I know who you are." said the Snake, watching Barlow's body language, looking for signs of weakness. Dammit, the guy was really on guard and any movement would trigger his survival instincts, which would hurt Allison. The Snake would have to be careful how he proceeded and would have to try to find an opportunity to get Allison away from Barlow. In the meantime though, it'd probably be best if he didn't antagonize Barlow.

"I'm sorry that I invaded your home." said the Snake in his most beseeching tone. "I wouldn't have done that if I knew I had to face Owen Barlow."

"Oh really?" said Barlow, his snarl turning into a smile.

"Oh yeah," the Snake answered, lowering his gun a little, trying to appear non-threatening. "You're Owen Barlow, former running back for the Denver Broncos and New York Giants, and winner of four different Super Bowls. You retired three years ago, and now you're on the board of three Fortune 500 companies."

"Actually, it's two companies." said Barlow, his smile becoming a frown again. "I got kicked off the board of the Pepsi Company last week. They didn't like that one of their board members had been accused of crimes that he didn't commit."

"Well, I'm sorry to hear that." said the Snake, trying to sound sympathetic. "And I'm sorry I came into your home uninvited. I mean, you're THE Owen Barlow. God, I can't believe I'm so stupid. I'm supposed to be smarter than to take on a living god!"

"A living god?" said Barlow, his smile returning. "You got that right, kid." Barlow laughed a little. "I am a bit of a living god. And you do seem pretty stupid."

"Of course." said the Snake, trying to keep his panic under wraps. Surely there was an opportunity to get Allison back from this self-obsessed monster—wait a minute. Suddenly the Snake had an idea. For now though, he had to keep stoking Barlow's pride. Clearing his throat, he continued complimenting Barlow.

"Come on! You're Owen Barlow!" said the Snake, gesturing with his free hand at Barlow. "People worship you—and they still should, after the charges get thrown out. Half the guys on the football team at school became football players because they grew up watching you! You can't do anything wrong. Your wife must be looking for a big divorce settlement or something."

Barlow smiled. "You know, you're actually pretty smart, kid." said Barlow. "I'm almost sorry I have to kill you for seeing all this. Who are you, by the way? You know me because everyone knows me, but I don't know you except as this girl's boyfriend." Barlow reached a hand up and stroked Allison's cheek, causing Allison to shudder violently. "Awww," cooed Barlow, seeing Allison shudder. "Don't be scared. I'm not going to hurt you…much."

The Snake felt his anger rise again. Now was the time to strike. "I'm actually pretty famous too," he said, keeping his voice even.

Barlow looked at the Snake, surprised. "Oh?"

"Yeah, I've been in the news lately." the Snake continued, tightening his grip on his gun. "They've been calling me the New York Mafia Killer."

Barlow's eyes widened and he said, "You? You're the New York Mafia Killer? You're really him?"

"Yes I am." said the Snake, his Russian accent creeping in. "By the way, which game did you get that scar on your foot from?"

Barlow glanced down at his feet. "What scar?" he said. The Snake grinned. Barlow worshipped himself. The idea that he'd missed a single imperfection or battle scar was unthinkable for him. And now that the man's attention had been taken away from the threat in front of him, even for a second, the Snake could act.

The Snake lifted his gun and shot a lamp next to the bed, the lamp exploding into twenty different pieces. Barlow and Allison both jumped, Barlow looking surprised while Allison looking twice as scared as before. Slipping the mask onto his face, the Snake fired another bullet into the bathroom, where it ricocheted a few times before embedding itself in the tiles. Barlow and Allison jumped again, and the Snake saw Barlow's grip on Allison loosen even more.

Encouraged, the Snake fired a shot into the ceiling, distracting Barlow and loosening his grip on Allison even more. Seeing his opportunity, the Snake shouted, "Allison! Run!" Allison broke free of Barlow's grip and ran behind the Snake; Barlow looked down and seemed surprised that Allison wasn't there anymore. The giant man looked up again and had enough time to register that Allison was behind the Snake before the Snake fired a bullet into Barlow's head.

Barlow's head leaned back, and the large man rocked on his heels for a moment before falling back against the wall with a loud crash. Striding forward toward Barlow, the Snake fired another shot, and then another, and another, each bullet going into Barlow's body. Each time he fired a shot, Barlow's body flopped a little before continuing its slide down towards the ground. The Snake did not stop firing until he became aware of the lackluster reaction of the trigger as he squeezed it and realized he had run out of bullets.

The Snake stared at the bullet-riddled body of Owen Barlow for a moment before turning to Allison, who was standing a few feet behind him, looking like she was about to collapse from shock and fear. The Snake put his gun in his jacket and walked over to her, opening his arms to embrace her. Allison fell into his arms again, crying loudly as the Snake held her, whispering comforting words for her while he listened for the sounds of sirens and helicopters nearby.

This night was far from over for the both of them.

Chapter Sixty-Three

The Snake allowed Allison to cry a little longer before saying, "We have to go."

Allison looked up at him and said, "Go? Go where?" The Snake looked into Alison's eyes and saw the fear and desperation there. He could see that she'd been horribly traumatized over the past two weeks, and being held captive by Barlow had only worsened it. And even though he'd saved Allison from Barlow, the Snake had a feeling that it hadn't done much to make her feel any safer.

"Somewhere safe," the Snake assured Allison in his regular voice, placing a hand on her cheek. "Nobody will find us or try to hurt you. Don't worry, I'll handle everything. You wait by the front door, okay? I've got some stuff to do in here."

"What are you going to do?" asked Allison.

"I'm going to destroy any evidence we were here." said the Snake, pulling up his mask. "Now you go downstairs and wait for me, okay?"

Allison looked like she wanted to stay by his side, but then she hugged her chest and ran out of the room, her feet making light *tmp! tmp! tmp!* noises on the carpet as she ran. The Snake waited till he could no longer hear her before he pulled his mask back on and took his hunting knife from his jacket. He would have to let the world know that Owen Barlow was more of a monster than they'd previously thought before he destroyed any evidence, that Barlow was enough of the depraved deviant to arouse the wrath of the New York Mafia Killer. But he had to do it before Allison came back to look for him.

Bending his knees and adjusting the position of the body, the Snake plunged the knife into Barlow's chest and carved the first letter, creating the S in four jagged lines. Then he pulled the knife out and stabbed Barlow's chest again, this time creating an N in three lines next to the S. Again, the Snake stabbed Barlow's chest, creating the A, and then the K, and then the E. The Snake had gotten so used to carving the letters he was finished within a minute.

Wiping the blood on the knife off with the bedsheets, the Snake replaced the knife in his jacket and reached for Barlow's head. *So, you wanted to break Allison's neck?* thought the Snake, his right hand on the top of Barlow's head and his left hand on Barlow's chin. *Let's see how you like it!* The Snake twisted and Barlow's neck cracked, the head looking to the left at an awkward angle.

The Snake grabbed Barlow's shoulder and broke that too, then the arm and hand and fingers. When all those were broken, the Snake took the next arm broke the bones in that arm too before moving onto Barlow's chest. The Snake went about destroying Barlow's body in pure silence, remembering how he'd done the same thing to James Sanonia two weeks ago, only with a few slight differences.

After several more broken bones the Snake stood up and admired his work. With all the broken bones and the letters carved onto his chest, Barlow seemed almost more hideous to his eyes. Looking at the mutilated and twisted corpse, the Snake felt a sense of satisfaction. If only he had some time to castrate Barlow like he had Luiso, just for a little shock value.

But like I just said, I don't have enough time. The Snake left the bedroom and walked down the stairs, where Allison was waiting for him wearing an orange and white coat and a worried expression, her fingernails firmly planted between her lips.

"Are you done?" she asked as the Snake walked right past her and headed to the kitchen.

"Not yet." said the Snake, going to a small fridge underneath the counter next to the cabinet he'd spotted when he'd first went exploring the kitchen. "Looks like we're going to need something big to get rid of everything."

"Something big?" Allison repeated.

"Yes," said the Snake, pulling out a bottle of wine from the fridge. "Something big." The Snake uncorked the wine and, starting from outside the front door, poured out the wine, working his way up the stairs and to the bedroom before running out and having to go to the kitchen to grab a bottle of scotch. Then, taking the bottle of scotch, the Snake poured it around the bedroom, on the bed, over the lower half of the body, on the carpet and even in the bathroom.

As the Snake came downstairs, he found Allison sitting on the couch. She looked up at him, her expression more tired than scared now. If the Snake had to guess, he'd say that Allison's fear and adrenaline had worn off and now she was just exhausted from being terrified for so long. "Can we go now?" she asked.

The Snake looked at Allison again, and had the sudden thought that he was forgetting something. What he'd forgotten though, he couldn't say. He felt that if he looked at Allison on the couch long enough, he could figure it out, but even if there was time for it, he didn't want to keep Allison here longer than necessary.

"Sure." said the Snake, extending his hand to Allison, who gladly took it. Lifting herself off the couch with the Snake's help, Allison asked the Snake, "How does alcohol erase evidence that we were here?"

"It's not the alcohol that'll erase the evidence," the Snake explained, leading her to the kitchen and going through the cabinets. Finally the Snake found a wand-type lighter and clicked it on, the flame dancing at the tip of the barrel. "What we do once we light it up will erase the evidence."

"Light it up?"

"Oh yeah." The Snake led Allison out the door, cautioning her to beware of stepping in the alcohol. As they stepped out of the apartment, the Snake bent down and put the tip of the lighter in the wine trail. Immediately the wine lit up, the flame moving quickly out of the reception area and into the apartment.

"Come on," said the Snake. "Let's get out of here."

"Where are we going?" asked Allison.

"Anywhere but here." The Snake pulled Allison to the stairs and led her down, skipping two steps at a time. After more flights than the Snake cared to count, they emerged into the garage, heading towards the Mercedes. Allison became hesitant at the sight of it, but with a little encouragement the Snake managed to get her to go to the car.

"Are we going to use this to get to where we're going?" asked Allison.

"For part of the way." said the Snake, pulling out his bump key and opening the driver door. Unlocking the passenger door for Allison, the Snake slipped into the driver's seat and opened up the cover over the wheel. As Allison slipped into the passenger seat, the Snake twisted one wire over the other and the engine roared to life.

"Where'd you learn to do that?" asked Allison.

"You don't want to know," the Snake replied, pulling out and driving towards the exit. As the grate came into view, the Snake looked around the car before finding a remote clipped to the sun visor, which lifted the grate up and out of sight. Driving out of the garage, the Snake turned left and started heading towards the highway, taking an alternate route as fire trucks came into view.

As the Snake turned onto the highway, Allison said his name and then said, "Can I ask you something?"

"Ask me anything." said the Snake, pulling off his mask.

"What did you mean back there?" Allison looked at him, and the Snake saw a face that didn't want to be lied to. "You told that man...Barlow...you told him that you were the New York Mafia Killer. What were you talking about?"

The Snake blinked when he heard the question. He'd forgotten he had said that in the heat of the moment, too focused on trying to save Allison, but now he remembered. There was no hiding from Allison now what he was. Well, he'd shot a guy in front of her, so she probably had a good idea already what he was. And now that the subject had come up, the Snake felt that might as well tell her the whole truth, or as much as he thought she could take.

The Snake took a deep breath and said, "After you called me two weeks ago, I went to see your father. I thought he might know what was going on, but he...he hadn't even called the police.

He'd been threatened with your death if he called. I told him to call anyway, and he was about to when…when—"

"He was killed." Allison finished. "I know. They told me. While I was being held captive." Allison was silent for a second, and then said, "You saw it, didn't you?" When the Snake nodded, she said, "How did he die?"

"Sniper shot." said the Snake. "I'm sorry."

The car was silent for a little while. Finally Allison said, "What happened after that?"

"I went a little crazy." The Snake looked out the front window, unable to meet Allison's eyes. "I—I started hallucinating or something. I don't know how to explain it, but afterwards…I'd changed. I'd become some sort of…monster, something that could beat the Camerlengos. I'd become the Snake in the Garden of Eden, and I would bring the downfall of the Camerlengos by finding you and destroying the Camerlengos to keep you safe.

"I left home. I started searching for you. I killed members of the Camerlengos, six of them, and the police officer who betrayed you, Kasmet." Allison winced at the sound of Kasmet's name, and the Snake guessed she knew how very close she'd gotten to living as a sex slave for the rest of her life because of that man.

The Snake continued telling Allison his story, telling her in brief and without details about each of his victims. "Every time I killed someone, I got a little closer to you." said the Snake after a while. "It was tough and I was nearly killed once or twice, but I kept searching. And tonight, I found you."

"And you became known as the New York Mafia Killer?" asked Allison.

"That's what they're calling me on the news and in the papers," the Snake replied. "I only called myself that because I didn't think Barlow would recognize me if I told him I was the Snake, or that I carve the word 'Snake' into my victims' chests."

The Snake realized what he'd just said, how it made him look like the freak he was, and wished he could take it back. Allison stared at him for a while, not saying a word. The Snake sat there, feeling himself sweat as Allison continued to stare quietly at him. What did she think about him now? Was she scared of him, or did she actually admire him for what he'd done? Most likely it was the former.

He was about to ask her what was on her mind, even if only to just break the silence, when Allison looked back out the window and said, "That's why you erased the evidence at the apartment. You didn't want anyone to know who you are, or try to find us."

"If they found me, they'd try to stop me," said the Snake, glad she wasn't asking him about his murders. "And if they tried to stop me, then the Camerlengos would find a way to kill me."

"And I might fall back into the Camerlengos' hands," Allison added, shivering at the thought.

"Probably," said the Snake, reaching out and touching Allison's shoulder. Allison didn't shrug it off, but she didn't act like she noticed it either. "So what happened to you? What did they do to you?"

"Are you going to hurt somebody because of it?" asked Allison. Before the Snake could think of an answer, Allison said, "I was brought back to the hotel after they caught me. They wouldn't let me see my father. I was brought to Mr. Camerlengo, and he said that since he'd known me since I was little, he'd let me live if I behaved for a little while. I was so scared when I saw him. Mr. Camerlengo always made me think of a raging bull, just waiting to let loose.

"Anyway, they gave me a change of clothes and sent me to this phone sex service called—"

"Naughty Princess Industries," said the Snake. "I met Carla Scarusco when I was looking for you. She wanted me to tell you that she's sorry she couldn't do more to help you. She's safe, by the way. Probably in California right about now."

"Oh," said Allison. The Snake waited for her to say more, but instead of commenting she went on with her story, "It was nice, I suppose. I mean, I hated having to act like I enjoyed talking dirty or imagine that some old man was spanking me or trying to do an English accent for some Bond geek, but the staff was nice enough, and I stayed in the same apartment as Ms. Scarusco. She called me 'Little A'. I hated that nickname. It annoyed me more than 'Al', especially since I know they weren't calling me 'Little A' because they care about me or anything."

"What happened?" asked the Snake, though he already knew the answer.

"Kasmet." Allison replied, pulling her legs up on the seat and hugging her knees to her chest. "I thought he'd help me, but instead, I ended up in a cell with no human contact. They kept me locked up, I couldn't bathe or change clothes, I was always cold, and I...I had to use the bathroom in a bucket." Allison started to cry, hugging her knees tighter. "And there was this one guy with an earring, I think his name was Joe, he watched me when I used the bathroom. He was a monster. When they made me get ready for the auction, he teased me the whole time and he even...he even kissed me. I didn't think it could get any worse until I saw who bought me."

The Snake gripped the steering wheel tightly and promised that if he ever found the man with the earring, he'd put him through nine circles of Hell before he killed him. "Well, you're safe now." said the Snake, extending his arm to hug Allison. "You're not with them anymore. You're with me."

Allison was silent for a while, not reacting as the Snake pulled her against him. After some time had passed she asked, "What happens now?"

The Snake was at a loss for an answer. Finally he just said, "Let's just get somewhere safe for now", and left it at that. They did not say another word to each other until the Snake stopped and got out of the car, and only then to notify Allison that they were changing cars. Allison didn't say a word.

Chapter Sixty-Four

The Snake led Allison up the stairs of his apartment building, holding her hand tightly in his. Allison held onto his arm, looking around warily at every closed door as if whoever or whatever was behind each door was only there to hurt her. The Snake was talking incessantly, trying to get Allison's mind off of her experience and make her feel less afraid. He wasn't sure if it was working, but at least they were getting close to his floor.

"I had to leave home, because I couldn't search for you if it somehow endangered Ruby, and because I didn't trust my dad to let me do what I had to do. But this place works well for me. Only a few people know I'm here, and I really don't think they'll tell anyone. Plus the landlord is easy to bribe, so I can keep Linda here and not get background-checked or anything. Well, here we are."

The Snake took out his key and opened the door, letting it swing open with a soft creak. As the door opened, a giant grey form shot out and jumped onto Allison, placing two massive paws on her shoulders and licking her face with a wet, pink tongue. Allison gave a loud shriek, which quickly turned into giggles. "Linda!" she said, laughing. "It's good to see you too." Allison hugged the giant dog, who whined happily as she rubbed her head against Allison's face, poking out her tongue every few seconds. The Snake watched with a smile on his face, letting Allison and Linda get reacquainted. At least the dog was getting Allison's mind off her problems.

Finally Linda stepped down from Allison's shoulders and turned to greet her master, stepping on his shoulders and rubbing her head against his head. "Oh now you remember me?" said the Snake with a laugh, rubbing her head back. "I'm happy to see you too. Come on, *sobaka*." Linda loped back into the apartment, followed by Allison and the Snake, who locked the door behind them as they stepped in.

The Snake gestured at the small apartment and said, "It's not much, but it's cozy." The Snake took Allison's hand in both of his, pulling her attention from the apartment to him. "And it's safe," the Snake added, letting go of one hand to stroke Allison's hair. "Nobody will hurt you here. I'll protect you."

For a moment Allison didn't say anything for a moment. Then she said, "May I use your shower? I-I'm kind of tired and I want to go to bed."

The Snake was surprised by the request but said, "Okay," anyway. Leading her to the bedroom, the Snake pointed to the adjoining bathroom and said, "You can leave your clothes wherever. If you want me to I'll get rid of them the first possible chance. And you can use some of my clothes until I can get you something else to wear."

"Th-Thanks," she replied, not looking at him. "I'd like that."

An uncomfortable silence settled in, and finally the Snake said, "Well, I'll give you some privacy. Call me if you need anything."

"Thanks." said Allison, still not looking at him. "I will."

The Snake left the bedroom, telling in Linda in Russian to stay with Allison. The big dog jumped onto the bed, laying her head over the edge to look at Allison as the Snake closed the bedroom door behind him. Going to the kitchen and pouring himself a glass of water, the Snake took a big gulp and looked back at the bedroom door.

Poor Al, the Snake thought, thinking of her face. That face had had more than exhaustion in it, including pinches of fear and wary alertness mixed in. What was she afraid of now that she was free? The Camerlengos? The Snake? Both? For once the Snake couldn't tell what she was thinking, and that frightened him, but even more frightening to him, the Snake couldn't tell how she felt about him and about being free thanks to him.

She's been through so much, the Snake thought, taking another gulp of water. *Some people might not be able to take all that.* And for the Snake, wondering if even Allison, who was normally so strong and stubborn, would be broken down by her experience was the most frightening thing of all.

Chapter Sixty-Five

Allison waited till her boyfriend had left the room and closed the door behind him before she shrugged off the coat and took off the gold bikini, throwing it on the ground without a second thought. *I'll be happy if I never see another skimpy bikini again!* Allison thought, heading into the bathroom and turning on the lights and fan. *Especially a gold one.*

Allison waited for the water to warm up before stepping in, letting the hot water roll over her still-freezing legs and the rest of her body. The water was almost scalding to her skin, but that was fine. She wanted to feel the heat. She'd been cold the whole time she'd been kept captive in that warehouse, and they'd only let her shower once, for a few minutes before the photo session.

As the falling droplets of water warmed her body and the drumming of the shower water hitting the tiles and the humming of the fan blended into a hypnotic rhythm, Allison felt some of the tension in her body melt away. Hugging her chest, she looked up at the shower head and thought about her boyfriend, who was just a few feet away from her, wearing clothes he'd killed people in, gloves with which he'd held weapons he'd used to carve words into people's chests—

And he touched me while wearing those clothes. Allison shivered at the thought of it. *He touched me with clothes that might've touched some dead guy, probably several dead guys. And he acts like he doesn't care!*

Allison leaned her forehead against the shower wall and started to cry again, letting the water from the shower fall on her back. What had happened to him? Had he really gone off the deep end and become a serial killer, like the ones out of those awful movies of his? She'd always considered his interest in horror movies and thriller novels a little morbid—after all, wasn't there something wrong about being drawn to movies and books where the main thrill came from some creep killing people?—but she'd put up with it because he put up with her tastes and other than that, they got along great.

But to think he'd be acting out those movies just to find her! And to admit it without any guilt or remorse. Not even any embarrassment! His take on it was total calm. It terrified her that he'd take life like that, and not care about it like he wouldn't care about killing off a minor character. In fact, it was the part of him that terrified her the most.

I can't stay here. Allison decided, standing up straight. *He said he'd protect me, but what if I do something he doesn't like, or if I get in his way? He could torture me. He could kill me! As soon as I get the chance, I'm going to bolt from this place and go—*

Allison stopped herself. Go? Go where? She had no family to turn to, and her boyfriend knew all her friends, so if she went to one of them, she might be putting them in danger. Perhaps if she went to the police—

Allison stopped herself again. *If I even get to the police, how can they guarantee my safety?* she wondered, falling to her knees and hugging her breasts like she did after the photo shoot, shaking. *What if there's someone like Officer Kasmet there, someone who's working for Mr. Camerlengo? They'll hurt me, they'll kill me, they'll make sure no one ever finds my body!*

Allison pushed that train of thought aside and tried to think of something else she could do. Perhaps if she went to a hotel or a youth hostel to hide and tried to formulate a plan—no good, she had no money and besides, she had no idea where to find a hotel she could hide in with no questions asked. Perhaps if she went to a church and asked for sanctuary...would they even believe her? If she told them she'd been kidnapped by the Camerlengo Family and then rescued by her boyfriend, who also happened to be the New York Mafia Killer, whose sole purpose in killing God only knew how many people was to save her? Just listening to it in her head, Allison admitted it sounded crazy. She'd get sanctuary, but then she'd get sent to a mental hospital. And then maybe they'd send the police to interview her, just in case she knew something. More likely though they'd come to see if she knew something she shouldn't.

She was stuck with him. She was stuck with her boyfriend, the Snake in the Garden of Eden, the New York Mafia Killer, who carved his name into the chests of his victims! And if she tried to leave, she risked being stalked by both him and the Camerlengos. It felt like she'd been thrown from the fire, into the frying pan, and was now being cooked rotisserie style in an oven!

Suddenly there was a knock on the door, causing Allison to jump where she sat. "Al, you alright in there?" It was his voice, tinged with concern that she wished she could trust as sincere. "You've been in there nearly half an hour."

"Er—yeah, I'm okay." Allison called back, trying to not sound as startled as she was. "I'll be out in a sec, okay?"

"'Kay." he replied. "Oh, and I put some clothes of mine on the bed next to Linda. You can mix and match or whatever, I don't care."

"Okay. Thanks." said Allison, standing up shakily. After she was sure that he was gone, she turned off the water and grabbed a towel off the rack. Once she'd dried herself off, Allison wrapped the towel around her middle and peeked outside the door. The room was empty, save for Linda snoozing on the bed. The jacket she'd stolen from Barlow's apartment and the gold bikini were no longer in the room. Stepping out of the bathroom and turning off the lights and the fan, Allison went to the bed, where several T-shirts, sleep shorts and a few other items of clothing had been left for her. Going through the pile, Allison selected a pair of grey sleep pants and a yellow T-shirt and put them on.

When she'd returned the towel to the bathroom and had put the extra clothes on top of a cabinet, Allison opened the door, where she found him looking at something on his smartphone. He was also wearing different clothes than before, a pair of nay-blue sleep pants and a black wife-beater. There was almost no trace of the serial killer that had appeared in Barlow's apartment, which both relieved and scared her at the same time.

Clearing her throat, Allison said, "I'm out."

Looking up, her boyfriend put his phone down and said, "Alright. If you'll just let me wash up, we can all go to bed." he said, as casually as if this was the most normal night of all. "I'll take the couch, and you can have Linda stay with you if you want to. Just warning you though, you might wake up with her paw on your face."

Despite herself, Allison found herself laughing a little. "Yeah sure." she said. "No problem."

Her boyfriend went into the bathroom while Allison crawled into the bed, letting the thick, comfortable sheets wrap around and warm her. Linda yawned as Allison slid her legs next to the large dog, but other than that, she did not stir.

A minute later he came out of the bathroom, looking directly at her. Allison was afraid he might insist on something from her, maybe ask her to do something as a thank-you for saving her. Instead he said, "Well, if you need anything, I'll be on the couch. Don't hesitate to ask me. Okay?"

"Um…sure." said Allison. "I'll let you know. Thanks."

He nodded and turned to leave the room. As Allison watched him go, she felt an overwhelming anxiety well up in her. As the door was about to close behind him, Allison called out, "Wait!"

The door stopped, and her boyfriend poked his head back in. "Yeah?" he asked

Allison didn't know why she'd stopped him. She opened her mouth to say, "Nothing, forget about it", but instead what came out was, "Will you stay with me?" As soon as she'd asked it, Allison realized what she had said and wondered why she said it.

By the door, her boyfriend was looking at her with a look she knew all too well, the one where he was studying her body language, where every curve of an expression and every shift of the body were up for study and dissection. How much could he tell from that look alone? Could he tell how freaked she was by her situation, or how she had no idea why she asked him to stay with her? Most importantly, could he tell how vulnerable she was, how everything around her scared her and she had no idea if she was truly safe or not?

Finally he said, "Okay," and closed the door behind him. Sliding on top of the covers, he reached over and pulled her towards him, much to Allison's surprise. "This okay?" he asked.

"Y-Yeah." she answered, feeling less scared than expected and even less...vulnerable? How was that even possible? "This is just fine."

Her boyfriend reached over and turned off the lamp next to the bed, bathing the room in total darkness. Allison felt his arm encircle her again, and a kiss on top of her head. "It's okay, Al." he whispered. "You're not with them anymore. You're with me. I'll keep you safe, so you don't have to worry about them."

Strangely, his words actually made Allison feel slightly better. Then she realized, as much as she was scared of him now, he still made her feel safe. He loved her, and he would do anything to protect her. And right now, as scared as she was, she needed that love and protective feeling to allow her to to get some sleep and to hold onto her sanity. Allison leaned into his arms and rested her head against his chest, her ear resting right above his heart, which was beating with a fast *th-thump, th-thump*. Allison wondered if that meant he was nervous too, even if for entirely different reasons.

My only source of safety and security is my serial killer boyfriend, Allison thought, listening to his heartbeat. *And I'm relying on him to scare away boogeymen in his bedroom. How screwed up is that?*

Even so, Allison didn't try to move out of his arms, and slowly she found exhaustion overtaking her fears, finally allowing her to drift off to sleep.

Chapter Sixty-Six

Outside the apartment building, Uri Denikin lit up a cigarette and walked back to the blue Audi waiting two blocks down from where he stood. As he approached, he saw his surveillance partner and good friend Anton waiting for him, also smoking a cigarette. Anton saw him coming and sat up off the hood of the Audi and ambled over to him. "What news?" asked Anton in Russian.

"It was some kid." said Uri, referring to the driver of the minivan they'd been tasked to tail, the same driver who'd dumped the minivan, had managed to sneak into an expensive high-rise apartment building, and then leave with an expensive Mercedes, later dumping it and getting into a beat up Volkswagen with some girl. The driver and the girl had later dumped the Volkswagen a few blocks away from the apartment building that Uri had just snuck out of. "The person we were chasing was some kid. He couldn't have been more than twenty. Same for his girlfriend."

"Are you kidding me?" asked Anton.

"Does this face look like it is kidding to you?" Uri replied, blowing out smoke from his nostrils. "Why do you ask?"

"I was listening to the news after you left to follow that guy and his girlfriend." Anton explained, pointing behind him to the blue Audi. "That building the guy snuck into? There was a big fire there after we left. That newswoman my brother's so in love with, Candace Berman? She says that police who arrived at the building are also working on the New York Mafia Killer case."

Uri's nostrils flared at the mention of the New York Mafia Killer. The serial killer whose modus operandi resembled methods used in the past my Russian families, and that had drawn attention to their own operation. This had made the New York Mafia Killer a source of controversy in the organization. On the one hand, some more conservative members were angered that an outsider would try to imitate them, especially since it was unknown whether or not he was really Russian, and that he might lead to more police investigations of the organization and maybe even reprisals from other families. On the other hand, there were those who thought that the New York Mafia Killer might be doing the family a hidden favor, weakening the power of the Camerlengos and giving the organization an unexpected boost in power and wealth. Uri was more of the conservative opinion, so he was wary of the New York

Mafia Killer, and the fact that he might've been following the serial killer himself without even realizing it was almost mind-boggling.

"Are they sure?" asked Uri, leaning closer to Anton. "Are they certain it's him?"

"No one's certain of anything, so don't go getting your gun and teaching the boy a lesson." Anton answered.

"Let us call the boss, then." Uri suggested. "He'll make the final call."

Anton nodded. "I'll make the call," he said, and pulled out his cell phone. Flipping it open, he speed-dialed a number and brought the phone to his ears. A moment later someone picked up, and Anton said, "Sir, I have news."

Somehow, Uri had a feeling something big was going to happen.

PART FOUR

ALLIANCE

Chapter Sixty-Seven

"Why is there so much press here?" asked Harnist, leaning forward in his seat. "We haven't even begun investigating yet."

"I'm not sure," said Murtz, turning off the engine a block from the building. "But whatever the reason, it must be a big one."

Harnist and Murtz jogged to the police tape, ducking underneath it and heading into the building before they could be hailed by the journalists surrounding the front entrance.

"Hey Agent Fallmouth!" said Murtz, running up to the familiar face. "Why is the press already on our front porch? We only just got notified that this guy is the latest victim!"

"Do you know who this guy is?" asked Agent Fallmouth.

" No, we don't" said Harnist, pulling out his phone and unlocking the touch screen. "I only just got the email that was sent as we were pulling up—oh shit."

"What?" asked Murtz, looking at Harnist.

"I just saw the name of our vic." Harnist replied, looking up from the screen. "It's Owen Barlow."

"The football player who allegedly beat his wife and molested his daughters?" said Murtz, eyebrows raised.

"Didn't need to leave an ID in the victim's mouth." Fallmouth commented, looking up towards the top floor of the apartment building. "That face is famous enough."

"Goodness," said Murtz. "This is out of character for our perp though. There's no obvious connection to the Camerlengo or any other family. Could it be a copycat?"

"If it is, he's incredibly well-informed," said Fallmouth. "Come inside, I'll show you."

"Yeah, let's get inside." said Harnist. "Before the press hears something they shouldn't."

Fallmouth led them to the elevators inside the front lobby, pressing for the top floor of the building. As the elevator hummed upwards, Fallmouth got them up to speed on the investigation. "Call came in after midnight about a fire on the top floor of this building from a couple driving home from their anniversary dinner. When first responders put out the fire, they found the body, and saw the bullet wounds. And yes, I said bullet wounds. There were the usual broken bones and the carving on the chest, but there are multiple bullets, and the ones that didn't get burned from the fire have no burns around the entry wounds, meaning our perp shot this guy from a few feet away. And get this, there are a few other shots around the room, meaning the killer fired several bullets before he finally shot Barlow."

"Anything else? "asked Harnist.

"You mean besides the usual chances of finding some good evidence?" Fallmouth replied. "The CSU teams are just happy that most of the first floor wasn't burned to a crisp. And does it seem unfair to you that this guy throws around footballs and molests his kids and he has two floors in his apartment? Meanwhile, yet we can just barely make rent while protecting our fellow citizens. Where's the justice in that?"

Before either Harnist or Murtz could give an answer, the elevator doors opened into a large hallway, the door to the one room on this floor open wide with the sounds of camera shutters and busy agents coming through. As Murtz and Harnist entered, the first thing they were struck by was the smell of burnt carpet and another foul stench that was wafting to them from underneath the smell of burnt carpet. CSU techs were around the room, taking photos and shining ultraviolet lights on every unburned surface.

"Our guy used alcohol from the minibar." Fallmouth explained as he handed Murtz and Harnist two pairs of gloves and led them inside. "Used about two or three different kinds of drink to start a trail from outside the hallway, all the way across the living room to the stairs, and up the stairs to the master bedroom, where the real inferno was waiting. He wanted time to get away."

"Any cameras?" asked Murtz.

"Near the front door and in the elevator, but they haven't been activated yet. This building's actually not supposed to be open yet. The only reason Barlow's here is because his company owns the building, so he has access and the penthouse all to himself." Fallmouth started climbing the stairs, speaking as he gestured for Harnist and Murtz to follow. "As best we can tell, our perp left the building after he killed Barlow, stole his Mercedes, used it as a getaway ride. We've got uniforms canvassing for it now, though I don't think we'll have long to wait till we find it."

"Has anything been found connecting Barlow to the mafia?" asked Harnist.

"I don't think so, but ever since that story broke out about his wife and daughters, I'm not sure what to think." Fallmouth replied. "It's still early though, so we might find something. Heck, we already found some leather shackles and a collar and chain, so that's pretty telling in itself."

"Not to mention disturbing." Murtz remarked.

"That too." said Fallmouth. "Well, here we are."

The odor that had been an undertone in the living room became an intolerable stink in the master bedroom, the scent of bad meat burning and lying out for all to smell, and Murtz and Harnist had to take a moment to get used to it. As they stepped into the bedroom, they saw that the source of the burning-meat smell was the half-burned body of Owen Barlow lying against the wall. Standing over Barlow was Dr. Mohawk, examining the body and muttering under his breath as he wrote down notes on a clipboard.

"Rather terrible stuff to be woken up for in the middle of the night, isn't it?" said Dr. Mohawk as he noticed Harnist and Murtz. "This is the sort of stuff that makes me want to switch jobs."

Harnist and Murtz looked at the body and couldn't help but agree: the body was burned up to the chest, everything below blackened and charred like wood in a fireplace. The body above the chest wasn't much better off, with bloody bullet wounds from the chest and head as well as disjointed and twisted arms and shoulders.

"Is it the same guy?" asked Harnist. "Or is it a copycat?"

"Do I look like a mobile CSU lab?" replied Dr. Mohawk. "As far as I can tell, this is our same freak. Forty-five millimeter bullets, *zamochit*-style torture, the same sort of handwriting on the chest. It's just the multiple bullets and the victim that doesn't make sense. Once I get a look at the bullets back at the lab, I'll know more. But you know what it means if this is the same guy, right?"

"That Owen Barlow had some sort of connection to the Camerlengo family." Murtz replied. "Otherwise, why go after a disgraced football player who was likely to get sent to jail for assault and rape?"

"Maybe there's another reason why he was killed by the Snake killer?" Harnist offered, giving a little shrug. "I mean, what do we know this guy? The only evidence he leaves is the evidence that he was here and that he killed the vic. He could have had a different reason for killing Barlow, but didn't feel the need to change his MO for it. And you've been saying you've felt like you've been missing something."

Murtz look troubled but murmured "True" anyway.

Suddenly Fallmouth came in, his phone on his ear. "The Mercedes's been found." he said. "A couple of juvenile delinquents were about to take it for a joyride before we found it. Said they found it by the side of the road with the doors unlocked and the key in the ignition. They've been taken in for statements and we're checking out traffic cams to confirm their story. The arresting officer doesn't think any of them is the New York Mafia Killer. A CSU team is on its way to check it out just in case. Oh and get this: they found a hair downstairs on the sofa."

"A hair?" said Murtz.

"That's more than usual." said Dr. Mohawk as his assistant helped him put Barlow's body in a body bag.

"Exactly, Doctor." said Fallmouth, nodding at the medical examiner. "And get this: it's long, straight and red. Barlow's hair is short, curly, and brown, and his wife's shoulder-length and blonde.

So are the daughters. And the furniture was delivered after Barlow made bail two weeks ago, so it had to have been left here recently. It could be connected to our murder."

"Or it could be a coincidence." said Harnist. "Maybe Barlow had a prostitute here or something the other night to give him the girlfriend experience. But yeah, let's hope it leads somewhere."

Dr. Mohawk wheeled the body out of the room, and as she watched it go, Murtz hoped that the hair led to something. She also hoped that the CSU team would be able to find evidence connecting Barlow to organized crime as well. Otherwise, Murtz had no idea how this connected to her profile, or if her profile was even anywhere near correct. Once again, she had that sinking feeling she was missing something vitally important, and she wished she knew what.

Chapter Sixty-Eight

The Snake heard voices speaking softly and his eyes shot open, wondering if someone was in the apartment. Sitting up in bed, Allison started next to him, the remote control to the television falling from her hands. "Oh, you're awake." she said, a hand over her heart.

The Snake looked at her and then at the television, where near the bottom of the screen, the headline NEW YORK MAFIA KILLER TARGETS SCANDALIZED FOOTBALL PLAYER. On the screen, Candace Berman was narrating a summary of what had been found by police and released to the media, which wasn't much. After finishing the summary, she began speaking on the public's reaction to the New York Mafia Killer and his latest kill. Berman was trying to make it sound horrifying and tragic, but the Snake could tell she was enjoying every minute of this.

"She's a typical reporter," the Snake commented.

"What?" said Allison, still looking at him with a startled expression on her face.

"Candace Berman." The Snake pointed at the screen with his thumb, where the woman in question was still reporting. "She's trying to make it sound like I'm a monster, but her shoulders are a little too relaxed to be anywhere close to angry. She's happy that I killed Barlow, because it means her story is going to get bigger."

"Oh." said Allison. There was a silence, during which the Snake checked the clock. It was just seven in the morning, yet it still felt like night. The Snake wanted to go back to sleep. He'd already gotten up once during the night to retrieve his gun, knife and mask from the front room right after Allison had fallen asleep, and another time to get something to drink because his throat had been dry, during which Linda had gotten up and wanted to take a walk. He'd wanted to sleep next to Allison like a real couple for so long, and now that it had happened, he felt like he hadn't really been given a chance to savor it. He knew that it was selfish to think about such things after Allison had been through so much, but he really wanted to go back to sleep with Allison in his arms and—

The Snake became aware that Allison was talking to him and returned his gaze to her. "I'm sorry?" he said.

"I asked...er...what did you do to the...to the people...the people you—"

"The people that I killed?" guessed the Snake. Allison nodded. The Snake wondered how he should best respond before saying, "Are you sure you want to know about that?"

"Y-Yes." said Allison, but the Snake saw her blink several times and how forced her smile seemed. Allison noticed the Snake looking at her and fell back against her pillow, turning over so that he couldn't see her face. "You know what? Never mind." she said. "I'm not sure I want to know."

"You know that's not going to work, right?" said the Snake, rolling his eyes.

"What's not going to work?" asked Allison, still not looking at him.

"Come on Al." said the Snake, reaching over to her. "You're talking to the person who can't be lied to—Allison?"

As the Snake tried to put a hand on Allison's shoulder, Allison gave a violent shudder, and curled up into a ball. She almost reminded the Snake of a small animal trying to seem inconspicuous. The Snake withdrew his hand, confused. Why would Allison do that? Unless…

"Al?" said the Snake, hoping he was wrong. "Are you afraid of me?"

Allison turned over to look at him. The Snake was shocked to see tears in her eyes. "Why shouldn't I be?" she said, struggling to keep her voice even. "You killed eight people! There's someone the news doesn't even know about! You said it yourself, didn't you?"

"Allison, I—" The Snake broke off, listening intently. Had he just heard the door?

Allison saw the expression on his face and said, "What's wrong?"

"Shush!" said the Snake, putting a finger to his lips. He listened, and then he heard the front door open with a soft creak. Allison and the Snake looked at each other. Allison looked terrified while the Snake wore the face of a beast whose territory had been breached by a predator. At the foot of the bed Linda woke up and began to growl, standing up so that she faced the door.

"Linda." the Snake whispered, speaking quietly enough that only the dog could hear him. Linda stopped growling and looked at her master, as if imploring him to let her attack. The Snake gestured to the bathroom with a hand and whispered something to her in Russian. Without a sound Linda padded over to the bathroom, standing in the doorway as if to block it.

"Allison." the Snake whispered, looking at her. "You go wait in the bathroom with Linda. I'm going to go see what this is about."

"But I—!" Allison tried to protest, but before she could the Snake had reached for his mask and gun on the bedside table and had put the mask on while turning off the gun's safety. Seeing the gun and the mask, Allison closed her mouth and slipped out of bed to join Linda in the bathroom, closing the door to sit in the dark.

With Allison and Linda in the bathroom and out of sight, the Snake reached a foot off the bed and onto the bare floorboards, putting his toe first to test for creaks. When the wood didn't creak, the Snake put his whole foot on the ground, and then he put the other foot down. Slowly he walked towards the closed door, putting his big toes first to softly test the floorboards for creaking like he'd seen soldiers and police do in movies. When he was at the door, he slipped to the other side of the doorframe, reached for the door handle, and hiding behind the wall, opened the door.

The Snake waited beside the door, expecting a barrage of bullets to pass through the door. Instead he heard low whispers, too low for him to make out clearly, yet something about the whispering triggered something in his brain, like there was something in the whispering that he should recognize and understand. Ignoring the bell that was ringing exasperatingly in the back of his head, the Snake counted to three and jumped through the doorway and into the main room.

Nothing happened. No bullets, no knives, no shouting voices. Instead, the Snake saw three men standing in the kitchen. The one on the left looked cautious and weary, the one on the right stuck his head out from underneath the kitchen counter like he'd been caught with his hand in a cookie jar, and the one in the middle, a large, jovial man with thinning hair and a stubbly beard, regarded the Snake with amused detachment.

"Well, aren't you cautious." said the large man with a Russian accent. "But then again, I knew you would be. You are the New York Mafia Killer, after all."

Chapter Sixty-Nine

The Snake stared at the large man, who was leaning against the kitchen counter as if he owned the place. The Snake's eyes flicked between the two men on either side of him, who were standing like they were ready to jump in front of the large man at a moment's notice. *He must be the leader.* thought the Snake, his eyes focusing on the large man again. *If he's wounded, they will have to do their best to make sure he gets treatment. Killing me will become secondary. I'm glad I remembered to reload the magazine while Al was in the shower.*

The Snake cleared his throat and said with his Russian accent, "Who the hell are you and what are you doing here?"

The large man's eyes widened, as well as the eyes of the two men who flanked him. However unlike his two friends, the large man burst out laughing. "Now *that* is a Russian accent." he said, holding a hand to his gut. "I mean, I know now you're an American, but that accent of yours is amazing. You could easily pass for a native on the streets of Moscow."

"I'm flattered." said the Snake flatly. No wonder he'd thought he recognized something in the whispers he'd heard from the door. They were speaking in Russian. "Now answer my question and tell me who you are!"

"Ah yes, forgive me." said the large man, still smiling. "Where are my manners? My name is Nikolai Scherbakov. I don't suppose you've heard of me?" When the Snake didn't answer, the large man Scherbakov just nodded as if he understood and said, "Well, let's just say I like to compete with the Camerlengo Family."

The Snake raised his eyebrows, suspicious and surprised. Did this man just say he competed with the Camerlengos? As in—

"Yes, I head a... a certain organization with questionable business practices." said Scherbakov. "Of course, I never deal in the sex trade. You Americans treat your prostitutes with such disdain. In the country of my fathers, prostitutes are noble beings, women of valor. I don't treat them like products like Mr. Camerlengo."

"But you're a rival of his?" said the Snake, curious.

"Rival is too great a term for my organization at the moment." Scherbakov replied. "My family is allowed to exist because it is convenient for the Camerlengos to have rivals whom the police and federal agents can investigate, and it is convenient for those families to have us so they cannot be investigated. But yes, I compete occasionally with Mr. Camerlengo. And it seems I've had a new opportunity to compete with him lately, thanks to you."

"Me?" said the Snake. "What did I do?"

"What did you do? Ha!" Scherbakov's smile was so big the Snake wondered if it would just pop off of his face. "You've put the criminal underworld in a frenzy. Naturally we've been asked if we put out a hit on the Camerlengos, but we've told them no, and they've found nothing to support that we're lying, so they can't go after us without starting something, which would not be smart with you out there killing random Camerlengo soldiers.

"But do you not see?" said Scherbakov, clapping his hands together for emphasis. "You're garnering my family prestige! You are using Russian *zamochit*! That is enough to put eyes on us. And that can only help our stature."

"Or get you in trouble with another family." the Snake pointed out.

Scherbakov shrugged. "True, this is why I've had all my men be extra careful these past two weeks, in case of unwarranted reprisals upon the family. But I can be optimistic, can't I?"

The Snake was confused. This man's family might be in jeopardy because of the Snake's actions, but he was happy about it? The Snake decided to change the direction of the conversation before he was confused any further and said, "How'd you find me?"

Scherbakov walked around the table and reached for an apple in the fruit bowl without answering the Snake's question. Scherbakov's men looked anxious as the Snake's gun followed the mob boss, but made no move to stop the Snake or cover their boss.

"Ah yes." said Scherbakov finally, taking a bite out of the apple. "That is one of the bigger questions, is it not? How did I find the New York Mafia Killer? Well, it was quite on accident, to tell you the truth: one of my men saw you leaving the auction pick-up site in a minivan and phoned it in. We set a tail on you, and then watched as you went to Owen Barlow's apartment, left in his Mercedes, and then switched it for another car that you dumped about eight blocks north of here, and then as you ran with a young lady on your back to this apartment. It only took listening to the radio to make the connection between the person in this apartment and the murderer of Owen Barlow and seven of Camerlengo's men."

The Snake wanted to point out that he'd actually killed eight, but decided against it. Instead he said, "So why come all the way here? I don't sense any malice towards me, and I doubt that a man such as yourself, Mr. Scherbakov, came all the way here just to praise my contributions to your family or to gloat on how your men found me before the police did."

"Well, before I answer that, I'd like to pose you a question, if I may." said Scherbakov, munching lazily on the apple. "What happened to the young lady my men spotted in your company last night? Is she here in this apartment right now?"

The Snake narrowed his eyes but didn't answer. Why did this man want to know about Allison? And if he kept asking after her, would the Snake have to take him out?

As he was wondering this, Scherbakov's eyes grew wide and he said, "Oh, I see. She is your lover. The Camerlengos were intending to sell her, and you sought to save her from all the pain and misery of being a sex slave. That, my friend, is very noble. Tell me, what would happen if I commanded my men to go look for her in this apartment?"

"Don't you dare touch her!" the Snake shouted, startling Scherbakov's men. Scherbakov just stared at the Snake with the same detached air that he had been exuding since this strange conversation had begun. "Don't you dare try and harm her. If you do, your family will suffer the same fate as the Camerlengos!"

"How dare you!" said one of the bodyguards, reaching into his coat jacket. Before the Snake could point his weapon at him though, Scherbakov raised a hand and said, "Peace, Grigor. There is no need to become violent."

"But sir—!"

"I said no, Grigor." Scherbakov frowned for the first time since the Snake had met him, the wrinkles on his forehead dipping downwards to give his brow an angry-looking scrunch. The bodyguard, whom Scherbakov had called Grigor, practically wilted under the gaze of that frown and took his hand out of his jacket, letting it fall limp to his side.

Satisfied that his subordinate wouldn't disobey him, Scherbakov turned back to the Snake and said, "You are truly in love with this woman. I can tell by how forceful you are, and how adamantly you wish to protect her. You'd even kill for her, though that fact goes without saying."

"Let's not get her involved with this," said the Snake, trying to sound like he wasn't pleading with the man. "I just want her to be happy. I'm pretty sure mob business isn't conducive to happiness."

"You are quite right to say she is scared out of her mind." said Scherbakov, finishing the apple and going to the trashcan to throw the core away. "If the police haven't found her, the Camerlengos may go looking for her to protect their secrets. The only true way to make sure they don't is to erase the Camerlengos, obliterate them completely." Scherbakov stuck his hands in his pockets and sauntered casually over to the Snake, a small grin on his face. "And that my friend," Scherbakov said as he came to stop in front of the Snake's pointed gun, "is where we share a common goal."

The Snake was silent for a moment, too surprised to speak. Finally he lowered his gun, and while the two bodyguards exhaled relief that he wasn't pointing a gun at their boss any longer, he said, "You want us to team up."

Scherbakov nodded, his smile growing wider. "You've already done so much to the Camerlengos and the criminal underworld on your own." said Scherbakov. "Imagine what you could do with my family's resources. We may not be as powerful as the Camerlengos, but we are strong enough. Together, you and I can obliterate the Camerlengos, reduce them to nothing."

"And you can enjoy the power and prestige that they used to have." said the Snake. "But what if I don't want to help you? You know my identity, so what's to keep you from using that as leverage against me?"

"My word that I won't use your identity against you." Scherbakov replied, as if it was the easiest answer in the world to give. "And when a man of my family gives their word, it is not easily broken. In fact, bones break more easily. Of course, you know how easily bones can break, but you get the idea."

The Snake didn't reply, but instead looked over Scherbakov's face and body language, trying to discern if there was a lie in anything he said. As far as the Snake could tell, this man wasn't lying when he said he wouldn't divulge the Snake's identity. At the very least, there wasn't anything from his expression or posture that hinted at betrayal. Still, the Snake didn't know whether or not he should trust this man.

After a moment, Scherbakov sighed and said, "You know what? Why don't you think on it a little while? Let my offer sink in a little bit. I'll even leave you my number. How about that?" Before the Snake could answer, Scherbakov had reached into the pocket of his suit jacket and handed him a tiny card with the initials NS and a phone number with the area code for Brooklyn on it. Without breaking eye contact, the Snake took the card and shoved it into his pants pocket.

An uncomfortable silence followed, after which Scherbakov cleared his throat and said, "Well, I must be on my way. I have a busy day today, you know. Things to do, places to go, people to see. Call me when you've made your decision."

Scherbakov walked away from the Snake and headed for the door, snapping his fingers twice as he did so. The two bodyguards rushed to their boss's sides, looking warily at the Snake as they did. As Scherbakov reached the door, he turned around and said, "Oh, before I forget, I noticed this pile of clothes here by the door. Tell me, does that jacket belong to the late Owen Barlow by any chance?"

The Snake flashed to when he'd left the Denver Broncos jacket and the gold bikini by the front door, intending to take it somewhere to be dumped when he was sure Allison could handle a few minutes alone without him. "Yes it is." said the Snake.

"I'll take it off your hands for you." said Scherbakov, reaching down and gathering up the pile of clothes in his arms. "It wouldn't do to have evidence in your own home."

"You don't have to do that—"

"Oh, but I insist." said Scherbakov, his voice at its friendliest and its most deceitful.

"You touch them and you'll have a hole in your hand." the Snake warned. He wasn't going to let that piece of evidence into Scherbakov's hands. That would be too dangerous.

"I see." Scherbakov replied, looking slightly disappointed. "But please do think on my offer. We could do so much together. Now good day to you, Mr.—"

"Call me Snake." said the Snake, interrupting Scherbakov. "I'd prefer it if you didn't use my real name. After all, you want the serial killer, not the man, right?"

Scherbakov nodded after a second. "True." he said. "Very well then. Good day to you, Snake. I look forward to hearing from you soon."

Scherbakov and his men left, closing the door behind them. The Snake waited until he could no longer hear their footsteps before letting go of the nervous tension that had been building up within him the whole time the mob boss had been in the apartment with him. Taking off his mask, the Snake turned around and to his surprise saw Allison standing in the doorway to the bedroom, tears in her eyes.

Chapter Seventy

Time seemed to hold still while Allison and the Snake looked at each other. The Snake opened his mouth to speak several times, but each time he couldn't think of anything to say and closed it. *She was listening!* the Snake thought, panicked. *She heard that guy Scherbakov offer me a deal! Or I think she did. What did she hear? Does she think we can trust Scherbakov? But then she's scared of me! I should read her body language, maybe then I'll know how she's feeling. Wait, she knows the face I make when I'm trying to read her body language. She'll do what she did earlier and try to hide from me. Goddammit, what am I supposed to do?*

The Snake took a deep breath and opened his mouth again. This time he could actually find his voice to speak. "Allison, I—"

Before the Snake could get any farther Allison was running to him, slipping on the Snake's too-long pajama pants she was wearing as she walked. The Snake dropped his mask and ran to catch her before she fell, hooking his arms underneath her shoulders as she fell forward.

"Al! What's wrong?" When the Snake saw the tears falling down Allison's cheeks, he said, "Al! Why are you crying?"

"I-I'm so sorry!" said Allison, standing up straight and, to the Snake's surprise, wrapping her arms around him, pinning his arms to his side. "I was so scared when you told me you'd lost your—when you had a break with…when you said you'd become a serial killer. I was afraid you'd kill me if I did something you didn't like or if I tried to run away or…"

"Al, I would never hurt you." said the Snake, freeing his arms from Allison's grip and hugging her. "I'm crazy about you."

Allison looked up at him with a surprised face. Catching himself, the Snake said, "That's a bad choice of words, but you get the idea."

Allison gave a small laugh. "Yeah, I do." she said with a sniff. "I get it now. But when I didn't, when I'd just found out what you'd been up to, I…I was just so scared. And then I heard you talking with that man…oh, can you ever forgive me?"

"I already have." said the Snake. "But you do get the prize for cheesiest line I've ever heard outside a movie."

"Huh?" said Allison, confused.

"'Oh, can you ever forgive me'?" the Snake repeated. "Al, I hate to tell you this, but that's in just about every sappy story with a fighting couple I've ever heard—"

"Oh, would you shut up!" Allison stood up on her tiptoes and kissed the Snake, cutting him off. The Snake was surprised for half a second, but then the surprise melted away, leaving behind a happy contentment. Hugging Allison closer to him, he kissed her back, only breaking away when Allison did.

"Why do you do that?" asked Allison, leaning her head against his shoulder. "Why do you tease me and call me 'Al', even though you know I don't like it?"

"I've told you, you're cute when you're annoyed." said the Snake. "That and I think a small part of you likes being teased."

"You're lying."

"No I'm not." said the Snake. "You stand up a little taller and stick your chest out when I tease you and call you Al. It makes me think you like it."

"Either that, or I'm trying to intimidate you and let you know that I don't like that nickname." Allison remarked.

The Snake thought about it for a second and said, "That could be it as well."

They held each other for a while, letting the moment sink in. "Are you hungry?" asked the Snake finally.

"A little. Why, are you?"

"Not as much as Linda probably is." The Snake pointed at the bedroom doorway, where Linda was looking at them like she was waiting to be called. Allison looked back at the bedroom and laughed. "I didn't even realize she was there." she said.

"Let me just feed her and then I'll make you whatever you want for breakfast." said the Snake. "Then I'll see about getting you something to wear."

The Snake broke away reluctantly from Allison and moved to the kitchen, calling to Linda as he did. As he pulled out the bag of dog food and poured it into Linda's bowl, he heard Allison say, "Are you going to take that man's offer?"

The Snake paused in pouring the dog food. Looking up, he saw Allison looking intently at him. "Scherbakov, you mean?" asked the Snake. Allison nodded. Sighing, the Snake said, "I saw nothing in him that said we couldn't trust him. However, that doesn't mean we should." Putting down the bag of dog food, the Snake reached underneath the counter and felt something made out of plastic that hadn't been there before. Pulling it out, the Snake found a small device with a tiny red light. The Snake recognized immediately as a bug.

The Snake crushed it in his hand and threw the pieces into the garbage can. "So that's why that guy was messing around in the cabinet." he said, more to himself than to Allison or Linda.

"I thought he said we could trust him." said Allison angrily. "Why did he do that—?"

"Perhaps that's just business for him." the Snake suggested. "In either case, I'll really have to think about that deal before I decide whether or not I'll take it."

Allison stared at him, her eyes growing wide. "He bugged your kitchen and you're still thinking about taking his deal?" she asked, incredulous.

"Like I said, that bug might just be business for him." the Snake explained, putting a new bowl of water down in front of Linda. "And I didn't see anything untrustworthy in him. Taking a deal with him might just be the thing we need to get rid of the Camerlengos and find ourselves some peace."

"You're still thinking about fighting the Camerlengos?" said Allison. "You've already saved me, why can't you—"

"Stop killing?"

Allison looked away, muttering, "You know that's not what I meant."

"Allison, I want to stop." said the Snake, going to her. "But the Camerlengos are still looking for you. You have secrets they don't want getting out, and I'm not going to have you live in fear for the rest of your life."

"So you're going to—" said Allison, unable to finish her sentence.

The Snake didn't answer, but instead he gave her a long hug before letting go and going to make breakfast.

Chapter Seventy-One

The task force command center was quiet for once, which surprised Murtz. She had expected a lot of conversation on the Snake killer's choice to murder Owen Barlow early last night, but instead she only saw tired faces drinking bad coffee, and wondered if the exhausted investigators had already tossed around enough theories and were too tired to rehash even the most likely theories.

Harnist yawned next to her and whispered, "I wonder what's taking so long to start this meeting." he whispered. "Where's the captain and Gramer?"

"Probably held up by their superiors or reporters or something." Murtz whispered back. "Why are we whispering?"

Before Harnist could shrug and say, "I don't know", the door opened and Patton and Gramer fast-walked in and headed to the back of the room, followed by a technician wearing a TARU jacket who took a seat near the back. As heads turned to watch them, Murtz felt energy pass through the room, as if the two heads of the investigation had done more than a ton of caffeine could do for the members of the task force. Even Murtz felt a little more awake seeing Patton and Gramer standing in front of the entire assembled group of police officers and federal agents.

"Sorry we're late," began Gramer, "but apparently Barlow's wife was in town to pick up stuff from her old home and we thought we'd ask her about her whereabouts last night. Turns out she had nothing to do with the murder: she was speaking late into the night with a psychologist friend. The conversation was still going on when Barlow was killed."

"So there goes the family angle." said an officer in the room.

"Not necessarily." said Patton. "Apparently one of the wife's brothers was in Buffalo for a reunion with some Army buddies, and apparently he's old enough to fit Agent Murtz's profile. We've already sent a unit to Buffalo to interview the brother, and we've got law enforcement in Colorado and Arizona checking on the rest of the family just to make sure nobody made an unexpected trip to New York."

"Now, lab did confirm that the bullets used to kill Barlow were the same ones used to kill the Snake killer's other victims." said Gramer, taking up the thread. "However the bullet's in the abdomen and chest were shot post-mortem after the head shot, which did the killing. There were also some bullets in the walls and ceiling of the bedroom and bathroom. He may have been trying to shoot Barlow, but Barlow was a tricky target."

"Or he could've been doing it to distract Barlow." offered a federal agent. "I played football in high school and college. We're trained not to get distracted by screaming fans or anything going on to the side of the field. It would take a lot to distract a veteran professional like Barlow."

"Like several random shots?" said Harnist, looking at Murtz. "Would he do that?"

"I wish I knew." said Murtz. "We don't have any clue what went down at Barlow's apartment, except that someone had the same gun as our suspect and that he killed Owen Barlow and then lit the apartment up like a bonfire. I suppose it's possible, but there's no way to know definitively."

"There are too many uncertainties with this case." said Gramer, cutting through the growing chatter. "We're still not sure why Barlow was hit by a poker and then shot several times before his bones were broken. It is very confusing."

"We do know something definitively about Owen Barlow, something we didn't know before." said Patton, gesturing to the TARU tech that had come in with them. "I'll let Officer Mehta explain."

The TARU tech stood and strode to the front of the task force, clearing his throat as he got there. "Thanks for having me." he said. "Barlow's tablet device was found in his kitchen at his apartment, thankfully with only a cracked screen. We looked over recent activity on the tablet, and we found something interesting.

Apparently Barlow did have mob ties, but not the type we expected."

"What do you mean, 'not the type we expected'?" asked an officer.

"Apparently Barlow was taking part in one of the Camerlengos' special online auctions." explained the TARU tech. "The family uses a programmer to create an online auction room that's all but impenetrable from the outside. You use a username and password to get in, and then you bid without fear that someone will find you bidding on human beings. It's the new thing for selling valuable illegal goods, with the auction taking place online and the items sold given to the buyers at a different location. After the auction's over, the site destroys itself, leaving barely any trace it was there. The NYPD and the FBI have found these sites occasionally, but have never gotten in, and this is the first time we've found somebody who actually took part in the auction, and it looks like he spent a lot of money on someone."

"Does this mean the killer was in on the auction and somehow used it to find Barlow?" asked an officer.

"It's possible." said Mehta. "He could've also found the programmer and used him to find Barlow, but there's no way to know for sure just by looking at a dead website on a victim's tablet."

"Is it possible that the programmer might be working with the killer?" asked Harnist. "He's worked with others before."

"Yeah, but that was with law enforcement who sympathized with the killer." Murtz pointed out. "If this person is responsible for the trafficking and selling of human beings, then it's much more likely that the killer never went near him, or if he did, he threatened the programmer and then killed him."

"So we have a possible eighth victim?"

"This is mostly theoretical, so let's not start spinning stories we can't prove." Patton interrupted. "What we do know is that Barlow took part in an auction, probably bought a human being, and brought that person to that apartment. The killer followed Barlow, and then killed him."

"How do we know Barlow bought someone?" asked a federal agent.

"We'll explain that in a moment." said Gramer. Turning to Mehta, he said, "Thanks Officer Mehta, you may be seated." The TARU tech nodded and returned to his seat in the back, letting Gramer and Patton take the reins of the meeting again.

"At the crime scene, CSU found a single hair on the couch in the living room." said Gramer, pulling a remote out of his pocket and pressing a button on it. The projector on the ceiling turned on and the wall lit up with an image of the hair in a bag with an evidence label on it. "We ran it through the databases, and actually got a hit from the Army's DNA files. Wait, don't get excited, it's only a familial match."

"Dr. William Langland." said Patton, as Gramer pressed the remote button again and the image changed. On the wall, a blown-up photo of an older man with a greying mustache and a balding head looked with tired eyes out at the task force. "He's a general practice doctor for New York's wealthy, some of whom have rumored or confirmed connections to the mob. We do know he was in the Army, and before that he went to a military academy with Christopher Camerlengo, where the two made a friendship."

"Now, the doctor has been missing for nearly two weeks." said Gramer. "His secretary reported him missing the same day as when James Sanonia's body was found. In addition, he's just past the age on Agent Murtz's profile and he's a doctor, so he'd know how to break bones."

"The hair was a fifty-percent match to Dr. Langland, so most likely it was a child of his." said Patton. "Dr. Langland's only living relative is his daughter, Allison." Gramer pressed a button on the remote, and a photo of a pretty teenage girl with red hair wearing a school uniform appeared next to Dr. Langland's photo. "Most likely, this hair is hers. And get this: the same day Dr. Langland was reported missing, so was his daughter."

A ripple went through the task force, and whispers broke out among the members. One voice was heard above the rest saying, "Was the doctor looking for his daughter? Was she kidnapped and sold by the Camerlengos and he went to get her back?"

"We can't be sure," said Patton, "but it is a possibility, and we will pursue it. Dr. Murtz, what's your opinion?"

Murtz stood up and strode closer to the two photos, trying to get a sense of the people captured within them. Dr. William Langland and his daughter, Allison Langland.

Could the doctor be the killer?

Chapter Seventy-Two

Nikolai Scherbakov sat in his office, a small but comfy room with a view of the Hudson from the window behind him. At the moment, Scherbakov was texting his wife while he was talking to one of his lieutenants. "So the surprise we sent to the Camerlengos is set up?" he said in Russian. His lieutenant Yulian, a thin man with ash-blonde hair and a protruding jawline, nodded and consulted his smartphone.

"According to our mole, the surprise is set up to go off after the engine's been on after at least ten minutes." said Yulian. "Hopefully that means it'll go off around the time they get on the highway."

Scherbakov nodded and put his phone down. His wife was pregnant again. *Bozhe moy*, he'd need to get a new house for the new baby. Well, that would come later. Now he'd have to take care of official business.

"May I ask you something sir?" asked Yulian. When Scherbakov nodded, Yulian said, "It's about the New York Mafia Killer—I mean the Snake, sir. Are you sure we should make an alliance with him? He's a teenager who went on a killing spree because he's lovestruck. I'm not sure he makes the best ally."

"Then it's a good thing I made the decision to offer the alliance, Yulian." said Scherbakov. He was not easily angered, preferring to stay calm and collected. However he'd seen messages in one form or another from his lieutenants and his advisors that they were uneasy, if not downright disapproving, of the Snake and this alliance Scherbakov had offered him. If Scherbakov heard one more complaint today, he might lose his composure, which was something very few had seen and which nobody wanted to see again.

"I realize you do not like the Snake, though you're quite fond of what he's done." Scherbakov continued, picking up his phone again. "But I prefer to think in terms of looking for every opportunity and creating my own luck. Instead of worrying about reprisals, I've made the Snake into an opportunity to improve our stature, and it has worked. We are not looked down upon by other families now. We are feared and respected, because nobody is certain if the killer is with us or not. The connection though, makes us seem powerful and dangerous, and that is something I like.

"Now whether or not the Snake takes our alliance, I believe he can help us. That should be enough for you, Yulian."

"But sir—"

"Yulian!"

"Very good sir." Yulian left Scherbakov's office, leaving Scherbakov alone with his phone and his wife. Sighing, the mob boss lifted himself out of his seat and looked out the window. At this point he felt he should be feeling omnipotent, knowing the identity of the New York Mafia Killer. But the bug he'd planted in his apartment had been found and destroyed within minutes of his leaving, and the boy had threatened his organization. Judging by what was happening to the Camerlengos, Scherbakov knew the boy could inflict serious damage if he decided Scherbakov was better off dead than an ally.

Well, it was in God's hands now. He could only hope that things would work out in the end, as he'd always done. And he could hope the Snake could forgive him for planting the listening device under the sink.

There was a ring from Scherbakov's phone. Turning away from the window, Scherbakov looked at his wife's text and quickly replied that he'd talk to a realtor before putting his phone in his pocket and heading to speak with one of his smugglers about some long-overdue fees.

Chapter Seventy-Three

Christopher Camerlengo sat on his living room couch, watching through the window of his million-dollar mansion as his wife and two younger children loaded their luggage into the back of the brand-new Jaguar he'd gotten her for Christmas. As his wife Sheila closed the car trunk and headed to the front seat, she looked towards the living room window and raised a hand to wave at him. Already feeling heartsick that his wife was leaving, Camerlengo raised his hand and waved back at her.

Camerlengo rarely let himself feel anything such as affection or attachment, but for his wife and his children there was an exception. He adored them more than he thought possible for himself, and in good times and in bad they were what kept him going in this cutthroat business of his.

Getting into the car, Sheila drove down the long, gravel driveway and out of the gate, escorted by black Audis in front and behind. Camerlengo watched as the Jaguar and Audis turned left around the corner and disappeared from sight, on their way to JFK and then to Florida. It was good that his family was getting out of New York and heading to their vacation home, where they would be safe. With Owen Barlow's death, the Camerlengos' business partners—politicians, police, smugglers, overseas contacts—were withdrawing their support now that they knew just being associated loosely to the family could lead to one's death. The reminders that

Camerlengo's lieutenants had sent to the other families had been forgotten and again the family was under attack, both physically and financially. To say the least, he was in tough straits.

Killing my subordinates, taking away my business interests, thought Camerlengo, putting a hand over his head. *I can't believe one freak can cause this much trouble. At least Sheila and the kids will be out of town while we sort this out. If it gets any worse though, I may need to call in him.* Camerlengo felt a sense of dread that things were getting to the point that he might need to call that man. After all, that man was the only person for whom Camerlengo felt anything close to fear.

Still, even if the situation wasn't desperate enough for that man to be called, he wanted his family far away before things got that way. If anything happened to them, he didn't know what he'd do, which was why they were being sent to Florida before something did happen to them.

Deciding that he needed to get his mind off his family, Camerlengo pulled a paperback off the shelf his wife had been bugging him to read for a while and started reading. Before he knew it, he was engrossed in the book, only looking up when he sneezed and realized a full twenty minutes had passed. Realizing the book was good for getting his mind off his problems, Camerlengo turned back to the book, only for a knock on the door to interrupt him.

Alex Rocca entered the room, looking slightly apologetic for having interrupted his boss. "Sir, your son just called. He says he's on his way to the airport right now and he'll join your wife and kids in Tampa in about five hours." Rocca gulped and said, "He also wanted me to give you a message."

"What sort of message?"

"He said..." Rocca gulped again before continuing, "He said you're a jerk for making him leave school when you know how busy he is, but he still loves you."

To Rocca's surprise and fright, Camerlengo laughed heartily. "Sounds like Phillip." he said, setting the paperback on the couch. "I'll call him when his plane arrives, make sure he's doing well."

"Very good sir." said Rocca. "Do you need anything else?"

"Actually..." Camerlengo began, but changed his mind and shook his head. It was still too early to call him. Better wait a little while and see if this situation could resolve itself first. "No, you can go. I'd like some time by myself, if you don't mind."

"Yes Mr. Camerlengo." Rocca turned to leave, but then one of the new security staff barged in, his face panicky and his eyes wide as saucers.

"Mr. Camerlengo!" said the guard, whose name Camerlengo couldn't remember. "It's your wife and the two children! They were getting on the highway when...when their car..."

Camerlengo rose from the couch and went to the maid, a sense of dread rising in his chest. His wife and kids...God, what could've happened to Sheila and Benjamin and Lisa? "What happened?" he said, squeezing the man's shoulders, trying not to hurt him in his trepidation. "What happened to Sheila? What happened to the kids?"

"Their car exploded!" the guard, looking up at Camerlengo through terrified eyes. "It blew up, just like that! No one survived! I just got the call from Eric in one of the Audis, he saw the whole thing happen!"

Camerlengo released the guard and stepped away from, shock spreading throughout his system. All else faded into the background. Sheila...Benjamin...Lisa...they were dead? In the car he'd gotten Sheila for Christmas? It wasn't possible. No, it couldn't be possible...

Coming back to his senses, Camerlengo said, "I want to speak to Eric. Or somebody who was there. I want to talk to them now!" The guard pulled out his cell phone, dialed a number and handed the phone to Camerlengo, who put it to his ear and listened as Eric picked up on the second ring.

"Hello?" said Eric.

"It's Christopher Camerlengo." Trying to control his tone of voice, he asked the dreaded question: "What happened to my wife and children?"

"Sir…I'm so sorry, Mr. Camerlengo." said Eric, sounding truly choked up. "We were just getting on the highway, and…the Jaguar just exploded. It burst into flames and then crashed into the rail. It nearly fell off the road. I'm sorry sir. Your family….none of them…they didn't—"

"That's enough." said Camerlengo. "Come back here as soon as possible. And thank you for telling me." Camerlengo hung up and dropped the phone to the ground, his mind threatening to fall into a state of shock. Somehow theough he was able to keep to his senses and told Rocca to have a team go and grab Phillip, to keep him safe at all costs. He wasn't going to lose his last remaining child. Then he commanded Rocca and the guard to get out and leave him alone. As the two left, Camerlengo reached for a vase and threw it at the wall. Giving a guttural scream, he lifted the couch and turned it over, sending it crashing into a table with a glass sculpture Sheila had always loved. Ripping his jacket and shirt off his chest, Camerlengo threw books off the wall, sent a bottle of expensive scotch into the fireplace, and tore down the chandelier.

When he was done, Camerlengo stood in the center of the trashed living room, panting heavily. This was all the New York

Mafia Killer's fault. Camerlengo knew it to be true! Before the killer had messed up the status quo, there had been barely any deaths in his family, one or two a year tops. His people were arrested and released more than they were killed, for Christ's sake!

But that bloody freak had just kept on killing, and no matter how much they tried, they couldn't get a handle on him, couldn't find out where he was hiding or who he was. And as he kept killing, the other families were emboldened to rebel against him, against the freedom he allowed them to live under. And now his own family had become casualties of this damned war! Perhaps the New York Mafia Killer had done it, perhaps the act was the work of some arrogant family head looking to make moves on his turf. Either way, they'd taken his family from him! And it was all because of that fucking serial killing freak!

"If I ever get my hands on the New York Mafia Killer, I'll strangle him with my own two hands." Camerlengo swore under his breath.

Reaching into his pants, Camerlengo pulled out his cell phone and dialed a number. Now, more than he had before, he needed Frissora's help.

Chapter Seventy-Four

"Go Linda!" Allison yelled, throwing the Frisbee. "Fetch!" With a bark Linda ran after the Frisbee, her legs pumping as she ran. Bending and unbending her legs, Linda jumped into the air and caught the Frisbee in her mouth before crashing into a leafy shrub and scaring a woodchuck out of hiding. Before Allison and the Snake could check to see if Linda was okay, the large wolfhound had stood up, spit out the Frisbee and had started racing after the woodchuck. The Snake and Allison watched as the woodchuck skirted up a tree and into the braches, leaving Linda at the base barking loudly and trying to climb up the tree with her front paws.

Allison and the Snake watched from a distance as Linda put her legs down and started circling the tree, watching the woodchuck. Finally she seemed to grow bored and went to go look for the Frisbee, which she brought back to Allison with a proud look on her face.

"I don't believe it." she said, taking the Frisbee from Linda's mouth.

"I know." said the Snake, rubbing Linda's head. "I thought she'd catch that woodchuck."

Allison looked at the Snake with a dubious look before bursting into laughter. The Snake saw and heard her laughter and felt his mood brighten considerably. This was the first time since breakfast—hell, this was the first time since he'd saved her from Barlow that he'd seen Allison truly laughing. It was a wonderful sound, better than birdsong and he was happy that she could still remember how to laugh.

And even better, the Snake hadn't thought about obliterating the Camerlengos once since breakfast. Not once! He wasn't sure if he was too preoccupied with helping Allison or if he was just too happy to be in her presence to even think about it, but he counted the lack of rumination as a good sign. It meant he could focus on Allison, and focusing on her was much more fun than thinking about killing anyone.

Allison threw the Frisbee again, watching as Linda ran over the Central Park grass and caught it without crashing into another bush. Then she looked at the Snake and said, "What's with that funny look on your face?"

"Nothing." said the Snake. "Just happy." It was the truth.

Allison raised an eyebrow. "Really?" she said. "Are you sure that's all?"

"What more do you want me to say?" asked the Snake. "That you look good in that new blue coat? Because that's the truth too."

"Well, I picked it out." said Allison, putting her hands on her hips. "Of course I look good in it. And where did you find that shop with the one-day delivery, by the way? I didn't even know those sort of places existed."

"You kidding me?" said the Snake. "I handle all of Ruby's clothes-shopping. There has been more than one occasion when I've had to get her clothes for some shit she's doing when she's only given me an hour's notice."

"Are you sure you're only a high school senior?" asked Allison. "You're more responsible than most guys our age."

"I have to be." said the Snake. "Have you seen my dad?"

"Unfortunately." said Allison. Then she said, "How's Ruby doing these days?"

The Snake felt some of the joy go out of him as Allison mentioned his sister. "She misses us." said the Snake. "And when I say 'us', I mean all three of us. You, me, Linda. We're family to her, and without us in her life…"

"She's just not complete." Allison finished. the Snake nodded. There was a pause before Allison continued, "I wish we could make it up to her somehow."

"Um…We are going to make it up to her." said the Snake with a cough. "I already promised her that we would take her to Coney Island and then take her to see a movie."

"What?!" said Allison.

"Sorry."

"Damn you!" For a moment Allison looked seriously annoyed, but then her face burst into a smile and she laughed again. The Snake laughed too and put an arm around Allison. "Oh, a whole day watching over Ruby at a theme park and then a kid's film." said Allison. "How will we survive?"

"How will *we* survive? How will *I* survive?" said the Snake. "I can stand the theme park, but can I handle a kid's film with singing and brawny men who get all sentimental when asked about their dreams?"

"Oh come on, you know you like seeing her happy." said Allison. "And besides, it's not all bad. We can tire her out early and then we can spend some time by ourselves. We'll let Linda babysit her."

"Is that so wise?" the Snake asked, pointing to where the giant dog was now. During their conversation, Linda had spotted the woodchuck again and had gone chasing after it, circling one tree before going to another as the woodchuck jumped from branch to branch. Allison watched Linda but didn't answer, only giving a small, contented smile.

After they'd watched the large dog lose the woodchuck again, the Snake said, "Are you hungry?"

Allison nodded. "Is there a hot dog stand nearby? I could go for one with some relish."

"Your wish is my command." said the Snake with a theatrical bow. "You stay right here." The Snake kissed Allison and left, heading to a hot dog stand he'd seen when they'd entered the park. Sure enough, the hot dog stand was still there, and it only had a few people in line despite the fact it was close to lunchtime. Getting into line, the Snake let out a quiet sigh of relief. He'd been worried that Allison would be too afraid to leave the apartment after all that had happened to her. But after he'd ordered her a new set of clothes, he'd managed to get her out of the house and had taken her to Central Park with Linda, taking her to an area far away from where Paul Sanonia's body had been found. To the Snake's delight, playing with Linda had brightened Allison's mood and consequently brightened the Snake's mood.

Even better, Allison was talking like she and the Snake were more than just a couple of high schoolers going steady with each other, but like an adult couple, living together and managing the young child they both took care of. It was a strange feeling to the Snake, but it was one he liked. He wondered if that meant that Allison was possibly—

The Snake shook his head. That was ridiculous, and they were still only in high school besides. It would be a while before they could even discuss that!

As the Snake's turn in line came up, the vendor asked him what he wanted. "Yeah, can I get two dogs, one with relish, one without a bun, and one veggie dog?" asked the Snake. The vendor pulled out the hot dogs and the Snake got out his wallet to pay. As the Snake pulled out the bills, there was a sudden gunshot and several screams from behind him. The Snake turned around and felt his throat constrict.

The area that the gunshot had come from was where Allison was.

Chapter Seventy-Five

The Snake slipped his wallet back into his pants and bolted, running towards the sound of the gunshot. His blood was on fire, his heart was pounding, his mind was in a whirlwind of emotions. Had the Camerlengos found Allison? How? Were they planning on killing her in the middle of broad daylight? Why the hell would they do that? What the fuck was going on?!

As the place they'd been playing with Linda came into view, the Snake spotted Allison by a tree and on her knees hugging Linda while the large dog growled at...a man with a gun. A man with a gun standing not five yards away from where Allison huddled in fear.

That was all the Snake needed. As people ran past him screaming in terror, the Snake ran at the man, tackling him just as the man realized someone was coming at him from behind. The man let out a surprised yell as he fell to the ground and dropped the gun, then screamed as the Snake grabbed the man's wrist and twisted, breaking the bone. As the man looked up at the Snake in shock and fear, the Snake started hitting the man's face and head, his wild fury going into every punch. *Camerlengo bastard!* the Snake thought, pinning the man's arms down. *Don't you dare touch Allison!*

The Snake was lost in his rage, only aware of the man under him and the swings of his fists. At some point the Snake became aware of someone tugging on his shoulder and he looked up into Allison's face. Only then did his senses return to him and he looked down at the man he'd attacked.

It wasn't a Camerlengo soldier. It wasn't even a soldier from any family! Instead the Snake saw a man with cornrows and a goatee, staring up at him with tears in his eyes and blood flowing from his nose and mouth. "What the fuck's wrong with you, man?" said the man, his voice coming out as a moan-filled whine. The Snake stared directly into the man's eyes, feeling as if something horrible had happened. But what? What had he done?

The Snake reached up to touch his face and realized he wasn't wearing his mask. His mask! How could he have forgotten his mask? That meant that—

—this isn't a movie, oh my God this isn't a movie, I actually hurt someone, I can't distance myself from this, oh holy shit, what have I done?—

Nearby the Snake heard screams and looked up to see a woman in her late pregnancy screaming and pointing at the Snake (or was she pointing at the man underneath him?). "Why'd you do that?" she shouted, sobbing loudly. "He didn't mean no harm. He's just an idiot. Why'd you do that?" The woman repeated "why'd you do that" again, her voice dissolving into a weak, keening moan.

The Snake sat on top of the man, frozen. *I can't distance myself from this.* thought the Snake, a sense of numbness sinking into him. *I got scared for Allison and I ended up forgetting to put on my mask. I broke this bastard's wrist like I would break a twig. This is bad, very bad—!*

The Snake felt himself lifted up as Allison pulled him by the arm. "Come on!" she was saying, a note of desperation in her voice. "We have to get out of here!" She pulled the Snake along, but soon he'd come back to the world enough that he was running beside her, Linda following next to them as they ran away from the man with the gun and the pregnant woman and the possible bystander or two who were shooting video with cellphones and tablets what they'd just seen and uploading it onto the Internet.

The Snake didn't care about any of that, though. All he could think of was that he had done something horrible. Something he couldn't distance himself from. Dammit!

Chapter Seventy-Six

The Snake allowed Allison to lead him from the park and to a small outdoor restaurant several blocks away from the man he'd just assaulted, stopping along the way at a pond to wash the blood off of the Snake's hands, face and coat and then wiping them dry with Allison's scarf. Then they left again before anyone could see them and figure out that the Snake was the one who'd attack the gunman a few minutes ago. Thankfully nobody noticed them as they left the park, preferring to notice the giant dog, and once they were out of the park and on the streets, they were just like anyone else out on the street. They just happened to have a big dog with them.

Once they were out of the park and at the café, Allison put Linda back on her leash and tied her to a table right next to the café doors. As the Snake sat down she sat across from him, looking at him worriedly. The Snake just stared past her and into space, his thoughts seeming to go on a continuous loop. *I can't get away from this, it won't be like the other times, what if I'd killed him, then I'd be in deep shit, I can't get away from this—*

The Snake was jolted back to reality as he felt a sharp pain his foot. Looking underneath the table, he saw the heel of Allison's brown boot smashed firmly into the toes of his black Army boot. Looking back across the table, he could see Allison staring back at him with an worried look on her face. Imagine! Allison was worried for him, when he should've been the one worrying over her. Today was just full of surprises, and none of them were any bit pleasant.

"What was that for?" said the Snake.

"What was that for?" Allison repeated. "I asked you what happened at the park, and you just spaced out on me. I had to get your attention somehow!"

"Nothing happened." the Snake insisted, trying not to seem defensive. "I just…was a little surprised when I saw it wasn't a Camerlengo creep trying to hurt you."

Allison raised an eyebrow, as if she didn't know whether or not she should believe him. "Is that really what happened?" she asked as if she already knew the answer. For all the Snake knew, she probably did.

The Snake let her eyes bore into him, trying to withstand the brunt of her stare by looking away, watching people walk by the restaurant, not even looking at the waitress as he ordered a small coffee. When he looked back though, he saw beneath that stare how deep her worry was, and he knew he couldn't keep the truth from her. Sighing deeply, the Snake said, "I should've been wearing my mask."

Allison blinked. "Your mask?" she said. "What does that got to do with anything?"

"That mask does more than hide my identity." he explained, resting his elbows on the table and his forehead in his hands. "That mask, it...it distances me from what I do. When I wear it, I'm no different than most slasher movie killers. I'm just a character in a movie who happens to be identified by his iconic mask. But without it...it's just too hard for me, and I find I'm unable to hurt anyone. I can't do what I can to protect you.

"So when I hurt that guy...God, I thought he was after you! I didn't know what was going on. All I knew was there was a gunshot, and I was scared shitless for you. There wasn't time to change in the middle of the street. I just got there, I saw a man with a gun, and I...ended up hurting a guy who wasn't even involved in our problems."

"Yeah? Well, I'm glad you did do something about that guy." said Allison, taking the surprising the Snake. "That pregnant woman showed up after you'd left, and that guy not too long afterwards. I got the sense from the way they were shouting at each other that he was her boyfriend and that he thought the kid was someone else's, and she kept saying he should trust the mother of his child. Then he pulled out the gun and started threatening her unless she told the truth. He even fired a warning shot, right into the air. You were doing everybody a favor when you took him down."

"Well, that actually makes me feel a little better." said the Snake, meaning it. Maybe he couldn't totally distance himself from what he'd done, but with Allison's explanations of events, at least he could justify his actions. "Thanks for telling me about it."

Their coffees came and Allison and the Snake paused to each take a warm sip, Allison telling the waitress they were still deciding on what they wanted for lunch. As the Snake tilted his head back and felt the hot mocha rush down his throat, the Snake heard Allison ask, "Did you do it before? You know, hurt someone without the mask?"

The Snake was surprised by the question. Putting his mug down, the Snake said, "Yeah, once. It was James Sanonia, the first guy I killed. I knew he was the public spokesman for the Camerlengos, so I tracked him down the same day I left the house and moved into the apartment. I found him and I cornered him in the alleyway outside his favorite bar."

The Snake went silent remembering it all. After a short while Allison cleared her throat and said, "Go on."

"It was like a nightmare." said the Snake, staring off into the distance, feeling like he was talking more to himself than to Allison as he relived it, seeing himself in that sparsely-lit alleyway with the smell of rotting garbage and too much alcohol all around him. "I was just standing there with this gun I'd bought illegally and with a silencer I'd had to literally strong-arm the dealer into giving me. And I was scared shitless. I mean, I'd resigned myself already to killing in order to find you, but the thought of actually taking a life…you can't have any idea what that's like! To suddenly have the power to take a life right in your hands and to decide whether or not to use it, while wondering if you actually have the power, the fortitude, the potential, the fucking balls to take that life! It's as scary as it is intoxicating.

"And there was Sanonia, making fun of me. I think he was a little drunk and thought I was some sort of mugger who didn't know who he was mugging and was probably new to the game. He was taunting me, saying all sorts of horrible things. And I was just getting madder and madder. I told him to shut up, but the drunk son of a bitch just wouldn't shut up.

"And then I asked about you. I tried to make it sound cool, like in all the movies, but I probably stammered, I can't really remember. And he asked me what you meant to me before he just went and said…he said you were fucking some guy's brains out and having the time of your life while you were at it. I just sort of lost it there. I fired a shot before I knew what I was doing. The guy just wobbled on his feet with this look of weird surprise on his face and fell flat on his back in a pile of garbage.

"After that I went a little crazy with rage. I just started breaking his bones, and then I carved my name—the name 'Snake'—into his chest. I couldn't tell if I was angrier at myself or at him, I was just so scared and confused. And then I realized what I'd done. I'd killed someone and maimed their body. I'd done all that. That realization...it just shocked me. Really shocked me, like the kind you need to go to the hospital for. It took just about all my energy and what was left of my sanity just to get the body into a car and dump him in the Hudson."

"What happened after you dumped him?" Allison whispered, leaning in and looking to make sure no one else was listening.

"I just walked around." said the Snake with a shrug. "I just walked around with the gun in my coat and didn't think about anything else but the murder I'd just botched until I passed by this small little bondage shop hidden between a bakery and a hair salon. I just passed by the window and stopped. I looked back in and I saw it. My mask, the mask I needed. I knew then I needed the mask, that it would make killing easier for me. It was almost as if it was calling for me! As soon as the store opened I went in, saw the mask was on sale, and bought two or three of them, just in case one was lost or ruined.

"When I dumped Sanonia's body, his cousin Paul had texted him about some 'new merchandise' that'd be coming in that weekend." the Snake continued, looking at Allison for the first time since he'd started telling her about what had happened to him that night. "I knew that couldn't be anything good and that he must be involved in the Camerlengos too, so I kept an eye on him, thinking I might learn something from him. When it came time to...to interrogate him, I put on the mask and…it was as if everything changed for me, like I was playing a role in a movie and everything was acting in front of the camera. I've worn the mask when I've had to hurt people ever since."

The Snake looked at Allison, waiting for her to say something, not trying to read her body language because he knew how uncomfortable that made her. When she didn't immediately reply, he looked away and said, "God, you must think I'm so messed up."

"We're both messed up." said Allison. The Snake looked back at her and saw a sad look on her face. No pity, just sadness, and it amazed him to think she might be suffering too, probably worse than he was, yet she was still concerning herself with his problems. "You're a serial killer, and I've probably got PTSD or anxiety disorder or something now." Allison looked like she was about to cry as she said, "Do you think we'll ever be normal again?"

The Snake didn't answer, because he knew the answer already and so did she, even if she didn't want to believe it. They didn't have time to answer anyway: the sound of sirens were coming their way. It would only be a matter of time before the cops started canvassing the shops and cafes in this area. Leaving a ten on the table, the Snake, Allison, and Linda left before anyone could take a second glance at them.

Later when police came by, the waitress remembered the two teens and the dog, but couldn't give many other details. Nobody else remembered the teens, but they remembered the dog, and that it was big and grey. With the ten already put into the register and then handed back to a woman who paid with a twenty for a latte and no security cameras, the cops moved on to other shops, wondering if they'd find clues to the young man's identity somewhere else. Secretly though they applauded the guy who'd taken down the gunman, who had a rap sheet a mile long and was out on probation after serving five years on a fifteen-year sentence for assault. With what had happened in the park, he'd be going back to prison, and thanks to the guy who'd stopped him, nobody but the gunman had gotten hurt in the process. Despite the guy's recklessness and his use of his fists, the police believed that whoever had taken down the gunman was a hero, and should be treated as such.

Chapter Seventy-Seven

Murtz heaved a big sigh as she typed out her opinion of Doctor William Langland and the likelihood that he was the Snake killer. Clicking Save and forwarding it in an email to the rest of the task force, Murtz sat back in her chair and stretched. It was nearly five in the afternoon and Murtz still had a few more hours before she could even think about getting a shower and some rest.

And the murder of Camerlengo's wife and kids doesn't help, Murtz thought, rubbing her tired eyes. She knew she should feel more sympathy for those poor souls—family of a mob boss or not, they were still probably innocent of any crimes, especially the children—but in her tired and sleep-deprived state, it was difficult to feel anything close to sympathy.

"You look like you could use a little pick-me-up." Murtz looked up to see Gramer standing next to her chair with a cup of coffee—even better, a cup of coffeehouse coffee instead of the swill brewed in the office—held out towards her. Smiling, Murtz took it in her hands and drank a long, happy, refreshing gulp of the stuff.

"Section Chief Alan Gramer, my knight in shining armor." she said after she'd drunk nearly a fourth of the cup in one sip. "How can I ever repay you?"

"How about before I meet up with Captain Patton, you give me the details of Dr. Langland's profile?" Gramer suggested.

Immediately after hearing Gramer's request, Murtz felt the wind she'd felt enter her sails disappear, and her tired annoyance returned.

"What's there to give?" she asked. "He's not a good suspect. I'd say it's more likely that he and Camerlengo got into an argument, and Camerlengo brutally murdered his friend and tried to sell the daughter, which ended up a disaster for the buyer."

"You think so?" said Gramer, head cocked to the side. "But I thought he fit some of the aspects of your profile."

"Some, but not even that makes him a good suspect." Murtz pointed out. Gesturing at a large stack of files at her desk, she said, "I just looked through his military records dating back to his days as a student at the military academy he went to with Camerlengo. Turns out he wasn't exactly the best soldier."

"What do you mean?"

"The reports say the doctor was nowhere close to athletic or combat material and was better with academics than with military training." Murtz explained. "Apparently he used to lead tutoring sessions with some of the other cadets. One of his teachers said that if the doctor's own father wasn't a retired Army captain himself, Dr. Langland would've likely gone to some school for the gifted."

"More of a life-saver than a fighter, in other words." said Gramer.

"That's one way of putting it." said Murtz. "Not only that, but the doctor was the most nonviolent person you could ever meet. According to his file, he used his time on active duty to be a doctor at Fort Bragg. Strictly boring, not a bit of excitement or anything worse than a misfired rifle to the leg."

"Well, maybe he was just quiet." Gramer suggested. "Plenty of serial killers are."

"Yes, but there's just one problem." said Murtz. "I checked the audio of the recordings from the phone calls the killer left at the newspaper presses and television studios and checked it against the voice message on Dr. Langland's office phone. No match for tones, cadence, or anything else."

Now it looked like Gramer's sails had lost their air. "Well, there goes our first suspect this whole investigation." he said wistfully. "And now we're back to square one."

"Sorry Alan." said Murtz with a shrug. "Just doing my job."

"I understand." said Gramer. "Hey, go get some rest, okay? You look like you're ready to murder someone with an axe."

"Don't give me any ideas, sir." said Murtz with a laugh. Leaving Gramer in the task force room, Murtz headed for the elevators. As she passed the break room's open door though, something she saw out of the corner of her eye made her stop.

Walking into the break room, Murtz watched with a few other members of the task force as the news played on a small flat screen in a corner.

Murtz sat down in a chair and watched as the reporter on the television opened the report, saying a shooting in Central Park had taken an unconventional turn when a citizen had stopped the shooter. An amateur clip taken by a cell phone showed a man pulling out a gun, firing it while shouting, and then being tackled by someone from behind.

As Murtz watched though, she saw something in the corner of the screen that made her breath catch. To be more specific, it was some*one* in the corner of the screen.

Allison Langland. Dr. William Langland's daughter, the girl sold to Owen Barlow and then apparently saved by the Snake killer. She was in the corner of the screen, huddling in fear by a large dog that was growling at the shooter.

The clip continued, showing the shooter on his stomach being beaten by the man who had attacked him, and then Allison Langland tugging on the shoulder of the man on top of the shooter. As Murtz saw the man, who had an ordinary appearance and looked rather unremarkable, she realized the man was more like a boy, probably a little older than Allison herself.

Murtz watched as Allison, her head cut off in the video, led the boy away from the shooter, running away and off-screen while the video focused on the shooter. A moment later the dog followed Allison and the boy after making sure the shooter wouldn't follow, watching the shooter on the ground warily before running away.

As the clip ended and the reporter asked for all those who had information on the shooting and on the strange boy who had intervened to call police investigators, Murtz realized there was more to that clip than met the eye.

"Hey, is that clip online?" Murtz asked one of the agents in the break room. The agent shrugged and said, "Probably. Isn't everything these days?"

Without a word, Murtz ran out of the break room and headed back to the task force command center. She had to watch that clip again.

And while she was at it, she had to find out more about Allison Langland.

Chapter Seventy-Eight

Allison handed the Snake a plate, which the Snake started scrubbing in the sink, soaking it in sudsy water before rinsing it off. Placing the plate on the drying rack, the Snake wiped his hands with the towel draped over his shoulder. "Finished." he said. "What do you want to do now?"

"Nothing too exciting." said Allison. "I ate too much of that pasta dish. What'd you call it again?"

"Penne Arrabiata." said the Snake. "I thought you'd like it. Ruby adores it."

"I'm not surprised." said Allison. "Say, you want to just stay in and watch a movie?"

"Is there anything on?"

Allison shrugged. "I don't know. I thought we'd just channel surf and see what's on."

"Sounds good to me." said the Snake. "But Linda needs to go for a walk first. You want to come with?"

Allison shook her head. "Nah, you go on ahead." she said. "I'll see if I can find something to watch for when you get back."

"Sounds good to me." said the Snake, giving Allison a quick kiss as Linda starting hopping with excitement by the door.

Grabbing his coat and putting Linda on her leash, the Snake walked out of the apartment and down the stairs to the street. It was only when he was outside the building that he allowed himself a sigh of relief.

After the incident in the park, the Snake had felt anxious for most of the day, waiting for somebody to recognize him, to remind him that he'd been mistaken, to remind him that he'd fucked up big time in front of everyone and that he'd hurt an innocent person (*or not so innocent*, he reminded himself, wondering if he would actually believe that at any point). It had taken him all his energy to stay calm around Allison, and when she'd mentioned that she didn't want to do anything exciting, he thought she'd been making a reference to what happened earlier.

At least her mind was on her stomach, the Snake thought, watching as Linda raised a leg and peed on a parking meter. The Snake walked Linda up the block and west for about another two blocks before circling back to the apartment building and up the stairs.

As the Snake let Linda and himself in, Linda went to sit by the heater while the Snake undid his jacket and set it on the rack. "Allison!" he called. "Found anything interesting?"

"Just some romantic spy film called *Never Let the Curtain Fall*." Allison called back from the bedroom. The Snake poked his head in and found her sitting cross-legged on top of the comforter, leaning against the pillow as a back support. As she saw him, she said, "The movie's plot is a little silly, but the acting is pretty good so far. You want to watch?"

The Snake sat down next to Allison and looked at the screen, where two men with hairstyles and suits from the 1970s were talking in low voices on a rooftop while looking down at a party on another rooftop with binoculars. The Snake shrugged and put an arm around Allison. "If you don't mind, I don't. But why'd you call it a romantic spy film? Looks like a regular spy film to me."

"Because apparently the TV station is having a marathon of action films with big romantic elements all week." Allison explained. "They're calling it 'Seven Days to Saint Valentine's Celebration'. Oh, can you do me a favor and not do your movie critic commentary while we watch?"

"How about after the movie?" asked the Snake, earning him an elbow to the rib cage from Allison.

As he sat back with Allison and watched the characters in the movie, the Snake found himself getting drawn into the story. Like most old spy films, the plot was ridiculous to the point of being hilarious, but the characters seemed strangely real, more so than most actors that the Snake had seen acting.

During one scene when everything seemed to be going wrong for the characters and the love interest for both spies was lamenting at how bleak the situation was, the Snake felt himself identifying with the junior spy as he tried to cheer her spirits. It was almost like what he was doing with Allison and what she'd done for him earlier today. He looked over at Allison, willing to risk her ire by interrupting the movie and commenting on this similarity…and saw tears in her eyes as she stared at the love interest character.

Wrapping his arms around her, the Snake watched with Allison as the scene changed and showed all three characters taking down the antagonist and preventing him from setting off his nuclear bomb. The film ended and the Snake turned off the television. "That film was actually okay." said the Snake, looking at Allison. "I didn't think I'd like it, but it has its good points—"

The Snake stopped as he saw Allison looking up at him, her expression something he'd never seen in her before. It was part fear, part love, but mostly it was…yearning. The Snake lifted one hand and brushed a strand of stray hair away from Allison's cheek. He remembered the unease and dread he was constantly feeling, the unease that someone would take Allison away again and he'd never see her again, coupled with the scar the incident from the park had created within him. The Snake knew that Allison was also uneasy, though her unease came from a much different but very real threat.

And the Snake knew that they both wanted their worries to go away.

The Snake flashed back to that one scene from the movie they'd watched, the one where the junior spy character had promised the antagonist's daughter that he'd always protect her, no matter what happened to them. What was the line the sidekick character had said?

"Things aren't going to get worse." said the Snake, remembering the line. "I'm going to make sure of that. Just stand with me, and we'll make it out of this together."

Allison's expression didn't change, but she said, "For a top-notch director and a serial killer, you can be a really horrible actor when you're not playing the villain."

"Hey, at least I—"

Before the Snake could finish, Allison was kissing him, her eyes closed and her hand on his cheek. The Snake felt her lips pressed against his, hard and searching, and he felt a feeling of tenderness well up in him. Hugging her closer to him, the Snake kissed her back, losing himself in the passion and feeling.

Allison pressed herself closer to the Snake so that her hips were against his, increasing the Snake's excitement. Oh, how he loved her, how he wanted to always be with her and always wanted to see her smile and to kiss her like he was kissing her now. Leaning forward, the Snake pushed Allison down onto the bed, her head sinking into the folds of the comforter.

The Snake came up for air and gasped, feeling electricity flowing through his body. Looking down at Allison, he saw a dreamy expression on her face that he'd never seen before, her eyes half-open as she gazed up at him. He could tell just from looking at her, she was feeling the same sort of electricity that he was. The Snake kissed her again, his eyes staring directly into Allison's, wishing to float into them, to disappear into their beautiful green depths.

The Snake kissed her cheek, her earlobe, her neck. Allison gave a soft moan underneath him, which only made the Snake more excited than before. Reaching down, the Snake lifted up Allison's sweater over her head, kissing her shoulder as it came free of the sweater. The Snake breathed in Allison's sweet scent as he reached underneath her back and undid her bra, slipping the straps off her arms and throwing them across the bed. Allison stared up at him, her breasts bare before him and her arms at her side, her expression totally trusting.

The Snake kissed Allison's lips again and whispered, "I love you." Cupping her breasts in his hands, the Snake massaged the soft, elastic skin while he kissed Allison's lips, Allison moaning as he pinched her nipples playfully. Kissing her neck again, the Snake moved slowly downward to her shoulders, her armpit, and then finally over the rise of her soft breast and onto the nipple, sucking it softly between his teeth. Allison cried out his name as his hand rubbed and massaged the other breast and as his tongue tickled the hard tip.

Unable to stop himself, the Snake reached down again and unbuttoned her pants. Slowly pulling down the zipper, the Snake's hand rested first on Allison's side, then on her hip, and finally between Allison's legs. Still sucking on her nipple, the Snake pressed a finger against the fabric of Allison's underwear, eliciting a soft gasp from her. Pressing his fingers against her slit, the Snake began to rub his fingers up and down against the fabric, which was sticky to the touch. Beneath him Allison moaned, spreading her arms and legs out as if to let the feeling diffuse itself over her entire body.

The Snake stopped massaging Allison's breast and sent his left hand to join the right. Pulling her pants and underwear down her thighs, the Snake let two of his fingers enter inside Allison and stroke. Allison's soft little cries became a loud shout of pleasure as her back arched against him.

"Where…Where did—Where did you learn to do *thiiis?!*" Allison gasped, the last word coming out as a shout of joy.

"You kidding me?" said the Snake, finally releasing Allison's nipple and looking at her face, already shining with sweat. "You'd be surprised what sort of stuff you find in the books I read. You get a feel for things."

"And that's why I don't like those books!" said Allison as the Snake continued stroking her insides. The Snake only smiled and kissed her neck, sucking on a vein as he felt her pulse underneath his lips. Allison screamed again, wrapping her arms around the Snake's back as he moved along her neck to her cheek and back to her lips, cutting off her cries.

Allison's thighs squeezed his arm as his hand stroked her harder, their breathing matching inhale to exhale, their hearts matching beat for beat. The Snake felt the warm, electric feeling inside him growing with every passing second, becoming unbearable. Finally he couldn't take any more waiting. Taking his fingers out, the Snake undid his pants and slid them off, followed soon after by his boxers. Taking Allison's underwear in his fist and sliding it down the rest of the way, the Snake leaned his body forward, his hard, throbbing member searching for her. Wrapping her legs around him and squeezing, Allison guided him in. With a thrust, he entered her.

As the Snake went in, he felt a powerful sensation in his genitals, as if every cell was alive and singing. As Allison's insides wrapped around the tip of his member, he felt the sensation intensify, every square inch of his throbbing sword being squeezed and caressed by every square inch of Allison's accepting sheath. Thrusting in deeper, the Snake let out a long, low moan, feeling his entire self flooded with a burning, inescapable pleasure. Another thrust and he was all the way in, his body on top of Allison's, his every thrust and push causing Allison to give a yelping cry for more.

"Allison!" the Snake shouted, planting his hands on either side of her as he lifted himself off of her body. "Allison! Allison!" Beneath him Allison was shouting out his name, her back and hips arched towards him, her nipples pointing in the air. Hearing her shout his name the Snake increased his thrusting, turning Allison's shouts into one long scream.

Finally the Snake slowed down, his member deep within her. Leaning forward, he kissed her shoulder, her neck. The books had never prepared him for this, this sharing of...he didn't know what to call it. Maybe "cosmic energy" was a good term to use, or "life force", or maybe even "love energy". They were sharing it in their bodies, and it was amazing, almost mystical in nature. It reminded him of when he first began to grasp what sex really was, more than just teens in movies rolling naked in a bed, but a force for life-bearing. Girls had seemed magical to him now, full of mystery and a power he could never attain.

Here in the bed, Allison was allowing him to take part in the power, in that great mystery. And he could only count himself lucky, purely lucky that she was giving someone as unworthy as himself a glimpse of something much greater than himself, something that was at the core of their love but permeated everything in the universe. It was so humbling and exciting at the same time.

The Snake felt the pressure in his member rising to an almost painful throb at the exact same time as Allison's insides began to squeeze and tighten around him. With a final shout the Snake released into her, his mind becoming aware only of himself and of Allison and of their shared joy and pleasure and the energy that was exploding in that single moment. With a loud gasp, he Snake fell on top of her, sucking in lungfuls of air as he continued releasing into her. Finally when he felt his breath return, he whispered, "That was…amazing."

Allison didn't reply, instead placing her hands on his shoulders and pushing the Snake onto his back. Before the Snake knew what was happening Allison was kissing him, her tongue slipping between her lips, past his teeth and around his tongue. As he felt the excitement and passion return to him, the Snake wrapped his tongue around Allison's, her taste mixing with his within his mouth.

As Allison moaned happily she began to pull his shirt off, breaking away from their kiss as it came over the Snake's head and bringing their lips and tongues together as soon as the shirt was out of the way. Feeling his member swelling to attention again, the Snake placed one hand on her shoulder blade and the other on the small of her back, crushing her naked body against him.

Before he knew what was happening Allison had reached down and taken him in her hand, the sensation of her soft palm and fingers around his hot member enough to make him almost come again. Slipping her tongue out of his mouth, Allison sat up on top of him as she guided his member back into her. As it went in, the Snake felt the warm, wet sensation again and let out a shout of sheer joy, grabbing Allison's hips in his as she cried out on top of him, her body moving up and down along his member with every thrust of her pelvis. Lifting his upper body off the bed, the Snake pulled himself close to Allison, his hands cupping her breasts as he kissed her lips, her nose, her eyes, her forehead, her ears, her cheeks.

Their bodies thrust together, their cries and breaths in time, their heartbeats beating at the same pace. Looking into her eyes, the Snake felt it, knew what it was like to be one with another person, to be one with Allison, to be a part of the mystery she embodied within her. It was a pure, wonderful feeling, made of love and trust and a connection that went beyond the physical, into a realm where words were meaningless and unnecessary. It was sheer bliss!

As Allison's insides tightened around him, the Snake let go of her breasts and instead squeezed her to him, one hand on the small of her back and the other cradling the back of her head. Allison wrapped her arms around his neck and her legs around his waist, whispering his name to him. "Oh my God." she said. "Don't stop. Oh, please don't stop!"

The Snake kissed her, their tongues wrapping around each other in the space between their lips. With a final thrust he released into her again, and they screamed together as the feeling of being one with each other spiked and then slowly fell away. With a soft sigh Allison fell against his chest, panting heavily as she whispered "I love you" to him.

Kissing the top of her head, the Snake laid Allison on her back, her head resting against the pillow. Kissing her belly, the Snake moved slowly downward, eventually reaching her special spot. As Allison's breath began to quicken again, the Snake stuck his tongue out and reached in.

Near the head of the bed, the Snake heard Allison give another cry of delight.

Chapter Seventy-Nine

The Snake was aware of how warm he was, how rested and how relaxed he felt, and of the warm body that was laying on top of him. Opening his eyes, the Snake saw Allison's head resting on his shoulder, her red hair surrounding her face almost like a veil. The Snake looked with fascination as Allison slept on top of him, naked and beautiful and as innocent-looking as a child. To the Snake, it was like an angel had come to rest on top of him.

I don't deserve this. he thought, twirling a strand of Allison's hair between his fingers. *I'm so lucky. I hope this can last forever.*

Which was why the Snake would have to do what he knew Allison didn't want him to do. It was the best way to protect her and keep her with him, and that was the whole reason he'd become a serial killer. He just hoped he wasn't making another deal for his soul.

As he was thinking this, the Snake heard Allison groan and her eyes flutter open. Looking up at him, Allison looked confused for a second before a change came over her face, signaling to the Snake that she'd remember what had happened the night before. Smiling at him, she asked, "What time is it?"

The Snake looked over at the clock on the bedside table. "A little after eight." he said.

"Well, good morning then." said Allison, planting a kiss on the Snake's cheek. The Snake smiled and turned his head back to her, planting a kiss on her lips. "Good morning to you too." he said. "How late did we stay up doing…you know?"

"Um…I think I looked at the clock at some point." said Allison. "I think it was maybe…two thirty? I was looking at it for barely a second. Why do you ask?"

"No reason." said the Snake. "Just…that was my first time. And it was…wonderful. You were wonderful."

Allison looked away from him, as if she were embarrassed by his compliment. "Well, that was my first time too." she said. "And you were wonderful as well."

"I'm happy to hear that."

"No, you don't understand." said Allison, resting her head back on the Snake's shoulder with a sigh of contentment. "You know what a girl always is afraid of when she has her first time, besides that the guy she's with will be a jerk afterwards or that she'll get pregnant or an STD or something? She's afraid it'll hurt when she has sex, that instead of feeling good it'll hurt and that she'll have to endure that pain every time she has sex.

"And last night, when you…well, when you went in, it didn't hurt at all. All I felt was…you know."

"No pain?" said the Snake. "None at all?"

"Well, I might be a little sore for the rest of the day." Allison and the Snake laughed, Allison falling off the Snake and landing next to him. From the next room came a bark, followed by the sound of paws scratching on wood.

"Sounds like Linda's up." said the Snake. "Probably hungry too. I'll go feed her."

"You do that." said Allison. "I'm going to freshen up a little."

"Sure thing." said the Snake, slipping out of the bed and searching for his underwear. When he couldn't find last night's pair and instead put on a new pair of boxers, the Snake opened the door and was greeted by Linda, who walked up to him and stood on her hind legs with her front paws on the Snake's shoulder.

"Whoa girl!" said the Snake as Linda whined at him. "I'm happy to see you too. Alright, get down. *Vneez devochka.*" Linda jumped down and scampered to the kitchen, whining at the Snake to feed her. The Snake sighed and went to feed her, pouring a more-than-generous amount of dog food into Linda's bowl. Linda stuck her nose into the bowl and started chomping down noisily. Satisfied that Linda was being taken care of, the Snake went back into the bedroom, found his pants, and pulled out his phone and wallet

437

I hope this decision doesn't come back to bite me in the zhopa. the Snake thought for the second time since he'd woken up as he opened his wallet. Sifting through the wallet, he found what he was looking for and dialed the number on the card. *Even if this is necessary.*

Walking out of the bedroom, the Snake pressed SEND and brought the phone up to his ear. Two rings in and there was a click as someone picked up. "*Pree-vet?*" said Scherbakov.

"I'm glad to see you are awake this early in the morning," said the Snake in Russian, his voice deepening and the accent coming out. "But then again, I guess mob bosses must have the same hours as regular people too."

Scherbakov must've recognized his voice, because then he said in Russian, "Are you taking my deal, my young friend?"

"Not yet." said the Snake. "First, I'd like to meet. In a public place with lots of visibility and witnesses. And when I say 'witnesses', I don't mean people on your payroll. Do you understand me?"

"You are cautious." said Scherbakov. "I like that. It would be a shame if you were stupid."

"If I was stupid, you and I would never have had the pleasure of meeting." the Snake pointed out. "Do you agree to my terms?"

"How about we meet at the MoMA?" suggested Scherbakov. "I believe that fulfills all your terms."

The Snake thought about it for a moment, and then said, "Fine. What time?"

"Three o'clock." said Scherbakov. "In front of the entrance. You can bring your girlfriend with you."

"You'll be more likely to meet my dog." the Snake replied. "And trust me, she's no lapdog."

"I look forward to it." said Scherbakov with a laugh. "See you at three. Oh, and one more thing."

"What's that?"

"Your Russian is impeccable! I just can't get over how realistic you sound. How did you learn to speak the language so well?"

"Very carefully, one word at a time." the Snake replied. "See you at three."

The Snake cut the call and put the phone and card on the counter. Rubbing his forehead as if he felt a headache coming on, the Snake wondered if he was making a deal with the devil again.

"Was that that Scherbakov man?" The Snake turned around and saw Allison leaning against the doorframe of the bedroom, wearing her bra, panties, and a frown that the Snake did not like.

"Yes it was." said the Snake in English, in his voice normal and unaccented.

"What did you talk about?" asked Allison, stepping off the doorframe and walking towards him. "Did you take his deal?"

"No." said the Snake truthfully. "I just agreed to meet with him in front of the MoMA. We're going to talk."

"Talk?" repeated Allison.

"Yes, just talk." said the Snake, taking Allison into his arms. Allison gratefully accepted his arms and hugged him, her ear pressed against his chest like she wanted to hear his heartbeat, which the Snake thought was probably the case. "We'll be in front of a lot of people, we'll be in public. Nothing bad will happen."

"Nothing bad will happen?!" Allison repeated, looking up at his face. He hesitated, and then immediately the Snake knew he'd waited too long to answer as Allison continued talking. "He's a mob boss! You can't trust him. How do you know something won't happen?"

"Because Scherbakov has agreed to all my demands so far, and because I can't see a single lie in anything he says to me." said the Snake. "Besides, I'll have Linda with me."

"Oh, a dog and a knack for reading people! Yeah, real great protection against men with guns." Allison broke away from the Snake and turned away, her arms crossed against her chest. "Did you think about how I might feel about you making a deal with that man? Did you think I might want you to tell him no and just not bother with him? Especially after he planted that bug under the counter?"

"I did." said the Snake. "I also considered the fact that the Camerlengos are still out there, they are still looking for the both of us, and that as long as the Camerlengos are out there and still looking for us, we won't get any peace!"

"Why can't you just forget about the Camerlengos all together and just stop killing?" asked Allison, her voice rising as she continued to look away from him. "Or if you have to kill, why can't you—"

"—do the same goddamn thing I've been doing?" finished the Snake. "Allison, did you see the wound on my shoulder?"

There was a pause, during which Allison said nothing. Finally she turned to look at him and said, "What about it?"

"I got shot!" said the Snake, turning around to let her see the still-healing wound, hidden under a square of cotton the Snake had taped onto his shoulder. "I got shot escaping from the police after I killed Roman Veretti, the guy who finally told me about the phone sex service. I was barely able to get away from that place, and if I hadn't had help from a state trooper who sympathized with me, I'd have been caught and killed while in booking and you'd be with Owen Barlow right now!"

Allison flinched at the sound of the dead football player's name. The Snake saw a pained and fearful expression on her face and felt bad that he'd had to remind her of this fact, even if it was necessary. Deciding to finish his point with a gentler tone, the Snake said, "Al, I don't want to get shot again. I don't want to be captured or caught in the act or discovered. Because if something were to happen to me, you'd be all alone. And I know neither of us wants that."

Allison nodded, tears welling up in her eyes. "I'm just so scared," she said, her voice coming out in a whisper. "If I lose you...what'll happen to me?"

The Snake went up to her and hugged her tight. "I don't want to even think about that." said the Snake. "Which is why I'm going to go see Scherbakov. There's strength in numbers, and if that man's resources are half of what he claims, then it'll be an advantage I'll make full use of."

"And then?" asked Allison. "What happens after the Camerlengos are gone? What if we're still afraid?"

"Things aren't going to get worse." said the Snake, quoting from last night's movie again. "I'm going to make sure of that. Just stand with me, and we'll make it out of this together."

Allison groaned. "I'm seriously starting to regret finding that movie." she said. "Okay, go meet that Scherbakov man. But take me with you and Linda."

The Snake stared at Allison, trying to think of a million ways to keep her from going to that meeting. "Allison, I really don't think—"

"Take me with you!" Allison insisted, her face the picture of resolute determination. "Otherwise I won't let you go. You got it?"

The Snake struggled on how best to handle this demand. Finally he just sighed and said, "Fine, you can go." Allison smiled and nodded her head, her way of saying the issue was resolved. Silently the Snake looked up towards the ceiling and beyond and prayed that Allison wouldn't make any more demands of him like this one.

Allison went back into the bedroom while the Snake went to the kitchen and started pulling out coffee and pancake mix. As he heard the shower turn on and water flow through the pipes, he wondered again if he was taking a very bad deal, even if it was necessary, and if it would come to harm not just him, but Allison too.

Chapter Eighty

Camerlengo struggled to keep his hands steady as he poured wine into the glass. As he spilled a little bit of wine over the lip of the glass, his guest said, "Let me get that for you."

"No, you are a guest in my home." Camerlengo insisted, forcing his hands to steady and managing to pour the rest of the wine without spilling a drop. Handing the glass to Frissora, Camerlengo raised his own glass in a toast and poured back the wine. Frissora merely sipped the wine, looking quietly dignified as he drank, even though he only wore jeans and a light-gray hoodie over his massive frame.

"You know why I've called you here." said Camerlengo, putting the glass down and wiping his mouth with the back of his hand. "You know this is a difficult time for me, and for my organization."

"Indeed I do," said Frissora, his mouth and eyes the only parts of his face visible from within the hood he wore over his head. "I am sorry about your family, by the way. You have my condolences."

Camerlengo knew that Frissora had no idea of the meaning of the word "sorry", let alone had any idea what Camerlengo was going through right now. The man before Camerlengo was more intelligent beast than expert assassin. Nevertheless, Camerlengo said, "Thank you, Frissora. You don't know how much I appreciate that."

"It's the least I can do." said Frissora, pulling back his hood to reveal a dark-skinned face with burn scars along the left side. The scarring on Frissora's face was what led to the creation of Frissora's nickname among some of Camerlengo's underlings: Freddy. Camelengo could see why this nickname was so popular among his men. Not only was Frissora scary to behold, especially his face, but he was also a ruthless killer, employed by various terrorist and crime organizations around the world. If they were willing to pay his fee, Frissora would do what they wanted, though Camerlengo secretly suspected that what Frissora really liked was the death and destruction he caused and that the fee was just a formality.

"So," said Frissora, taking another sip of wine, still looking highly dignified despite his scars and dress, "tell me about this New York Mafia Killer."

"You've seen the news reports." said Camerlengo, sitting in his chair. Frissora sat down in the chair on the other side of Camerlengo's desk, the chair making a loud protesting creak as it took Frissora's full weight. "And you've heard what our police mole was able to dig up before he was murdered. He likes to carve 'Snake' into his victims' chests and break their bones till they can't take anymore."

"*Zamochit*." said Frissora. "I'm familiar with it. It was used mostly in the Soviet era though, originating in the seventies."

Camerlengo raised an eyebrow. "I didn't know that." he said. "So this guy could be in his mid-40s or something? That's what the police's shrink seems to think, anyway."

"It's possible." said Frissora. "I'd be more concerned with the Owen Barlow killing. It's an aberration in his pattern."

"What do you mean?" asked Camerlengo, curious.

"The Snake killer, as your men call him, went exclusively for people on your payroll." said Frissora, swirling the wine in his glass as he talked. "Your *consligiere*, your pimps, your lieutenant and your mole. But then a football player who bought a girl from one of your auctions…he could've gone for anyone from that auction, or even ignored the auction entirely. Why the football player?"

Camerlengo realized what Frissora was talking about with a shock. "Something about Barlow stood out to him." said Camerlengo. The man in front of him was a beast, without question, but at least he was a highly intelligent beast. "That's why he went after him!"

Frissora nodded. "I'm a killer, so I know a thing or two about them." said Frissora, taking another sip of wine. "I kill when I get my orders from my employers, and the Snake killer kills when he sees something that makes someone a target. If we can figure out what exactly stood out to the Snake killer about Barlow, what made Barlow a target, we may be able to find the person who calls himself the Snake killer."

"Any ideas about what attracted this guy to Barlow?" asked Camerlengo.

"Perhaps the Snake killer was molested by his father as a boy." said Frissora with a shrug. "Him or someone he knows. Or perhaps it's the girl Barlow bought. Was there anything special about her?"

Camerlengo wondered how best to answer before saying, "She had some information we wanted to keep secret. We gave her a chance to live under our care, but...well, she couldn't keep her mouth shut."

"Why didn't you just kill her?" asked Frissora.

"I wanted to make use of her." said Camerlengo. "She was a virgin and she was defiant, which some customers like. You can't blame me for wanting to see the little bitch be useful, can you?"

"I suppose not." said Frissora with a deep chuckle. "Well, I think that girl might be a weapon of sorts for the Snake killer. He'll use her information against you, if he can."

"Then we'd better hurry and find them both." said Camerlengo. "And if you bring them to me alive, I'll double your usual rate."

Frissora smiled. "Where do you want me to start looking?" he asked, his shiny white teeth reminding Camerlengo of fangs.

Chapter Eighty-One

The Snake spotted Scherbakov from across the street, standing casually by the entrance of the MoMA and talking on his cellphone. Looking around, the Snake couldn't find anyone who looked like they were guarding Scherbakov or standing watch for the Snake, but that didn't mean there wasn't anyone nearby doing those things. Standing next to him, Allison squeezed his hand and whispered, "Are you sure this is a good idea?"

"I'm not sure of anything at this point." the Snake answered. "But I'm willing to take a chance and trust this guy. If you want, I can hail you a cab and you can go home."

Allison shook her head at him. "No, I'm staying with you." she said. "We're in this together, remember? 'Sides, you said I could hold onto Linda, remember?"

"I remember." said the Snake. "I just hope you remember those Russian commands I gave you."

"You're not the only one." said Allison. Taking a deep breath, she said, "Okay, let's do this."

The Snake nodded and led them across Fifty-Third Street, Allison holding onto the dog leash while the Snake held onto Allison's hand. As they approached Scherbakov, two men came out of the museum entrance and headed straight for the Snake and Allison. As they approached, Linda started growling, and the Snake became aware that Allison was squeezing his hand so tightly it felt a little painful.

"Really?" said the Snake in Russian as the men came within earshot. "I hope you're not thinking of frisking me in public. You'd both look very strange doing it."

The two men stopped in their tracks and looked at each other as if unsure of what to do. Pushing past them, the Snake walked with Allison and Linda towards Scherbakov, who quickly ended his call and put his cellphone in his pocket as he saw the Snake coming.

"Ah, I'm glad to see you without the mask on." said Scherbakov in English, extending his hand. The Snake only narrowed his eyes and stared seriously at Scherbakov, who seemed to get the message and put his hand back at his side. "You're right," said Scherbakov, "we're not exactly friends yet, are we? Let us wait until I explain my idea before we shake hands, shall we?"

"Sounds good to me." said the Snake, using his normal voice.

Scherbakov nodded his head and then, to the Snake's chagrin, turned to Allison. "And how are you, young lady? I don't believe we've had the pleasure of meeting."

"If I had my way, you would never meet at all." said the Snake, his teeth gritted. "Now, did we come here to make pleasantries or are we actually going to get down to business?"

"Of course," said Scherbakov amiably. "It is obvious you still do not trust me. Maybe this meeting will change your mind. Especially when I tell you what I've learned."

"What have you learned?" asked the Snake.

Scherbakov shook his head. "Walk with me, Snake." he said. "You too, Ms. Langland. You both should hear this."

"I don't remember giving you my name." Allison pointed out as they started walking away from the entrance and down the street.

"You didn't have to." Scherbakov explained, pulling out a cigar and lighter. As he lit the cigar, he continued, "I checked out your boyfriend's Facebook page after we met yesterday. Your name and face was plastered all over it. It wasn't too hard to put two and two together, as you Americans like to say."

The Snake groaned. "Sorry, Al." he said. "Looks like I fucked up there."

"It's not your fault." said Allison.

"She's right." Scherbakov added, blowing smoke rings as he took the cigar out of his mouth. "I would have found out eventually about your girlfriend. After all, I already have your name. With just that, so much information is available with just a few clicks of a keyboard."

"I hope knowing Allison's identity isn't the important piece of information you wanted to share with us." said the Snake. "Because it only makes me more wary of you."

"Then I'm sure you'll appreciate what I'm about to tell you." said Scherbakov. "The Camerlengos have called on Frissora."

"What's a Frissora?" asked the Snake.

"Not 'what', but 'who'." corrected Scherbakov. "Frissora is a mercenary, a professional hitman who's done jobs for organized crime families and terrorist organizations the world over. Not much is known about him, except rumors that he came from some conflict or another in the north of Africa, and that he's so good that law enforcement officials have never even heard of him. In any case, he's well-known in underground circles, and Camerlengo has employed him before. The fact that Frissora was called in shows how dangerous Camerlengo considers you and how far he's willing to go to get rid of you."

"He's really that dangerous?" asked Allison, squeezing the Snake's hand again.

"Indeed he is, Ms. Langland." said Scherbakov. "Not only that, but he is extremely intelligent and quite the detective. I'd say it's only a matter of time before he tracks you both down."

"How do you know that?" asked the Snake.

"You see the evening news yesterday?" asked Scherbakov.

"No we didn't." said the Snake, hoping he wasn't blushing as he remembered what happened last night. "We were otherwise occupied."

"Well, that thing in Central Park with the shooter yesterday made the news." said Scherbakov. "A video was filmed on a witness's cellphone. And in the video, you can clearly be seen tackling him, Snake. I don't think they saw you breaking the man's arms, but they definitely saw you attack and hit him. Not only that, but Ms. Langland can be seen in the video for a little bit."

"What?" said the Snake, feeling panic rising within him. Instinctively the Snake let go of Allison's hand and wrapped his arm around her shoulders, pulling her close to him as if to shield her from the world.

"She's only seen for a few seconds in the left-hand corner, hugging the dog." Scherbakkov gestured to Linda, who was staring past him and watching the foot traffic on Fifty-third. "Later when she drags you away from the shooter, her face cut off in the frame.

However, she can be seen in the video, and both law enforcement and the Camerlengos are looking for you two."

"Law enforcement?" repeated the Snake. "What do they want with Allison—oh, you've got to be kidding me! I knew I was forgetting something."

"I see you realize what happened." said Scherbakov, looking from the Snake to Allison. "Ms. Langland, you left some of your DNA in Owen Barlow's apartment. It may have been only a hair or maybe even an eyelash, but the point is, the police found something, and that led them to you. Word from an informant on the investigation said your report from Missing Persons was brought to the task force, and now they believe you are with the New York Mafia Killer."

"They got that right." said the Snake.

"But they don't know for sure, do they?" asked Allison anxiously. "Or that I'm with him, right?"

"Not likely." said Scherbakov. "But I doubt it would make much difference, anyway. Your boyfriend is a dangerous killer, Ms. Langland. The police just want to capture him at this point, so they'll assume anything about your relationship if it can lead to an arrest. And the Camerlengos want to kill their greatest threat in years and the girl who they tried to get rid of only to have her slip through their fingers and into the hands of their enemy, so they'll also be on the lookout for any sign of you, Ms. Langland."

"*Bozhe moy*" said the Snake. "Soemone's got to have noticed by now that Allison and I are in that video."

"And whoever does notice you will start looking for the both of you." Scherbakov finished. "And I can guarantee you things will go badly when that happens, especially if Camerlengo and Frissora are the ones who find you. I thought you should be aware of that fact."

The Snake hesitated with what he said next, but he opened his mouth anyway and said, "Thanks. I didn't know I was in that much trouble."

"You're welcome." said Scherbakov. "I bet you also didn't know that *zamochit* isn't used so much these days in the Russian mob."

The Snake stared at Scherbakov as if he'd just shown the Snake he could levitate. "What? I heard that *zamochit* was popular in the Russian mob—!"

"During the Soviet era, yes it was." said Scherbakov. "But since there are so many mob families of Russian descent these days, and we all have such control over the Russian economy, *zamochit* isn't as useful to send messages anymore. Too many people have used it, so it's gone out of popularity. Today we lean on…newer methods to get our messages across."

"What sort of methods?"

Scherbakov only smiled and said, "Shall we discuss my plans for our partnership, Snake?"

The Snake was surprised by the turn the conversation had gone, but said, "Tell me what you want to do."

"Well, I'd like to first get you to a new location." said Scherbakov. "Now that your security is in jeopardy, it'd be better if we moved you to somewhere only we knew about."

Scherbakov paused, during which time the Snake processed the information in his head. So far, he hadn't been given a reason to distrust this man, so either he was a good actor or he was really trying to get the Snake on his side and was being an honorable person while doing it.

"Go on." said the Snake. "What happens next?"

Scherbakov's smile grew wider. As the mob boss explained his plan, the Snake listened with interest. Finally when Scherbakov was done, the Snake said, "It sounds pretty good. But you could do this sort of plan without me. I don't necessarily have to be there for the Camerlengos to be interested and come."

"But that would be too big a lie to tell." said Scherbakov. "And it would be so much better to have you on my side and working actively with me, especially if we both wish to destroy the Camerlengos. Besides, my family's prestige will grow if you're there and this succeeds."

The Snake thought about it and decided that what Scherbakov was talking about made sense. And if the plan worked, not only will the Snake have gained a powerful ally, it would make destroying the Camerlengos that much easier.

The Snake looked down at Allison, who was looking up at him. The look in her eyes said, *If you're okay with it, so am I. Just don't separate me from you.*

Finally the Snake looked at Scherbakov and said, "When this goes down, I want Allison to be nearby. You understand me?"

Scherbakov's face lit up like a Christmas tree. "Of course." he said. "In fact, I can think of several places at the site that Ms. Langland can be hidden safely while still be near you."

The Snake smiled and extended his hand. "It's a deal." he said.

Scherbakov took the hand and shook it. "Deal." he said. "Now how about we go to your apartment and get your things? I'll arrange for use of a safe house for the both of you to use."

Scherbakov raised his hand in the air as if he were about to hail a taxi. What appeared instead was a black town car, which pulled up to the side of the street with its engine humming softly. Scherbakov opened the door and gestured for the Snake, Allison and Linda to get in. As the Snake sat down on the fine leather seats, he wondered again if this second deal with the devil would bite him in the ass…and then let the thought go.

Chapter Eighty-Two

Murtz marched into the task room feeling more energetic than she had in days. Walking right past other members of the task force who called out afternoon greetings to her, she went straight for Harnist, Patton, and Gramer, who were deep in conversation while looking at a whiteboard with the timeline of the murders written on it, along with various photos of the victims and other pieces of information and evidence tacked on with magnets. Stopping right behind them, Murtz cleared her throat and said, "Excuse me gentlemen."

Harnist, Patton and Gramer all spun around, hands over their hearts like they'd just been given huge electric shocks. Murtz was feeling so cheerful, she couldn't help but laugh. "Sorry boys." she said. "Didn't mean to frighten you."

"It's okay, Murtz." said Patton, resuming his normal commandeering manner. "Anyway, you came at the right time. We've been trying to figure out if there was something we missed before, so we've been basically looking at the whiteboard for the past couple of hours."

"Where've you been anyway, Murtz?" asked Harnist. "I haven't seen you since yesterday afternoon."

"Yeah, sorry about that." Murtz looked left and right to make sure no one was listening before leaning in and whispering, "I think I've found the Snake killer's identity."

"What?" said Harnist, Patton, and Gramer in unison, their voices a little louder than normal. Murtz winced as several faces turned to look at them in confusion. Lowering his voice, Patton whispered, "Let's go in my office."

They quickly retreated to the room that had been made Patton's temporary office while he was working at FBI headquarters, a small room with glass windows and a high-tech computer system with a large interactive flat-screen along an entire wall. Locking the door and closing the blinds, Patton turned to Murtz and said, "Alright, tell us what you've come up with, Murtz."

"Love to, but can we first set that thing up?" asked Murtz, gesturing to the computer system on the wall. With a few clicks Patton had set up the main computer and the interactive whiteboard. Thanking him, Murtz went to the computer and plugged in a flash drive, which lit up as soon as it was inserted into the slot. A moment later Murtz's flash drive appeared in its own window with several files listed with various abbreviations and nicknames. Clicking on one particular file, Murtz brought up a picture of a young man with unremarkable features save for a pair of brilliant blue eyes on the whiteboard, staring out at the camera while wearing a smart school uniform.

Harnist, Patton, and Gramer looked at Murtz with their eyebrows raised. "Um…Agent Murtz?" said Gramer. "I hate to ask this…but are you kidding me?"

"No." said Murtz confidently. "I'm not kidding you. That there's the New York Mafia Killer, with this photo taken back in November at picture day at Mardukas Academy."

Harnist read the name listed under the photograph and said, "Murtz, are you saying that the New York Mafia Killer…is a teenager? I thought you said that he was at least in his thirties. You put it in your own profile!"

"And like I said, the profile is only a lot of educated guesswork." Murtz reminded them, sitting down in the chair in front of the system's keyboard. "It's not until we actually sit down and talk to the suspect that we can see the true killer, the true nutcase committing the crimes. But I think this guy might be our perp after all."

"How do you figure that?" asked Gramer.

"You remember I said that I felt like I was missing something?" asked Murtz. "Like there was something missing from my profile? Well, I found what I was missing, but I didn't realize it until I saw this." Murtz pressed a key on the computer and the photograph of the young man in the school uniform switched to the news clip of the shooting in Central Park yesterday. Murtz watched with Harnist, Patton, and Gramer as the video played out. As it ended, Murtz said, "See anything interesting?"

"That boy from the photo." said Gramer. "He was the one who attacked the shooter."

"Indeed he was." said Murtz. "But did you notice the girl who pulled him away from the shooter? I'll play the clip again. Pay attention to the left-hand corner of the video." Murtz pressed a key and the clip looped back to the beginning, showing the shooter attacking his girlfriend, followed by the boy from the photo attacking the shooter, and then the shooter being led away. Murtz turned to look at her colleagues and was pleased to see looks of surprised recognition on their faces.

"That's Allison Langland." said Harnist. "The missing doctor's daughter, the one whose hair we found at Owen Barlow's apartment."

"Correct." said Murtz. "And guess what? That boy in the clip is no mere acquaintance of Allison. That's her boyfriend." Murtz pressed another key and a picture appeared on the screen showing the two teenagers in beachwear, the boy holding a surfboard in one arm and hugging Allison Langland to him with the other. "And she sure picked an interesting person for her boyfriend." Murtz added. "A very interesting person."

"What are you saying?" asked Patton.

"I saw that clip yesterday on the news and I noticed Allison in it." said Murtz. "She's sort of out of the way, so most might not have noticed her until she pulled her boyfriend away, and even then Allison's face is cut out of the frame. However the fact that she's there got me thinking. If the New York Mafia Killer is smart enough to kill several members of the Camerlengo family, erase the evidence, and even evade a whole task force when we've got him surrounded in an open field, surely he's smart enough to keep the girl who was kidnapped by the Camerlengos and then sold to Owen Barlow near him. After all, she's a chip he can use against them. But then if that's the case, what is she doing in Central Park?"

There were a couple nods as the men considered the question. Smiling, Murtz continued, "It doesn't make a lot of sense, unless the killer doesn't think of her as a chip. Doesn't *want* her to be a chip. He would rather her be free to go to a place like Central Park without feeling afraid. In other words, he may be a friend or a close acquaintance of hers. This led me to look at her Facebook page, and there I found our attacker, Allison's boyfriend."

"How do you know he's our attacker?" asked Harnist.

"I did a little digging about him." Murtz explained. "According to his school psychologist, his mother is out of the picture, and his father isn't very involved in his son's life. He's also president of his high school film club, which since he took the reins in his sophomore year, has taken a darker approach in its movies. In fact, last spring the film club submitted a documentary about the history of the mob in New York to a national film studies competition. The documentary won second place in its category. Get this though: the film covered some of the Russian mobs, and made specific mention of torture techniques such as *zamochit*. And during their fall semester this year, they made an hour-long film about Jack the Ripper, with Mr. Director here playing the killer as well."

"That doesn't prove he's the serial killer." Patton pointed out.

"Yes, but there's more." said Murtz. "According to friends of Allison and friends of her boyfriend, he's been into movies with serial killers since he was young. Not only that, but he's gotten into fights in the past, where he once put another teen in the hospital."

"He attacked the teen?" asked Gramer.

"No, the teen attacked a friend of his and he intervened." said Murtz. "But it's just like the New York Mafia Killer, who attacked the Camerlengos because nobody else can or will. That's not all, though: he's also fluent in several languages, including Russian, and is good at imitating accents, such as when he spoke Spanish with an exchange student and the student thought that Allison's boyfriend was from Spain as well."

"This is all circumstancial." said Patton. "And he's been at school this whole time—"

"No he hasn't." said Murtz. "I checked with his school: apparently he ran away from home around the same time as Dr. Langland and his daughter went missing. According to the psychologist, not too long after he ran away, his father disowned him over a disagreement and failed to file a missing person's report on the grounds it wasn't any of his business. I've been trying to contact the father, but so far none of my calls have been returned. But still, that's over two weeks of unaccounted time where we have no idea where the boyfriend is, which could mean—"

"That he was looking for his girlfriend." Gramer finished. "Are you saying the New York Mafia Killer went on a killing spree because they kidnapped his girlfriend?"

"And he was going through Camerlengo henchmen looking for clues to her." said Murtz. "I know it sounds like a stretch, but my gut is telling me—"

"And I respect your gut." said Patton. "I listen to mine all the time and I tell my subordinates to listen to their guts all the time. However we're going to need more evidence if we even want a search warrant for his father's place, let alone wherever this kid has been for the past several weeks. And for all we know, the New York Mafia Killer might've just run into the kid and given him his girlfriend before taking off."

"Or perhaps Allison got away from Barlow and the killer and then somehow met up with her boyfriend." Harnist pointed out.

"Or a dozen other possibilities." said Gramer. "Murtz, you're grasping at straws here. There's nothing here to tie this kid to the murders, let alone make him a person of interest."

"I know." said Murtz. "But I know this is our guy. And as soon as I have something to prove it, we're putting him away."

Before Harnist, Patton, and Gramer could say anything else and before Murtz could tell them to put away the sympathetic-but-disbelieving looks on their faces, there was a knock on the door and Fallmouth walked in, looking excited and nervous all at the same time. "Big news!" he said. "A contact in the Scherbakovs gave us some big info. They received some information about where the Snake killer will be in two nights!"

Murtz, Harnist, Patton, and Gramer all looked at each other in shock, the men looking surprised and excited. Murtz felt more than just excitement though: she felt opportunity. Perhaps she might have flimsy evidence to support her theory, but if this information on the Snake killer's location is correct, then she might have the chance to prove her theory.

Chapter Eighty-Three

Camerlengo had assembled all of his best men in his ballroom, his best lieutenants and soldiers, men with combat experience and undying loyalty to the family. Among them was Frissora, standing off to the side and chewing on a toothpick with a detached air to him, as if he was watching everything from a movie theater and Camerlengo and his men were characters in the film.

That was fine. For all Camerlengo could care, Frissora could have a bag of popcorn and a thirty-two ounce cup of soda. Since the death of Camerlengo's family, the police had been unable to figure out who had planted the car bomb on his wife's Jaguar, as the bomb had been made with household chemicals and parts that could be easily picked up at any electronics store and the explosion had destroyed anyh other helpful evidence. Even when Camerlengo's men had taken a look at the wreckage, they didn't find anything. With no one coming forward to claim the credit and no real suspects, Camerlengo could only point the accusing finger at the New York Mafia Killer, who had already taken away so much from him.

So Frissora could enjoy this show all he wanted. Just as long as he did as he was hired to do and delivered the son of a bitch into Camerlengo's hands. Only then would Camerlengo be satisfied.

Camerlengo strode over to the top of a makeshift podium he'd had assembled earlier today. At once the murmur in the room went quiet and all eyes turned to the podium. Camerlengo cleared his throat and eyed the crowd. For once, Camerlengo couldn't see any fear in any of the people here, and surprisingly he was happy about that. He needed these men to be ready, brave and strong for what lay ahead.

For the sake of Camerlengo's wife Sheila. For the sake of his children.

"You know why you've been brought here." said Camerlengo, waving his arms out at the crowd. "For the past several weeks, our organization—our family!—has been under attack by a man who hides in shadow and picks us off when it is convenient for him. A coward, who pretends he is some sort of hero so he can feel good about himself!

"And the media has dubbed this psychopath, this *freak*...the New York Mafia Killer!"

The air in the room intensified, rippling almost with anger. Camerlengo felt his pride grow as he saw the rage, the hate in his men's faces. "Until now, we have been unable to catch this killer!" Camerlengo continued. "But we have received information from a mole in the FBI where the New York Mafia Killer will be tomorrow night!"

The men started whispering amongst themselves, their voices filled with hushed awe and wonder. Camerlengo spoke over them, saying, "The New York Mafia Killer has allies, and he will be meeting with them in front of Hostos Community College in the Bronx, where they will plan how to kill several members of the family at once! You hear that? They are planning to meet and take out more of us!"

There were shouts from the soldiers, angry yells and threats to the Snake killer's life. The anger in the crowd was rising, and as it rose, so did Camerlengo's spirits. He could almost feel his wife's ghost near him, watching with joy as her husband worked to get revenge for her death.

"Are we going to let this man and his sick fans get away with taking more of our blood?" Camerlengo asked the crowd.

"No!" was the resounding answer.

"Do we want to get him and his allies?"

"Yes!"

"Then come tomorrow night, we will be waiting with the cops for the New York Mafia Killer!" shouted Camerlengo, his glee and rage uncontained. "Only instead of helping them arrest him, we will kill his allies! We will put them through the same hell that he put our comrades through!"

The soldiers screamed with excitement, bloodlust and wrath. Camerlengo's grin widened as he said, "And when you capture him, you will bring him to me. I will thrash him to within an inch of his life, and then I will destroy him! I will kill him and leave his body where all can see him! No one will ever try to fight the Camerlengos ever again!"

The screams that rose up from his men shook the room with their intensity. Camerlengo felt mad laughter bubble up from within him and burst out, mingling with the cheers and vengeful shouts of his men.

Soon, New York Mafia Killer. thought Camerlengo. *Soon, I'll have you where I want you. I'll snap your little neck with my own two hands! Nobody touches my family without paying the price!*

In the corner, Frissora grinned like a fanged child expecting to go to the carnival tomorrow night. It was almost as if Fate was working to bring his client his quarry and render Frissora ineffective. And that was what caught Frissora's attention, how timed this bit of news was. From what he understood, the Camerlengo Family had received their information from the authorities, who in turn had received their information from an informant in the Scherbakov Organization, and nobody in the Camerlengos knew where he'd heard it from or even who this informant was, only that he was trustworthy.

And all this had happened right as Frissora had started his investigation into the New York Mafia Killer.

Frissora had been a mercenary for nearly twenty-five years. He had seen and done enough to develop a sense for when things were off, and things were definitely off with this whole situation. Even if Camerlengo and his cronies were too angry and excited to see that they might be walking into a trap, Frissora knew that the possibility was more likely than not.

Even if he did know whether or not there was a trap waiting for him and the Camerlengo Family, Frissora was all too happy to walk into it. He craved excitement from the time he was a little boy, and walking into a trap willingly would be most exciting, if this New York Mafia Killer was as good as was said.

Leaning back against the wall, Frissora watched Camerlengo laughing like a lunatic on his little stage. He could not wait for tomorrow night.

PART FIVE
COILED

Chapter Eighty-Four

Murtz and Harnist waited in the black Crown Victoria hidden around the corner, sipping coffee as they stared out the window. At this time of night, Hostos Community College was empty, with not even a light or a maintenance worker in sight. It made Harnist realize why this place had been chosen for the Snake killer to meet his allies.

"I can't believe our luck." said Harnist, glancing over at Murtz. "Sure our bosses will probably take the credit for this catch, but we'll have a dangerous criminal off the streets who won't screw with our investigations anymore."

"Yeah." said Murtz noncommittally.

Harnist raised an eyebrow. "Everything okay, Doc?"

Murtz sighed and said, "I suppose."

Harnist wasn't convinced. Leaning over, he said, "Does this have anything to do with your theory about the boyfriend?"

"Maybe." said Murtz. "I mean, I just feel like it could be him, you know? I just have this gut feeling that tells me I'm on the right track. But then that tip comes in, and then the whole task force is rushing to get ready to capture the Snake killer in two nights. Kind of puts my theory on a back burner, if it's on the stove at all."

Harnist saw her point of view and nodded in understanding. "That's true." he said.

"And you know what? That's another thing."

"What's another thing?" asked Harnist.

"The tip!" said Murtz. "I mean, someone in the Scherbakovs calls in, says he knows the New York Mafia Killer, and says that he was tricked into helping him! Says he'll give away the location of the meeting and what sort of car he'll be driving if we promise him protection and not to prosecute him as an accessory to murder. It sounds a little too convenient, doesn't it?"

"But the tip was solid." said Harnist. "He even described things the Snake killer did, things we haven't released to the public yet. He even gave us Armentrout's name. We hid that name so that Armentrout would be safe until we prosecuted him!"

"I know." said Murtz. "Maybe I am grasping at straws after all. Maybe Allison Langland is with her boyfriend, and the Snake just happened to drop her off with him. Maybe the shooting in Central Park was just a boyfriend who got a little violent trying to protect his girlfriend from some idiot with a gun threatening the idiot's girlfriend, and I'm just saying the Snake killer is the boyfriend because I feel like I'm missing something and I'm not sure what."

"Well, there's one thing we can be sure of." said Harnist.

"What's that?" asked Murtz.

"We'll know who the killer is in a few minutes." Harnist pointed out the window, where a black van was rolling up to the curb in front of the college entrance. Over the car radio, Patton could be heard saying, "Target is in sight, exactly as the source described. Be ready people, it's almost showtime. Wait until he's turned off the car lights before moving out."

Murtz and Harnist reached for their weapons and set them to semi-automatic. Slipping quietly out of the Crown Victoria, Harnist and Murtz tiptoed to the street corner. Around the street, other agents were doing the same. As the lights on the front of the van clicked off, Harnist raised his hand in the air with three fingers up. Slowly he curled his ring finger down, and then he put his middle finger down. As he was curling his index finger down, there were several loud reports and the side of the van became riddled with large holes.

Bullet holes.

Before Harnist could look to see who had fired before he could give the command, the black van roared to life and sped away from the college, its tires squealing on the pavement. A moment later a line of expensive-looking all-terrain vehicles were speeding after the van, several with men leaning out of the windows holding large machine guns.

Harnist and Murtz looked at each other, each wearing an expression of horrified realization. The Camerlengos had known about the meeting, and they were literally gunning for blood.

Chapter Eighty-Five

Frissora drove after the black van, his hands gripping the steering wheel tightly. Next to him, a young soldier who couldn't have been more than twenty-five was sticking his upper half out the window and shouting wildly. Frissora let him shout and wave his gun around like a big boy. Soon, they'd have the target in their hands, and the killer and his friends would all feel the Camerlengos' retribution. It was okay for the boy next to him to feel a little excited.

Of course, that was assuming this wasn't a trap. Then anything was possible, including the youth's life being cut dramatically short.

As the Camerlengos drove after the Snake killer, several of them leaning out the windows and trying to get a clear shot, there were the sounds of police sirens from behind. Looking in the rearview mirror, Frissora saw several plainclothes cars on their trail with flashing red bubbles on their tail. Feeling slightly annoyed, Frissora tapped on the youth's leg. The kid slipped his head back in and said, "What's up?"

"Shoot at the police officers." said Frissora. The kid looked at Frissora with wide eyes, like he couldn't believe what he'd said. "Go ahead," urged Frissora, gesturing for the kid to stick his head back out the window. "If you start shooting, the others will follow, and you won't be the only one shooting. They won't be able to know who started it or who finished it." A change came over the kid as he absorbed Frissora's words, and he put his forefinger and thumb together in a circle, the American sign for "OK". Slipping his head back out the window, the kid looked behind the car and starting shooting at the police cars. A moment later there were several more gunshots in the direction of the police cruisers, followed by a screech, a loud crash, and an explosion.

Frissora winced as he heard the explosion. Nevertheless he was smiling, and gladly gave the kid a high-five as he ducked his head back in again. This was proving to be as exciting as Frissora had hoped it would be.

"That was awesome!" said the kid. "Now the cops won't be able to interfere for at least...um—"

"Five to ten minutes." Frissora answered, keeping his eyes on the road. The black van was gathering speed ahead of them, and it was only a matter of time before it crossed the East One-Forty-Fifth Bridge into Manhattan. Gunning the accelerator, Frissora pulled ahead of the Camerlengo pack and managed to pull alongside the black van.

"Hang on!" Frissora shouted. Jerking the wheel hard to the left, Frissora rammed the car into the van's side. The van swerved along the road, nearly hitting the bridge barrier. Somehow though the driver was able to right the course of the van and pull ahead, attempting to leave Frissora behind.

Frissora grinned. "He's a worthy opponent." said Frissora to the kid, who was high on exhilaration and adrenaline, leaning forward in his seat as if he could get closer to the Snake's van that way. "Let's see if we can knock him down a few pegs, though." Frissora slammed his foot down on the accelerator, ramming the front of the car into the back of the van. The van lurched forward, the back bumper bent and the license plate knocked loose. Flooring the accelerator again, Frissora rammed the car into the back of the van again, this time freeing the back bumper from the van and sending it clattering down the road.

"We almost got him!" said the kid, bouncing up and down in his seat.

Frissora gunned the accelerator again, smashing the car into the van a third time. "Almost." he said, more to himself than to the kid. "But not quite." Frissora eased his foot off the accelerator as the end of the bridge approached, watching to see if the van would make a sudden turn. Sure enough, the van turned off of One-Forty-Fifth Street in Manhattan and onto Lenox Avenue heading south. Jerking the wheel sharply to the left again, Frissora followed the van down Lenox Avenue, followed by the rest of the Camerlengos in a huge herd.

As the van swerved down Lenox Avenue, passing by angry honking cars and angrier shouting motorists, Frissora struggled to keep up, scratching against other cars and nearly ramming twice into the back ends of innocent motorists as he tried to catch up with the Snake killer. Somewhere in the distance he could hear the sound of the police finally beginning to catch up with them, but they were still too far away to do anything useful.

A few cars ahead the van looked like it was about to keep going along Lenox, but to Frissora's surprise and glee the van swerved from the middle lane to the right lane and then turned right onto West One-Thirty-Ninth Street and out of sight. With a competitive growl Frissora managed to get into the right-turning lane and followed the van onto West One-Thirty-Ninth, speeding as he attempted to get close to the van again.

Up ahead the van turned right into the open gate of a construction lot and out of sight. As Frissora followed the van, he was joined by the rest of the Camerlengos, who followed him into the construction lot. At the base of the building, which at this point was nothing more than floors and support columns, the van sat, its engine steaming translucent white smoke.

Frissora pulled up his car near the van. As the Camerlengos pulled up beside him, their engines roaring loudly as the tires squealed to a halt. Frissora was about to get out when he saw something that surprised him. Looking around, he saw several hundred people standing in the structure, wearing suits and bulletproof vests and wielding guns.

And there was one man on an upper floor, wearing black clothes and a mask. Frissora couldn't pick out any details but he guessed that the man in the mask was feeling deep satisfaction.

As Camerlengos slowly got out of their cars and became aware of the situation, Frissora heard the squeaking and clanking of a gate on rollers being closed behind them.

Frissora got out of the car and surveryed the situation. They were trapped.

Interesting.

Chapter Eighty-Six

Scherbakov checked his phone and whispered in Russian, "They've spotted the dummy vehicle and are pursuing it here. We should see it sometime within the next ten minutes."

"Good." the Snake replied in Russian. "I am looking forward to this." The Snake gripped the two machine guns that Scherbakov had loaned him, their shoulder straps crisscrossing his chest. "By the way, thanks for the weapons. They'll come in handy when I go face-to-face with Camerlengo."

"Camerlengo will not be here tonight." said Scherbakov, as if that were the final word on the matter.

The Snake looked at Scherbakov perplexedly. "How come?" asked the Snake.

"Because Camerlengo may be their leader, but he is not the kind who would put himself in the line of fire." said Scherbakov. "He prefers to delegate and watch from the sidelines, to let those lower on the ladder do his dirty work. He's probably given orders to bring you to him, dead or alive."

"I take that you standing here with me means you're a different type of leader?" said the Snake as he let Scherbakov's explanation sink in.

"In the days of the small nation of Rus, when kings formed their kingdoms from the ashes of war, the best general was usually the one who became king." said Scherbakov, checking his phone again. "Not just because he was the best strategist, but also because he fought alongside his troops, encouraged those with potential, rewarded those who garnered the most glory in battle." Scherbakov looked at the Snake and continued, "I may not live in those times anymore, but I believe in the way of the leaders of those times. *They were true leaders.*"

Underneath his mask, the Snake grinned. "You should've run for office." said the Snake.

Scherbakov laughed. "And be like the politicians I already manipulate?" said Scherbakov. "No, thank you! I prefer the job I have right now."

The Snake nodded in understanding. A short pause followed, which the Snake ended when he said, "Thank you, Nikolai."

"For what?" asked Scherbakov.

"For everything you've done for me these past two days." said the Snake. "You became my ally, you gave Allison and me shelter, and you're allowing me to finish my mission. Hell, even Allison is grateful, though she won't say it."

Scherbakov chuckled. "You're welcome, Snake." said Scherbakov. "I enjoyed having you stay as a guest in my home. And my wife enjoyed your presence too, which is something considering she usually doesn't trust non-Russians."

"Oh, that reminds me, I'm going to have to get that recipe for mushroom lapsha that your wife made last night." said the Snake. "It was delicious. I wonder what spices she used in it."

"I'm not sure, but you can ask." said Scherbakov. "Doesn't guarantee she'll tell you, though. Oh, and before I forget, I have something else I want to give you. Yulian, bring the gift!"

"Gift?" said the Snake, confused. "What gift—? Oh."

One of Scherbakov's subordinates came forward carrying something the Snake knew well. Taking the machete out of its sheath, the Snake held it up so that its steel blade reflected in the moonlight. "It's beautiful." said the Snake. Looking at Scherbakov, he said with full gratitude, "Thank you."

Scherbakov shrugged. "Call it a good luck charm for tonight." he said. "Besides, you mentioned you were an admirer of the movie serial killer Jason Voorhees, did you not?"

"Yes, I did," said the Snake, sheathing the machete and tying the sheath's strap under the straps of the machine gun. "And you just made tonight a whole lot more fun."

Scherbakov smiled, but then his face became serious again as he looked down at his phone. "They're almost here." he said. A moment later the black van pulled into the lot and screeched to a stop, followed by several all-terrain vehicles that pulled to a stop behind the black van. As the people in the cars slowly got out, Scherbakov pressed a button on his phone, and the gate into the lot rolled shut.

The Snake looked down at the Camerlengos, seeing their confused and horrified faces. *This is, without a doubt, the best movie I've had a role in yet.* he thought.

Scherbakov raised his arm in the air and swung it forward in a chopping motion. "*Nahpahst*!" he yelled. *Attack!*

There was the sound of gunfire, shouts and roars, with Scherbakov's men rushing forward or climbing down ropes to fight the Camerlengos. The Snake grabbed onto a rope and slid down, already firing one gun as the ground approached. The whole time, he was grinning like a goblin under his mask.

Chapter Eighty-Seven

Harnist watched wide-eyed as the Snake killer's van disappeared, then the Camerlengos' cars disappeared, and finally there was silence. Snapping himself back into action with a shake of his head, Harnist shouted, "Follow them!" while running back to his car with Murtz. Placing a strobe light on the roof of the car and switching it on before sitting down in the front seat, Harnist started the car and started driving after the Camerlengos.

"Damn those Camerlengo bastards!" snarled Harnist, pounding the dashboard as he drove. All around him other plainclothes vehicles with flashing bulbs on their roofs were driving after the Camerlengo cars. Up ahead Harnist could barely make out the black van, which was pulling farther and farther ahead and out of sight. "How did they know that we were going to be here?"

"They must've placed another mole inside the task force." said Murtz. "We'll worry about that later though. Look what they're doing to the van."

Out of several of the cars, men were leaning out with automatics and machine guns and were shooting at the black van, riddling its back doors with bullet holes. Harnist groaned, trying to control his panic at the sight of all those guns pointed at them. "They really are out for blood, aren't they?" he said. "They don't even care about civilian deaths!"

"There's nothing we can do about it now except our jobs, so stay focused on that.. Look, he's turning onto the bridge!" said Murtz. Sure enough, the van turned onto the East One-Forty-Fifth Bridge heading towards Manhattan. "We're going to lose him if we don't find a way to get past these Camerlengos—"

"Get down!" shouted Harnis. All of a sudden one of the Camerlengo cars ahead was shooting towards the task force, damaging windows and causing some cars to swerve. Harnist and Murtz ducked down, Harnist's head barely poking out between the spokes of the wheel. "Dammit." said Harnist. "They could've killed us!"

"You think they'd want our help." said Murtz sardonically. "Well, looks like they stopped—"

Suddenly several of the gunmen leaning out of the car windows turned away from the black van and began shooting a wave of bullets at the task force. Several more cars swerved as they took damage. One of the cars was swerving more wildly than the others, finally veering to the left and crashing against the entrance to the bridge, blocking the way onto the bridge. Harnist slammed his foot on the brakes, stopping just short of hitting a car in front of him. Harnist and Murtz flew forward before being pulled back against their seats by the seatbelts. His head hurting, Harnist looked at Murtz and said, "You alright?"

Murtz nodded her head and held up a thumb, her hair wild and plastered against her forehead with sweat. Harnist smiled at her before saying, "You spoke too soon."

"All available units!" squawked the car radio. "All available units, take alternate route on Madison Avenue Bridge!

Repeat, all units head to alternate route on Madison Avenue Bridge!"

Harnist turned the wheel as the space around him widened and headed south, gripping the wheel tightly as he drove. Turning onto the bridge, Harnist turned left onto Harlem River Drive as the task force split up on the Manhattan side of the bridge, looking for the Camerlengos and the Snake killer.

As Harnist drove down Harlem River, a report came in through the car radio. "Shots fired!" said Patton's voice. "We've got reports of several shots fired at a construction site! Repeat! We've got reports of several shots fired at a construction site!"

As Harnist heard the address, he looked at Murtz. "It's him," he said. Murtz nodded as Harnist turned the wheel and drove towards the address, joining several other cars with flashing lights as they hurried to the construction site. As they converged on the site though, Patton's voice came through on the radio. "Stand down!" he said. "I repeat, stand down! Do not go in there!"

"What the hell?" said Murtz, looking between Harnist and the radio. "Why not?" Harnist tried to see into the construction site, but there was black, gauzy fabric attached to the chain-link gate, and instead of a chain-link fence a tall, wooden fence had been placed around the site, blocking any view of what was going on inside. All Harnist could tell was that inside the construction site, there was a lot of shouting and shooting going on.

"This is Agent Fallmouth," said the radio suddenly. "I'm here on the police chopper. You're not going to believe this. There's a gang war going on down there. I repeat, there's a gang war down there."

"Explain that one." said Harnist into the radio's receiver. "What do you mean, 'gang war'?"

"I mean gang war!" said Fallmouth. "There are people fighting each other down there, not just one against several people. Not even a couple against several people. It's a whole ton of people fighting with guns against a whole bunch of people fighting with guns!"

"Oh my God." said Murtz, a look of realization dawning on her face. "He's got allies in there. The Snake killer has allies. A whole ton of them. They weren't meeting at Hostos. That was all just a diversion to get the Camerlengos here!"

Harnist looked at Murtz and nodded, a deep dread sinking in. "And to take them all out at once." said Harnist. "Just one question: who are his allies?"

Chapter Eighty-Eight

Allison watched from the manager's trailer as the battle raged on outside, hugging Linda's neck in fear before letting go and looking out the front door window, catching a few seconds of action, and then ducking back down again. As she watched, thoughts buzzed around her head, scaring her, reminding her of all the things that could happen, reminding her of all the things she could stand to lose, of all the things that could happen to him out there.

What would happen if he died out there? Or what if he survived but the cops found him? What if the cops didn't find him but some Camerlengo soldier or Camerlengo himself found them? What if he killed everybody after them? What if he didn't stop killing even after everyone after them was dead? What if he liked killing? What if while he was out there killing now, someone came in here and killed her? What if—?

Allison banged her head against the door, trying to drown out her thoughts. As she hit her head, Linda whined and licked her face, trying as best she could to comfort the human she'd been told to guard.

Allison looked at Linda and hugged her again, burying her face in the wiry hair of Linda's neck. "Oh Linda." said Allison. "I feel like something's squeezing me from the inside, crushing me like a grape. It doesn't matter whether I'm here or with Mrs.

Scherbakov, I'm still scared shitless." Allison raised her head out of Linda's neck and sat back against the door, looking towards the harsh fluorescent lights glowing on the ceiling. "Why did this happen?" she asked aloud. "I never asked for any of this. I just wanted a quiet, normal life. Why did I have to get kidnapped? Why did he have to become a serial killer to get me back? This makes no sense."

As Linda licked her face, Allison thought about the past few days. Ever since she'd been kidnapped nearly three weeks ago, she'd slowly begun to feel like she wasn't herself, like she was losing the parts of her that made her Allison Langland. Being kidnapped, taking those calls from disgusting men and a few women, she'd felt her pride weaken and her urge to fight back at the things that bothered her dissipated. Oh, she'd felt like she'd come back again when Kasmet had called her and she thought she'd found a way out, and Allison really felt like herself when they'd tried to carry her out of the service office like a rolled-up rug, but then she'd been locked in that room…starved…forced to use a bucket as a bathroom…watched…forced to do horrible things in front of a camera…harassed by that Camerlengo soldier…nearly raped…

Allison tried to shake her train of thought again and looked out the trailer door window. To her surprise she could easily pick him out of the large crowd, standing on top of a car and shooting at Camerlengos with two large machine guns. A second later he'd jumped off the car roof and was out of sight. Yet seeing him,

Allison felt so much better. It wasn't just that he gave her a sense of security that she'd desperately needed since she'd been rescued, though that was a big part of it. It wasn't even that he was good in bed, though that was a perk. No, it was as if with him, she could find herself again, be Allison Langland again. *I want to be with him so much.* Allison thought, pressing her hand to the window glass, as if to reach out through the darkness to him. *Because when I'm with him, I feel so complete—*

Allison blinked, surprised at herself. She hadn't realized she had fallen so deeply in love with him.

As she looked out again, trying to spot him again, Allison saw a face she recognized and felt a cold stab of fear. The person turned towards the trailer and their eyes connected. Allison felt her heart go cold as the man started running towards the trailer, bending low to avoid bullets.

It's the guy with the earring. thought Allison, backing away from the door. *It's Joe, the guy who watched me use the bucket and kissed me at the warehouse.* There was a bang against the door, and Allison let out a scream. Scampering behind the manager's desk and crouching down behind the chair, Allison watched as Joe banged against the door again, bending it forward a little in the frame. Linda stood in front of the door, growling loudly.

Please shoot him in the back. Allison prayed, hoping that any being that could help her would help her. *Please shoot him in the back, please shoot him in the back, pleeease shoot him—*

The door swung open and Joe jumped in, closing the door behind him. "Oh red!" said Joe, grinning ear to ear. "I'm home—what the hell?"

As the door swung close, Linda jumped on Joe and pushed him against the door, snarling as she tried to bite Joe's throat. Joe wrestled with the large dog, pushing on her forepaws as he tried to create space between him and Linda. From her hiding spot, Allison silently cheered on Linda as Joe's fight against Linda began to turn in Linda's favor.

Suddenly Joe ducked out from in front of Linda and kicked Linda in the chest. There was a sickening crack and Linda fell over on her side, whimpering loudly as she tried to get up and failed. Turning away from Linda, Joe looked towards Allison and grinned. "Hey red." said Joe, fingering his earring. "Miss me?"

Joe ran towards the desk as Allison tried to run around it, blocking her escape. Allison tried to run the other way, but Joe was there too, grinning from ear to ear. Suddenly Joe put his hands on the desk and pushed everything off, leaning closer to Allison, who backed against the wall as Joe swung his legs over the desk and in front of her.

"I don't know what you're doing here, but it looks like you and I can still have some fun, red." said Joe, licking his lips. Allison whimpered as his shadow completely covered her. "Don't worry, I'll be gentle with you. Hey, you think if I ask nicely they'll let me keep you at my place? They might, 'specially if I catch you and you're pregnant with my kid—Ooh! Ow! Ungh!"

As Allison heard him speaking about keeping her, something in her snapped. Rushing forward, Allison kicked Joe in the balls and punched him in the stomach and chin. Joe fell back onto the desk, holding his chin and groin like they were going to fall off. Allison raced around the desk, looking for something, anything she could use as a weapon—

Allison saw the paper cutter on its back, the blade half-detached from the body. Grabbing the handle of the blade, Allison pulled on it, working to loosen the blade from the base as she heard Joe groaning. There was a final crack from the paper cutter and Allison felt a rise in her spirits before two giant hands grabbed her shoulder. Before she could cry out, Allison was spun around and looking up into the seething face of Joe, an ugly black bruise forming on his chin.

"You little bitch!" he growled, reaching for her neck. "Now I'll really let you have it—!"

Allison swung her arm upwards in a round arc, sending the blade into Joe's skull. Joe cried out as blood spurted from the side of his head, tottering on his huge, trunk-like legs. Allison watched as the big man swayed in every direction before falling on his side, the guillotine blade sticking out from Joe's skull.

Allison stared at Joe for a moment before grabbing the blade and pulling it from Joe's skull. Raising it high, she brought it down on his head. Then Allison raised it again and brought it down again. And again. And again, channeling all her anger, her fear, all the pent up emotions of the past several days into the blade as it went into Joe's head, turning his face into a bloody, mashed-up pulp.

Breathing hard and crying, Allison looked at what she'd done, feeling strangely deflated, like something had been let out of her. *I wonder if he feels like this when he's the Snake.* Allison thought, walking around the body and to Linda. *Not horrified, not scared. Just spent. It's a weird feeling.*

As she looked longer at the body though, the deflated feeling began to pass and revulsion welled up within her. Turning away from Joe's body, Allison bent down and rubbed Linda's head, whispering to the whining dog. "Hey." Allison whispered. "Don't get up. You did well, you did really well. I have to go now, I can't stay here, not with him over there. You just lie here, and we'll get you help, 'kay? Good girl."

Allison stood up and looked out the window, trying to find her boyfriend. When she spotted him though, she felt fear. Not fear for herself, but fear for him, and she felt fear for him because of the person approaching him, looking like a large, hulking ogre in a hoodie.

Chapter Eighty-Nine

The Snake jumped off the top of a car and aimed at a young Camerlengo, firing several shots into his body. The Camerlengo shook like a puppet having its strings jerked before falling down in a bloody heap. Not stopping to check the body, the Snake moved onto the next target, shooting down a Camerlengo who had his back to him. Then he aimed a shot at the gate, where a police officer was trying to climb over the chain-link barrier. The police officer started as the bullet sailed above his head, falling back behind the gate and out of sight.

The Snake laughed beneath his mask and ran between the cars, dodging bullets and shooting at anyone who shot at him. *This is amazing!* the Snake thought, shooting at a Camerlengo who was trying to climb a rope to the upper levels of the structure for safety. The climber fell off the rope with a scream, disappearing into the warring crowd. *I may not have the time to mark any of my victims, but I'm getting rid of more people than I killed in the past three weeks! And Nikolai's gang is winning the battle with barely any casualties, thanks to the jackets we're all wearing.*

The Snake grabbed a Camerlengo soldier who was running by him and snapped his neck, throwing the body onto the ground even as the Snake focused on another Camerlengo and began to shoot.

"Now that is some deep sociopathic behavior." said a voice behind the Snake. The Snake turned around, but as he did someone punched him hard in the face, knocking him to the ground. Looking up the Snake saw a huge man wearing a grey hoodie and jeans leaning over him, his face hidden in darkness. "Not as deep and sociopathic as my behavior, though."

The Snake backed away from the man, clambering on his hands and feet like a crab. "Who are you?" asked the Snake, feeling suddenly afraid, as if he were seeing not a man but a monster in a man's skin, a monster worse than the Snake himself.

"Me?" said the man in the hoodie, pulling back the hood to reveal a dark-skinned face with horrible burn scars on the left side. "People call me Frissora."

The Snake blinked as he heard the name, remembering what he'd heard from Scherbakov. "I've been told about you." said the Snake. "I didn't know about your facial scars, though. You should call yourself Freddy."

Frissora laughed humorlessly. "You Americans and your bloody horror films." said Frissora. "You prefer to sit back and stay away from real horrors. I grew up surrounded by real horrors! But when I survived those horrors, I learned something. I learned that I had become the horror, and that I had forgotten how to be afraid." Frissora drew a large, saber-like knife from his hoodie, holding it in his hand like he was waving a candy bar in front of a small child.

"Compared to me, your horror movies are just comedies, they make me laugh so hard."

"Funny you should mention that." said the Snake.

"Why's that?" said Frissora.

"Because horror movies are my teachers." explained the Snake, lifting his guns up and aiming at Frissora's abdomen. "They made me the monster *I* am, and made me realize how much I want to kill my father." The Snake squeezed the triggers on the guns, shooting at Frissora as the large mercenary jumped behind a car and dodged the bullets. Repositioning himself on the ground, the Snake fired underneath the car at Frissora's feet, barely missing as Frissora jumped and rolled away.

As Frissora bounced up near where the black van had been abandoned by its driver, the Snake stood up and faced him. "*Do svidanya*, Mr. Frissora." The Snake squeezed the triggers, but instead of the roar of bullets, all the Snake heard were empty clicking noises. Frissora grinned as the Snake looked down at the guns, amazed he'd run out of ammunition so fast. Throwing the now-useless weapons down to the ground, the Snake pulled the machete out of its sheath on his back, twirling the handle in his hand like a baton as he approached Frissora.

Frissora laughed as he held his knife in front of him. "I'm going to enjoy this fight." he said with a mad grin.

The Snake rushed forward with a roar, swinging the machete at Frissora's head. Frissora parried with his knife, throwing a punch from below with his left hand. The Snake went flying, spinning over a car and onto his stomach. As he stood up the Snake saw Frissora marching towards him with that same mad grin on his face. Fear clutched at the Snake's chest and he ran, jumping over cars and dodging soldiers as he headed for the structure.

He's too much! thought the Snake. He knew it, he could tell from the punch, it was too dangerous to face Frissora like this. The man was like a terrible beast, something far worse than the Snake, and they both knew it too.

As the Snake was about to reach the structure, he suddenly felt himself being pushed into the elevator, almost as if a rhinoceros had hit him from the side. The Snake managed to raise his head as Frissora drove him like a football player into the elevator. The Snake tried to stop him, but he couldn't find a purchase on the ground and the arm with the machete was pinned against his side by Frissora.

As Frissora pushed him into the elevator, the Snake crashed into the wall. Dazed, the Snake shook his head to refocus himself and saw Frissora close the elevator door and press for the top floor of the structure. Frissora turned to the Snake, holding up his knife as he grinned. "Now, now." he said. "Don't want you going anywhere, do we? After all, I plan on having some fun with you before I give you to Camerlengo to play with."

Frissora thrust the knife at the Snake, who was only just barely able to dodge the path of the blade. Frissora laughed as he said, "Doesn't mean I can't scratch you up a bit first." The Snake raised the machete again and brought it down on Frissora's arm, who jerked his arm back a moment before the Snake would've cut it off. Frissora counterattacked with a jab, the Snake blocking with the machete above his face. The Snake tried to get at Frissora with a stroke from the side, but Frissora jumped in the path of the machete, sent the machete bouncing up with a parry from his knife, and barreled into the Snake with his side.

"You see, this is the problem with fighting with sharp weapons in an elevator." said Frissora, crushing the Snake against the elevator wall. "Even big guys like you, or bigger guys like me, have an advantage when we use small weapons in a small space. Bigger weapons need so much room to be successful. Smaller weapons though…that's another matter entirely." Frissora brought his knife down and stabbed the Snake in the side, thrusting the knife in up to the hilt. The Snake groaned as the knife cut into him, waves of pain emanating from the wound.

The elevator reached the top floor of the structure with a loud clang. Frissora threw open the elevator door and pushed the Snake out of the elevator. The Snake stumbled and fell onto the floor, cradling his wound with his free hand. Turning over, the Snake's eyes widened as Frissora loomed over him, the mad grin on his face wider and madder than it had been before.

"Oh, Christopher is going to *loooove* torturing you." said Frissora. "He blames you for the death of his family, you know. Which means he's going to make sure you don't die until he's exhausted his anger on you." Frissora raised his foot high and brought it down on the Snake's leg. The Snake heard a snapping sound a second before he felt the wave of pain rush up his leg and through his body. "Looks like I'll have to get as much as I can out of you while I still have the time."

The Snake watched, his heart pounding in his ears, as Frissora raised the knife again, this time with a direct aim at his bladder.

"Don't you dare touch him!" There was a scream and Frissora turned as something came flying into his neck. Frissora staggered away, making a gurgling noise as a spurt of blood flew from his throat. The Snake stared as d he saw Allison standing behind Frissora, covered in blood and breathing hard.

"Allison?" he said, his astonishment apparent.

Allison turned to him and extended a hand to him. "You alright?" she said as he took it and was lifted back onto his fee. The Snake felt his leg give a scream of protest but stayed up anyway.

"I've been better." said the Snake. "Al, what're you doing here?"

"Talk later." said Allison. "I just saved your ass, so please do your job and kill that guy!"

Frissora was walking back to them, pulling whatever Allison had hit him with out of his neck as he walked. "The blade of a paper cutter." said Frissora, holding the blade in his hand as blood poured out of the base of the neck, staining his hoodie. "How original. And Allison Langland is here too! What luck for me."

"We'll see about that." said the Snake. Ignoring the angry screaming in his leg, the Snake ran forward, swinging the machete. Frissora raised the blade to defend himself, but as he did the giant man tottered like a wave of dizziness had hit him. The guillotine blade faltered, and the Snake drove the machete deep into the side of Frissora's abdomen before pulling it out again.

Frissora hopped to the side, dropping the paper cutter blade to the ground as he placed a hand on his bleeding side. The Snake smiled, raised his machete again, and drove it straight into Frissora's chest. Frissora stared wide eyes at the Snake as the Snake twisted the blade in Frissora's chest. "You know what's good about being a horror like me?" said the Snake, looking back at Allison. "I've got people like her on my side."

The Snake pulled the machete out and reached into his jacket. "That, and I'm consistent." said the Snake, pulling out his gun and shooting Frissora in the head. The great giant fell backwards, shaking the ground as he hit the concrete.

Allison came to stand next to the Snake, who put an arm around her and said, "Did you really put a paper cutter blade in his neck?"

Allison nodded. "Yeah, right after I used it on the guy who was harassing me when I was being kept captive." said Allison. "He found me, and…you get the idea."

The Snake took one look at Allison, then pulled off his mask and hugged her. "That's probably the sexiest thing you've ever said to me." said the Snake, kissing the top of her head.

Chapter Ninety

As the Snake held Allison, he looked at her…and realized somebody was missing. Looking around, the Snake saw she wasn't there and said, "Where's Linda?"

"Linda was injured trying to defend me from the guy I…from him." said Allison. "I think she might've broken a rib."

"Oh God." said the Snake. "Where is she now?"

"Two of my men have already gone to retrieve her." said a familiar voice. Allison and the Snake turned to see Scherbakov walking up to them, his clothes riddled with bullet holes and his forehead cut, but otherwise alright. Next to him was the Yulian, the soldier who had given the Snake his new machete, just as beat up and tired as his boss. Scherbakov came up to the Snake and Allison and then stared at the body lying on the ground, blood pooling steadily around it.

"Is that who I think it is?" said Scherbakov.

"Indeed." said the Snake. "Frissora. I wouldn't have been able to kill him if it hadn't been for Allison, though." The Snake gave Allison's midriff a soft squeeze as he said, "The big bastard would've killed me if Al hadn't come and given him a good whack in the neck."

"Do you have to call it 'a whack in the neck'?" asked Allison. "You make me sound like Lizzie Borden."

"Sorry." said the Snake, looking oddly at Allison. There was something different about the girl in his arms. What was it though? The Snake was having a hard time putting it down in words, but something had changed since the last time he had seen her.

As he was thinking this Allison looked down and screamed. "Oh my God, you're bleeding!" she said, pointing at the blood. The Snake looked down and saw that she was pointing at the wound in his side. "Ah damn." he said, remembering that Frissora had stabbed him earlier and putting a hand over the wound. "My leg was giving me so much crap, I forgot that guy tried to gut me like a pig."

"W-What should we do?" said Allison, looking around like there might be a doctor hidden around a support column or a corner.

"Here, take this." said Scherbakov, reaching into his pants and pulling it out. "It's my old license. It may not look like it, but these things can stop a bleeding knife wound for hours until you can get to the hospital."

The Snake took the card and stuck it under his jacket. "Thanks." he said, sliding the card into the wound. There was a brief flare of pain, but then the Snake felt along the wound and felt the flow of blood slow to a trickle and then stop. "Once again, you've done me a huge favor. How will I get out of your debt?"

"Once the Camerlengos are toppled, then we'll be even." said Scherbakov. "And I don't think it'll take much more to do that."

From below there was a sudden hissing noise. Limping with Allison towards the edge of the structure, the Snake saw a thick white gas covering the construction lot, hiding the ant-like people below in the mist. "Wow, you really mass-produced my smokescreen formula." said the Snake. "I can't see a thing down there."

"Well, we're Russians." said Scherbakov sardonically. "We can mix a little bit of chemistry too from time to time."

The Snake laughed as he turned toward and limped over to the body. "I'm going to mark this body. Let the world know that the New York Mafia Killer took down the great Frissora."

"Only because his girlfriend happened to be around with a paper cutter blade." Allison pointed out.

"Yeah, speaking of which, you might want to wipe that thing down for DNA." said the Snake, trying to pinpoint how Allison had changed. "Don't want the police implicating you in this guy's death." He was sure that Allison had changed, but what was it—? Oh, there it was!

"It's enough that the New York Mafia Killer killed Frissora." said Scherbakov. "The Snake's stature in the criminal underworld will rise astronomically. Frissora was as feared as he was respected, which was why he commanded such a high fee for his services. The Camerlengos' power will be further shaken and we will be able to eliminate them."

"You want to stick around and watch, Al?" asked the Snake.

"Uh…no!" said Allison, ducking out from the Snake's embrace. "I'll leave the macabre to you."

The Snake smiled and pulled Allison back into an embrace. "You're back to yourself." said the Snake.

Allison smiled and kissed him. "Yes I am." she said. "Just took getting rid of some of the causes of my nightmares. Now you get carving and meet me downstairs. I want that leg of yours looked at."

"Yes Mom," said the Snake as Allison ran off towards the stairs, grabbing the paper cutter blade as she left. As she disappeared, Scherbakov turned to the Snake and said, "Let me help you over to the body. She's right, you're probably going to need surgery on that leg."

"It won't stop me from cutting Christopher Camerlengo's life short." said the Snake, putting his mask back on. "Come on, let's get carving."

"I can't let that happen." said a voice. The Snake, Scherbakov, and Yulian turned to see two people with guns appear from behind a support column, one a young man with a hard look, the other a dark-skinned woman. "New York Mafia Killer!" said the man, who the Snake recognized as the person who had spoken a moment earlier. "Nikolai Scherbakov! Both of you and your friend are under arrest!"

"Police?" said Scherbakov. "I don't remember inviting them onto my property."

"And yet they are here." said the Snake. "We'll have to get rid of them somehow."

"Good luck with that." said Yulian suddenly, pulling out a pistol and pointing it at Scherbakov and the Snake. "You two are going away for a long time."

Chapter Ninety-One

The Snake and Scherbakov looked at Yulian like he was telling some sort of joke. "Yulian, this is not the time for this." said Scherbakov, gesturing at Yulian's gun. "Now, if you could kindly put away the gun—"

"I'm afraid I can't do that." said Yulian, still pointing the gun at Scherbakov and the Snake. Scherbakov's eyes widened as both he and the Snake realized that Yulian wasn't joking.

"Yulian?" said Scherbakov. "What are you doing? Why would do this?"

"Because my name's not Yulian, it's Officer Frank Acker." said Yulian, his Russian accent disappearing completely. "I'm an undercover cop with the New York Police Department's Organized Crime Control Bureau. And who knew that getting planted in a small-time family would lead to the biggest arrest in my career?"

"Acker!" said one of the cops. The Snake raised an eyebrow in surprise as he recognized the voice of the cop: it was Harnist, the cop that Armentrout had attacked and knocked out by the highway. "I didn't recognize you earlier with the dyed hair."

"Good to see you too, Detective Harnist." said Yulian, looking at Harnist and the dark-skinned woman. "Congratulations on your promotion, by the way. I wouldn't be surprised if after we arrest these guys, we both get bumped up to sergeant or lieutenant or something."

"Yulian!" said Scherbakov, growling at the man with a face as red as a tomato. "How dare you! I took you in and you lied to me this whole time! Trust me, nobody double-crosses me after I treat them like family!"

"Oh, would you shut up!" said Yulian—no, his name was Acker, not Yulian—rolling his eyes. "I was never working for you to begin with! I still can't believe you fell for that false history about me being an orphan in Moscow who was smuggled into America by slave traders!"

"I didn't believe it." said Scherbakov. "But I believed you were a kid in trouble, so I tried to help you by bringing you into this family. I even covered for you with the Ukranian!"

"What Ukranian?" asked Harnist.

"Never mind that." said Acker. "You're not going to believe who the New York Mafia Killer is once I tell you. I couldn't believe it myself when I found out!"

"I think I know who it is, though." said the dark-skinned woman. The next moment she said a name. The Snake's name.

The Snake's eyes widened underneath his mask. How did this woman know who he was?

The woman smiled at him and said, "Harnist, you see that? His eyes are widening. I was right."

"Son of a bitch." said Harnist, his own eyes widening in surprise.

"Well, this is a let-down." said Acker. "I was so looking forward to revealing the New York Mafia Killer's identity to the NYPD. Can we share the glory?"

"You won't be sharing anything but a jail cell, Yulian." said Scherbakov suddenly. "Especially after I tell them about the Ukranian."

"What is this Ukranian?" asked the Snake, his voice still deep and heavily accented. He wasn't sure how the woman had found out about his identity, but he had to act normal and make sure they didn't see his face or get any hard proof they could use against him. And that meant pretending that the name hadn't affected him at all.

"Oh, just a woman Yulian here raped sometime after he joined my family." said Scherbakov, as if he was talking about a friend's ex. "She was a pretty young thing, just arrived from Europe and thinking Yulian here was a nice young man."

"Shut up!" said Acker suddenly, pointing his gun at Scherbakov's head. "Don't go making any lies about me."

The Snake's eyes narrowed as he looked at Acker's body language. The tension in his forehead and limbs indicated to the Snake that Scherbakov wasn't lying. Acker had raped someone. The Snake turned his attention back to Shcerbakov, who was still talking despite Acker's threat. Why was he telling them all this?

"Apparently he did quite the number on her, too." Scherbakov was saying as he studied his fingernails. "Beat her and then forced her to suck his cock. He peed in her mouth afterwards, and then forced her onto her stomach so he could have sex with her."

"Is all of this true?" said Harnist, his eyes narrowed with suspicion as he looked from Scherbakov to Acker, who was sweating now. All of a sudden, with Scherbakov's testimony, the whole scenario had changed, giving a new tension to the atmosphere, a tension that did not favor Acker at all. "Did Acker really rape some girl?"

"Don't believe him!" shouted Acker. "He'll lie to save his own ass."

"She's buried by a highway, you know." said Scherbakov, unperturbed. "Yulian forced himself on her again before he killed her. I told him where to bury her so she wouldn't be discovered, and when to do it too. I only told him because he told me she'd robbed him after he'd paid her, but now that I think about it, there were several things that didn't add up then—"

"Shut up, you stupid fuck!"

"No Acker. You shut up!" said Harnist. "We'll deal with you after these two are taken care of."

"Oh come on, man!" said Acker. "You seriously believe this crap? He's just trying to sow tensions between us! He wants to get away scot-free!"

No. thought the Snake. *That's not what he's doing.* The Snake stared at Acker, not seeing him as a cop or a mobster, but as a corrupted human being and a rapist. Which meant Acker was somebody the Snake could kill. Slowly the Snake pulled out his knife while everyone's attention was on Frank Acker and looked around. How best to handle this situation—aha!

As Harnist, Acker, and the woman finally noticed the knife, the Snake threw it at one of the cables on the ceiling, piercing through it and cutting several of the wires. There were several sparks and the lights on the ceiling went out, bathing them in darkness.

With a grin, the Snake rushed in the direction of Acker. Lowering himself so that he was pushing his full weight into the man, the Snake pushed Acker to the edge of the structure, Acker unable to put his feet on the ground or get any balance as the Snake pushed. As the edge came into view, the Snake stopped, pulled out his gun, and shot Acker in the gut. Acker stumbled backward, his feet slipped over the edge, and a moment later he was gone, his screams echoing off the concrete before being cut short.

The Snake turned away from the edge and slipped back into the darkness of the floor, his leg screaming with every step. Despite that, the Snake felt powerful and exhilarated. *I am the Snake in the Garden of Eden.* he thought. *And the Garden is burning. I can't let myself be stopped now.*

The Snake pulled out his gun and fired off a round into the ceiling. In the brief flash of light offered by the shot, the Snake saw where Scherbakov, Harnist, and the woman were, and rushed at Harnist. The Snake tackled him and sent him to the floor, Harnist's gun skittering away as the Snake began punching Harnist's gut and chest. Harnist groaned underneath him, trying to break free of the Snake.

Suddenly something hit the Snake in the head and he fell off of Harnist, holding his temple as white pain burst out onto his forehead. Despite that, the Snake stood up shakily and looked around, trying to find the source of what kicked him. As he did, he heard the woman said, "Harnist, you okay?"

Oh, she must've kicked me. thought the Snake. The Snake fired off another round and saw the woman helping Harnist stand up. The Snake rushed at her as the flash from the gunshot died, pushing her away from Harnist and lifting her up by the front of her coat. The woman's gun clattered to the ground as the Snake brought her face close to his. Although in the dark the Snake couldn't see the woman's face, he could tell she was afraid.

"You have no idea whom you're messing with." said the Snake, throwing the woman back to where Harnist was. There was the sound of two bodies colliding followed by several grunts and groans. The Snake followed the sounds to Harnist and the woman, and then put his gun to the temple of someone's forehead. "I'll let you live." said the Snake as the person in front of him froze. "But I won't be so merciful next time. Leave."

"Please do as he says." There was a click and Scherbakov appeared in the dark holding a flashlight in his hand. "After all, you're on private property. I'd really like you to get off of it, if you would."

The Snake followed the beam of light from the flashlight and saw he was holding the gun to Harnist's forehead. Murtz was standing a few feet away, looking terrified and angry at the same time.

"Harnist." said the woman. "Let's go. We can still catch them if we say we found out the identity of the New York Mafia Killer and have his accomplice here! We may even be forgiven for sneaking in!"

"You snuck in?" said the Snake. "I wondered why there weren't more cops. Well, it doesn't matter. You won't arrest me"

"But your eyes—"

"Is that all you have?" said Scherbakov. "Good luck getting that in court. At the very most, the person whose name you mentioned may be investigated, but it'll be difficult to get him or me or anyone else you want to arrest into court. And if I do find myself in court, let me be clear that my lawyers and I will fight tooth and nail to keep me and anyone you decide to arrest out of prison. Do you understand?"

The woman didn't reply, but the Snake saw from her body language that what Scherbakov was saying bothered her. And the Snake had no doubt Scherbakov could make an investigation or any trial that resulted from it extremely difficult for the authorities. Especially after the gains made tonight.

The Snake pushed Harnist to the elevator, using his gun as added incentive to move. The woman followed behind, looking very conflicted as she joined Harnist on the elevator. Even so, she closed the gate and pressed the down button, sending her and Harnist down and away from the Snake. The Snake watched them go before turning back to Scherbakov.

"Well, that was close." he said.

"I'll say." said Scherbakov, grabbing something off the ground and giving it to the Snake. The Snake saw it was his knife and put it in his coat with a curt "Thanks" in Russian.

"Shall we get going?" said the Snake.

"Let's." said Scherbakov, putting an arm around the Snake and helping him get to the stairs. They passed Frissora's body with barely a glance and a minute later they were down the stairs and heading towards a sewer access that Scherbakov's men were guarding. As they approached it, the Snake became aware of how much his leg hurt, and how glad he would be when he could get off his feet.

As they reached the sewer access, the Snake was helped in by Scherbakov's men while Scherbakov brought his phone out of his pocket and looked up at the naked structure of concrete and metal.

"The insurance company will never believe what has happened here." said Scherbakov, glancing at the gate, where police and FBI were climbing over to meet the forms of Harnist and the woman. "But I guess that's okay, when you weigh that against the benefits of tonight."

Scherbakov dialed a number as he stepped into the sewer access. A moment later the structure exploded in a fiery blast, sending concrete and metal debris flying everywhere. The cops pulled back while the Snake and Scherbakov disappeared into the sewer access, sliding the heavy metal cover over the access before they left.

PART SIX
THE TASTE OF SNAKE VENOM

Chapter Ninety-Two

Christopher Camerlengo was seething, barely able to keep his emotions in check as he left FBI headquarters. Right after he'd laid Sheila, Benjamin and Lisa to rest, two stooges from the feds had showed up and told him that they needed him to come down to Federal Plaza for questioning. Questioning! About that incident at the construction site in Harlem, for chrissakes! And he had to leave Phillip to go home by himself! Didn't those government pigs know anything about sensitivity?

With the help of his private lawyer and *consigliere* Martinelli, Camerlengo had been able to get out of the Federal Building quickly, but he was still angry that they'd interrupted his mourning just for some nigger cop and his federal buddy to ask him pointless questions about why so many of his men were found dead at the construction site and try to charge him when they didn't have anything to use against him.

Not to mention that Camerlengo was still humiliated from the incident in Harlem a week ago. All the soldiers he'd sent in to bring the Snake were lured into a trap and then slaughtered! Even worse, only a few of the people who had lured them into the trap had died, men from the Scherbakov family, and yet Scherbakov and his men hadn't been called into the federal building! Now the Red bastard was probably swaggering around the Russian neighborhoods, boasting about how his men had showed the great

Camerlengos, about how he was best friends with the New York Mafia Killer.

Well, Camerlengo would show him. Already, he and his lieutenants were planning on how best to get revenge on Scherbakov. It was just a matter of pulling together enough men, which meant the family had started doing a lot of recruiting. The problem was, people from the Italian communities seemed much more reluctant than before to join up. It was almost as if they thought the family was cursed by a murderous demon, and were staying far away.

But it's not a murderous demon! thought Camerlengo, grinding his teeth together. No, it was just a serial killer with allies who had murdered Camerlengo's underlings and then had tricked his entire organization so that he could then mass murder them!

And I lost Frissora too! thought Camerlengo. *How the fuck did that freak kill Frissora? That's not supposed to even be possible!*

"Um...sir?" said a voice. Camerlengo was jarred from his thoughts and looked at Martinelli, who was looking up at him with big, watery eyes. "Do—Do you still need me, sir?"

Camerlengo sighed and rubbed his brow as if he were trying to get rid of a headache. "No Martinelli." said Camerlengo.

"I'm going to go home and have some dinner with my son. You go home. I'll talk to you tomorrow."

All of Martinelli's five-foot-four-inches gave a big sigh of relief and he said, "Yes, see you tomorrow sir." The small man scuttled off, making Camerlengo wonder if Martinelli was planning on jumping ship. Several other men in his organization had already done so, going into hiding or refusing to come to work or leaving town and even the country because a "relative" had suddenly gotten sick and needed family there. It had been happening at all levels of the organization, and Camerlengo was having trouble stopping it. If he didn't do something soon, his organization would be totally and utterly destroyed.

Camelengo's town car pulled up to the curb and he slid into the back seat. "Take me home." he said. The driver nodded his head and, without looking anywhere but the road, drove away from the federal building and toward the highway. As the town car joined the evening traffic, Camerlengo leaned back in his chair and rubbed his brow again. What was he going to do? How could he gain back the prestige and power his family once enjoyed as soon as possible if he couldn't get to the New York Mafia Killer and string him up like a fish for the world to see? How was he supposed to avenge his wife? His children? His men?

Not to mention that the police and the feds had been probing his people and his organization more than usual lately. Ever since the incident, they had become nosy, interpreting his recent losses as an excuse to be bold and stick their business where it didn't belong. Stupid fools! They would know better soon enough, if Camerlengo had his way. And Christopher Camerlengo always had his way in the end.

As Camerlengo looked out the window, he realized he wasn't on the highway, but instead heading into a part of town he had never been in before. Looking out both windows, he saw several signs in storefronts and on community bulletin boards in Cyrillic. Looking at the driver upfront, Camerlengo said, "What the hell is this? I want to go home!"

The driver didn't reply, but just continued to drive as if Camerlengo hadn't said anything. Enraged, Camerlengo leaned forward and growled, "Hey you idiot, are you deaf or something?"

As Camerlengo leaned forward, the driver stepped on the brake suddenly, sending Camerlengo crashing face-first into the back of the driver's seat. Rubbing his nose, Camerlengo felt his anger rise to almost boiling levels. "Hey you idiot, what the fuck do you think you're doing—?"

Camerlengo was cut short as the driver turned around and pointed a pistol at him. Camerlengo sat back in his seat, eyeing the pistol warily before looking at the driver. To Camerlengo's shock, it wasn't his usual driver. Instead it was a different person, someone who was as Italian as a Martian.

"You do not want to be calling me names right now." said the driver, speaking with a Russian accent.

Russian accent...?

All of a sudden the car doors opened and two people sat down on either side of Camerlengo. One was Nikolai Scherbakov, whom Camerlengo recognized and was both surprised and angry to see. The other was a man in a mask wearing entirely black. Even though he couldn't see his face, Camerlengo had a pretty good idea who this masked man was.

"Christopher Camerlengo." said Scherbakov, lighting a cigar. "It's time we had a long overdue discussion."

The New York Mafia Killer reached into his jacket and pulled out a hunting knife. "A *very* long, overdue discussion," he said, twirling the knife between his fingers.

Chapter Ninety-Three

Christopher Camerlengo. The Snake had waited nearly a month to finally come face-to-face with this man, and he was just as ugly as Allison had described him. It would be very difficult to make him even more disgusting to behold. Of course, the Snake would try his hardest to do so.

"So this is how it is?" said Camerlengo. "You're going to slaughter me? Right here in this car? You're very cold, Scherbakov. Colder than I thought. But then again, you employed this lunatic. Shouldn't surprise me in the least."

"He didn't try to bribe us." the Snake remarked, referring to Camerlengo as he twirled his knife between his fingers. "I like that. I hate it when they try to beg their way out with bribes or threats. Shows this man has character."

"Does that matter to you when you kill?" asked Scherbakov.

The Snake shrugged. "Not really." said the Snake. "But it'll make things more fun for what we have in mind. Oh, and Mr. Camerlengo, Nikolai doesn't employ me. He and I are allies and friends, but one does not employ the other. Understand?"

Camerlengo seemed disturbed by this revelation for some reason, or perhaps he was just disturbed to be in his town car with the cause of his troubles lately and couldn't do anything about it. Either way he nodded and said, "I understand."

Scherbakov nodded. "Excellent." he said, opening the door and sliding out of the car. Gesturing to Camerlengo, he said, "Please get out."

Now Camerlengo looked surprised and confused. "What?" he said. "You're not going to kill me?"

"In this car?" said Scherbakov, as if Camerlengo had said something highly illogical. "No, we're not killing you here. That'd be too easy...and it would ruin the leather."

"There's a nice little butcher shop a few blocks away from here, Mr. Camerlengo." said the Snake, stroking the side of Camerlengo's face, enjoying the look of fear and disgust as Camerlengo shivered at his touch. "It'll be the perfect place to chop you up. There will even be a chainsaw!"

"You're freakier than I imagined." said Camerlengo. "That's just great."

"Oh, that's so sweet of you to say." said the Snake, putting his hand back on his lap. "But it won't make things easier for you with the compliments. So how about we get going?"

"I have a better idea." said Camerlengo. Suddenly the big man shoved Scherbakov out of the town car and jumped onto the street, dodging an SUV and running down a street. Further away, the sound of screams and shouts started coming back to the car, giving the Snake an idea of what Camerlengo was up to at the moment. As the Snake jumped out of the car and helped Scherbakov back to his feet, the Snake gave a loud sigh.

"Looks like I'll have go after him." said the Snake. "Call the butcher, tell him we'll have to use his services some other time."

"You sure your leg can handle it?" asked Scherbakov.

"No, but that won't stop me." said the Snake. "See you in a bit. Oh, and—"

"Let Allison know you're okay?"

"Damn, you're good." The Snake ran in the direction that Christopher Camerlengo had gone in, pulling his machete out of its sheath. There weren't many people on the streets, but those that were seemed to be very afraid, probably more of the Snake than of Camerlengo. The Snake shrugged his shoulders and continued searching, trying to find Camerlengo. As he looked, he heard a can rattling behind him and spun around only to see a cat running across the street.

With an annoyed sigh the Snake turned back around and saw Christopher Camerlengo raising a fist and letting it swing forward into the Snake's chest. The Snake sailed through the air, flipping over and landing on his stomach with a thud. Standing up shakily, the Snake turned to face Camerlengo, who was breathing and staring at the Snake like a bull with a red flag being waved in front of him.

"Do you know what you did to me?" said Camerlengo, his teeth gritted together as he spoke. "I lost everything because of you! My wife, my children, my men, my power! Everything I'd spent my whole life creating, you tore down! I won't forgive you for it! I'll destroy you!"

The Snake held his machete in front of him, watching Camerlengo's body language for any clues as to what the giant of a man might do. To his surprise, the Snake was having trouble reading Camerlengo's body language, which meant whatever happened would be instinctive and impulsive.

Not good.

Camerlengo rushed at the Snake, his giant hands balled into fists. The Snake felt the ground shake underneath his feet with every step Camerlengo took and jumped out of the way. To his surprise Camerlengo stopped right as he passed the Snake, turned around, and sent a fist flying at the Snake's head. The Snake dropped down, letting the fist sail well over his head, and swung the machete's blade at Camerlengo's leg. There was a squishing noise as the blade sunk into Camerlengo's calf, releasing a small spurt of blood as it went in. Camerlengo cried out in pain even as he looked down at the Snake, more ogre-like than before in his anger.

The Snake pulled the machete out of Camerlengo's leg and readjusted himself so that he was in a crab-like sitting position in front of Camerlengo. Swinging his leg up, the Snake connected with Camerlengo's groin even as his leg gave a shriek of protest. Camerlengo bent over with a groan, holding his stomach as if his guts were about to fall out. Seeing an opportunity, the Snake crawled out from underneath Camerlengo and started running backwards, putting as much distance between him and Camerlengo as possible.

Dammit, why did I just start running? the Snake wondered, stopping his feet and looking at Camerlengo, who was standing up to his full height again and was looking murderously at the Snake. *I could've killed him right there!*

You know the answer to that. said a voice in the Snake's head. The Snake saw something to the left and looked to see himself in a shop mirror. As he looked he realized there was something different about the reflection, just as there had been something different about the reflection in Dr. Langland's apartment. *You can't win just yet.* the reflection continued, pointing a thumb at Camerlengo. *You have to make him suffer a lot more before you deliver the final blow. Isn't that right? Because that's how the Snake does it, isn't it? So go get him and make him hurt!*

The Snake glanced at Camerlengo, and then turned back to his reflection. Smiling under his mask, the Snake nodded and held up his machete like a miniature sword. "*Ti zigda znayesh shto skazat pravda.*" said the Snake. *You always know the right thing to say.*

"What does that mean?" said Camerlengo. "I don't speak fucking Russian!"

"Oh, I was just talking to myself." said the Snake. "You should try it sometime. It really puts things into perspective for you."

"Freak." growled Camerlengo, rushing towards the Snake. The Snake felt the approach of Camerlengo in the ground, and then dodged at the last second, swinging his machete and cutting Camerlengo's hip as the gargantuan man ran past him. Camerlengo tripped and fell as he let out an agonized cry, his hand on his bleeding hip. The Snake nearly fell forward himself as Camerlengo's impact with the ground shook the street underneath them.

Keeping his balance, the Snake watched as Camerlengo slowly stood back up, one hand over his hip as he turned back to face the Snake. "I won't let you win!" he growled. "I won't let it happen!"

"Then you might actually want to hurt me a little." said the Snake. "Or perhaps you might want to run away, wait until you're better prepared to face me. After all, you can't do anything without your men, can you? That's why I didn't see you last week in Harlem. Otherwise, we wouldn't be talking right now."

Camerlengo looked at the Snake like he wanted to throttle him, but then the giant mob boss's face changed and he pointed behind the Snake. "Maybe I don't like getting my hands dirty, sure." said Camerlengo. "But you're wrong about one thing: I don't always rely on my men."

Before the Snake could ask what Camerlengo was talking about, there was a horn blast from behind the Snake, and it was close. Turning around, the Snake saw a large produce truck barreling down the street towards them, and it didn't look like it was going to stop. Jumping out of the way, the Snake rolled into the doorway of a flower shop and stopped when he hit the glass door. Standing up and looking for Camerlengo. To the Snake's astonishment, the giant mob boss had disappeared.

There was a loud laugh, and the Snake saw Camerlengo riding in the produce truck's bed, waving at him as the produce drove away and got into a turning lane. "*Arrivederci*, New York Mafia Killer!" called Camerlengo as the produce truck made a right turn. "We'll finish this the next time we meet! And next time, you'll be the one who's unprepared!"

The Snake's eyes narrowed. "I don't think so, Camerlengo." said the Snake. Seeing a man on a motorbike waiting at the corner, the Snake ran to the motorist and pushed him off the bike. Before the motorist could stand up again and stop him, the Snake was driving off with the motorbike, turning right and following closely after the truck. As the produce truck got closer, the Snake could see Camerlengo standing in the truck's bed, looking murderous as the Snake approached.

The Snake sped up, trying to get closer to the produce van. It was only a few yards ahead of him. If he could only get a bit closer, he could at least try stabbing at Camerlengo's feet.

Suddenly the produce truck braked hard, nearly causing the Snake to crash into the truck's back bumper. As the Snake and Camerlengo looked over the side of the truck to see why the truck had stopped, the driver jumped out of the driver's seat, shouting at Camerlengo in Russian. Camerlengo rolled his eyes and swore in Italian before jumping over the side of the truck's bed and in front of the driver. Before the Snake could even get off the bike or reach for his gun, Camerlengo had snapped the driver's neck and was running to the front of the produce truck and the driver's side door.

Oh no you don't! thought the Snake, finally getting his gun out of his jacket and aiming at the back tires. The Snake fired twice, poking a hole into each tire. A raspberry-like noise came from the tires as they deflated, detaching from the rest of the wheels with a melancholy final sputter of gas. Camerlengo froze and turned around, staring at the dead tires before looking at the Snake.

"Did you think I'd make it that easy for you?" asked the Snake, sheathing his machete and revving the engine. "Now start running. I'll give you a head start."

Camerlengo skipped round the produce truck door and began to run, pushing past people on the street who'd come to see what had happened. The Snake counted to thirty in his head before gunning the engine and following Camerlengo, who was just thirty yards away and heading downhill towards the boardwalk and the beach.

The Snake sped up till he was ten feet behind Camerlengo and then slowed down, waiting for Camerlengo to tire out or trip and fall. How long could the mob boss go? Where could he hope to go? And what did he plan to do about the monster following behind him and ready at any moment to strike him down?

Camerlengo reached the boardwalk, which was empty at this time of night with so low a temperature. He looked left and right for an escape route, and as he did, the Snake sped up, heading straight for Camerlengo, who saw the Snake coming and jumped out of the way a mere second before the motorcycle could hit him.

Slowing down and pulling up a few yards away from Camerlengo, the Snake stood up off the motorcycle and put down the kickstand. "It's over, Camerlengo." said the Snake. "You can't run anymore. You have to face me and fight or die like a coward."

"And don't forget about me." There was a loud, metallic crack and a white orb went spinning through the air into Camerlengo's skull. The mob boss groaned and tottered on his elephantine legs as the orb fell to the ground and rolled along the boards towards the Snake. To his surprise, the Snake saw that the orb was a softball, pure white except for a red dash of blood.

Camerlengo and the Snake looked in the direction where the softball had come and saw a lone, redheaded figure with a totebag over her shoulders and wielding a baseball bat. The redheaded figure looked up and flashed the Snake a smile.

"Wow, I didn't think I'd actually hit his head." said Allison, hitting the bat against the palm of her hand. "Now, let's finish this."

Chapter Ninety-Four

Camerlengo gaped as he looked at Allison, while the Snake was mildly but happily surprised. "Al, you told me that you were going to sit this one out and wait for me to take care of this guy." the Snake called to her. "Were you just trying to surprise me?"

Allison nodded her head and called back, "Did it work?"

"Oh yes." said the Snake. "And it was the perfect timing too."

"Allison Langland?" said Camerlengo. "You're here to help this freak too? After all I did for you?"

"Yes, I'm helping my boyfriend." said Allison, fishing a softball out of her totebag and walking towards the Snake and Camerlengo. "After all you did to me, you deserve everything we're going to give you."

"Too bad we couldn't bring the dog with us." said the Snake, unsheathing his machete. "But I didn't want poor Linda to overexert herself with her ribs still healing."

"Wait a damn minute." said Camerlengo, looking at the Snake. "Did she just call you her...boyfriend?"

The Snake nodded his head before reaching up and taking his mask off. Camerlengo stared at him as if there were antlers growing out of the side of the Snake's head. "You...you're just a kid." said Camerlengo. "You're younger than my son. And yet you…how the hell did you become—?"

"That's a very long story." said the Snake. "But to keep it simple, what your people did to Allison and her father was what pushed me over the edge." The Snake put his mask back on and held up his machete. "And now we're going to finish you once and for all."

"We're giving you back all the pain and fear you put us through." added Allison, bouncing the softball in the palm of her hand.

"Not if I have anything to say about it!" snarled Camerlengo. The giant man started running towards the edge of the boardwalk, his footfalls shaking the boards beneath his feet. Allison threw up the softball and swung the bat as it came down, sending the ball straight for Camerlengo's head. Once again she made a direct hit, but Camerlengo kept running as if he hadn't noticed the ball. Reaching the boardwalk railing, Camerlengo heaved himself over and fell towards the beach, making a loud grunt as his feet hit the sand below.

The Snake looked in Allison's direction and shouted, "Take the stairs! I got this!" Allison nodded and ran towards the stairs to the beach, while the Snake followed Camerlengo and jumped over the railing onto the beach below.

As he landed, the Snake felt a tremor of pain vibrate up his bad leg, causing it to buckle. Pushing himself up with his machete, the Snake chased after Camerlengo, who was running along the beach towards the stairs. As he got closer, the Snake could make out Allison heading down the stairs, jumping them two at a time as she went.

The Snake was closing in on Camerlengo. Twenty feet...fifteen feet...*The Garden of Eden will be destroyed!*...ten feet...five...

The Snake swung his machete across Camerlengo's back, opening up a huge slit from his shoulder to his hip bone, where the blade was stopped with a loud *think*ing sound. Camerlengo fell over with a cry, landing face first in the sand. The Snake walked around him, intending to push him over, but then Camerlengo jumped up and wrapped the Snake in his huge arms, squeezing him. The Snake groaned as he felt the arms squeezing on his rib cage, threatening to break him. Dropping the machete, the Snake struggled to get air into his lungs while Camerlengo squeezed harder.

Allison ran up to Camerlengo and started whacking him with the bat. "Let him go!" she shouted. "Let him go!"

Camerlengo scoffed. "Fat chance of that!" he said, sliding his leg out in a wide arc. Allison's legs were swept from under her by Camerlengo and she fell to the ground, crying out as she landed flat on her back. As if he hadn't missed a step, Camerlengo

538

continued to squeeze the Snake, putting more and more strain on the Snake's body.

Camerlengo's breathing quickened as he squeezed, his eyes staring madly at the Snake. "This is for my wife Sheila, you little freak." he said. "Now she can rest in peace."

The Snake was losing oxygen quickly. If he didn't do something soon, he'd faint or his ribs would break, he wasn't sure which would happen first. As one last-ditch attempt, the Snake drew back his leg and, summoning what little strength remained, kicked Camerlengo between the legs.

Camerlengo cried out and his grip on the Snake relaxed for just a fraction of a second. Seeing his opportunity, the Snake pulled his arms free of Camerlengo's grasp and head-butted Camerlengo's giant forehead. The Snake saw stars for a second before he felt the sensation of nothing supporting him and fell to the ground, landing on his ass.

Sucking in great gulps of air, the Snake stood up and backed away from Camerlengo, helping Allison up and giving them some distance from the behemoth of a man. As Camerelngo fell on one knee while clutching his groin, the Snake locked eyes with Allison.

It was time to finish this.

The Snake rushed at Camerlengo and swung the machete down on Camerlengo's shoulder. Camerlengo screamed in pain as blood spurted out of the wound and onto the sand, the arm attached to the shoulder becoming limp and useless.

With a yell, Allison ran and swung the bat at Camerlengo's face, knocking out a tooth and sending a spurt of blood from his noise. Allison raised the bat again and swung it, this time swinging low and into Camerlengo's stomach. Camerlengo groaned, falling flat on his face. Smiling, the Snake withdrew the machete from the mob boss's shoulder. Kicking Camerlengo over onto his back, the Snake raised the machete and stabbed Camerlengo in the stomach, twisting the blade round and round. Camerlengo screamed in agony as a wet puddle of blood spread across his front.

Satisfied, the Snake withdrew the machete from Camerlengo's stomach and sheathed it in exchange for his gun. Gesturing at Allison to come over to him, the Snake looped an arm around her and pointed the gun at Camerlengo's head.

"This is the end." said the Snake, turning the safety off and cocking the hammer back.

"Are you sure?" said Allison.

"He's going to go soon." said the Snake. "It's time to end this. Though I wouldn't have minded drawing this out a little longer."

"Don't say creepy shit like that." said Allison, covering the hand with the gun with her own hands and wrapping her finger with the Snake's around the trigger. "It's just weird."

As the Snake aimed the gun at Camerlengo's forehead, Camerlengo looked at them with an undying fury. "You won't get away with this." said Camerlengo, spitting up some blood. "I'll get my revenge on you, even if it's beyond the grave."

"Well when that happens, we'll get an exorcist." said the Snake. To Allison, he said, "You ready?"

Allison nodded her head. Together, Allison and the Snake squeezed the trigger. There was a bang, the bullet zoomed out of the silencer, and a small hole appeared in Camerlengo's forehead. A trickle of blood bubbled out of the hole. Beyond that, Camerlengo's corpse did not move.

The Snake and Allison lowered the gun and looked at each other before embracing, Allison burying her head in the crevice between the Snake's shoulder while the Snake stroked her hair. "We did it, Al." said the Snake. "We won."

Chapter Ninety-Five

"Well, that didn't take very long." said a voice. The Snake and Allison looked up and saw Scherbakov on the boardwalk, looking like he was watching the waves rather than looking down on the Snake, Allison, and Camerlengo's body. "I had a bet with one of my lieutenants that Camerlengo would take an hour to find. You found him in ten and killed him in less."

"What can I say, Nikolai?" said the Snake with a shrug. "I'm not exactly known for long hours of torture. I just do what I have to."

Scherbakov nodded in understanding. "So what do you plan to do now?" he asked. "Going to mark the corpse like usual and then throw it in the ocean?"

The Snake smiled underneath his mask as he broke away from Allison and went to the body. "No, not like usual." said the Snake. "I plan to do something special with this body."

"Something special?" Allison repeated. "What do you mean by that?"

The Snake opened up Camerlengo's shirt and pulled out his hunting knife. "I'm sending one final message with this one." said the Snake, carving in the S. Behind him the Snake heard Allison gagging as he pulled the knife out and began working on the N. "So it's going to take a little while before he's ready to even be tossed in a body of water."

"And what message would that be?" asked Scherbakov.

The Snake didn't look up at Scherbakov to answer, instead making the final stroke on the N and moving onto the A. "It's a simple message." said the Snake. "What you reap is what you sow."

EPILOGUE

Chapter Ninety-Six

The Snake whistled as he walked into a small restaurant, feeling like he'd been on a drug high for a week without taking any drugs. And considering what had happened last night, the Snake's high couldn't get any higher than it already was. Spotting Scherbakov, the Snake made his way to Scherbakov's booth, where the mob boss stood up and hugged him. "How are you today, my dear friend?" asked Scherbakov in Russian.

"Nikolai, I feel like a kid on Christmas." said the Snake, replying in Russian. "Well, Christmas in a normal family. Anyway, I am doing extremely well."

"So you're saying...?" The Snake nodded, and Scherbakov's face broke out in a big smile. "Congratulations, my friend. I wish you both plenty of happy years together."

"Thank you Nikolai." said the Snake, sitting down in the booth with Scherbakov. "Of course, it won't happen immediately. We'll probably wait till after we've graduated from college before we do it. But I can wait. I've got Allison with me and I'll soon have my sister back with me too. That's all I need to be content."

"You're a lucky man to be so content with what you have." said Scherbakov. "I've met plenty of people who aren't so content with what they have. I wish they could be more like you."

"Ah, thanks Nikolai." said the Snake. "That means a lot to me."

"Well, you've done a lot for me and my organization." said Scherbakov. "Ever since Camerlengo's corpse was hung from that streetlamp, the Camerlengos have all but disintegrated. The other gangs have been moving into their territories, taking as much as they can before everyone else can. My organization has taken up a majority of the Camerlengo's former assets, by the way. My Lucia couldn't be more thrilled with our new home, thanks to the boost."

"Let me guess, you won't touch the prostitutes?" said the Snake.

"Like I said, prostitutes are to be respected." said Scherbakov. "My lieutenants do say we may want to…dabble in the trade. If we do, and it's a very slim chance, it'll be radically different than what the Camerlengos did, I can assure you."

The Snake shrugged. "I guess I can't ask for more." he said. "Just don't tell Allison, okay? She's still trying to come around to the fact that she likes you a little, but if she hears you're considering dabbling in the sex trade, she may try to make sure I never speak to you again."

Scherbakov laughed. "No, we wouldn't want that." he replied. "By the way, how is Ms. Langland doing? And your dog as well."

"Al is sleeping better, thank God." said the Snake. "She's basically back to her old self, though we're a lot more…cuddly than before. Linda's doing pretty good, too. The doctor says that by the end of the month, we can probably take off her bandages and she'll be able to run around like she always did."

"What about Allison's father?" asked Scherbakov. "How is she dealing with that?"

"Well, so far it looks like his body hasn't been found." said the Snake. "At least that's what the police have told us."

"You met with the police?"

"That cop and his friend from the feds that we met at the construction site, Harnist and Murtz." said the Snake. "They met Allison and me at my apartment the other day. I think they're both pretty convinced that I was behind all the deaths."

"Can they prove it?" asked Scherbakov.

"Not with the evidence they have." said the Snake. "Or lack of it, to be exact. We spun them a story that I went searching for Allison, but the New York Mafia Killer got to her first and liberated her from Owen Barlow. Then when she was taken from Barlow's apartment building, she saw me on the street doing detective work and asked the New York Mafia Killer to be with me. He didn't want to babysit Allison, so he dropped her off with a promise of retribution if she gave up anything that would give him away."

"That's rich." laughed Scherbakov. "What did the police say?"

"That they didn't believe us." said the Snake. "But they can't prove it otherwise, now that the task force is being dismantled and reorganized to focus on the new landscape without the Camerlengos. And thanks to the interview with Candace Berman, Allison and my cover story is being accepted as the official story. Allison and I have been flooded with offers for TV interviews and book deals. Even Mardukas Academy wants us to speak to the entire school on perseverance or something like that! No way anybody is going to say that I'm actually the killer."

"Well, it seems that all's well that ends well." said Scherbakov. "Except for Camerlengo, that is. You know the video of his body on that streetlamp has over nine-hundred thousand views on YouTube right now."

"I think about thirty of those are mine." said the Snake. "What can I say? I'm an admirer of my own work."

"That's pretty disgusting to hear." said Scherbakov. "Especially since you cut off his penis and stuffed it in his mouth."

"Hey, you brought up the subject, not me." said the Snake. "But if you would like to change the topic, how about some tips to get my sister back form my monster-father? Because at this point, my best bet is to go through a lengthy custody battle, and I don't want to put Ruby through that, especially with the amount of mud-slinging that will inevitably occur during the course of the trial."

"Now there's a conversation I'd be happy to talk to you about." said Scherbakov. "In fact, I have just the thing to help you with your little problem. It may also get you another interview with Ms. Berman."

"Oh really?" said the Snake. "What's that?"

"This." Scherbakov reached into his suit jacket and pulled out a small, leather-bound book, which he handed over to the Snake. On the front cover were the words LEDGER, and within the book someone had placed the bookmark at a particular page. The Snake looked up at Scherbakov, who motioned for him to open it.

Curious, the Snake opened the book to the bookmarked page and was surprised to see his father's name at the top. Reading through the next couple of pages, the Snake had become aware that his eyes had grown wide. *So that's what those accounts were for!* thought the Snake.

Looking up from the book, he flashed a smiling Scherbakov his own devious grin. "Thanks, Nikolai." he said, closing the book. "this is exactly what I needed."

"You're welcome, but that's not all, my friend." said Scherbakov. "You should see the rest of his file."

Chapter Ninety-Seven

His nickname around the office was The Beast. He rather enjoyed having that nickname. The very sound of it brought to mind the power he enjoyed as an investment broker with access to others' money, the ruthlessness he used when exploiting loopholes and exploiting his clients, and the awesome strength and power he felt when he bedded women who would do anything he told them to do. Ever since he had earned the moniker, The Beast had enjoyed calling himself by that nickname in his head, and he always got a thrill when he was called The Beast, whether to his face or when he overheard it spoken by people in whispered conversations.

As The Beast was walking into his office from a wonderful lunch at the Waldorf with one of his biggest and dumbest clients and the client's latest piece of arm candy, his secretary stopped him from her desk. "Sir, there's a phone call for you in your office." said Tessa, standing up as she saw him. The Beast looked her over, noticing how tight her shirt was and how many buttons had been unbuttoned from it before he said, "Who's the call from?"

"I'm not sure, sir." said Tessa. "The caller just said he had pertinent information for you and if you didn't pick up soon, something about your son would be released to the media."

The Beast stopped in his tracks. His son…that ungrateful little cockroach! The Beast wondered who was calling him about the little brute and if it had anything to do with his son's sick little habit.

If it did, he would personally track down that boy and strangle him, famed serial killer or not.

"I'll take the call in my office." said The Beast. "Did anything about the caller stand out to you? Anything at all?"

"Only that he said he's been on TV once or twice." said Tessa. "I thought it might be your son, but his voice was deep and it had a Spanish accent. Does that mean anything to you?"

The Beast felt his violent temper rising as he replied, "More than you know." The Beast slammed the door behind him, went to his desk and picked up the phone. "What do you want?"

"You know, this is the first time I've ever called your office?" said The Beast's son, infuriating his father with his casual tone and irritatingly convincing Spanish accent. "You shouldn't have such a hot secretary with such a sexy voice behind your front desk, Dad. Thoughts of screwing her might distract you from your call girls."

The Beast stiffened. *...your call girls.* That's what the brat had said, wasn't it? How did that little shit know about that?

"Oh, are you surprised?" The Beast's son laughed with his normal voice before his tone turned serious. "I have a friend who hooked me up with a ledger full of days, places, girls, and the cash you paid to fuck random girls. I couldn't believe how busy you've been since Mom up and left! And then my friend showed me the unabridged version."

"The unabridged version?"

"Yeah, these girls were required to put down what they did with their clients. You know, most people would be freaked out reading what their parents do in the bed, but I just found it plain entertaining. It was my *Fifty Shades of Grey* in a way, especially with the Asian girls you fucked."

You have all this?" said The Beast.

"Oh yeah." said the brat. "And if you don't do what I say, your dirty affairs are going on page one of a major newspaper tomorrow, with all the lurid details for everyone to see."

"What do you want?" asked The Beast, his voice coming out as a growl.

"Well, I found out the most interesting thing today from the buddy who hooked me up with the goods." said the brat, as if he were a gossiping woman talking with her gossiping best friend. "It turns out that if you take a piece of paper, follow the proper rules, and list all your assets in it, it counts as a proper will. That got me thinking, why don't you create a will? One that lists me as Ruby's guardian and that says you bequeath all of your property to Ruby and me, with Ruby's share being in the form of a trust fund that she gets when she graduates from college."

"Graduates from college?" repeated The Beast.

"Well, she's a good kid, but how many good kids have been corrupted by money? Better make sure she's earned the money before she gets it."

"Isn't there a little flaw with your plan?" asked The Beast. "Like, a lawyer and witnesses?"

"Not if it's handwritten." said the brat. "And not if you follow my directions."

"I won't do this." said The Beast. "This is utterly insane."

"Do you want these photos of you with the Nicaraguan chick to go to the Post or the Times?"

"They have photos?!"

"Yes, taken with secret cameras in their purses. I think it was insurance for a rainy day, if you get my drift. Now do you want them to go to the Times or the Post?"

"Okay, I'll write out the damn will!" said The Beast. "What do you want me to write?"

Over the next half-hour, the brat coached The Beast on how to write his new will, begrudgingly writing it down on a legal pad. When he finished with his signature, The Beast said, "I filled out the fucking will. Now what do you want me to do?"

"Put it in an envelope, and give it to your secretary." said the brat. "Tell her not to open it unless something happens to you."

"What do you mean, 'unless something happens to me'?" said The Beast. "Are you planning my funeral or something, you little shit?!"

"You know, I'm looking at this photo of you with the blonde and the Asian." said the brat. "The blonde can't be older than fourteen, and the Asian's younger. Where do you find these girls, man? And can they put this stuff on the nightly news?"

The Beast groaned and pulled out an envelope from his desk drawer. Sealing the will in the envelope, The Beast did as he was told and gave it to his secretary, who put it in her purse with a dubious look on her face, as if she wasn't sure what to make of this unusual request. Returning to his office, The Beast picked up the phone and said, "Alright, it's done. You won't publish that stuff."

"I won't." said the brat.

"Good." said The Beast. "But just so you know, it only works unless I die sometime soon."

"I'm counting on that." said the brat. "Look out your window."

The Beast raised his eyebrows in confusion but looked out the window just the same. Outside, he saw nothing out of the ordinary. But then the brat said, "You see the black Crown Victoria down below?"

The Beast looked down and did see a black Crown Victoria, pulling into a parking space in front of The Beast's building. Two men in trench coats got out of the car and started walking towards the building, disappearing as they fell out of sight underneath the window. "Who was in the Vic?" asked The Beast.

"Detectives." said the brat. "With the Special Victims Unit and Vice departments, to be exact. They're here to arrest you on over five hundred counts of solicitation, statutory rape, sexual assault of a minor, and plenty of other felonies that'll get you into prison for the rest of your life."

"But you said—!"

"That I wouldn't take this information to the media." said the brat. "I never said anything about going to the police. It's your fault for not asking about the police or checking to see if I already went to them. And now you're going to go to jail. How sad is that?"

"You tricked me!" shouted The Beast, squeezing the phone handle tightly in his hands. "You fucking tricked me!"

"And now you're going to be a bitch." said the brat. "Yeah, the guys in prison are going to love raping your ass. They'd just love to have a rich white man suck their cock. Unless they find out you've been screwing kids; then they'll just beat your ass."

"You son of a bitch!" snarled The Beast. "I'll kill you! No, even better, I'll reveal that you're the New York Mafia Killer!"

"The police already tried to pin that on me, and it didn't work then." said the brat. "What makes you think it's going to work for you? You don't exactly have any proof besides that conversation in the apartment, which I can always refute. And have you seen the news? You'll just sound like you're recycling garbage from the news media that nobody will want to believe because everyone prefers the romantic love story. So you can talk all you want, for all the good it'll do you.

"And why would you speak to the cops? You and I both know that's not going to happen. They care too much about pinning you for all those girls you fucked, so they'll just treat you like the trash they deal with every day. And that's not you. I mean really, are you seriously going to let them treat you like that? You're too important to go to jail, which is where you'll be heading soon.

"Well, I have to get going before the cops show up at your office." said the brat with a laugh. "I'd say it's been fun, but it hasn't. See you in hell."

The brat hung up, leaving only silence in his wake. The Beast looked at the phone before hanging up. He knew what he had to do now that he knew those detectives were coming for him. The Beast picked up his chair and, lifting it up with a great heave, threw it at the window. The window smashed into a million pieces, the chair falling to the ground with the glass. Feeling the wind flowing into his office, The Beast climbed out onto the edge of the window and looked down.

There's no way I'm going to jail. thought The Beast. *There's no way.*

The feeling of ground beneath his feet disappeared.

Chapter Ninety-Eight

Had it been only some weeks ago that he'd dumped Paul Sanonia's body in that lake over there? Had it only been two weeks before that the Snake and Allison had been casually walking Linda and enjoying each other's company without any clue of what would come? It seemed almost like a strange dream. But what was happening right now…

"Hey Al?" said the Snake. "If I'm dreaming, don't wake me up."

"I think I can do that for you." said Allison, snuggling up to the Snake on the bench. Not too far away Ruby was playing with Linda, the latter of whom looking very happy to have her bandages off and to be able to play in the outdoors again. "Just don't wake me up if I'm the one dreaming."

"Sounds good to me." said the Snake. As he said this Ruby and Linda ran over to them and Ruby clambered onto the Snake's lap, squeezing him and Allison together. The Snake and Allison laughed as they hugged her back, the Snake giving her a kiss on top of her head.

"Isn't this wonderful?" said Ruby, as Linda put her forepaws onto the bench and joined in on the hugging and kissing. "Linda, stop it! That tickles! Isn't this all just wonderful?"

"What's so wonderful?" asked the Snake.

"Everything!" said Ruby. "You and Linda came home, Allison's going to be living with us, and you two are going to get married!"

"Yeah, but the whole marrying part isn't going to happen anytime soon." said Allison, rubbing Ruby's head. "We're going to wait a few years."

"Why?"

"Because we want to go to college first." said the Snake. "Don't worry, you'll be with us when we go to college."

"Really?"

"You think we're going anywhere without you?" asked Allison. "Who's going to take care of Linda when we're on a date?"

"Alberta?"

The Snake looked at Allison and said, "Can we convince her to move with us wherever we go to college?"

"If we pay for her new home, maybe." said Allison. "That shouldn't be too hard to do, though. Right?"

"Right." said Ruby. "Daddy gave you all his money, so you can pay for Alberta's new home! By the way, how did Daddy die?"

"Um…heart attack." said the Snake. "You get them when you're angry all the time."

"Okay." said Ruby. "Oh look, a hot dog stand! I'm starved."

"How about you go get in line with Linda?" Allison suggested. "We'll catch up with you two and join you."

"Come on Linda!" Ruby jumped off the Snake's lap and ran with Linda to the hot dog stand, getting in line behind a woman with a big fur coat and a businessman talking on his phone. As they scampered off, Allison looked at the Snake and said, "How much did you have to do with your father's suicide?"

"Why do you ask?"

"Oh, I knew it." said Allison, displeased and scared. "You're lucky the police aren't investigating you for that mysterious phone call from the pay phone."

"What pay phone?" asked the Snake. "The one near Nikolai's place that I used when we were over there for lunch?"

"Oh, that's why you and Linda were gone for so long!" said Allison. "I knew it!"

"Looks like you're too smart for me." said the Snake with a shrug. "But hey, you're not going to fault me with getting rid of a sociopathic sex offender who had custody of my sister, are you?"

Allison only replied by standing up and pulling the Snake after her to join Ruby and Linda at the hot dog stand. Before they joined Ruby and Linda in line though, Allison stopped and said, "Just promise me one thing."

"What's that?" said the Snake. "From now on, no more killing."

"At all?" said the Snake, meaning it as a joke.

"I'm serious!" said Allison, surprising the Snake with the desperate look in her eyes. "We were lucky this time! The police may not have been able to prove that you were the New York Mafia Killer, but what will happen next time? You could be caught! You could be killed! I don't want to live without you, so no more killing. And…" Allison rubbed tears out of her eyes before continuing, "And when I killed Joe…and when we took down Frissora…and Camerlengo…I-I felt excited. I felt pleasure. I felt all my fear and anger going away…and yet I was scared. I was afraid I'd grow to enjoy it. And then I was afraid for you. Because I know a part of you enjoyed it too. Do you know how much that frightens me? The possibility that we could become killers? Just for the pleasure of it?"

"It was only a small part of me, Al." said the Snake. "Most of it was in anger. And I was desperate to find you. And you were scared and needed catharsis. That's all it was. You probably won't kill again, will you? You won't even think of it as a joke."

"But what if you kill again?" asked Allison. "What if you get addicted to it, like the mercenaries and killers in your books? I'm afraid I'll lose you, not the Snake, but the real you, the man I fell in love with, and all that will be left is the monster. So please stop killing. Not just for me, but for Ruby too."

As he looked at her face close to tears, the Snake felt his heart go out to her and hugged Allison to him. "I can't resist that look on your face." he said, kissing her. "Alright, I'll give up the killer lifestyle. It's too much work, anyway. I can't tell you how heavy a body is when you're moving it all by yourself."

"I don't want to know."

"Do you have anything else you want me to promise you?" asked the Snake.

"Well, I wouldn't mind you continuing to buy my birth control." said Allison, the desperate look in her eyes gone and replaced with joyous relief. "And when it comes to what we watch together in the evenings, we do rock-paper-scissors to see who decides what we watch."

"Sounds good to me." said the Snake. "But can we apply that rock-paper-scissors thing to all our arguments when we're trying to make a big decision? It would save a ton of time."

"Let's see if it works out." said Allison. "Come on, Ruby's waiting for us. You know, she's taking your dad's death very well. She's not even asking for any big details."

"It's hard to feel a loss when you never felt attached to a person in the first place." said the Snake. "Ruby's considered me more of a parent than our dad, so she's just happy that I'm staying with her from now on."

"Does that make me the mom or the cool older sister or something?" Before the Snake could answer, Allison laughed and said, "If it's Ruby, I think I can manage."

The Snake smiled as they joined Ruby and Linda in line. Things were definitely going to be better from now on.

Chapter Ninety-Nine

Murtz looked around the task force office one last time as files were placed into boxes, computer systems were shut down and whiteboards were erased. Watching it, Murtz felt a loss, like she'd been so close to earning a big prize only to have it swept away from her. Right now the New York Mafia Killer was still out there and probably enjoying his life with Allison Langland and his younger sister. And the media had made them out to be some sort of happy love story nearly done in by the mafia. What was the world coming to?

"I know it's not fair." Harnist stood next to Murtz, sipping coffee while watching the other task force members clean up their desks. "We found the guy, but we can't prove that he's the killer. If we could just figure out how to prove it was him—"

"I wish we could too." said Murtz, sighing. "But the criminal underworld is shifting in ways we can't predict, and besides, Camerlengo's body had a message on his back: 'THE END'. Since Camerlengo was the head of his organization and his organization has basically collapsed, it's assumed that the killer will stop. At least, that's what our bosses want to believe, so that's how we're going to proceed with the case from here on out.

"And with drug cartels moving their products into the lower-income neighborhoods, hitmen killing other hitmen, and families starting new schemes to get rich and powerful, who has time for a killer who's supposedly stopped killing?" Murtz finished with a huff.

"Tell me about it." said Harnist. "How's your boss taking his new orders?"

"Alan?" said Murtz. "He's not happy that he now has to focus on the harbor smugglers for the next few months, but he'll do it. Besides, it'll help us figure out the new lay of the land, so who's to complain? How about your boss?"

"Captain Patton will probably think about this for a while, but he'll move on." Harnist replied. "At least until some new information comes in. In the meantime, we've got smugglers to catch and cartels to bust and dogfighting rings to locate. It's part of our never-ending war on organized crime."

"Tell me about it." said Murtz. "I've already been called to Washington to look at a rapist who may have been crossing state lines. It's going to be crazy."

"Good luck." said Harnist. "Hey Murtz, if you want, I can treat you a drink. I think we could both go for it."

"Thanks but I'll pass." said Murtz. "I've got a flight to Washington in two hours anyway. I appreciate the offer though. And it was great working with you, Detective Harnist. You're a fine detective."

"Thanks, Dr. Murtz." said Harnist, extending a hand. "It was great working with you too, and you are an ingenious profiler."

"Either that or lucky." said Murtz. "And we may get lucky again."

"What do you mean?" asked Harnist.

"Well, don't think I'm wishing for someone to die," said Murtz, "but serial killers are not the type to start killing and then just stop there. They find it hard to stop, and when they do, they're just waiting for the right opportunity to kill again. We'll get this guy again. We'll just have to wait for our opportunity. Maybe then we'll be able to catch the New York Mafia Killer."

Chapter One Hundred

The Snake opened up the attaché case he'd bought, an aluminum box with two five-digit security locks on either side of the lid. Following the directions, the Snake set the locks to Allison and Ruby's birthdays, testing to make sure the locks worked properly. Unable to open it with just his hands, the Snake put in the combinations and opened the lid, feeling the fabric on the inside.

The Snake picked up his hunting knife first, holding it between his fingers like he was examining a fine antique. The Snake committed the shine of the blade, the grip of the handle, and the sharp point of the tip to his memory before placing it in the attaché case The Snake then picked up his gun, looking over it, remembering every curve and every edge, the cold plastic against his palm, the smell of gunpowder and cleaning oil. The Snake placed the gun components carefully, tenderly in the attaché case, placing two magazines next to the gun.

Finally the Snake held up his mask and looked at it. So simple in design and make, yet it had such an effect when he wore it. Looking through its eyes, the Snake had seen the world in a whole new light, had become a movie character with the most awesome role in the movie, the iconic killer. And not only that, he had saved the day, gotten the girl, and made his mark on the world.

The Snake folded the mask up, tucking the sides in before folding it horizontally and placing it like a blanket on top of the knife and gun parts. The Snake touched the leather with his fingers one last time and then finally he closed the lid of the attaché case and spun the dials.

The Snake hid the attaché case in his closet with his machete, covering them with an old sweatshirt and the cape he'd worn when he'd played Jack the Ripper back in autumn. Then the Snake closed his closet and ran downstairs to the living room. On the couch, he found his heart growing warm as he saw Allison reading to Ruby, the latter of which was growing sleepier and sleepier the more Allison read to her. At Allison's feet Linda was lying with her legs splayed out, but she got up as soon as the Snake came in and went to greet him.

Allison looked up from the book and saw him. Smiling, she closed the book and said, "I think that's enough for tonight."

"But I'm not even ti—I'm not even tired." Ruby yawned.

"Yes you are." said the Snake, joining them on the couch. "Now come on, we've got a big day tomorrow. We're going to Coney Island, remember? And then after dinner, we'll go see that anime movie you told me about."

"Mm-hmm." said Ruby, her head drooping. "I can't wait."

"I know you can't." said the Snake, picking Ruby up in his arms and carrying her to her room, Allison and Linda following behind them. As they tucked Ruby into bed, Linda lay down next to the bed and spread her legs out again, her way of saying she wanted to be with Ruby tonight. The Snake and Allison left Ruby's bedroom, leaving the door open a little in case Linda wanted to leave. As the fact that they were alone came over them, Allison and the Snake embraced and kissed.

"We're alone now." said Allison. "What do you want to do?"

"Considering that we'll be supervising an energetic six-year-old all day tomorrow, I'd like to sleep." said the Snake. "What about you?"

"The same." said Allison with a laugh. Holding up her left hand in front of her face, Allison looked at the engagement ring the Snake had given her only a few days ago, the light bouncing off the ring and onto Allison's face. "God, you just got this rock on my finger and moved me into your room and I'm already acting like the responsible older sister. It's such a weird feeling, but it's also kind of nice."

"Welcome to my world." said the Snake. "Come on, how about a roll in the hay and then bed?"

"We shouldn't with tomorrow happening but…okay." said Allison, placing a hand on the Snake's crotch. Feeling his excitement rise, the Snake led Allison to his bedroom. Closing the door behind them and shutting off the lights, the Snake and Allison sat down on the bed, their arms encircling each other.

"I'm so glad this is all over." said Allison in the dark, pushing up the Snake's shirt. "Now all we have to worry about is catching up at school."

"I'm sure we'll be make it up over spring break." said the Snake, taking off Allison's top. "Given what we've both been through, they'll probably have us make up the credit by speaking to the student body."

"What about us living together?" Allison pointed out, pulling down the Snake's pants. "The school might not like that, even if we're engaged."

"We'll figure something out." said the Snake, unhooking the back of Allison's bra. "After all, we're at the age of consent and engaged to be married. The administrators can't complain or preach morality at us…unless they want a lawsuit."

"That sounds like a good idea." said Allison, running her hand up the Snake's chest slowly, sensuously. "In any case, we'll put everything behind us. Get out of New York and start a new life together. Forget all that's happened to us."

"You can't forget the past, Al." said the Snake, reaching into Allison's shorts. "Especially since we'll be staying in contact with Nikolai, right?"

Allison's hand stopped on his chest. "True," she said contemplatively. Sighing, she said, "I guess we can't forget the past, can we?"

"Nah, just move on." said the Snake, taking off Allison's shorts. "And we'll do it together, one step at a time. I'm already moving on, starting with moving on to your underwear."

The Snake growled playfully as he kissed Allison's neck, pushing her down as he reached for her underwear. Allison laughed as she arched her hips to him, her hands reaching down towards his groin. Finally the Snake kissed Allison, cutting off her laughs and cries as they embraced and their bodies became one.

Later, the Snake would watch Allison sleep and think about leaving the past behind them. They couldn't leave the past behind of course, it would be impossible. After all, the Snake was keeping his gun, his knife and his mask. The Snake knew Allison didn't want him to keep them, but what could he do? He'd made a reputation for himself and probably several enemies that wanted his blood. The Snake was sure a few of them would try to seek them out. It was better to be prepared for a possible jam than to be caught in one without anything to get them out of it.

Besides, you always had to plan for a possible sequel.

June 10, 2012—December 16, 2012

Acknowledgments

A novel is the child of an author's imagination and labor, but the author always has a wonderful network of people supporting him in that regard. I would like to thank some of those people now.

First, I would be remiss to not thank Angela Misri (whom I swear Angela Murtz is not named after), author and friend. Her meticulous notes and suggestion on Snake are laced throughout the novel, and it would not be the story it is without her patience and her vivid foresight into the many flaws that are common in novels before they're ready for publication. I can't wait to read Jewel of the Thames, Angela. I bet it'll be great!

I'd also like to thank Dr. John Tilley, who took my request for help with the profiles on the Snake and gave me the best profiles I ever got outside of a TV show or novel. I hope you liked the final product, John.

I would also like to thank the makers of *Taken*, who helped to inspire *Snake* (I bet you were all thinking I got inspired by *Dexter*, didn't you? At the time I'm writing this, I've never seen an episode of *Dexter*, though I plan to watch it eventually). I'd also like to thank my family and friends for all their support and love. A special thank you to all the people, websites, and organizations that provided me with quick info for small details that added up to big results at the end of the day.

A special shout out to The Holy One, Blessed Be He. I can't thank Him enough for all He's done in my life.

And finally, thank you dear reader. It makes me happy to know you decided to pick up or download this book. I hope we have further adventures together someday.

Hoping you are well,

Rami Ungar

February 3, 2014

Rami Ungar is a student at Ohio State University who is studying History and English. For Rami, scaring people and writing are two of his greatest talents, so merging them is like a marriage of two great loves. His influences include Stephen King, Anne Rice, and James Patterson. When not writing, Rami enjoys reading, watching TV, and sneaking up on people when they least expect it.

You can also find Rami at these places:

His blog: ramiungarthewriter.wordpress.com

Facebook: Rami Ungar the Writer

Twitter: @RamiUngarWriter

Made in the USA
Monee, IL
24 September 2022